COLD-BLOODED KILLER

The Congregational Church was packed to capacity, the sanctuary and the vestibule. A crowd had gathered outside on the front steps and down the sidewalk. She knew that these people weren't here to show their respects to Jamie. Not many people had liked Jamie. Quite a few had despised him. And several had hated him, as she had. The huge outpouring of sympathy was for Big Jim and Miss Reba.

The sheriff and the chief of police were here, reminding everyone that Jamie had been murdered. Tortured and tormented. Made to suffer. Punished for his sins. She'd seen to that. She'd made sure he would never hurt her, her child, or any other woman—not ever again.

Jazzy Talbot was conspicuously absent. Good. She'd hated to think that worthless slut would dare show her face.

As she watched while others paraded by Jamie's closed casket, she had to fight the urge to smile—even laugh. She had destroyed his pretty face and silenced his lying mouth. And now Jazzy was suffering.

But not nearly as much as she would suffer.

The woman had to die.

Deserved to die.

Would die.

But not yet.

When this all came to an end and everything was as it should be, Jazzy would be the last to die . . .

Books by Beverly Barton

AFTER DARK

EVERY MOVE SHE MAKES

WHAT SHE DOESN'T KNOW

THE FIFTH VICTIM

THE LAST TO DIE

Published by Zebra Books

THE LAST TO DIE

Beverly Barton

ZEBRA BOOKS
KENSINGTON PUBLISHING CORP.
http://www.kensingtonbooks.com

In memory of a very special lady, an avid reader and a fellow Tuscumbian who never missed one of my autographings,
JAN WHITTLE

and

In memory of my dear cousin
LOUISE GIBBS THORNE,
a fellow writer whose weekly column appeared in
The Colbert County Reporter
for many years.

A very special thank you to my wonderful editor
JOHN SCOGNAMIGLIO

And several dear friends who understand
the life of a writer
and help keep me sane,
LINDA, LJ, WENDY, and PAULA

Prologue

He pounded on her door and shouted her name. *Go away*, she wanted to scream. *Leave me the hell alone.* But she knew he wouldn't go. Not unless someone came and dragged him away.

Maybe she should call Jacob and tell him that Jamie was harassing her again. As the county sheriff, he could hold Jamie in jail overnight. Or she could phone Caleb and ask for his help in getting rid of an unwanted midnight visitor. Caleb had gotten plenty of practice lately as the bouncer at Jazzy's Joint. He'd thrown Jamie out of the place several times recently.

But for some reason, she just couldn't bring herself to pick up the telephone. It wasn't that she wanted to see Jamie. Not tonight of all nights. But she'd been expecting him, had known somewhere deep down inside her that he would pay her a visit after his engagement party ended.

"Jazzy . . . lover, please, let me in."

His voice was slightly slurred, no doubt the result of numerous glasses of champagne, and not the twenty-dollars-a-bottle stuff either. Probably Moet's Dom Perignon or Taittinger Comtes des Champagnes. Or possibly Roederer Cristal or Pommery Cuvee Louise. Something that cost no less than eighty bucks a bottle. In hosting the big bash celebrating their only grandchild's upcoming nuptials, Big Jim and Reba Upton had spared no expense. Everybody in Cherokee Pointe had been talking of nothing else. The Uptons had hired a catering service out of Knoxville for the engagement party and the rehearsal dinner, the same service the bride's parents had chosen to cater the wedding reception next month.

While Jamie continued banging on the door and pleading with her to talk to him, Jazzy curled up tightly on the sofa and placed her hands over her ears. Jamie had been engaged twice before and hadn't followed through with wedding plans either time. But it looked as if his engagement to Laura Willis might actually end in marriage. If for one minute she believed Jamie's marrying another woman would put an end to his obsession with her, she'd be the first in line to offer them congratulations.

Sure, there had been a time when she'd dreamed of becoming Jamie's wife, but that had been years ago, when she'd been young and foolish. That stupid dream had died a slow, painful death as maturity had given her a firm grip on reality. No way would Jamie's rich and socially prominent family ever accept her; they still saw her as nothing but a white trash tramp who'd gotten pregnant at sixteen.

Did she still care about Jamie? Yeah, somewhere in her heart remnants of that passionate first love still existed. Only a few years ago, she had still been as obsessed with Jamie as he was with her. For the past ten years he had floated in and out of her life, just as he had floated in and out of town. But this time, when he'd returned a few months ago with a new fiancée in tow, Jazzy had turned him away when he'd come to her. And one night, when he hadn't taken no for an answer, she had threatened his life. Or, to be more precise, she'd threatened his manhood. And what truly frightened her was the realization that she would have shot him—shot his balls off—if he'd come after her again.

"Jazzy . . . don't be mean. Please, doll baby, let me come in. Just one last time. Don't you know how much I love you?"

No, damn you, no! You don't love me! You never did. You're not capable of loving anyone except yourself.

While she sat on the sofa, hugging herself, wishing she could block out the sound of Jamie's pleading, memories washed over her, flooding her senses. The first time Jamie had kissed her. The junior/senior prom, when she'd given him her virginity and had known she would love Jamie forever. The day he'd cried when he told her he couldn't marry her even though she was carrying his child. The night he had returned to Cherokee Pointe after his first year of college. They'd made love repeatedly for forty-eight hours, leaving bed only when necessary. The first return visit, years ago, when he'd brought home his first fiancée—and Jazzy had welcomed him into her arms, into her bed, not caring about his bride to be.

How many times had she forgiven Jamie? How many times had she given him just one more chance? Time had run out for them. She knew it, even if he didn't. She'd turn thirty soon; she had wasted enough of her life waiting for Jamie Upton to give her what she wanted, what she'd always wanted from him. Marriage.

"Jazzy . . . Jazzy . . . baby, please, talk to me. Even if I marry Laura, it doesn't mean we can't still be together."

A cold, deadly calm settled over her heart. She stood,

squared her shoulders and walked to the door. Her hand hovered over the knob. *You're the only one who can end this thing once and for all,* she told herself. *Do what you have to do to free yourself from Jamie.*

Simultaneously Jazzy unlocked the deadbolt and turned the knob. When she eased open the door, Jamie took full advantage and shoved his way into her apartment. Before she could say a word, he grabbed her and kissed her. Impatiently. Brutally. His tongue thrust inside her mouth. For a split second, she savored his savage possession. Then common sense took charge. She broke away from him, her breathing ragged. He reached out for her, but she sidestepped his grasp.

"I need you, Jazzy. I'm aching, I want you so bad."

"What we once had is over," she told him. "It's been over for a long time. I've accepted that fact. It's time you did."

"I don't love her. I'm marrying her because Big Mama is giving me no other choice. She expects me to marry Laura."

Jazzy laughed, mirthless chuckles. "And God forbid you ever go against what Big Mama wants."

"I'm sorry." His shoulders slumped. "I know I'm a spineless bastard. But if I don't keep Big Mama happy, I could lose everything. Big Daddy's done told me this is my last chance. If I screw things up with Laura, he'll write me out of his will."

Jazzy almost felt sorry for him. Almost. "You know I'll never be your mistress. I draw the line at fooling around with a married man."

Lifting his gaze from where he'd been staring at the floor, he looked directly at her. "Would you let me stay tonight? Just for a little while. A couple of hours." He held up his arms in an "I surrender" gesture. "Just let me hold you. I swear, I won't do anything you don't want me to do. I need you, Jazzy. One last time. Please, lover. Please."

Against her better judgment, she nodded. "You can stay an hour. That's all." When he opened his arms to her, she shook her head. "Sit down on the sofa. I'll fix us some coffee. I think you could use some. You should sober up before you head home and try to explain to your fiancée where you've been."

"Hey, honey, if you're planning on getting your gun while the coffee is brewing, there's no need. Believe it or not, I want us to be friends. I'd prefer lovers, but I'll settle for friends. I just can't imagine my life without you in it."

Oh, hell. Why had he said that? *Don't go soft. Not now. You've heard Jamie's line of bull before. You know the guy can sweet talk his way out of any jam—or into any woman's bed.* But not her bed. Not ever again.

"You aren't going to get to me," she told him. "Remember, I've heard it all before. I'm the girl you honed your persuasion skills on."

"You may not believe me, Jazzy, but . . ." He came up behind her, but didn't touch her, just stood very close, his breath warm on her neck. "In my own selfish way, I do love you. I always have. And I always will."

Odd how a part of her wanted to believe him, maybe even needed to believe him. When she turned to him, he reached out and caressed her cheek. She sucked in her breath.

"Please, Jazzy." He looked at her with those sexy hazel eyes, his expression one of intense longing. "Baby . . . please."

She didn't protest when he pulled her close. Gently. And kissed her. Tenderly. All the old feelings resurfaced and for a moment—just a moment—she wanted him in the same old way. He allowed her to end the kiss. Then he stood there staring at her, waiting for her judgment call.

"I can offer you coffee and conversation for an hour," she told him. "That's it. Take it or leave it."

"I'll take it." A sly, seductive grin curved the corners of his lips as he turned and walked over to the sofa, then sat and crossed one leg over the other knee.

You're a fool, Jazzy told herself as she rushed into the kitchen and prepared the coffeemaker. Being nice to Jamie wasn't the answer. But God in heaven, old habits died hard.

Tonight she would say good-bye to Jamie. This time would be the last time. And if he ever came to her again, she knew what she'd have to do. She'd have no choice, not if she wanted to save herself.

The man had to die! It wasn't that she wanted to kill him or anyone else, but he had left her no other choice. Not only would he have to die, but she feared others would have to forfeit their lives, also, if they interfered. Of course, it wasn't entirely his fault; after all, he was only human, a mere man, with all the weaknesses inherent to his sex. But he was the worst of his kind, spineless and weak. He gave in to his baser instincts without regard to how his actions might harm others. He reveled in the depravity that plagued most men and many women.

Her hand settled over her belly. In order to protect herself—and her baby—she needed to plan a strategy that would put suspicion on someone else. But not just anyone. She wanted that woman to pay with her life, and what better justice than to have her executed for murdering her lover? After all, the whole town knew she'd threatened to kill him.

She stood in the shadows, waiting and watching, knowing where he was and what he was doing. He was with that woman, making love to her. How could he do this? He had sworn his love was true. Lies. All lies! They were fornicators. Sinners. Evil to the core. Both of them deserved to die. To be punished.

She shouldn't act hastily, in the heat of the moment. That was the way mistakes were made. She had made mistakes in the past, but not this time. She had trusted when she shouldn't have, but never again. She needed to be calm and in control when she ended the son of a bitch's life. There was no need for her to kill him tonight. As long as she eliminated him before his wedding day, everything would be all right.

She would not kill him quickly. A quick death was too good for him. He needed to die slowly, painfully, tortured and tormented. The thought of listening to his agonizing screams excited her. Her mind filled with vividly gruesome impressions of his last hours on earth.

"Everything I do, I do for you, my sweet baby. I won't let anyone hurt you. They think we aren't good enough for them. They think they can sweep us out the door and pretend we don't exist. But I won't let that happen. You don't have anything to worry about. Not now. Not ever. Mother's here . . . Mother's here."

Chapter 1

The man writhed in agony, his naked torso helplessly bound, his legs spread-eagled. Tight rope manacled his ankles to either side of the heavy spikes in the wooden floor. She removed the thick cotton rag used to gag him effectively and mute his tortured cries. Self-satisfied and excited, she stood over him, the bloody knife clutched tightly in her steady hand. The dim glow of the lone lamp burning in the room cast shadows across her face, revealing nothing about her except a few flyaway tendrils of burnished red hair. As she lowered the knife, the man's eyes widened in terror. He knew what she was going to do. He struggled futilely against his captivity. Sweat dotted his forehead, his upper lip, and dripped along the side of his face. When she placed the knife between his thighs, red with blood from where she'd tormented him, she laughed.

"'Whatsoever ye sow, that shall ye reap.'"

He mumbled pleadingly as he shivered, his head thrashing side to side, panic seizing him completely. Fear consumed him.

"You will never hurt anyone ever again," she told him. "I will punish you for your many sins and rid the world of your evil." She brought the knife back, reached under him and lifted

his scrotum, then, with one swift, deadly slice, castrated her
victim. "I am your angel of death, whoremonger!"

Genny Madoc screamed. When she shot straight up in bed, her fiancé, Dallas Sloan, came up beside her a split second later. He wrapped his arms around her and held her as she trembled.

"What happened?" he asked, then brushed his lips along her temple. "Was it a nightmare or a vision?"

She gave herself over completely to his comforting care, having come to depend on him with total trust these past few months. "Both. A nightmare vision."

"You haven't been bothered with visions since . . ." He let his words trail off. She suspected that he, as she, preferred not to dwell on the events of this past January, when she'd come very close to being a maniacal serial killer's fifth victim here in Cherokee County.

Although it was early April in the mountains, the nighttime and early morning temperatures remained in the high thirties and low forties. Genny shivered as a cold chill racked her body. Dallas lifted the heavy quilt from the foot of their bed and wrapped it around her, then pulled her back down into the bed beside him. She cuddled against him and sighed heavily.

"Want to tell me about it?" he asked.

"I'd rather forget it . . . but I can't. I believe the vision was a forewarning. I saw a man being murdered."

"Did you recognize either the victim or the killer?" Dallas asked.

"Yes and no, but . . ." She pulled away from him and rolled out of bed.

Dallas leaned over, just enough to loosen the covers from his upper body. Genny looked at him, at this man she loved more than life itself, and wished more fervently than she ever had before that she wasn't cursed with the *gift of sight*. Loving her, living with her, marrying her come June, Dallas had to deal with her special talents as only the mate of a true psychic would have to do.

Genny discarded the heavy quilt, dropping it to the floor as she slipped into her robe and house shoes, her movements slow and unsteady. She turned to Dallas. "I won't be able to sleep. I think I'll fix myself some coffee and go outside to watch the sunrise. You stay here and go back to sleep."

Totally naked, Dallas emerged from the bed in all his masculine glory, a morning erection jutting out between his thighs. "You're so weak you can barely walk. You aren't going anywhere without me." He grabbed his discarded jeans and shirt off a nearby chair. "I'll fix coffee. Then if you want to go outside, I'll go with you."

"I'm just a little weak. The vision drained some of my strength, but it was a brief vision and I'm not exhausted. Really I'm not."

Not bothering to put on his socks, he stuffed his feet into his shoes, put his arm around her shoulders and guided her out of the bedroom. "You need to talk about it. If it was a premonition of someone's death, then maybe there's something we can do to prevent it from happening."

Genny loved the way he said "we" so naturally, without giving it any thought. Almost instantly, from the first night they met, they had become one spirit.

Fifteen minutes later, Dallas and Genny, coffee mugs in hand, stood on the front porch of her old Tennessee farmhouse and watched the sunrise. Dallas's strong arms encompassed her as he stood behind her, his big body warming her. Pale and pink, like the tips of a hundred torches barely beginning to brighten the horizon, the first glimmer of morning sunlight lit the Eastern sky.

"No matter how many times I see this, it never ceases to take my breath away," she told him.

"I know exactly what you mean." One of his big hands clamped down on her shoulder.

When she glanced back and up at him, he wasn't looking at the sunrise, but at her. And she knew that she, not nature's beauty, was what captivated him.

Genny glanced up at the sky, leaned her body back, closer into Dallas, and lifted the strong, dark brew to her lips. The Colombian Supreme had a rich, mellow flavor, and she, like Dallas, took her coffee black.

"The man was Jamie Upton," Genny said, her voice not much more than a whisper, as if she thought by not saying his name too loudly, it might somehow protect him.

"You saw someone kill Jamie Upton?" Dallas nuzzled the side of her neck with his nose. "I'm not surprised. I figure it's only a matter of time before he pisses off the wrong woman."

"Please don't say that."

Dallas took a swig of coffee, then set his mug on the windowsill behind him. When Genny took several steps toward the edge of the porch, he followed and wrapped his arms around her again. "Tell me what's frightened you so. There has to be more to your vision than simply seeing Jamie killed."

"Isn't that enough?"

"Depends."

"On what?" she asked.

"On how he was murdered and on who killed him."

"I don't know who she was, but—"

"So I was right, huh? I figured it was a woman. After all, it would be only poetic justice if some woman chops off his balls."

Genny gasped. Dallas clutched her shoulders and whirled her around to face him.

"Is that what happened?"

Feeling suddenly cold and knowing the color had drained from her face, Genny nodded. "And—and there was something about the woman."

"I thought you said you didn't recognize her."

"I didn't see her face, but I saw a few strands of her hair."

"So?" Dallas stared at her quizzically.

"Her hair was red."

"Red? Good God, honey, you don't think it was Jazzy, do you?" When she couldn't bring herself to respond, Dallas grunted. "You think you saw Jazzy murder Jamie, don't you?"

"No, of course not. Jazzy isn't capable of murder."

"That's where you're wrong. Every human being is capable of killing, given the right provocation. But if Jazzy was going to kill Jamie, she'd already have done it. Long ago."

Genny took a deep breath, then exhaled as she nodded agreement. "I don't think the woman who killed Jamie in my vision was Jazzy, but my instincts warn me that somehow Jamie's death will bring great trouble to her."

"So should we forewarn Jamie?"

Genny shook her head. "No. He'd never believe me. He'd only laugh at me. But I'm going to tell Jazzy. She needs to stay as far away from Jamie as she possibly can."

"That might be a problem, considering how he hounds her all the time."

"I think she needs to take out a restraining order against him." Genny looked directly at Dallas. "Now that you're the chief of police, you can handle that for her, can't you?"

"Yeah, sure, but Jamie being Jamie, I doubt a restraining order will keep him away from her."

"Then maybe I should speak to Caleb McCord."

"McCord? The bouncer at Jazzy's Joint?"

"Yes, that Caleb McCord."

"Am I missing something? Why would you tell—"

"That's right, I didn't tell you, did I?"

"Tell me what?"

"Caleb is in love with Jazzy."

"He is?"

"Yes, he is. He just doesn't know it yet."

Dallas chuckled. Genny turned her attention back to the morning sky as she sipped her coffee and allowed her fiancé to pull her down in his lap as he sat in one of the four rocking chairs on the front porch.

Laura Willis rested on the window seat in the guest bedroom she shared with her younger sister, Sheridan, at the Upton estate outside Cherokee Pointe. She'd been living here since Jamie brought her to meet his grandparents three months ago. Until her sister and parents had arrived two days ago for her engagement party, she had shared Jamie's bed many nights. The nights he stayed at home. His grandmother, Miss Reba, assured her that Jamie wasn't with other women on those nights he stayed out until dawn, but she knew better. Her Jamie was a ladies' man. And there was one lady—and she used the term loosely—Jamie found irresistible. Jazzy Talbot.

Maybe she was a fool to believe that once she and Jamie were married he'd be faithful to her. But he had solemnly vowed to her that once they said their "I dos," he would be true to her. Perhaps she had to believe he'd keep his word because she loved him so much.

And he loved her. She knew he did. He could be tender and considerate and loving, as well as wildly passionate. She was lucky that he intended to marry her. He'd been engaged twice before, but this time would be different. In three weeks they would say their vows and she would become Mrs. James Upton III. And if Jazzy Talbot didn't stay away from her husband, she'd . . . what would she do? She'd kill her, that's what she'd do. *No, no, Laura, you don't mean that. You could never kill another human being. Not even Jazzy.*

The eastern sky brightened as dawn colored the horizon with muted pastels. Laura could see the front drive from her window as well as the expansive front lawn. Quiet, empty, nothing more than the spring breeze stirring at this time of day.

You're with her, aren't you, Jamie? You spent the night with her. Touching her, kissing her, making love to her the same way you do me. No, no, no! It's not the same. He loves me. He only wants to fuck her.

Tears gathered in Laura's eyes. She swallowed hard and willed the tears away. It wasn't too late to call off the wedding. But what good would that do? Jamie had already broken her heart. And she knew that without him, she'd die. He was everything to her. Her whole world. The only way she'd ever be free of him was if she died. Or if they both died.

"Where do you suppose that fiancé of yours went?" Sheridan asked as she approached the window seat.

Not realizing her sister was even awake, let alone out of bed, Laura gasped. "I'm sorry if I woke you. I couldn't sleep."

"I wouldn't be able to sleep either if my fiancé had left our engagement party before it ended and stayed out all night." Sheridan sat down beside Laura and glanced out the window. "You do know what people were saying, don't you?"

"I do not want to hear gossip!"

Laura wished her sister would leave her alone, but she knew Sheridan would needle her until she'd drawn

blood. Figuratively drawn blood, of course. Sheridan
had a knack for it, especially where Laura was concerned.
Her sister seemed to derive some perverse pleasure from
pointing out all of Laura's shortcomings.

"You know, I wondered how you'd caught yourself such
a prize," Sheridan said. "Someone like Jamie. Someone
in our social circle, very rich, handsome, charming. But
I'm beginning to understand. Your fiancé has a major
character flaw, doesn't he?"

"I don't know what you're talking about." *Please, God,
make her leave me alone. I don't want to despise my own sister,
but sometimes . . .*

Sheridan laughed. Laura hated the sound. She'd hated
that mocking laughter since they'd been children and
Sheridan had pointed out to Laura that "Mommy loves
me best." Maybe Mother did love Sheridan best. God
knew sometimes it seemed that way. But Laura knew
she was her father's favorite, something Sheridan punished her for, even though it wasn't her fault.

"I suppose it's only fair that both you and your fiancé
aren't quite perfect."

Laura forced herself to confront her sister. Their
gazes met forcefully—and this time Laura didn't blink,
didn't back down as she so often did. "I've never claimed
to be perfect—"

"Good thing . . . considering."

"Considering what? That I'm crazy?"

"You said it, I didn't."

"I'm not crazy. I'm not! I'm high-strung and nervous. I'm more emotionally sensitive than the average
person. That's all. Daddy said that I'm all right. Even
the doctors said I'm okay." Why did Sheridan have to
keep reminding her about her past mental and emotional problems?

"Does Jamie know?" Sheridan asked. "Is he aware

that his little bride-to-be could easily go completely berserk at any given moment?"

"What a cruel thing to say to me."

"Maybe someone told him about you and he's run away before—"

"He's gone to her!" Laura cried out. "That's what you wanted to hear, isn't it? You wanted me to admit that he left our engagement party to go to her."

"Then you do know all about her, don't you?"

"Yes, I know all about Jasmine Talbot."

Sheridan smirked, the expression hardening her cute cheerleader brunette beauty. Her big brown eyes twinkled with delight. "If Jamie was my fiancé, he wouldn't have to go to an old girlfriend for what he needed. I'd give it to him. I'd keep him so satisfied that he'd never even look at another woman." Sheridan paused, smiled wickedly, and licked her lips. "Why he chose you instead of me, I'll never know. Maybe he thought you were a virgin." Sheridan chuckled softly. "Of course, he knows from firsthand experience that I'm not."

The meaning of her sister's taunt hit Laura full force. Before she realized what she was doing, she slapped Sheridan, who simply continued smiling as she rubbed her red cheek. Laura jumped up and ran toward the door, tears clouding her vision.

"Where are you going?" Sheridan called after her.

Laura paused after she opened the bedroom door. "Anywhere away from you."

"Why don't you drive into town? You might find Jamie still in bed with his old lover. Or have you already been to town? Is that where you disappeared to last night after the party ended?"

Laura walked out into the hall and headed toward the stairs. Maybe she could find sanctuary in Big Jim's study. Surely Sheridan had tormented her enough and wouldn't follow her. As she descended the spiral staircase, her sister's last question played itself over in her head. *Or have you already been to town? Is that where you disappeared to last night after the party ended?*

What was Sheridan talking about? Laura had no memory of going anywhere after her engagement party ended. Why would she have driven into town alone? She wouldn't have, would she? *Don't think about it. Just because you have no memory of the time between when you said good night to your parents and when you came to your room two hours later doesn't mean you went to Cherokee Pointe to search for Jamie.*

But what if she had followed him to Jazzy's apartment? What if during those two missing hours she'd done something stupid? Something terrible? She'd been so hurt and angry when she realized Jamie had deserted her on their special night and embarrassed that most of the people attending the engagement party suspected he'd left her to go to Jazzy.

Just because years ago she lost several hours and had no memory of where she'd gone or what she'd done didn't mean it had happened again. Just because she had done something bad that time didn't mean she had this time. She wasn't crazy!

But what if I am? a frightened little voice inside her asked.

Jazzy hadn't slept a wink after Jamie finally left. He'd stayed two hours—an hour longer than she'd told him he could stay. And he'd tried his level best to convince her to let him spend the night in her bed. And truth be told, she'd been tempted. Maybe with Jamie, she always would be.

But a person could overcome temptation. Although

being tempted posed a problem, it was giving in to that temptation that wreaked havoc in her life. She supposed she was addicted to Jamie, the way another person might be addicted to tobacco or booze or drugs. You knew it was bad for you, knew it could kill you, but you still craved it.

Although each time she turned Jamie away, it became just a little easier the next time, she knew in her soul that only death—his or hers—would ever free her completely. At this point in her life, she hated Jamie more than she'd ever loved him. And the perverse, sinister part of her wished him dead—but only in those darkest, most frightening moments when her instincts for survival overcame her common decency.

There was no point mooning around in her apartment, wearing out the rug in her living room. All the restless pacing in the world wouldn't take her mind off her predicament. She had to find a way—short of murder—to keep Jamie out of her life. Permanently. She could have Jacob or Dallas issue a restraining order, but that would probably have an adverse effect. Jamie would see it as a sign of weakness on her part and pursue her all the more, even if it meant his being arrested. With Big Jim Upton's money, Jamie could afford the best lawyers and unlimited bail money.

What she needed was to get out of the house, go down to Jasmine's for breakfast, find as much work to do in the office this morning as possible. Jazzy showered hurriedly, then slung on jeans and a long-sleeved gold shirt. She grabbed a beige chenille sweater and her purse as she headed out the door. The air was crisp and chilly, the sky clear and bright. Already at six o'clock the little town was showing signs of activity. When she reached the bottom of the outside stairs that led from her upstairs apartment to the sidewalk that ran along the back of Jazzy's Joint, she heard a horn honk. When she glanced up, she saw Dr. MacNair toss up his hand and wave at her. She waved back as he turned his SUV into a parking place in front of Jasmine's, the restaurant she owned that was located beside her honky-tonk on the corner of Florence Avenue and Loden Street.

Now why couldn't she fall for a nice guy like Galvin MacNair? She'd bet her last dollar that he'd been as faithful as an old dog to his wife before she up and left him for her former high school sweetheart a couple of months ago. Why was it that nice guys seemed to finish last, when assholes like Jamie came out on top time and again?

Poor Galvin. The whole town knew his personal business, knew his wife had left town, moved in with her former lover, and filed for divorce. Every motherly old woman in Cherokee County had made it her mission in life to console him and try to fix him up with their daughter or niece. So why didn't she ask Galvin out? A new man in her life was just what she needed. But not Galvin. He just wasn't her type. He was too damn nice. Too sweet.

"Morning, Jazzy," Galvin said as he got out of his truck. "You're out and about mighty early."

"So are you," she replied. "You don't usually eat breakfast at Jasmine's. What's wrong, tired of hospital food?"

"I decided to eat out to celebrate." When Jazzy eyed him speculatively, he explained. "Nina went to Reno for a quickie divorce. It seems she couldn't wait."

"Gee, Galvin, I don't know what to say. Should I say congratulations or I'm sorry?"

He shrugged. "Neither, I guess."

She placed her hand on his shoulder. "Come on inside. Breakfast is on me."

"That's awfully nice of you, but not necessary." He followed her into Jasmine's.

When she saw Tiffany, one of her waitresses, she called out to her, "Dr. MacNair's breakfast is on the house."

"Sure thing." Tiffany smiled warmly and showed the doctor to a table.

Maybe Tiffany and Dr. MacNair might make a good couple. *Forget it,* she told herself. *Don't try to play matchmaker. You need to find yourself a man, somebody who'll take your mind off Jamie.*

No sooner had the thought been processed than the door opened and Sheriff Butler entered the restaurant. Big, rugged Jacob. A six-five quarter breed who'd once been a Navy SEAL. Now there was a man for you. A real man, one hundred percent, through and through. She'd known Jacob all her life and loved him—like a brother. They'd tried dating back last year and found out after only a couple of months the reason they'd never dated before then. No sparks. Absolutely no sexual chemistry. She wouldn't go as far as to say kissing him had been like kissing a brother, but they'd both figured out pretty quick that they were better off remaining good friends than risking their friendship by sleeping together.

"Good God, has hell frozen over?" Jacob asked teasingly in his deep baritone voice.

"Okay, so I recently said that hell would freeze over before I'd get up before seven, but there's no need to be sarcastic so early in the morning."

Jacob removed his Stetson and nodded toward a booth in the back. "Join me for breakfast?"

"Coffee, maybe."

By the time they slid into opposite sides of the booth, Tiffany appeared with a coffeepot. After she poured their cups full and took Jacob's breakfast order, she headed toward the kitchen.

"Want to tell me about it?" Jacob asked.

"About what?"

"I saw Jamie Upton's Mercedes parked in front of Jazzy's Joint in the middle of the night, after the place had closed."

"So?"

"I thought you were finished with him."

Jazzy forced a smile. "Why couldn't you and I have fallen in love? It would have made my life so much simpler. And so much better."

"I know it's none of my business, but . . . did you let him spend the night?"

"You're right—it's none of your business. But no, he stayed two hours and left. I have no doubt that he found somebody to soothe his disappointment."

"Maybe he went home to his fiancée. He is getting married in a few weeks, isn't he?" Jacob lifted his cup to his lips.

"That's what they say."

After taking several swigs, he set the cup down. "Genny called me right before I left the house. I figure she'll be getting in touch with you today."

"Is something wrong?"

"She had a vision before daybreak this morning."

A shudder rippled up Jazzy's spine. "She hasn't had a vision since . . . was it about—"

"It was about Jamie."

"What?"

"She saw someone kill Jamie. She believes it's a premonition."

"Who—who did she see kill Jamie? Was it me?"

Jacob reached across the table and took Jazzy's hand in his. "Are you planning on killing Jamie?"

She jerked her hand away. "No, of course not, but we both know I pulled a gun on him a few months ago. And we both know that, under the right circumstances, I might shoot him."

"Talk to Genny. Let her do a reading. She doesn't think you'll kill Jamie, but she believes that his death will create trouble for you."

"Why doesn't that surprise me? All Jamie Upton has ever been to me is trouble. Apparently he's trouble for me alive or dead."

"Stay away from him," Jacob advised. "And I'll make sure he stays away from you. I'll tell Caleb to keep an eye out for you and call me at the first sign of—"

"You think Genny's premonition is going to come true, don't you? And you're afraid she might be wrong and I'll be the one to kill Jamie."

When she looked into Jacob's moss green eyes, she saw the truth before he replied, "Better safe than sorry. No use taking any unnecessary risks."

Chapter 2

Erin Mercer cursed softly under her breath as she headed for the front door of her cabin. What the hell was Jim's grandson doing knocking on her door? She thought she had made it perfectly clear the last time he'd shown up—unannounced and unwelcome—that she wasn't buying what he was selling. As far as she was concerned, he was a worrisome brat someone should have disciplined years ago. Before she reached for the doorknob, she paused long enough to fasten the top two buttons on her blouse. No use giving Jamie an excuse to accuse her of trying to look sexy for him. Stupid boy. As if she'd ever be interested in someone as self-centered and immature as he, even with his undeniable youth and good looks. Too many women had fallen for the flashy exterior before discovering the ugliness of the interior man. She'd known his type and, when she'd been younger and foolish, she'd given her heart to someone a great deal like Jamie Upton.

If any other man stood outside her door this morning, she would take the time to check her appearance in the mirror, maybe even dab on a little blush and lipstick. After all, even though she was fifty, she took pride in her appearance and knew most men considered her an attractive woman.

Erin opened the door halfway and glared at the handsome devil standing on her doorstep. "What do you want?" she asked, her tone surly. She'd learned the first time Jim's grandson showed up at her cabin that he perceived any pleasantness on her part as an open invitation. Nothing would please him more than scoring with his grandfather's mistress.

"Wake up on the wrong side of the bed?" As he placed his hand on the door frame, he leaned forward. "If you'd woke up with me beside you, you'd be in a much better mood."

"It's early. I've had only one cup of coffee. I'm not in the mood for your games. I repeat, what do you want?"

When he moved toward her, she instinctively eased backward, not wanting their bodies to touch. She didn't trust this man, didn't feel entirely safe around him. She wasn't physically afraid of him, because she knew she could handle him, if it came to that. The fear she felt was more basic, a totally emotional response.

Once inside, Jamie headed straight for the living room. Erin huffed, resigned herself to enduring Jamie's presence for the time being, and shut the door. When she entered her living room, she found him already lounging on her sofa, with his feet propped up on the coffee table. He looked as if he'd been out all night. His tux was wrinkled, his bow tie missing, and his shirt buttoned up wrong. A hint of brown stubble on his pretty boy face gave him a rakish appearance. And that's what Jamie was all right—a rake. A bona fide, old-fashioned rake.

Of course, calling him a rake was a compliment in comparison to the other appropriate names that came to mind.

"I'm getting myself another cup of coffee. Would you care for some?" she asked as she passed through the living room and started toward the kitchen.

"I'll settle for coffee, but what I'd really like is some tea and sympathy. You know about that, don't you, Erin? It's when an older woman takes a younger man into her bed to comfort him."

Erin paused, but didn't bother looking back when she said, "My guess is that you've spent the night in someone's bed getting plenty of sympathy or whatever the hell you want to call it. I suggest that if you need more, you return to the generous lady who so willingly gave it to you earlier."

As she entered the kitchen, she heard him laughing. Damned obnoxious boy. Hurriedly she poured coffee into two mugs and returned to the living room. When she held out a mug for him, he patted the sofa.

"Sit with me."

She eyed him skeptically and shook her head.

He accepted the coffee. "I promise I won't bite."

"No, but I might. I might bite a plug out of that big head of yours and bring it back down to a normal size."

"You think I'm an egotistical bastard, don't you?"

"If the shoe fits . . ."

Erin took a seat opposite him, with the massive square oak cocktail table between them. "I suppose you know you'll have a great deal of explaining to do when you go home. The whole town is probably buzzing with gossip about your leaving your fiancée alone at your engagement party last night."

"I stayed for hours. I spoke to everyone, accepted

good wishes, presented myself as the dutiful fiancé. I didn't leave until nearly eleven."

"You left before half the guests did. How do you think that made your fiancée feel?"

"She knows I'm a cad . . . and loves me anyway." Jamie brought the coffee mug to his lips. "Strong and black. Just the way I like it."

"I feel sorry for Laura. She's so young and so in love with you. She deserves better. What's wrong with you, Jamie? Don't you have any idea how lucky you are? You have grandparents who adore you, all the money you could ever need, and a woman who is devoted to you."

"Laura's not the woman I want." He looked right at Erin, and for a split second she thought she saw genuine emotion in his hazel eyes. Sadness? Regret?

"Then why marry her? If she's not—"

"It's Jazzy," Jamie said. "It's always been Jazzy. It always will be."

"Then break off your engagement to Laura and marry Jazzy."

Jamie laughed, the sound hollow and emotionless. "You're a good one to talk. You're my grandfather's mistress. You know he'll never divorce Big Mama, yet you hang on to him anyway. Why don't you demand that he leave his wife and marry you?"

His accusation hit a nerve. Erin winced. "You're free. Jazzy's free. There's nothing to stop y'all from—"

"Big Mama would disown me if I married Jazzy. I'd have nothing. Not a dime to my name. I'd have to give up a fortune. I'm not willing to do that."

"Then you don't love Jazzy as much as you profess to love her."

"What do you know about it? I love her. I've loved her since we were teenagers. And just because Big Mama is forcing me to marry Laura doesn't mean I'm giving up Jazzy."

"Did you spend the night with Jazzy?"

"I went by to see her."

"And she turned you away."

"You're wrong. She didn't . . ." With his mug surrounded by both hands, Jamie leaned forward and held it between his spread thighs. He glanced at Erin. "She didn't let me stay, so I found a more willing lady, who shall remain nameless. After all, I don't kiss and tell. You might want to remember that for future reference."

"I don't think so."

Erin sipped on her coffee, finishing it off quickly. Why was Jamie really here? Why was he using her as a sounding board? As his mother confessor? It wasn't as if they were friends. She didn't even like him, and she wouldn't give him the time of day if he wasn't Jim's grandson. Unless he was a complete fool—which he wasn't—he had to know that she'd never have sex with him. Even if she wasn't in love with Big Jim, she wouldn't be crazy enough to become involved with Jamie. Any way you looked at it, he was bad news.

Jamie placed his cup on a coaster atop the cocktail table, then stood and went straight to Erin. Before she realized his intent, he dropped to his knees in front of her, grabbed her by the back of her neck and hauled her forward, just far enough to kiss her. He took her mouth demandingly. For a millisecond she froze, shocked by the unexpected assault. Then total awareness hit her. Her empty mug slipped out of her hand and hit the wooden floor with a splintering crash. She slipped her hand between their bodies and gave him a hard shove. He reeled backward and fell flat on his butt.

He looked up at her and grinned. "Now tell me that wasn't better than what you get from the old man."

"Your grandfather is twice the man you are—in every way. Now, get your sorry ass up off my floor and leave. I don't know what sort of game you're playing with me this morning, but I'm not interested. If I thought for one minute that I could help you . . . for Jim's sake, I would. But I think you're beyond help."

Jamie jumped to his feet like a jack-in-the-box. "Walk me to the door, darlin'."

"You know the way out."

"How about a good-bye kiss?"

"How about getting the hell out of my sight?"

"Now, sweet thing, don't be that way."

"Leave. Now!"

He winked at her, then sauntered out of the living room. She followed him and stood several feet away as he opened the front door. Before he left, he turned to her and said, "I'm going to accidently mention to my grandfather that I was with you this morning, sharing coffee, kissing . . ."

"You bastard!"

"I'd like to be able to tell the old son of a bitch that I'd screwed you, but I can imply as much and he might believe me. After all, if he asks you if I was here this morning, you won't lie to him, will you?"

Whistling as he walked toward his Mercedes, Jamie acted like a man who didn't have a care in the world, as if there weren't dozens of women who'd like to put a stake through his black heart. After getting inside the car, he lowered the window and blew Erin a kiss. As he backed out of the drive, she heard him laughing.

She should probably call Jim and tell him what had happened. Forewarn him. She wouldn't even bother if it wasn't for the fact that because of the difference in their ages, Jim wasn't as confident about their relationship as she was. God damn it, she hated to relay this incident to Jim, knowing how upset he'd be with Jamie. The boy, who should have been Jim's pride and joy, was an utter disappointment to him. A part of Erin wished she was still young enough to give Jim a child, even if at seventy-five he might not live to see the child grow up. But she was past the age of motherhood and Jim would probably laugh at the notion. Too bad he didn't have other grandchildren, at least one worthy of a man like Big Jim Upton.

For about the hundredth time since she left Chattanooga at daybreak that morning, Reve Sorrell asked herself why the hell she was doing this. Why did she feel compelled to come to Cherokee Pointe in search of a woman she'd never met? It wasn't as if she needed any more relatives. Since her mother died this past summer, cousins by the dozens had come out of the woodwork, all with an interest in the vast Sorrell fortune she'd inherited. One rather ungentlemanly cousin of her father's had actually had the balls to sue her, on the grounds that she was only Spencer and Lesley Sorrell's adopted child. The case had never gotten off the ground, since Reve's lawyer had convinced her cousin's lawyer that they'd be laughed out of court.

As she drove slowly along Main Street, she searched the faces of the citizens scurrying to and fro in the small downtown area. She had grown up in Chattanooga, a mid-size city, with just the right amount of hustle and bustle not to have remained a sleepy Southern town and yet not so large as to have lost its old-fashioned charm. She still lived in her parents' home on Lookout Mountain, in an old and prestigious neighborhood. Although not the Sorrells' biological child, she'd still been raised with their beliefs, traditions, and social snobbery. She was, in all but blood, a true Sorrell. And there wasn't a day that went by she didn't thank God for her good fortune.

As an infant of only weeks, she'd been blessed the day she was placed with the Sorrells. Her parents hadn't told her she was adopted until she was six, and in the telling, they'd made her feel very special and greatly loved. When at fourteen she'd asked them a lot of questions about her true parentage, they swore they knew nothing about her birth parents. It wasn't until she'd been awarded her bachelor's degree from UT that her then widowed mother told her she'd been found in a Dumpster in Sevierville, thrown away like trash when she was little more than a newborn.

It wasn't as if she had come to Cherokee Pointe today on a whim or that she'd simply taken Jamie Upton's word that she had a look-alike in this small mountain town. She'd met Jamie at a Christmas party late last year when he'd been visiting friends in Chattanooga. He'd done his best to charm her, and he had almost succeeded. She'd found the man utterly irresistible.

But once she'd discovered that he'd been fascinated by her because she resembled his teenage sweetheart, her common sense kicked into play. And if there was one thing Reve Sorrell was known for, it was her common sense. Never a playgirl, always a serious student as well as an obedient daughter and a lady who had been accused by many men of being an ice queen, Reve prided herself on not allowing emotions to rule her. She was an admitted control freak. Of course, knowing Jamie Upton for the charming scoundrel he was didn't mean she might not look him up while she was in the area. After all, hadn't he invited her to come for a visit and stay with his family on their estate outside town?

"I know a girl who could be your twin," Jamie had

told her. "You should come to Cherokee Pointe and meet Jasmine. She'd get a kick of meeting her look-alike."

Reve had hired a private investigation agency to compile a report on Jasmine Talbot. She and the woman were the same age, although their birthdays were almost a week apart; but then her parents hadn't known her exact birth date. And Jazzy, as her friends called her, had been raised by an aunt, an old woman known as the town kook.

Would a mother have given her sister one child and thrown the other into the garbage? Somehow it didn't seem likely. The private detective had included a dozen photographs of Jasmine Talbot when he'd handed in his report, and Reve had to admit that there was a striking resemblance between the two of them. Enough so that they could easily be sisters, perhaps even twins. She had put off meeting the woman face-to-face, unsure how she would react when she met Jazzy. If they were sisters, would she feel an instant bond, an immediate familial connection?

Reve parked half a block down from Jasmine's, got out of the Jag, locked it securely, and stepped up on the sidewalk. The air was crisp, fresh and cool, springtime morning cool. She checked her watch. Eight-fifteen. Still early enough to order breakfast at the restaurant. *Just go inside,* she told herself. *Order breakfast and see how the people who work for Jasmine react to you. If they don't go running to her with news that they've seen her twin and she doesn't come out to see for herself, then you'll have to ask to speak with her.*

When she arrived at the entrance to the restaurant, she paused, took a deep breath, then stiffened her spine and reached for the door handle. A large masculine hand shot out around her and grabbed the handle. Startled by the unexpected move, she gasped and glanced over her shoulder. A tall, lanky man with overly long brown hair and sexy golden eyes smiled at her. Her stomach did an involuntary flip-flop when he stared at her as if he wanted to kiss her. It wasn't that she didn't have a long line of eligible men knocking on her door. She did. But every single one of them knew she was a multi-millionaire. This man didn't know her, had no idea she was the heir to the Sorrell fortune. And he acted as if he was instantly interested in her.

His smile wavered. He shook his head. "Lady, has anyone ever told you that you've got a twin?"

"I beg your pardon?"

"Different hair style and your color is darker. More auburn. And your eyes are brown, not green, but then I'm pretty sure she wears colored contacts." He surveyed her from head to toe. "You're a few pounds heavier, maybe an inch taller. And your clothes are classier. But I'll be damned if you don't look enough like her to be—"

"And just who are *you*?" Reve asked, her tone deliberately stern.

"Sorry." He stepped back as she turned to face him. "I'm Caleb McCord." He held out his hand.

"Mr. McCord." She shook hands with him. "I'm Reve Sorrell. Does that name mean anything to you?"

He shook his head. "Nope. Should it?"

"No, I suppose not."

"Does the name Jasmine Talbot mean anything to you?" he asked. "You wouldn't by any chance be a relative I don't know about, would you?"

"Do you know Ms. Talbot well?"

"Well enough to know she doesn't have a sister, at least not one she knows anything about."

"That certainly makes two of us. As far as I know, I

don't have a sister. But a resident of Cherokee County I met at a party a few months ago mentioned I had a look-alike here in Cherokee Pointe, and since I was in the area anyway . . . well, I remembered his comments and I'm curious enough to want to meet her."

"And who would that be—the person who told you that you looked like Jazzy?"

"Jamie Upton. Do you know him?"

A dark frown erased all warmth from Caleb McCord's ruggedly handsome face. "So you're one of Jamie's women, huh? Something else you and Jazzy have in common."

"I take it that you don't especially like Jamie."

"Hate the guy's guts."

"Because?"

"Because being a man instead of a woman, I have the good fortune to see the son of a bitch for what he is."

"Which is?"

"He's a sorry, good-for-nothing louse whose hobby is breaking hearts and destroying lives."

Apparently this man cared for Jasmine Talbot and resented Jamie's connection to the lady. "You're jealous because Jasmine was his teenage sweetheart and she still loves him."

Caleb chuckled. "The guy did a number on you, too, didn't he? Is that the real reason you're in town? Jamie romanced you, screwed you, then left you to come back to Jazzy. And you're here in town to see what Jazzy's got that you don't have?"

"Mr. McCord, you have a very vivid imagination. Jamie didn't use and abuse me, although he would have if I'd given him a chance. I'm here strictly out of curiosity. I want to meet Jasmine Talbot."

"Then come right on in with me and I'll introduce

you to her." Caleb held open the door, then followed Reve into the restaurant.

The hostess, whose name tag read Tiffany, rushed forward, then stopped dead in her tracks. Her pink lips formed an oval as she gasped in surprise when he looked at Reve.

"We want a booth," Caleb said. "Two cups of coffee. Black?" he asked Reve.

"Cream, no sugar," she replied.

"And ask Jazzy to join us. Tell her I've got a little surprise for her."

"I'll say you do. Who is she?" Tiffany looked at Reve. "I mean, who are you, ma'am? I can't get over how much you look like Jazzy."

"So everyone keeps telling me."

"Second booth on the left, by the windows," Tiffany said. "I'll tell Jazzy and then get the coffee."

As they headed for the booth, several heads turned and more than one set of eyes stared unabashedly at Reve as she walked by. All of a sudden she wasn't so sure coming here like this had been such a good idea. Maybe she should have called Jasmine Talbot first and asked her a few questions. Maybe she should have telephoned Jamie and asked him to set up a meeting between her and her so-called twin.

By the time they sat down and Reve began to relax, whispers and murmurs surrounded them. Tiffany came rushing back to their booth, a coffeepot in hand. She flipped over the cups already on the table and poured the steaming brew, then reached in her apron and produced several small containers of half-and-half, which she placed by Reve's cup.

"Jazzy will be right out. She's just finishing up breakfast in her office with her aunt Sally and Ludie. Ludie brought in some pies she'd baked yesterday, so we'd have them for today's lunch crowd."

"Did you mention that I had a lady with me who just happens to be Jazzy's spitting image?" Caleb asked.

"I just told her that you wanted her to come out and meet a lady you had with you and that she was in for quite a surprise when she saw the lady."

No sooner had Tiffany walked away than Caleb stood up beside the booth, an odd grin on his face. Reve turned just enough to glance over her shoulder. The bottom dropped out of her stomach. The woman walking toward them wore skintight jeans, a bright yellow T-shirt that accentuated her large breasts, and sported a short, flyaway haircut that proclaimed her stylish and hip. Jasmine Talbot was strikingly attractive. And very sexy. Two things Reve Sorrell wasn't. But the body was similar to hers, although hers was well camouflaged beneath classically tailored pinstriped black slacks, a black blazer, and a white shirt. And the woman's every feature was a perfect match to Reve's. Same forehead, eyes, nose, mouth, ears, long neck, cheekbones, chin.

A cold fear encompassed Reve as Jazzy drew near. There was no way someone could look that much like another person without them being related. That meant this woman could very well be her sister, maybe her twin sister.

Jazzy stopped several feet away as Reve turned around fully and their gazes locked. She noted the same shock, the same uncertainty, and the same unanswered questions in Jasmine Talbot's eyes that plagued her. Green eyes, not brown, she noted. But what had McCord said? Something about Jazzy wearing contacts.

Caleb walked over to Jazzy and urged her into motion. "Come on over and meet another one of Jamie's lady friends. It seems you two have even more in common than just being Jamie Upton's type."

"What is this?" Jazzy asked as she came within a foot of Reve and glared at her. "Who are you?"

"Reve Sorrell."

Jazzy looked at Caleb. "How do you know this woman?"

"I just met her outside a few minutes ago. She mentioned that Jamie had suggested she come to Cherokee Pointe and meet you. It would seem that Jamie found an almost perfect substitute for you in Chattanooga."

While Caleb watched Jazzy speculatively, Reve picked up on a wild, angry tension smoldering inside him. God, what had she gotten herself into?

"Look," Reve said, "the reason I'm here really has nothing to do with Jamie, it's just that—"

"Why don't you tell the lady that Jamie no longer needs a substitute," Caleb said, "that as of last night, he's got the original back in his bed?"

Jazzy glowered at Caleb. Her cheeks flushed. "What were you doing, standing outside my apartment, watching me in the middle of the night?"

Jazzy glanced around, apparently checking to see if anyone was listening to their conversation. Since all eyes were focused on the three of them, it was obvious that anyone within hearing distance was privy to what was being said. Reve knew for sure and certain she had inadvertently walked into the middle of what seemed to be a lover's triangle: Caleb McCord, Jazzy Talbot, and Jamie Upton.

"I just happened to notice Upton's Mercedes at your place last night when I left work. I helped Lacy close up the place after you left," Caleb replied. "I don't give a shit who you screw, but from now on, don't pretend you want him out of your life. You've wasted my time and energy by getting me to throw him out of Jazzy's Joint time and again, when apparently all you were doing was titillating him, making him want you all the more. You know what that makes you in my book?"

Jazzy slapped Caleb McCord. Right there in the middle of the restaurant. Reve gasped, shocked by the woman's actions. A lady never reacted in such a coarse, crude manner. Certainly never in public. But then, from all accounts, Jazzy Talbot was no lady.

Being involved, even as a bystander, to this sort of crude behavior was not what she'd bargained for when she decided to make this trip. *Get the hell out of here now,* she told herself. *Go home to Chattanooga and forget there's a woman here in Cherokee Pointe who might be your twin. You don't want to be related to a woman like Jazzy Talbot.*

While the attentive clientele absorbed the scene between Jazzy and Caleb, Reve picked up her purse from the booth, then turned and all but ran from the restaurant. Before she reached the door, she heard a man's voice calling her name, but she didn't slow down, didn't look back to see who it was.

Just as she got outside and took a deep breath, a familiar hand clamped down on her shoulder. "Don't run off," Caleb said.

Reve swallowed, then turned to face him. "Please, leave me alone."

"I apologize for what happened back there. Jazzy and I tend to ignite sparks off each other. And I did deserve that slap she gave me. Come on back and—"

"No, thank you. I've seen quite enough of Jasmine Talbot."

"Don't judge Jazzy by what happened in there. If you'd give yourself a chance to get to know her, you'd like her. She's all right, you know. Her only problem is that she's addicted to Jamie Upton. And I suspect you might have that same addiction."

"I assure you, Mr. McCord, I do not."

Caleb laced Reve's arm through his. "If that's true, then maybe I've been trying to score points with the wrong redhead."

Chapter 3

The minute Jim Upton heard his grandson's Mercedes zoom into the circular drive in front of the house, he stomped out onto the veranda to head the boy off. He had a few choice words to say to Jamie, and he didn't want any of the ladies to overhear their conversation.

Reba had been so upset with their grandson's outrageous disappearance from his own engagement party last night that she'd gone to bed with a migraine. When he'd checked in on his wife this morning, she'd still been sleeping. He and Reba hadn't shared a bed in years. Her choice, not his.

Jim hadn't seen anything of the Willis family—Laura, her mother and father and younger sister. He assumed they were all still in bed. Of course, he wouldn't blame Cecil Willis if he insisted his daughter call off the wedding. Damn shame that such a sweet, fragile Southern belle had fallen in love with Jamie. The look on dear little Laura's face last night when she realized Jamie had just up and left had been enough to break a man's heart.

Jim stood on the veranda, his arms crossed over his chest, and watched his grandson meander up the steps, all the while whistling. When Jamie saw Jim, he threw up a hand and smiled broadly. *Damned good-for-nothing scoundrel,* Jim thought. What the boy lacked in every other aspect, he often made up for in charm. But charm was worthless in and of itself. Just about as worthless as Jamie. Why the Good Lord had seen fit to take away Jim's son and daughter and leave him with nothing but Jim Jr.'s only child, he'd never know. If only Jamie was more like his father. But he wasn't.

And to think that Jamie had been such a sweet, precocious child. Loving, beguiling, and seemingly as devoted to his grandparents as they were to him. But with each passing year, from twelve years old to the present, at twenty-nine, Jamie had become more and more of a disappointment.

If it hadn't been for Reba's pleading defense of the boy, Jim would have written him off as a lost cause a couple of years ago. But Jim realized that losing Jamie would break Reba's heart, and even if he didn't love his wife—had never really loved her the way a man should—he cared about her and believed she deserved what little happiness she derived from their grandson.

Reba had her heart set on Jamie's marrying Laura. And by God, if it meant beating sense into the boy to get him to straighten up, at least until after the wedding, then Jim was ready to whip his grandson's ass.

"We need to talk," Jim said as Jamie approached him.

"Ah, now, Big Daddy, what good is talking going to do? You'll chew me out, I'll say I'm sorry, then—"

Jim grabbed Jamie's arm, twisted it behind his back and said, "March your sorry ass around to the side of the house and into the gazebo. You and I are about to have a major come-to-Jesus-talk, boy."

Grunting in pain, Jamie struggled. Fruitlessly. Despite being seventy-five, Jim had the advantage of not only superior strength, but superior size. He was half a foot taller and fifty pounds heavier than his grandson. "Hellfire, Big Daddy, you're going to break my arm."

"I'd like to break your neck." Jim tightened his hold on Jamie's arm and marched him down the steps and onto the driveway.

Jamie stopped struggling, relaxed, and fell into step with Jim's pace. As soon as they drew near the large, ornately decorated gazebo at the side of the house, Jim gave Jamie a shove inside and motioned for him to sit down. Jamie sat in one of the two huge wicker chairs. Jim paced back and forth in front of his grandson, then took a deep breath and sat down in the other chair.

"Look, it's no big deal," Jamie said. "I'll apologize to Laura and to Big Mama and to Mr. and Mrs. Willis."

Jim clenched his teeth. *No big deal. I'll apologize.* "There comes a time when apologies just aren't enough. How the hell are you going to explain to Laura why you left your engagement party before it ended? Are you going to tell her that you had to go see Jazzy Talbot, that your hunger for another woman was so powerful that—"

"I can't give Jazzy up. Not entirely. Surely you, of all people, understand that."

"Don't compare the two of us, boy. I have never done anything that I knew would hurt your grandmother. I respect her too much, care about her too—"

"What about Erin? Don't you think that if Big Mama knew about your latest mistress, she'd be hurt?"

"She doesn't know and she never will."

"And Laura has no reason to ever—"

"Hell, boy, Laura knows about Jazzy. Everybody in Cherokee County knows about Jazzy."

Jamie glanced away, a sullen look marring his handsome features. "I'll marry Laura, just like Big Mama wants. And we'll give y'all some grandbabies. That should make Big Mama happy. But I can't love Laura. Not the way I love Jazzy."

Jim groaned. A part of him actually felt sorry for his grandson. Jamie truly believed that what he felt for Jazzy Talbot was love. Hell, maybe it was. Maybe he loved Jazzy as much as he was capable of loving another human being. But Jamie's love was weak and spineless, just the way he was.

"I thought Jazzy had pretty much told you to get lost," Jim said. " Is that what this is all about—you just can't take no for an answer? Her not wanting you makes you want her all the more?"

"She wants me." Jamie rose to his feet and walked over to the edge of the gazebo railing that circled the twenty-foot circular building.

"Did she let you stay the night?"

Jamie turned, a wicked grin on his face. "I stayed a couple of hours. We talked. We said our good-byes. But I know that sooner or later, she'll take me back. She always has."

"Not this time. She wants marriage, doesn't she? She knows you'll never marry her. I hear she dated Jacob Butler for a while. He's a fine man who'd make her a good husband. And I've been told that the new bouncer at Jazzy's Joint is very protective of her. He's thrown you out of the place more than once, hasn't he?"

"Jazzy broke it off with Butler . . . that big, ugly Indian. And as far as Caleb McCord—she wouldn't marry him anymore than she'd marry Butler. Neither man has what Jazzy wants."

"And that would be?"

"Money."

Jim snorted. "Maybe that's what she wanted when she

was sixteen and got herself pregnant with your baby, but Jazzy's grown up and turned into a damn fine businesswoman. My guess is her priorities have changed."

Jamie turned and glared at Jim. "Is this conversation over? I need some breakfast and a few hours' sleep."

Jim grabbed Jamie by the front of his fancy tuxedo shirt and hauled him closer. "Before you do anything, you find Laura and you fix things with her. You get down on your knees and beg her to forgive you, if that's what it takes. Come Saturday, three weeks from now, you're marrying that girl. And if you do anything—and I mean anything—to break your grandmother's heart, I'll break your damn fool neck. I've had all I'm going to take from you."

Jamie trembled. *Good,* Jim thought. *It's about time I made him afraid of me.* He released Jamie and shoved him toward the exit. "When you apologize to Laura, you'd better be convincing."

Locking his gaze to Jim's, Jamie smiled. "I didn't spend the night with Jazzy, but I did find solace in a lovely lady's arms. I think you might be interested in who I shared coffee and a kiss with less than half an hour ago."

"I couldn't care less what poor, stupid slut entertained you last night."

"Now is that any way to talk about Erin Mercer?"

Every nerve in Jim's body rioted, every muscle froze. "Try another lie, boy, because I don't believe that one."

Jamie shrugged. His grin broadened to show a set of perfect, pearly white teeth. "If you don't believe me, call her and ask her if we didn't share breakfast coffee and a smoldering good-bye kiss this morning."

Balling his hands into fists to keep from hitting his grandson, Jim inhaled deeply and exhaled slowly. "Get out of my sight. Now!"

Jamie laughed as he turned and sauntered lazily toward the house. Jim, who watched until the boy disappeared from view, wondered what he'd ever done to deserve a grandson like Jamie.

Sally Talbot and her best friend Ludie emerged from Jasmine's and headed up the street toward Jones's Market. Sally had a hankering for some catfish and she knew Jones's was the best place in town to get fresh catfish. They bought straight from Silas Monroe, who owned a pond-raised catfish farm here in Cherokee County. When they crossed the street, Sally gathered a mouthful of tobacco juice and pursed her lips. She spit out a stream of brown liquid just as they stepped up on the sidewalk.

"I wish you'd give up that nasty habit," Ludie said. "You're going to wind up with cancer of the mouth, mark my word. One of these days—"

"My God, look over there . . ." Sally grabbed Ludie's arm. She couldn't believe her eyes. But sure enough, right there across the street, only half a block from Jasmine's, a woman stood talking to Caleb McCord. A woman who looked a hell of a lot like Jazzy. A cold fear surged through Sally—a hidden fear that had plagued her for nearly thirty years.

"Where?" Ludie asked, glancing up and down the street.

"Over there by that fancy green car. I think it's one of them Jag-u-wars. Look at that woman talking to Caleb."

Ludie's keen black eyes zeroed in on the woman. Ludie gasped. "Dear God in heaven. She looks like . . . she could be Jazzy's twin. But how's that . . . oh, lordy, Sally, do you think she might be—"

"Yeah, I think she just might be. And if she is, you know what that means."

"It means our Jazzy is going to be asking a lot of questions."

"You got that damn straight." Sally munched on her tobacco, then spit on the sidewalk. "And just what do I tell her?"

"You could tell her the truth."

"She might hate me."

"She might," Ludie replied. "But knowing our Jazzy the way I do, I figure she loves you enough to forgive you."

"Come on." Sally motioned to her friend. "I got to see her up close. Let's go over there and get Caleb to introduce us. I might ask that lady a few questions before I worry too much. Maybe she don't know—"

"If she doesn't know she looks like Jazzy, she will soon enough. You know Caleb will tell her."

Sally yanked on Ludie's arm, then all but dragged her short, plump friend back across the street. As they drew near and were able to get a better look at the woman, Sally's heart sank. This gal had to be Jazzy's sister. *Lord, help me. I had no idea there were two babies. If I'd known . . .*

"Morning, Miss Sally." Caleb McCord, always cordial and mannerly, nodded in his friendly way. "Miss Ludie. How are you ladies this morning?"

"We're just fine," Ludie replied, all the while sizing up the woman beside Caleb. "Who's this pretty lady you got with you?"

Caleb chuckled. "Miss Ludie, Miss Sally, I'd like for y'all to meet Ms. Reve Sorrell, from Chattanooga, Tennessee."

"Howdy do, miss." Ludie smiled.

"What brings you to Cherokee Pointe?" Sally asked.

"I'd think that was obvious," Caleb said. "She came

here looking for a woman she was told resembled her enough to be her twin sister."

"Well, now that you mention it, she does favor our Jazzy some, don't she?" Sally extended her hand toward the woman. "I'm Jazzy's Aunt Sally."

Reve shook hands with Sally, all the while studying Sally as if she'd put her under a microscope for close scrutiny. "I met your niece and I agree that we do look a bit alike, but—"

"You know, they say that we all got a double out there in the world somewhere. Guess Jazzy's yours, huh?"

"Ms. Talbot, may I ask you a question?" Reve Sorrell looked Sally right in the eye.

Sally swallowed. *Don't blink,* she told herself. *Don't show any fear. You ain't done nothing wrong. Not thirty years ago. Not today.*

"What you want to ask, gal?"

"If Jazzy is your niece, then you'd know if . . . if she had a sister, wouldn't you?"

Sally chuckled, the sound just a bit off. She hoped nobody but Ludie heard the nervousness in her voice. "Yes, I'd know. And if you're thinking there's any chance you and Jazzy are sisters, then get that notion right out of your head. My younger sister—Jazzy's mama—had one baby girl. That's all."

"I see."

Sally could tell by Reve Sorrell's heaving sigh and her tentative smile that she was relieved not to be related to Jazzy. Judging the woman by the fancy clothes she wore and the expensive sports car she drove, Sally figured Ms. Sorrell came from money. Big money. And big bank accounts usually came attached to big snobbery. More than likely this gal was mighty glad to find out that she wasn't blood kin to the likes of Jazzy Talbot.

"What did Jazzy say when you two met?" Ludie asked, and Sally wanted to slap her friend senseless. *Damn it, Ludie, leave well enough alone.*

"We really didn't get a chance to talk," Reve said.

"I'm afraid Jazzy and I had a little difference of opinion," Caleb admitted.

"Let me guess." Sally huffed. "It was over Jamie Upton coming around last night, wasn't it?" Sally reached over and patted Caleb on the back. "You keep on giving her hell about it. When she told me she'd let that rascal in last night, I sure gave her hell for being so stupid."

"Jazzy told you that she was with Jamie?" Caleb asked.

Sally eyed him speculatively. "She didn't let him spend the night, you know. She ain't that stupid. She swore to me that it's over between them. And I believe her."

Reve cleared her throat. "If y'all will excuse me—"

"Ms. Sorrell is a friend of Jamie's, too," Caleb said. "He's the one who told her that she had a look-alike here in Cherokee Pointe."

"God help you, gal." Sally pinned Reve with a warning glare. "If you know what's good for you, you'll steer clear of Jamie Upton. He's nothing but trouble for any woman. Somebody should have skinned him alive years ago." Sally puckered her lips and spit a hunk of brown tobacco juice on the sidewalk. When she heard Reve Sorrell gasp and noticed her jump backward, Sally grinned. "Damn, I should have killed that good-for-nothing polecat back when he was a teenager. I could have saved Jazzy a heap of heartache." Sally slapped her hand down on Ms. Sorrell's shoulder. Wouldn't be a bad idea to scare the woman off. No sirree, not a bad idea at all. Even if Ms. Sorrell thought she might be Jazzy's sister, knowing somebody like Sally might be her aunt would run her off pronto. "If you been fucking around with Jamie, then you got my sympathy. Take my advice and stay away from him from now on."

"Ms. Talbot, I can assure you that I have not been—"

"Call me Sally. Everybody does." Sally interrupted before Reve finished her sentence, which undoubtedly was a denial of a sexual relationship with Jamie Upton.

"Sally, it's been . . . interesting meeting you. But I really must go." Reve backed away several feet. "Having met your niece . . . and you . . . and finding out that she and I are not related, despite our resemblance—"

"Did you really come here just to see if you and Jazzy might be related?" Sally asked. "Or did Jamie mention Jazzy and you came here figuring to see if she was competition? She ain't. Her and Jamie are finished. But you do know he's engaged . . . to be married."

"No, I didn't know, but I'm pleased for him. Believe me, Jamie Upton doesn't mean a thing to me. Now, if y'all will excuse me, I'll be going."

Sally spit again, this time creating a lot of noise before doing so, making the event seem even more gross to someone unaccustomed to being around an old woman who chewed tobacco and occasionally dipped snuff, too.

"Don't run off," Caleb called after Ms. Sorrell.

The lady in question didn't even bother saying good-bye. She unlocked her car, got in, and backed out of the parking place, all in a powerful hurry.

"So, what's going on?" Caleb asked Sally. "Why did you try to hard to run her off? Is she really Jazzy's sister?"

"What a fool thing to say," Sally told him. "My Jazzy ain't got no sister. My sister gave birth to one baby girl. Says so right on her birth certificate."

"Mm-hm . . . if you say so."

"I say so."

"Well, it's been quite a day already and it's not even ten o'clock." Caleb nodded cordially. "You ladies have a good one." Smiling, he turned and walked away.

Just as soon as Caleb was out of earshot, Ludie grabbed Sally's arm. "You might have run that Sorrell girl off pretty easy like, but we both know that Jazzy's going to ask you about her. And you just remember that Jazzy knows you. She'll be able to tell if you're lying to her."

"I didn't lie to that Sorrell woman and I won't be lying to Jazzy when I tell her that my sister, Corrine, gave birth to one little girl. Not twins. Corrine's baby didn't have no brothers or sisters."

"That's only a half truth and you know it."

"It's all the truth Jazzy ever needs to know."

"Something tells me that sooner or later Jazzy and that Sorrell girl are both going to start wondering more and more about why they look so much alike."

"There could be another reason, another explanation," Sally said. "I swear to you that I don't know nothing about there being two babies. All I ever knew about was my little Jasmine."

"I believe you." Ludie patted Sally on the back. "I been around all these years, all of Jazzy's life. I know everything you know."

Not quite everything, Sally thought. *There was one thing I never told you, my old friend. One thing I'll never tell a living soul.*

Morning sunlight warmed her as it streamed in through the floor-to-ceiling windows and caressed her body. She'd been thinking about what she had to do to protect her child. No more, no less than any mother would do to keep her child safe. Jamie Upton was a danger she planned to eliminate. He didn't deserve to live.

She had to be very careful. Her plans had to be well thought out, meticulous in details, so that not only would Jamie die a horrific death, but so that Jasmine Talbot would be accused of his murder. They were both sinners. Fornicators. They both deserved to die. Why did men think they could betray the women they professed to love and never be punished?

She had to act quickly. The wedding was in three weeks. Any time before then would be soon enough, but she didn't think she could wait. The thought of tormenting Jamie excited her. She didn't dare wait much longer. What if someone else killed him before she got the chance? And it was quite possible that might happen, because so many people hated Jamie. Even his beloved Jazzy professed to despise him. But she hadn't turned him away last night, had she? And for that alone, she deserved all the misery that was in store for her.

Chapter 4

Jamie felt damn good. He'd scored a direct hit on the old man. Even if Big Daddy knew he hadn't fucked Erin, some little fragment of doubt would remain in his mind about whether or not his mistress found his grandson a more interesting prospect. The more his grandfather worried about his own love life, the less time he'd have to interfere in Jamie's.

Of course, he'd have to cool things with other women for the next couple of months. Last night had been his final fling before walking down the aisle. After the honeymoon, he'd gradually ease back into Jazzy's life and into any other woman's bed he chose to pleasure him.

Jazzy might have convinced herself that they were through, but she was just kidding herself. The two of them were bound together forever, and nothing or nobody could ever permanently split them apart. Big Mama might be forcing him into a marriage he didn't want, but she couldn't make him love Laura. And neither she nor Big Daddy could make him give up Jazzy.

Whistling with an uneasy bravado—he wasn't sure he

could soothe Mr. and Mrs. Willis's ruffled feathers even if he squared things with Laura—Jamie headed up the stairs. By taking the back stairs, he ran less risk of running into his future in-laws before he spoke privately to Laura. Oh, she'd be spitting mad and all weepy. But a few kisses, a few well-chosen words, a promise to never stray again, and she'd be putty in his hands.

As he approached Laura's bedroom—the one she now shared with her younger sister— the door swung open, surprising him when Sheridan sashayed out of the room, wearing a bright pink springtime dress, looking much too sexy for a girl of not quite twenty. And that sexiness was more than just show. He knew, firsthand, that his fiancée's little sister was a hot and wild piece of ass. She had taken great delight in thinking she seduced him the very night he'd asked Laura to marry him, back at their home in Kentucky.

"Well, well, well. Look what the pussycat's dragged in," Sheridan said, a mischievous twinkle in her big brown eyes as she paused directly in front of Jamie and gave him a come-hither smile.

"Good morning to you, too, sister-in-law." Jamie leaned over and kissed her on the cheek.

Sheridan reached up and curled her hand around his neck, then stood on tiptoe and brought her mouth in alignment with his. She whispered against his lips, "You can do better than that, can't you?"

He removed her hand from his neck, swatted her behind, and chuckled. "Behave yourself, child. I've got enough trouble on my hands this morning without being caught with my tongue down your throat."

Sheridan offered him a seductive pout. "Mother and Daddy are very upset with you. And poor Laura cried her eyes out all night. I'm afraid she may call off the wedding."

"Not on your life. Your sister is going to become Mrs. James Upton III in three weeks. Big Mama has decreed it to be so, and what Reba Upton wants, she gets."

"Then you'd better start making lovey-dovey noises to Laura. And don't bother lying to her about where you were. She knows you went straight to Jasmine Talbot."

"I have no intention of denying where I went," Jamie said. "Once I explain to Laura why I was with Jazzy, she'll understand."

Sheridan's eyes widened in astonishment. "This I have to hear."

"Later," Jamie told her. "Meet me at the stables in an hour." He winked at her, then walked past her and knocked on Laura's bedroom door.

"Who is it?" Laura asked.

Jamie glanced over his shoulder and gave Sheridan another quick wink, then blew her a kiss. She smiled triumphantly before rushing off down the hall.

"Laura, darling, it's Jamie."

"Go away! I never want to see you again."

"Now, pet, don't be that way. I have to talk to you. I have to make you understand why I did what I did last night."

"I don't want to hear your explanations. I've forgiven you too many times already. If you want Jazzy Talbot, then you can have her. I'm calling off the wedding and—"

"You can't do that." Jamie turned the doorknob and flung open the door. Still wearing her nightgown, Laura sat on the edge of her bed. "You don't want to break my heart, do you?"

"Don't you dare come in here." Laura jumped up off the bed and pointed to the door. "Get out right this minute."

Jamie slammed the door shut, then locked it. "I'm not going anywhere. Not until you let me explain. Not until you forgive me for being a stupid jackass."

Laura lifted her pretty little head and hazarded a glance in his direction, but looked away quickly. That one swift glance told him that he had said just the right thing, given her just enough hope to make her listen to him. He would lie to her, tell her what she most wanted to hear. That was always the best policy with women. Tell a woman the truth and you're doomed. Lie to her, flatter her, tell her whatever her heart desires, and you'll have her eating out of your hand.

He took several tentative steps in her direction, then paused as if uncertain he had a right to approach her. *Act humble,* he told himself. *Pretend to be torn apart inside with the fear you might lose her.*

"Laura, I made a mistake in leaving our engagement party before it ended. I didn't realize at the time how it would look to you, your parents, and our guests." Jamie took another couple of steps toward her. "Chalk it up to my eagerness to do something I should have done a long time ago."

She looked at him again, this time for several seconds, before glancing down at the floor. "What—what are you talking about? What should you have done a long time ago?"

"Ended things with Jazzy."

Laura's head snapped up, her gaze focused directly on his face. He'd known that statement about Jazzy would gain him her full attention.

"I don't understand," Laura said.

He moved closer, bringing himself within touching distance of his eager-to-believe-him fiancée. "Last night at our engagement party, with our family and friends here to celebrate with us, I realized just how important this marriage is to me . . . how important you are to me. I want our marriage to work. I—I love you, Laura."

Tears gathered in her eyes as she stared at him, disbelief battling with hope in her expression. "You went to Jazzy and you spent the night with her."

"Yes, I went to Jazzy." He reached out for Laura. She pulled back, retreating from his touch. "I went to her to tell her that it's over between us. Now and forever. I told her that I love you. She understood. We talked for a couple of hours—just talked—then I left."

"If that's true, then where were you all night?"

"I drove around for a while, thinking, pondering my many mistakes, making plans for my—our future. Before I knew it, I found myself over in Knox County, nearly in downtown Knoxville. I thought about calling you, but hell, sugar, it was the wee hours of the morning. So I pulled off at a rest stop and got a few hours sleep before I headed back home."

"I want to believe you."

Jamie zeroed in on her, leaving her no room for escape. Knowing she wouldn't put up much of a fight, he pulled her into his arms and said, "Believe this, Laura. I love you. Only you." When he lowered his head to kiss her, she turned away from him. He grasped her chin and maneuvered her face around so that he could take her lips. Once he kissed her, she succumbed without even so much as a whimper. God, she was so easy. Dumb little cunt.

When he finally ended the kiss, she looked up at him with love and trust in her eyes. "Oh, Jamie, I love you so much."

"I know you do. And I love you even more. We're going to be the happiest young couple in the state of Tennessee come three weeks from Saturday." He lifted her into his arms and swung her around the room. "Hell, make that the happiest couple in the whole United States of America."

Reve wanted nothing more than to escape Cherokee Pointe as fast as she could. She'd been a fool for coming here, for seeking out Jasmine Talbot in the hopes the woman might prove to be her biological sister. Even though she didn't quite believe Sally Talbot's staunch denial that Sally's younger sister had given birth to more than one child, Reve couldn't accept the fact that she and a woman such as Jazzy Talbot might be blood related. The woman was trash. And from what she'd gathered on very brief acquaintance, Jazzy was a whore. Even if by some weird trick of fate she and Jazzy were related, Reve didn't want to pursue the truth. She didn't want to be the woman's sister. Hell, she didn't want them even to be cousins. And she certainly didn't want the likes of Sally Talbot to be her aunt!

As she zoomed her Jag along the highway leading out of town, she considered the can of worms she might have opened with her visit. Why had she told them her name? If any of them wanted to find her, it would be very easy. Everyone who was anyone in Chattanooga, in all of Hamilton County, knew who Reve Sorrell was. She was the heir to Sorrell fortune! People like Jazzy Talbot and her aunt Sally were the type to want money from a long-lost relative.

And what about Caleb McCord? She'd taken an instant liking to him, but she didn't kid herself about what sort of man he was. From the looks of him, he was a diamond in the rough, a poor boy from the wrong side of the tracks. A woman like Jazzy would know how to handle that kind of man, but Reve figured she would be out of her depths. She liked her gentlemen friends to be her social, intellectual, and financial equal. It didn't take a genius to figure out Caleb McCord didn't fit that bill, at least on two counts.

Would Caleb's curiosity about why Reve Sorrell and Jazzy Talbot looked enough alike to be twins translate into action? Would she have to pay him off so he would let the matter drop? And once they discovered how rich she was, what would it cost her to make Jazzy and Sally Talbot disappear from her life?

Cursing herself for allowing her desire to know the truth about her "double" to create a potentially embarrassing situation for her, Reve didn't realize how fast she was driving until she whizzed past a big black pickup truck going in the opposite direction. Suddenly she heard a siren. Damn! Glancing in her rearview mirror she saw the blue flashing light atop the truck, which had turned around in the middle of the road. Oh, great. Just great. Who was this guy? A policeman? A sheriff's deputy?

Slow down and pull off to the side of the road, she told herself. *Pay off this overeager lawman and be on your way.*

Before she could follow through with her plans to be a cooperative citizen, an enormous animal dashed across the road in front of her. Good God! A full-grown buck with an impressive rack that would gain the deer the admiration of any hunter. She swerved, trying to keep from hitting the magnificent animal, and in the process wound up running her Jag into the ditch. And not just a shallow ditch on the side of the road. No, it was a deep ditch, on the side of the mountain. Luckily she managed to bring the car to a full stop only seconds before it would have hit head-on into a massive oak tree. When she skidded to a halt, even her seat belt didn't prevent her from bouncing. Thankfully, the air bag didn't deploy.

With her heart beating wildly, her nerves screaming,

and a sudden headache pounding in her temples, Reve tried to undo her seat belt. Her nervous fingers couldn't manage the simple task. What was the matter with her? She wasn't hurt. Didn't have a scratch on her. Whatever damage had been done to the Jag could be repaired, and if not, she'd simply buy herself a new car and use one of the five others she owned in the meantime.

Why she was shaking like a leaf?

Shock. She was in shock. That had to be it.

A loud rapping on the driver's side window gained her immediate attention. When she looked through the window, she gasped when she saw the face of a dark-skinned savage, with black hair down to his shoulders, and a set of slanted green eyes peering at her. Maybe she'd hit her head and didn't remember. Surely she was hallucinating. This man couldn't be real.

Suddenly the driver's side door opened and the hallucination spoke to her. "Are you all right? Are you hurt?"

Reve gulped as she came face-to-face with the most brutally masculine man she'd ever seen in her entire life. A big, fierce warrior, with an angry look in his moss green eyes, reached out and began running his huge hands over her head, neck, shoulders, and arms.

"What the hell do you think you're doing?" she cried. "Get your hands off me."

He ceased his inspection and withdrew his hands. "I was trying to check you for injuries, since you didn't respond. If you're all right, let me help you get out and up the hill to my truck. I'll call a wrecker and—"

"Who are you?" She stared at the guy, noting that although he spoke with authority, he wasn't wearing any type of uniform. For all she knew he was a serial rapist who just happened to be in possession of a flashing blue police light.

"Sheriff Butler," he told her.

"You're the sheriff?" Inspecting him further, she realized he was Native American, at least part Native American. Of course half-breeds and quarter breeds probably weren't all that uncommon in this area, which wasn't that far from the Cherokee reservation just over the state line.

"I noticed you have a Hamilton County tag," he said. "You visiting somebody here or you just passing through?"

"Just passing through," she replied.

He reached over and undid her seat belt. "Think you can manage to get out, or should I help—"

"I can get out without any help, thank you very much."

After grabbing her purse off the other bucket seat, she shoved the sheriff aside and managed to exit the Jag, but the minute her high heels hit the soft, uneven ground, she lost her balance. He grabbed her around the waist, the action unintentionally bringing her body up against his rock-hard chest. She gasped, then looked up at him as her heartbeat drummed loudly in her ears. Their gazes locked instantly.

"Well, I'll be damned," he said as he stared at her, his mouth slightly parted.

"Take a picture, Sheriff, it'll last longer."

"Sorry." He apologized, but continued staring at her. "You remind me of a friend of mine. The two of you could be—"

"Twins," Reve finished his sentence for him.

"Yeah, how'd you know?"

"Just a wild guess." She pulled away from him and tried to walk up the steep embankment, but three-inch heels weren't made for mountain climbing.

Sheriff Butler came up beside her, put his arm around her waist, and all but hauled her up the hill. *How totally demoralizing,* she thought. Up until this moment in time, she'd never had so much as a parking ticket. And here she was being dragged away from the scene of an auto accident she had caused by her reckless driving. Well, not reckless, just speedy.

When they reached the side of the road, the sheriff released her instantly, as if he had no more desire to touch her than she had for him to have his hands on her. There was something unnerving about the man, something about him that sent off warning signals in her brain. And what disturbed her the most was that her reaction to him—to his touch—wasn't revulsion. No, it was something else. Something she couldn't name.

"We'll get a wrecker out here to bring your car up and take it to the garage," he told her. "You're lucky. It would have been a damn shame if your bad driving had totaled your little XKR. I guess that fancy sports car must have set you back at least eighty grand."

She didn't like his tone, didn't like his condescending attitude. Hell, she didn't like him! He was too bossy, too big, too masculine. "No big deal," she replied. "The only thing that matters is that no one was injured, not even the deer."

"Yeah, you're lucky, all right." He surveyed every inch of her, studying her closely as if he was memorizing her face and body. "Speeding the way you were doing often leads to serious accidents. Sometimes fatal."

"I wasn't driving that fast."

"My guess is you were doing over seventy-five in a fifty-five speed zone."

"You guess my car cost eighty grand. You guess I was doing over seventy-five." Reve crossed her arms over her chest and glared at the sheriff, giving him her best I'm-important-and-you're-not expression. "Do you know anything for certain, Sheriff, or do you just go through life making uneducated guesses?"

His gaze narrowed as he focused on her. She shivered. That stern, disapproving glare rattled her nerves.

"Get in the truck," he told her as he headed toward his vehicle. "I'm taking you to my office where I'll get all the information I need. Then, if I decide not to arrest you—"

"Arrest me!" Reve stormed around the hood of the truck, following him until she could grab his arm. "Now, you listen here to me, you big country hick Cochise wannabe, I'm not accustomed to being treated this way. I can easily contact the governor and—"

He turned around, grabbed her by the shoulders sternly but gently, and said, "Get your butt in the truck. Now. And if you want to call the governor when we get to my office, then you call him. Hell, call the president for all I care. The way I see it, you must have a screw loose to overreact to everything that's happened the way you have."

"Are you implying that I'm mentally incompetent?"

"Lady, I'm not implying anything. Now, get in the truck before I pick you up and put you in it."

Reve jerked away from him and planted her hands on her hips. "Do you have any idea who I am?"

"Nope. I don't have the foggiest idea of who you are, except that you're the spitting image of a lady much nicer than you are, by the name of Jazzy Talbot. And I sure hope for Jazzy's sake that you aren't some long-lost cousin or something."

"Is every man in Cherokee County a friend of Jazzy Talbot's?" The minute the question left her lips, Reve wished it back. Damn, now this infuriating man would realize she knew who Jazzy was. So much for her escaping Cherokee Pointe and any complications from her inquiries about Jazzy.

He eyed he skeptically. "I thought you said you were just passing through."

"I was. I am. And just as soon as we clear up this mess

about my speeding and about the accident, I plan to be on my way. The sooner I see the last of Cherokee Pointe, Jazzy Talbot, and you, the better."

"Then just shut up, get in the damn truck, and I'll do my level best to see that you get what you want!"

She loved that he was rough with her, hurting her just enough to make it exciting, to make her heart pound faster and her pussy drip with moisture. He wasn't like any lover she'd ever had and despite being only twenty—her next birthday in a few months—she'd already screwed at least two dozen guys, including her high school history teacher and a deacon in their church.

What she loved about Jamie was his sense of adventure, his willingness to take a risk. They were kindred souls. Why the hell he wanted to marry her sister she'd never figure out. She was a far better match for him. Laura would never dream of doing what she was doing. She'd never meet her sister's fiancé at the stables in the middle of the morning, strip buck naked, and fuck the guy's brains out in one of the empty stalls where anybody might come up on them. No, not sweet Laura. She was far too shy and sensitive, much too much of a Goody Two-shoes to ever be able to satisfy a man like Jamie Upton, who had all sorts of dirty, wicked desires.

It was that chance of discovery here in the stables that heightened the tension and gave her a climax only seconds after he first rammed himself inside her.

"Harder," she demanded. "And faster."

He lifted her hips and delved deeply, then withdrew. Just before he started jackhammering into her, he bit her shoulder. Bit her hard enough that she cried out in pain. But she loved the pain. She felt it in every fiber of her being. Every muscle. Every nerve. God, she wished he was bigger, wished every thrust brought the pleasurable pain that she craved. But he was big enough, hard enough, and wild enough to give her another orgasm. It was building now, her body tightening, the sensation increasing with each millisecond that passed. She bucked up against him, encouraging him to hold back nothing. She wanted to come again before he did—or at least by the time he did. She wanted it to be so fierce and hot that the top of her head would come off. It had been that way the first time they'd hidden in her closet at her parents' house and tore at each other like a couple of animals.

"Damn, girl, you're wild," Jamie told her as he increased his movements to a frenetic pace.

When he groaned deep in his throat, she knew he was fixing to spew into her. Her pubic lips swelled even more and moisture gushed out of her. And the very second he burst inside her, she unwound like crazy. Screaming with release, she clawed at his back, still covered by his white tuxedo shirt. While the aftershocks rippled through them, he collapsed on top of her, then rolled over and onto his side. She purred like the satisfied kitten she was, then rose up over him just enough to lick a wet trail from his right shoulder to his navel.

"You want to lick me clean, don't you, you little she cat?" Jamie grabbed her head and shoved her face against his penis. "Do it, darlin'. Get a good taste of me."

She struggled against his hold, but he was bigger and stronger and she couldn't escape. Sheridan Willis growled, bared her teeth and opened her mouth. She could bite him. Bite him hard. That's what he deserved. But, God, it would be such a shame to put him out of commission, even temporarily. She licked her lips, then placed her tongue on the tip of his sticky, deflated sex and licked off the mixture of their combined juices.

Chapter 5

"She's insane even to consider going through with the marriage," Andrea Willis told her husband in the privacy of their guest quarters at the Upton home.

When Laura had told them at lunch today that Jamie had explained—to her satisfaction—about his sudden absence from the engagement party last night and that the wedding was definitely on, everyone seemed as shocked as the bride's parents. Although a sweet, sometimes even docile child, Laura had always been difficult to understand. God knew Andrea had tried to bond with their eldest child, but it had proved an impossible task. Of course she loved Laura. Who wouldn't? But having to deal with the girl's ongoing emotional and mental problems often proved too much for Andrea.

"Never, ever use the word *insane* when you refer to Laura!" Cecil Willis glowered menacingly at his wife, his lightly tanned face splotching with color.

Andrea felt herself pale as she realized why he had gotten so upset over her use of the word *insane*. Most of the time she didn't think about that reason, preferring to wisely let the past stay buried, but apparently the past seldom left her husband's mind. Especially not where Laura was concerned.

"Cecil, I did not mean to imply that Laura is actually crazy, the way . . . Laura's just emotionally fragile. She's a true purebred, like her father." Andrea patted her husband's shoulder soothingly. "All I meant by my remark is that I find it incomprehensible that she'd actually marry Jamie knowing he went to another woman the very night of their engagement party. Not when the entire town knows where he was."

"I intend to talk to her, but I doubt it will do much good. I'm afraid if I forbid her to marry him, it will only make matters worse. She's been doing so well these past few years. I'm afraid if I press the issue, she might have a breakdown again."

"We're definitely in a difficult situation," Andrea agreed. "If we forbid her to marry him, it might push her over the edge. But we both know that if she marries him, sooner or later his philandering ways will destroy her emotionally."

"If this was another century, I could call the bastard out, challenge him to a duel, and kill him," Cecil said.

So like her husband to consider a once legal solution to protecting one's honor and acquiring justice when a family member had been wronged. Cecil was an old-fashioned Southern gentleman to his very core. Generations of good breeding went into making that kind of man, just as generations of good breeding produced the Kentucky Derby-winning thoroughbreds the Willis Farm produced.

"If I thought killing Jamie Upton would solve the problem, then I'd load the gun and hand it to you."

Andrea sighed. "But we know what his death would do to our Laura."

Something alerted Andrea that they weren't alone. She wasn't sure if she'd heard the door open or not, but when she glanced at the threshold, she saw her daughter Sheridan standing there. Beautiful, vivacious Sheridan, with her big brown eyes and chestnut brown hair so like Andrea's own. Her baby girl was a wild hellion, but as mentally stable as they came. No temper tantrums. No crying jags. No emotional breakdowns. Sheridan was made of tough stuff. And like her mother, when she saw something she wanted, she reached out and grabbed it.

"Whose death are you referring to?" Sheridan asked.

"How long have you been standing there, young lady?" Cecil frowned at his daughter.

"Long enough to know that you two were discussing murdering Jamie Upton."

"We were doing no such thing," Andrea told her.

"He is a total bastard, isn't he?" Sheridan grinned. "And much too much man for our sweet Laura."

"Despite the fact that we all agree on Upton's unworthiness, it doesn't alter the fact that Laura's in love with him," Cecil said. "I had so hoped she would find a nice young man, someone who would appreciate her and—"

"And take care of her," Sheridan finished her father's sentence.

"Yes," Cecil replied sadly. "Someone who would take care of her."

"She doesn't need a husband for that, Daddy. Not when you do such a great job of it yourself."

"Sheridan, don't start with that nonsense," Andrea warned. Since childhood, Sheridan had been jealous of Cecil's relationship with Laura, and no matter how much she tried to persuade their younger daughter that her father loved her just as much as he did Laura, she refused to believe it.

Cecil looked pleadingly at Sheridan. "You know full well that Laura needs—"

"Oh, yes, I know. Laura needs more attention. Laura needs more love. Laura needs more praise. Laura needs everything and I need nothing. So that's what you've given me, Daddy, absolutely nothing."

"That isn't true and you know it." Cecil reached out for Sheridan, but she easily sidestepped him. "Sweetheart, I've adored you since the day you were born. I've always been proud of you for being such a bright, strong, competent young lady."

"That's me all right. Strong and competent. And what has it gotten me? Not your time and attention. If I'd been more like Laura—more emotionally and mentally unstable—maybe you'd have paid attention to me."

"Don't ever refer to your sister as mentally unstable!" Cecil bellowed.

"Why not? That's what she is, and we all know it. She's had more than one nervous breakdown. My big sister is looney tunes, and that's a fact."

Cecil Willis lifted his hand to strike his daughter. Andrea stepped between him and Sheridan just in time to prevent disaster. Realizing what he'd been about to do, Cecil dropped his hand to his side and hung his head.

Andrea turned to Sheridan. "Your father is overwrought. He would never strike you. We're both very concerned about Laura marrying this terrible young man."

"Would you be so worried if I were the one marrying him?"

"Yes, of course we would be. What a silly thing to ask."

"Mm-hmm. Well, don't worry, Mother. After Laura

marries Jamie and has a severe nervous breakdown within six months, you and Daddy can pick up the pieces and try to put Humpty-Laura together again."

Before Andrea could reply, Sheridan whirled around and left the room.

"We've failed both of them," Cecil said. "And it's all my fault."

Andrea put her arm around her husband's slender waist and hugged him. She loved this man more than anything on earth. There had never been anyone else for her.

"You didn't fail them. You're a good father to both of your daughters."

No, Cecil wasn't at fault, Andrea thought. *All the blame lay elsewhere, with a woman long dead. A woman responsible for all the heartache their family had endured.*

"Am I free to go?" Reve asked Sheriff Butler, who had detained her for nearly three hours at the sheriff's department, located on the first floor of the Cherokee County courthouse. Of course, being a responsible officer of the law, he'd taken her by the local hospital's ER before dragging her here. Just as a precaution, he'd told her. More to humiliate her, she'd decided. This big moron had taken it upon himself to try to bring "Miss High and Mighty" down a peg or two. While she'd been twiddling her thumbs waiting for him to release her, she'd overheard him say those very words to one of his deputies.

"Why are you in such a big hurry to leave our fair city?" Butler asked her. "You might give us the idea you don't think much of our town or of us."

"I don't think anything one way or the other about you, this town, or the entire citizenry."

"Citizenry? That's one of them five-hundred-dollar words that you learn in college, ain't it?"

The two deputies on duty—Bobby Joe Harte and Tim Willingham—chuckled, but had the decency to look embarrassed when she glared at them. The two men had been staring at her since the moment the sheriff escorted her into the courthouse. With absolutely no tact, they'd asked her right out if she was Jazzy's long-lost sister. She'd replied, "Does this Jazzy person have a long-lost sister?"

Reve crossed her arms over her chest as she focused her attention on the sheriff. "If you've had your fun for the day, then just let me be on my way to the nearest car rental place, and I promise that you will never see me again."

"Closest car rental is out at the airport," Deputy Bobby Joe Harte told her.

"Thank you, Deputy Harte." She rewarded him with a warm smile. "If you'd please call a taxi for me—"

"We don't have a taxi service in Cherokee Pointe," Deputy Willingham informed her. "Not since old John Berryman died. Wasn't never enough business for him, so nobody wanted to take on the job."

"It's nearly lunchtime," the sheriff said. "Why don't you join me for a bite over at Jasmine's and afterward I'll drive you out to the airport?"

She'd rather eat glass than dine with Sheriff Butler, but she did need a ride to the airport. If there was a flight out to Chattanooga later today, she'd forget about renting a car. The sooner she escaped from this ill-advised little trip into the twilight zone, the better she'd like it.

"Isn't there any other place in town to eat?" she asked, not wanting to run into Jazzy Talbot again, possible biological sister or not.

"You have some reason for not wanting to eat at Jasmine's?"

Ah, hell, Reve, give up before you wear yourself out fighting a losing battle. It's destined for you to face your look-alike again, so just bite the bullet and go peacefully with the sheriff. Later, once you're back in Chattanooga, you can seek revenge. With one phone call to Senator Everett or Governor Neels, she could make Sheriff Jacob Butler rue the day he'd ever screwed with Reve Sorrell.

Damn! Bad choice of words. Putting Jacob Butler's name in the same sentence with hers and the word *screw* brought some rather graphic and totally unwanted images to her mind. *Totally unwanted,* she told herself again. This guy would be the last man on earth she'd ever—

"Ms. Sorrell?"

She snapped around and smiled, ever so sweetly. "I'd be delighted to join you for lunch at Jasmine's."

Butler eyed her suspiciously. So the guy was no fool. He knew she couldn't stand the sight of him, that from the moment he pecked on her car window after the wreck, she had taken an instant dislike to him.

"Okay, so delighted might be an overstatement," Reve admitted. "Let's just say I need a ride to the airport, and if eating lunch with you is the price I have to pay—"

"Humph. I just figured you and Jazzy ought to hook up before you rush out of town. It doesn't take a genius to figure out you two have to be related. My guess is you must be at least a little curious about a woman who looks enough like you to be your twin. And if I know Jazzy—"

"And you do know Jazzy, don't you, sheriff? Hell, every man in town knows Jazzy."

The two deputies cleared their throats simultaneously. Reve smiled mockingly.

"You implied that before, back at the accident site," Butler said. "Want to explain how you've jumped to that conclusion about a woman you don't know?"

Reve sighed loudly. "I met Jazzy, very briefly earlier

today. But we didn't have time to delve into the possibilities of being related. She was too busy arguing with a man named Caleb McCord about her having spent the night with Jamie Upton."

Reve could swear that Sheriff Butler growled, the sound somewhat like an enraged animal. Good Lord, was this man jealous over Jazzy Talbot, too?

"Was it something I said?" Reve asked sarcastically. "Did finding out that Jazzy's been two-timing you with more than one man upset you?"

"Come on, Ms. Sorrell." Butler picked up his Stetson, put it on, and then grabbed her arm. "I'll take you straight to the airport to pick yourself up a rental car or buy yourself a ticket out of town. I've decided that I wouldn't wish you on my worst enemy, let alone a good friend like Jazzy."

How dare he speak to her in such a manner! You'd think she wasn't good enough to kiss Jazzy Talbot's shoes, when in fact it was the other way around. Ms. Talbot was a white trash slut, reared by a tobacco-chewing bag lady.

"Nothing would suit me better." Reve jerked away from Butler, but kept pace with his long-legged stride as he escorted her out of the sheriff's department and into the courthouse corridor.

Just as Butler shoved open the door to the rear entrance, a whoosh of cool, damp air slapped them in the face. A misty drizzle pelted them the minute they walked outside. A loud clap of thunder rattled the windowpanes in the old building. *Great, just great,* Reve thought. *Just what I need—having to drive back to Chattanooga in a rental car during a springtime thunderstorm.*

They made a mad dash to Butler's truck, and much to her surprise the sheriff actually opened the passenger door for her and gave her a hand getting up and into the cab. She glanced over her shoulder to say thanks, but he was already rounding the hood. He jumped in on the driver's side, closed the door, and took off his Stetson. He shook the rain from his hat and returned it to his head, then stuck the key in the ignition and started the truck. While the engine idled, he turned to Reve.

"What?" she asked when he stared at her.

"Just to set the record straight, Jasmine Talbot is a good woman. She and I are friends. Nothing more. And Caleb McCord works for her at Jazzy's Joint. He's the bouncer. And he's become quite protective of her, just as I am, because Jamie Upton preys on women. He's hurt Jazzy in the past, and he'll hurt her again if she gives him the chance."

This eloquent defense of Jazzy Talbot wasn't what Reve had expected, and certainly not from a man she thought was a backwoods lout. If what Butler said was true, had she possibly misjudged the woman?

"I know Jamie Upton, and while I found him to be a charming scoundrel, I certainly didn't think he was—"

"You know Jamie?"

"Yes, we met at a Christmas party this past December."

"Another victim." Butler shook his head.

"See here, Sheriff, I am most certainly not a victim. Jamie Upton is an acquaintance. Nothing more."

"Don't tell me he didn't seduce you—or at least try to."

"Yes, of course he tried. But I'm not some gullible, love-starved female who—"

"Neither is Jazzy. But he got his hooks into her when she was only sixteen."

"He did mention that they'd been teenage sweethearts."

"He told you about Jazzy?" Butler's voice deepened with tension.

"Yes." Reve huffed. "And yes, that's why I came to Cherokee Pointe."

"Because of Jamie Upton. Humph. Just as I guessed."

"Well, you guessed wrong. I didn't come here because of Jamie. I came here to met Jazzy, to see if she and I might be related."

"Any reason other than the strong resemblance makes you think she could be a cousin or—"

"I believe it's possible she's my sister," Reve admitted.

"You should talk to Sally, Jazzy's aunt. She'd know if—"

"I talked to her earlier today. A chance meeting in the street," Reve explained. "She swears that Jazzy's mother gave birth to only one child."

"Why haven't you asked your own mama? Maybe—"

"I was adopted."

Butler's eyes widened.

"You see, I was abandoned when I was only a few days or perhaps few weeks old."

"Where?"

"Not here in Cherokee Pointe, if that's what you're thinking. I was found in Sevierville." No need to tell him exactly where. Sharing the information that she'd been placed in a Dumpster, disposed of like unwanted rubbish, wasn't something she'd willingly tell anyone, least of all Sheriff Jacob Butler.

"So why leave town without talking to Jazzy again?"

"Because after meeting her briefly, I realized I'd made a mistake coming here. We're obviously not sisters. And if we're cousins or something, it really doesn't matter. I mean, she and I have nothing in common, so there's no reason we'd want to become better acquainted."

"You're a first-class, blue-blood snob." Jacob glared at her with those hypnotic green eyes. "You think you're too good for the likes of Jazzy Talbot, don't you? Well, lady, the way I see it, it's definitely the other way around—she's twice the woman you are. There's not a selfish, cruel, or unkind bone in her body. You're as different as night and day. And you're right, there's no way on earth the two of you could be sisters. So it's a good thing for Jazzy's sake that you don't have the guts to stick around and find out for sure."

Reve grabbed the handle and opened the door. Butler clutched her arm.

"Where the hell do you think you're going?" he asked.

"I've changed my mind." She'd had a knee-jerk reaction to Butler's goading. This man didn't know her, couldn't have possibly realized that by daring her to stay and unearth the truth about her relationship with Jazzy, he had hit her weak spot. She'd been susceptible to dares ever since she'd been a kid. Tell her she couldn't do something, and she'd do it or die trying. "I'm not leaving Cherokee Pointe. At least not today. I'm going to check into the nearest hotel and—"

"Motels and cabins," Butler said.

"What?"

"Close the damn door before you get the interior of my truck soaked. I'll drive you over to Cherokee Cabin Rentals and drop you off. We don't have a hotel anywhere in Cherokee County, just motels and cabins for rent."

Reve closed the door. The right side of her body was dripping wet from the blowing rain. "Yes, a cabin will be fine, thank you. Something close to town so I can walk wherever I need to go. And sheriff, once you drop me off, let's make a point of never seeing each other again."

"Suits me fine," he said. "Only problem is that this is a small town, and we're bound to run into each other if you stay here for a while."

"Then let's try to avoid each other, and if by chance we see each other, let's pretend we didn't."

"For once, Ms. Sorrell, you and I are in total agreement."

Sally sat on the front porch of her small home up in the mountains. Peter and Paul, her bloodhounds, slept peacefully out in the yard, the afternoon sunshine warming their big red bodies. She spit a spray of brown juice off the side of the porch. Ludie had asked her a hundred questions after their talk with Reve Sorrell. Some she couldn't answer because she didn't know. She didn't know there had been another baby. How could she have known?

Hell, Sally old girl, you don't know for sure that this Sorrell woman is Jazzy's sister. Could be just a coincidence that they look so much alike. Yeah, sure, and God didn't make little green apples. She chuckled nervously. Of course, after all this time what difference did it make? Jazzy was a grown woman; she'd soon be thirty years old. Couldn't nobody take that gal away from her. They were bound together by love, by years of being the only family they each had. There wasn't nothing she wouldn't do for her Jasmine, the child of her heart, if not of her body. She'd die to protect Jazzy. She'd even kill to protect her.

But if Jazzy ever learned the truth, what would she think? How would she react? *Well, since you don't know the truth—the whole truth—then it's unlikely Jazzy or anybody else ever will, either.* The truth didn't matter. Whatever the whole truth was, it should stay buried in the past, along with all the lies Sally had told so nobody would try to take Jazzy away from her.

But what about Reve Sorrell? *She ain't the type to let sleeping dogs lie,* Sally thought. Nope, that gal seemed like the type who just might stir up trouble, in her own very cultured, highfalutin way. *What if she's determined to find out why she and Jazzy look so much alike? What if she starts asking questions, digging into the past? What if she puts doubts into Jazzy's head?*

What you gonna do then, Sally, ole girl? What you gonna do then?

Chapter 6

Jazzy saw them as they entered the restaurant. Jamie, his fiancée, and an older couple she assumed were the bride-to-be's parents—Mr. and Mrs. Willis, the wealthy horse breeders from Kentucky. For a split second, Jazzy froze to the spot. She glanced around, searching for a waitress who could take over her hostess duties immediately, but no one was close enough to summon before the party of four approached her. She had wanted to make her escape, but found it was too late.

"Good evening," the slender, distinguished gentleman with silvery gray hair and neatly trimmed beard said. "We'd like your best table for four, please. I telephoned earlier and was told reservations weren't necessary."

Doing her best to avoid making eye contact with Jamie, Jazzy replied, "That's right. We don't take reservations here at Jasmine's." She could feel Jamie's heated stare, knew he was watching her, and wondered if Laura noticed. Hazarding a quick sidelong glance at Jamie's fiancée, she found herself looking directly into the woman's speculative blue eyes. Their gazes collided, and Jazzy understood that this pretty, delicate girl was silently pleading with her. Jazzy could almost hear Laura saying, "Please let him go. You don't want him and I do."

With her nose titled upward, perfecting a haughty expression, Mrs. Willis inspected her surroundings. "This is a rather quaint little place. I do hope we can find something palatable on the menu." She skewered Jazzy with a sharp glare. "Everything isn't fried, is it? I detest fried food. Perhaps we should speak to the owner about having the chef prepare something that isn't fried."

"I'm the owner." Jazzy focused on Mrs. Willis. "Let me assure you that we have a wide variety on our menu, including broiled, boiled, baked, and grilled items."

"Well, that's a relief, isn't it, my dear?" Mr. Willis surveyed Jazzy from head to toe and smiled condescendingly. "So you're Jasmine." He paused for effect. "The proprietress."

Jazzy snapped her fingers at Tiffany who had just served a nearby table. The waitress rushed right over.

"Please give these customers a nice table"—she looked right at Mr. Willis—"or a booth if they prefer."

"We prefer a table," Mrs. Willis said.

Jazzy nodded.

Tiffany picked up four menus. "Please, follow me."

"And their dinner is on the house," Jazzy said.

That wiped the self-satisfied expressions off both Mr. and Mrs. Willis's faces.

"That's very generous of you, Ms. Talbot, but—" Mr. Willis said.

Jazzy offered the Willises a broad smile. "Your future son-in-law and I are old friends, so please consider this a wedding gift." Jazzy glanced at Laura, who looked rather flushed. She tried to convey, without words, her reassurance that she was no threat to Laura. Poor stupid girl. She knew only too well what it was like to love Jamie

Upton, to be so crazy about the guy that nothing else mattered.

"That's mighty nice of you," Jamie said.

"Yes, thank you," Laura added, her voice a whispery tremble.

"Enjoy your dinner." Jazzy turned around and headed for her office. She walked slowly, swaying her hips just a little, enough to make her movements both sexy and self-confident. Damn Mr. and Mrs. Willis. And damn Jamie, too.

As she passed by several tables, the customers glanced her way, some staring at her boldly, others doing it more subtly. Erin Mercer, an artist who lived in a cabin outside town and came to Jasmine's for dinner several evenings each week, purposefully avoided looking Jazzy's way. Jazzy caught a glimpse of the attractive older lady as she passed her table. She didn't know the woman well, but what she did know, she liked, despite the rumors she'd heard about Erin and Big Jim Upton. Of course, their affair was none of her business, but for the life of her she couldn't figure out why Erin would want the man, considering he was old enough to be her father. But then again maybe Erin wondered why Jazzy had wasted so much of her life giving Jamie numerous second chances.

At the table nearest the doors leading into the kitchen and down the hall to her office, another lone woman sat eating her dinner, totally ignoring Jazzy. She didn't know the woman's name, but she'd seen her in the restaurant several times over the past few weeks, and she was always alone. Another tourist enjoying herself in the mountains, Jazzy assumed. After all, it was springtime and tourist season had already begun. A keen observer of human nature, Jazzy got some odd vibes from this woman. She sensed the small, blonde lady was very sad.

Probably a recent widow or lonely divorcee, Jazzy decided.

Once she made it to her office, she closed the door and let out a sigh of relief. Was Jamie out of his mind coming here tonight? Or had dining at Jasmine's been someone else's idea? Mr. and Mrs. Willis's idea, perhaps. Surely not Laura's. She suspected Jamie's fiancée wasn't the type to seek confrontation, otherwise she would have already paid Jazzy a visit. Someone had a purpose for tonight's dinner, for bringing Laura and Jazzy face-to-face.

Going to the portable bar in the corner, Jazzy opened the bottle of Jack Daniels and poured enough for a couple of good belts, then took a swig. The whiskey burned a path from throat to belly, settling inside her like a hot brick. Within seconds the warmth spread through her whole body. She carried the glass over to her desk, placed it on top of a stack of bills, and pulled out her swivel chair. After sitting down, she leaned back her head and closed her eyes.

Don't stay here, she told herself. Tiffany could handle things. She should just slip out the back way and go on over to Jazzy's Joint. The loud music and rowdy crowd there might take her mind off everything she didn't want to think about—like Jamie and Laura's upcoming wedding, like wondering who the hell Reve Sorrell was. But over at Jazzy's Joint she'd be confronted with another problem—Caleb McCord. The man had been in town only a few months. He'd thrown Jamie out of Jazzy's Joint one night back in January when Jamie had tried to manhandle her. He had impressed her, the clientele, and her bartender, Lacy Fallon. Her regular bouncer hadn't shown up that night, something he had begun making a habit of doing. So she'd fired the unreliable guy and hired Caleb to take over the job. And he was very good at it, because he was not only strong as a bull, he possessed a killer stare that could stop most guys dead in their tracks. He wasn't as physically intimidating as Jacob Butler, whose six-five, two-eighty body put the fear of God into just about every man who crossed his path, but Caleb had that same earthy macho power that practically oozed from his pores.

The problem wasn't with Caleb's ability to do his job. No, the problem was that from the moment they met, there had been a sexual chemistry between the two of them. She'd be lying to herself if she denied being tempted. Her feminine instincts told her that he'd be a good lover. Probably a great lover. But despite her not altogether unwarranted bad-girl reputation, Jazzy didn't fall into the sack with every Tom, Dick, and Harry that came along. There had been a lot fewer men in her bed than most people thought. Actually, folks would be surprised to learn she really hadn't had all that many lovers.

It would be far too easy to give in to her desire for Caleb. The guy wanted her. He'd made that perfectly clear. And it was obvious that he was jealous of Jamie, which he shouldn't be. First of all, he had no claim on her, so he had no right to be jealous of any other man in her life. In the second place, Jamie was her past. She didn't love him. Okay, so he was a part of her past that kept hanging on, wouldn't let go, continued to complicate everything for her. And, yes, she did still love him. But not the way she used to. She wasn't crazy in love with Jamie anymore, but she couldn't deny that a part of her would always care about him. Hell, she knew he was a louse and considered herself well rid of that wild infatuation, but maybe a woman never quite got over her first love. Her first lover.

You need to give yourself a chance to find someone better. If you weren't so afraid of getting hurt, you might actually fall in love again. And it could be good. Maybe better than anything she'd ever known. Didn't she deserve to love and be loved with honesty, devotion, and commitment?

A soft knock on the door brought her quickly from her musings. "Yes?"

The door eased open partway and Laura Willis peeped into the office. "Ms. Talbot, may I speak to you?"

"Phone call for you," Lacy Fallon shouted to Caleb as she held up the phone located behind the bar.

He wasn't accustomed to getting calls at work. The few people he knew in Cherokee Pointe either dropped by to see him in person or telephoned him at home, if you could actually call his small rental cabin home. The place came fully furnished, and he'd done nothing to personalize it. He was a man who traveled light. All the extra baggage he carried was purely emotional, and he did his level best to never expose his vulnerabilities. He was a man without ties, free to pick up and leave anytime he chose to.

"Who is it?" Caleb asked the bartender.

"Chief Sloan," Lacy replied.

"Dallas Sloan?"

Now why would the recently hired chief of police want to talk to him? He knew Dallas on a personal basis only because the former FBI agent was now engaged to Jazzy's best friend, Genny Madoc. But he and Dallas weren't buddies, no more than he and Jacob Butler were. He liked and respected both men, but he'd given them a wide berth. He'd had his fill of lawmen back in Memphis. Hell, he'd had his fill of just about everything, including his job on the Memphis police force. But that had been another time, another place, another life. When he'd come to Cherokee Pointe back in

January, he'd come here searching for some answers about his past—about his mother's past. He'd had no intention of staying once he'd gotten those answers. But those plans had altered once he met Jasmine Talbot. The lady had gotten under his skin the moment they met.

Hell, admit it, McCord, you wanted to fuck her when you first laid eyes on her. Jazzy had hot and wild written all over her. And he wanted to be the man she gave all that hot wildness to—in and out of bed. That very first night when Jamie Upton had tried to manhandle her, Caleb had taken great pleasure in throwing the guy out of Jazzy's Joint. He'd hated seeing the fear in Jazzy's eyes. But he'd hated even more realizing she and Upton shared a lot of history. The lady brought out every possessive, protective instinct he had.

So he'd hung around, accepted a job as the bouncer at Jazzy's Joint, and decided to take his time unearthing the truth about his mother's past here in Cherokee County—and all because he had a hankering for a woman who probably would never get over her teenage crush on Jamie Upton.

Caleb made his way through the crowded room, packed to capacity because it was a Saturday night and locals as well as tourists found Jazzy's Joint the ideal place to let off a little steam. When he went behind the bar, Lacy nodded at the portable receiver she'd placed by the telephone base. After picking up the receiver, he escaped into the hallway that led to the storerooms on one side and Jazzy's office on the other. No way could he have heard anything if he'd stayed in the bar. Between the games going on at the pool tables, the music blasting from the live band, and the buzz of talk and laughter from the patrons, a guy couldn't hear himself think.

"McCord here."

"This is Dallas Sloan."

"Yeah, Chief, what can I do for you?"

Dallas cleared his throat. "Genny wanted me to call you."

Puzzled, Caleb asked, "Why would—"

"It's about Jazzy."

"What about her?"

"Hell, McCord, this is awkward for me," Dallas admitted. "But Genny had one of her visions this morning and she's worried about Jazzy."

"Why call me?" *Get real,* Caleb told himself. *Don't you think Dallas and Genny know you've got the hots for Jazzy?*

"Like I said, it wasn't my idea to get in touch with you. But my future wife can be very persuasive when she's determined to get her way. I'm contacting you because you and Jazzy are friends and you two spend a great deal of time together there at Jazzy's Joint. And because Genny feels that you care about Jazzy, enough to want to protect her."

"Protect her from what?"

"Jamie Upton."

"Look, tell your wife-to-be that there's only so much I can do. If Jazzy chooses to be with Upton, then—"

"Genny believes someone is going to kill Upton and that somehow Jazzy will be blamed for his murder."

"Are you shitting me?"

"Look, McCord, there was a time when I thought Genny's visions were a bunch of nonsense. But I've learned better."

"Why not call Upton and tell him he's a dead man walking?"

"He's not going to believe Genny. He's an arrogant fool, and we both know it."

"What does Genny want from me?"

"She wants you to keep an eye on Jazzy. If someone

does kill Upton, we don't want Jazzy involved in any way."

"Like I said, there's only so much I can do. It's not as if Jazzy and I live together. Hell, we aren't even dating."

"Hey, I'm just the messenger here. Genny doesn't want to frighten or upset Jazzy, but she does want someone helping us look out for her. Jacob's going to do his part to watch out for her and we've discussed keeping tabs on Upton, too. Unofficially, of course. Genny seems to think we can count on you to help us watch over Jazzy. Is she wrong?"

"No, she's not wrong."

"Okay then, that's it."

"Yeah, that's it." Caleb felt as awkward about this conversation as Chief Sloan did. They'd come damn near close to talking about their feelings. God, what a man would do for the woman he loved! And everybody in Cherokee County knew that Dallas Sloan loved his future wife about as much as a man could love a woman.

As he passed by the bar, Caleb handed the phone to Lacy, who looked at him questioningly. Ordinarily he didn't bother explaining himself to anyone, but Lacy had become a friend since he'd been working at Jazzy's Joint. The middle-aged brunette's lifetime smoker's gravelly voice, coarse skin, and deeply lined face belied her strong maternal instincts. She looked like an old barfly, with her long, frizzy hair, her double set of big silver hoop earrings, and her flashy, skintight clothes, but at heart Lacy Fallon was a mother. She'd never had any kids of her own. "Three husbands and not one baby," she'd told him. "My fault, not theirs. My equipment wasn't no good. I'm barren as the desert." She'd laughed when she'd said it, but he'd heard the hurt in her voice.

"Chief Sloan said Genny's worried about Jazzy. They want me to keep an eye on her," Caleb told Lacy.

"They want you to keep Jamie Upton away from her, don't they?"

Caleb nodded. "I told Sloan I'd do what I could, but if Jazzy wants to entertain the bastard in her apartment late at night, what am I supposed to do?"

"You're supposed to go up there and run his ass off. That's what you're supposed to do. She doesn't love him anymore. She honest to God wants things over with once and for all. But he keeps coming around and . . . well, Jamie's just a bad habit she's had a hard time breaking."

Caleb leaned across the bar and planted a kiss on Lacy's cheek.

"What was that for?" she asked.

"For being Jazzy's friend."

Jazzy looked directly at Laura Willis, rose slowly from her chair, and said, "Yes, of course, please come in."

Laura entered the cluttered office, looking totally out of place. Jamie's fiancée was a slender, delicate girl with luminous blue eyes and golden blond hair. The fairy princess type, Jazzy thought. But there was a fragility to the young woman—a hint of it was apparent in not only her pale, delicate appearance, but in the way she moved and talked.

"I told Jamie and my parents I was going to the ladies' room," Laura said in a soft, hushed voice.

"What did you want to speak to me about?" Jazzy asked, even though she had a really good idea. What else did the two of them have in common other than Jamie Upton?

"I—I know Jamie came to see you last night—"

"Look, Ms. Willis, I can assure you that—"

"He told me why he left our party and went directly to you. He explained that he felt last night—when we officially announced to the world that we're to be married—was the right time to say his good-byes to you, once and for all."

"Oh, yes, of course." Why was she surprised that Jamie had lied to this girl? She shouldn't have been. And why was she surprised that Laura Willis had believed him? Hadn't Jamie talked his way back into Jazzy's life time and time again, always with promises that he never kept?

"I'm well aware of your relationship with Jamie, that the two of you are . . . were lovers." Laura stayed close to the open door, as if she thought she might have to flee at any moment. "And I know there have been others. But Jamie wants our marriage to work. He loves me and I love him."

He doesn't love you, Jazzy wanted to say. *Jamie isn't capable of loving anyone except himself. But you love him, don't you, you poor girl? He's going to break your heart the way he broke mine, and it doesn't really matter that you'll be Mrs. Jamie Upton. He'll never be faithful to you. It's not in his nature.*

"I wish you well," Jazzy said. "I hope you'll be very happy."

"I believe we will be, that we can be if . . ." Laura's cheeks flushed. "Please, Ms. Talbot, let him go. Don't hold on to him. If he remains tied to you, in any way, he'll never be able to commit himself fully to me, to our marriage. Please, please . . . set him free."

Undoubtedly Jamie had told his fiancée that Jazzy was pursuing him and not the other way around. That, too, shouldn't have surprised her.

"You love him enough to forgive him for everything,

don't you?" Jazzy understood all too well that kind of foolish love.

"I know you love him, too, but he loves me now. He wants to marry me. I'm sorry if—"

Jazzy held up a restraining hand. "No, it's all right. I promise you that I will never pursue Jamie again. I did set him free. Last night." Only a little white lie, Jazzy thought. "He's all yours. You have nothing to fear from me."

Tears glistened in Laura's eyes. She swallowed, then smiled weakly. "I'll be a good wife to Jamie. I'll do every thing I can to make him happy."

"Yes, I'm sure you will. He's a very lucky man to have someone like you."

"Thank you, Ms. Talbot. Thank you." Bitting down on her lower lip in an obvious effort not to burst into tears, Laura continued smiling as she nodded her head, then turned and all but ran from Jazzy's office.

Jazzy sank down on the edge of her desk, took a deep, cleansing breath, and exhaled. She felt like crying herself. Odd, she thought, but she had truly meant what she'd said to Laura. Jamie was lucky to have someone like her love him. But Laura was very unlucky. It would take a miracle for Jamie Upton to change, to become the kind of man who could be faithful to one woman. And in that one moment, Jazzy experienced some sort of epiphany. She had seen herself in Laura, looked right in the face of hopeless, ill-fated love, and knew that but by the grace of God, she might be in Laura's shoes. How many years had she longed to be Jamie's wife? She had blamed Jamie's grandmother for keeping them apart. She had railed at cruel fate. She had made countless excuses for Jamie's behavior and kept on loving him, forgiving him, accepting him back into her life.

"Oh, God, if I had married Jamie when I was a teenager or even a few years ago, it would have been the biggest mistake of my life." Tears gathered in the corners of Jazzy's eyes as the hard, bitter truth hit her like a ton of bricks.

Jamie would have married her, but never been faithful. He would have lied to her day after day and betrayed her in every way possible. Why had she ever thought that marriage would have solved their problems? Jamie was the problem. He always had been. Marriage to him would have changed nothing.

Okay, so maybe mentally she'd known this fact for quite some time, but never before had her heart accepted it. For the first time since she'd fallen head over heels in love at sixteen, she faced the truth emotionally.

Please, please . . . set him free. Laura Willis's words replayed themselves in her mind. Over and over again.

But it wasn't Jamie she needed to set free. It never had been. She was the one she needed to set free. Now she could. Now she had.

Jazzy hugged herself as tears trickled down her cheeks. She laughed aloud, the sound reverberating inside her head, the sweetest music she'd ever heard.

She was free. Free of Jamie Upton. He could never hurt her again.

Chapter 7

Jazzy slipped into her fleece jacket, a light protection against the nighttime chill so prevalent in the mountains during the early spring. She'd leave Jasmine's in Tiffany's capable hands for the rest of the evening and go where she really wanted to be tonight—at Jazzy's Joint next door, with a loud, boisterous crowd of fun-loving folks. And with Caleb McCord. She'd kept the guy at arm's length for several months now for a couple of very good reasons. First and foremost, she hadn't wanted to use him to try to get Jamie out of her system. She had done that in the past and had broken a couple of hearts in the process. Secondly, she had wanted to protect herself by not getting involved with a man she knew she could probably care a lot about if she gave herself half a chance. She'd never truly been in love with anyone other than Jamie, and he'd been nothing but a heartache. Even though Genny had predicted a new love for her, a man who would make her happy, Jazzy wasn't sure she could ever trust love again. But that didn't mean she couldn't explore the possibilities, did it?

Feeling as if a heavy weight had been lifted from her heart and from her shoulders, Jazzy smiled to herself as she left her office. Maybe it was already too late for a chance with Caleb. Maybe he'd already gotten sick and tired of waiting for her. She really couldn't blame him if he told her she was offering him too little, too late.

Only a few steps into the hallway, she ran into a woman she instantly recognized as the small, blonde lady who had been frequenting Jasmine's for the past few weeks. Startled by Jazzy's appearance in the dimly lit corridor, the woman gasped and jumped simultaneously.

"May I help you?" Jazzy asked.

"Yes, I—I'm looking for the ladies' room."

"You went right past it," Jazzy said. "It's the first door on the left."

"How silly of me to walk past it. Thank you."

When the woman turned around, Jazzy called to her. "Hey, I'm Jazzy Talbot, the owner of Jasmine's. I've seen you here several times. Welcome to Cherokee Pointe. I hope you're enjoying your stay."

The woman paused, glanced over her shoulder and smiled. "Yes, this is a lovely town. I'm planning on staying a while longer."

When the woman started walking away, Jazzy followed her, then moved on past her when she entered the restroom. Just as the woman entered, Erin Mercer exited.

"How are you tonight, Ms. Mercer?" Jazzy asked.

"Just fine. How about you?"

"Better than I've been in a long time. Thank you for asking."

When Jazzy turned toward the door leading out into the alley, Erin asked, "Are you leaving for the night?"

"Going next door to Jazzy's Joint to check on things there."

"See you around." Erin studied Jazzy briefly, then returned to her table in the restaurant.

Jazzy had sensed rather strange vibes coming from Big Jim Upton's mistress. It was as if she'd wanted to say something personal to Jazzy but thought better of the idea. Maybe Erin Mercer knew all about Jazzy and Jamie's troubled love affair. Hell, who didn't? Maybe Ms. Mercer thought the reason Jazzy was leaving her restaurant so early in the evening was to get away from Jamie, his fiancée, and her parents, who had so obviously come to Jasmine's tonight so that Jazzy could witness the celebration. Did Ms. Mercer see her as a kindred spirit? Did she believe Jazzy would eventually become Jamie's mistress?

What difference did it make what anyone thought? She'd been damned for so many sins during her twenty-nine years that she couldn't remember which ones she was guilty of committing and of which she was innocent. Once a woman gained a bad reputation in a small town, deserved or undeserved, there was very little she could do to change people's opinions. The task was as impossible as reclaiming your virginity once you'd had sex.

Jazzy slipped out into the dark alley behind the adjoining establishments and hurried down the uneven brick walkway that led to the back entrance of the honky-tonk she owned. The nippy night air pinked her cheeks and sent a chill through her body. Even though the lids were closed, the large trash cans at the back of the restaurant emitted an unpleasant garbage odor and the nearby Dumpster reeked with the waste from all the businesses along the street.

Unexpectedly, a noise up the alleyway alerted her that she wasn't alone. Although Cherokee Pointe didn't have many vagrants, from time to time some homeless bum would rummage through the trash cans looking for food and other items of interest. She glanced left. Saw nothing. Looked right and caught a glimpse of a dark shadow that disappeared so quickly she wondered if she had imagined seeing it.

A shiver that had nothing to do with the weather shimmied up her spine. Jazzy rushed in through the back door. If it hadn't been a fire exit, she would have locked the door. *Don't overreact,* she told herself. *You're being silly. Just because you thought you saw someone in the alley doesn't mean there are bogey men lurking around every corner. And it certainly doesn't mean you are personally in any danger.*

She rushed past her office in Jazzy's Joint and went straight out front, where the action was. The place was jumping tonight. Filled nearly to capacity, the smoky interior pulsated with a let-the-good-times-roll rhythm. Tonight Jazzy felt quite susceptible to the rowdy ambience practically jarring the roof off the place. Yes, tonight she was in the mood for something wild . . . and maybe just a little dangerous. After all, she wanted to celebrate her liberation from years of emotional bondage.

Glancing around the room, from the pool tables in back to the dance floor up front, she searched for any sign of Caleb. Not finding him, she made her way toward the bar. That's when she noticed him standing at the end of the bar, his back to her, apparently talking to someone. When she approached the bar, Lacy Fallon motioned to her. Jazzy leaned across the bar so that she could hear Lacy over the din of music, talk, and laughter.

"We've got ourselves a kid with a phony ID," Lacy said.

"When I refused to serve her, she got belligerent. She kept demanding a drink, so Caleb's talking to her."

"Is she somebody we know?" Jazzy asked. "Should we call her parents?"

"Never seen her before, but from the looks of her clothes and her hoity-toity attitude, I'd say she comes from money. And I'd say she's definitely hot to trot. The minute she got a good look at Caleb, I'll bet you dollars to doughnuts that she creamed her pants. She can't seem to keep her hands off him, and he looks like it's making him damned uncomfortable."

"Maybe I should intervene." Jazzy couldn't hear what Caleb was saying to the young woman, but she noticed him shaking his head and sensed the tension in his broad shoulders.

"Watch out," Lacy warned. "The little hellcat probably bites and scratches."

Jazzy laughed. "Then I most definitely should intercede, since I doubt biting and scratching is in Caleb's repertoire of maneuvers to handle unruly customers."

As she moved closer, she heard Caleb suggesting to the young woman that she should leave peacefully or he'd be forced to call the police. Jazzy walked up to Caleb's side, which gave her an unrestricted view of the sexy girl who had her hand pressed against Caleb's chest and was staring at him as if she wanted to jump his bones. Slender, dark hair and eyes, and dressed in a white leather skirt and matching boots that probably cost a fortune, the underage customer rubbed her open palm in a circle over Caleb's shirt, totally ignoring Jazzy.

"I'll leave if you'll leave with me," the girl said. "You're the first interesting thing I've seen in Cherokee Pointe since we got here, and if I can't get a good stiff drink to drown my sorrows, then maybe a—"

"Mr. McCord is the bouncer here at Jazzy's Joint," Jazzy said. "His job is strictly to keep order. He's not available for any other services."

A set of large, pensive brown eyes settled on Jazzy. "What about when he's off duty? You aren't his mother or anything, are you?"

Jazzy laced her arm through Caleb's. "No, I'm his boss. And what he does on his own time is his business, but I doubt he's stupid enough to mess around with jail bait."

"I'm nineteen." As if realizing she had just admitted to not being legal drinking age, the girl frowned and huffed. Then she looked Jazzy over and a quirky little smile curved her full, rosy lips. "So you're Jazzy Talbot, huh? I know all about you. One man is never enough for you."

Who the hell was this kid? Jazzy wondered. She didn't know her and neither did Lacy, so that meant there was a ninety-five percent chance she wasn't local.

"Look, little girl, either you turn around and walk out of here peacefully or we'll call the police to escort you out and call your parents." Jazzy zeroed her warning glare in on the young woman's face, hoping to intimidate her.

"I'm Sheridan Willis. My older sister is engaged to Jamie Upton. You know Jamie, don't you? You were fucking him just last night, weren't you?"

The little bitch. So she was Laura Willis's sister, huh? The two didn't resemble each other in any way. Not in a physical way. And their personalities were definitely poles apart.

Jazzy squeezed Caleb's arm. "Go next door to Jasmine's and tell Mr. and Mrs. Willis that their younger daughter— Sheridan—is over here trying to pass herself off as twenty-one."

"No. Don't." Sheridan snatched her hand away from where she'd been caressing Caleb's chest. "There's no need to bother my parents. I'll go peacefully. I wouldn't want to interrupt their dinner with my sister and her fiancé." She took several backward steps, then looked directly at Caleb. "Tell me what time you get off work and I'll pick you up."

"Sorry, kid," Caleb replied. "If I were ten years younger, I'd take you up on your offer."

"I like older guys," Sheridan told him. "I've learned a lot from the ones I've screwed. And I'll just bet I could learn a lot from you."

"I don't give lessons," Caleb said.

Sheridan Willis shrugged. "Your loss." Then she tossed her long brown hair over her shoulder and with a prissy, take-a-good-look sway, walked through the crowd and straight to the front entrance.

"Interesting." Caleb motioned to Lacy, who immediately handed him a bottled cola. He downed half the bottle in one swig, then turned to Jazzy. "You're over here mighty early tonight. It wouldn't have anything to do with the fact that Jamie Upton and his fiancée are dining with her parents at Jasmine's, would it?"

"Only indirectly."

"Well, this is a good place to lose yourself for a few hours." He eased away from her. "I'll go do my job. I figure with this rowdy crowd it's only a matter of time before somebody gets out of hand."

"Somebody you can toss out on their ear if you can't talk sense to them." Jazzy nodded toward the entrance where Sheridan Willis had just exited.

"Gutsy kid. She's got spunk."

"Oh, she's got spunk all right. And unless my instincts are dead wrong, she's got a great deal in common with her future brother-in-law."

Caleb's brows rose questioningly.

"Just guessing," Jazzy said, "but I'd say little Miss Sheridan is a self-centered user."

"Is that how you see Jamie?"

"Mm-hmm."

Caleb nodded, the motion more one of speculation than agreement, as if slightly surprised that she'd admitted the truth about Jamie to him, of all people.

"If you need me, I won't be hard to find," he told her before walking away, meandering through the crowd.

"I need you," Jazzy whispered softly to herself.

Tim Willingham, an off-duty deputy, pecked on Jazzy's shoulder. "Howdy, Miss Jazzy. Would you care to dance?"

She'd known Tim all her life. He was a couple of years older than she, a divorced father of two, and an all-around good guy. Since his divorce last year, he'd started coming to Jazzy's Joint almost every Friday and Saturday night when he wasn't working.

"I'd love to dance," she replied. "I feel like kicking up my heels."

Dancing with Tim would be fun . . . and nonthreatening. Tim was about as dangerous as a strawberry lollipop. He was too "white bread" for her; she preferred her men rougher around the edges. But for now, safer was probably better. No sense rushing into anything with Caleb. A smarter course of action would be to move in on him gradually. Test the waters. Besides, if Caleb was the man Genny had foreseen in her future, the man destined to make her happy, then everything would work out in its own good time. And if it wasn't meant to be Caleb, then she'd be better off not getting involved and risk having her heart broken again.

She had considered waiting, but she realized there was more reason to act now instead of later. The longer she allowed him to live, the more harm he would do.

Her plans were made, every detail thought out. All

she needed to do was set things in motion. It shouldn't be difficult to get Jamie to go with her to the cabin. Once she had him there, a glass of drugged wine would do the trick. And when he awoke, he'd find himself quite vulnerable and completely at her mercy. But of course she would show him no mercy.

She laughed, loving the thought of making him pay for his sins. He had been cruel and unmerciful not only to her, but to others. Although she felt sorry for those other women, they really didn't matter. No one mattered except her baby. She had to protect her child. Poor, defenseless little thing.

She hugged herself and swayed back and forth there in the shadowy darkness. Alone. She was so alone. No one to love her. No one to care. But she wouldn't be alone for much longer. She'd soon have her baby with her. Her little girl would love her. But first she had to kill Jamie Upton.

She'd like nothing better than to destroy Jazzy Talbot— the slut! But Jazzy could wait. Killing Jamie had to come first in order to protect her child. Once Jamie was dead, she could take care of everything else. It wasn't that she enjoyed killing people. It was the pleasure of making them suffer that excited her. But some people didn't deserve to live. If only she had been able to act sooner. If only they hadn't stopped her. They should pay, too. Both of them. But she couldn't punish them, not yet. Not until she was sure her baby was safe.

Reve's evening meal had consisted of a diet cola and a pack of peanut butter and crackers, with a Snickers candy bar for dessert. Those delectable items had been available at Cherokee Cabin Rentals' main office, where she'd used her credit card to pay for three nights in a cabin located in town, within walking distance of everything. She had decided not to go back out tonight, but to stay in her small, one-bedroom cabin and figure out exactly what she planned to do. Had staying here in Cherokee Pointe been a dreadful mistake, one she would regret in the morning? Had she simply allowed Sheriff Butler to goad her into staying?

Flipping through the TV channels, she paused on the local cable station that offered tourists a schedule of events in and around the town, as well as within a seventy-five-mile radius. What caught her attention was the advertisement for Jasmine's Restaurant, located in downtown Cherokee Pointe. The picture of Jasmine Talbot welcoming guests flashed across the screen. Reve studied the woman's face, the cheerful expression, the made-for-sin body. *Admit the truth,* Reve told herself. *You know that she's at the very least related to you and very probably your sister.*

Okay, so maybe Jazzy Talbot was her sister—her twin sister. Did that mean they should get to know each other, that they should explore the history of their births together? Somebody was lying about something. Probably about everything. Sally Talbot swore her sister gave birth to only one child. Jazzy. Why would the old woman lie? Was she ashamed because her sister had thrown away one child and kept the other? Or had Sally been the one who had dumped the unwanted baby into the garbage heap in nearby Sevierville?

Ever since the day her mother had told her about where she'd been found as an infant, Reve had battled with myriad unwanted emotions. And now, learning that she might well be a twin, she had to face a horrible truth: someone had thought she wasn't worthy of living and that her sister was. That fact alone was reason enough to dislike Jazzy. Illogical. Based solely on an emotional reaction. And totally unlike Reve Sorrell. Ever since childhood she'd been a sensible young lady, not prone to temper tantrums or emotional outbursts. A quiet child. Obedient. Mannerly. And as dull as dishwater.

Except when challenged. Her one major vice was stubbornness. Her father had always told her that she had gumption. God, how she missed Daddy. And Mother. The Sorrells had been her true parents in every way that mattered.

A completely ridiculous thought crossed her mind. Had something been wrong with her at birth? Had her biological mother chosen to rid herself of the less desirable child? Stupid notion. But if there was even a shred of truth to it, wasn't that a good reason to dislike Jazzy? Of course, she didn't really know the woman at all. Maybe Jacob Butler's assessment of Jazzy was correct. Maybe she was a good woman. Didn't she deserve the benefit of the doubt?

Reve punched the OFF button on the remote and threw it into a nearby chair. Enough already! Tomorrow she'd go see Jazzy Talbot and confront her own fears. Nothing she found out about her birth and biological parents could be any worse than the things she had imagined. And just because Jazzy might turn out to be her twin didn't mean the two of them had to form a sisterly bond.

Chapter 8

The doors at Jazzy's Joint closed shortly after one on Saturday nights. Liquor couldn't be served after midnight, so most of the crowd left by twelve-thirty. A few stragglers who were there to dance or shoot pool stayed behind. But when the band left at one, the few remaining customers made their way home—or, in the case of some couples, made their way to the nearest motel. As she emerged from her office, where she'd spent the last hour going over the liquor order she would place on Monday, Jazzy glanced at the clock behind the bar and noted the time. One-fifteen. She'd divided her time between her office, taking care of several things she could have left until Monday, and mixing and mingling with friends and acquaintances who frequented Jazzy's Joint.

When she'd danced the second time with Tim Willingham, who so obviously had a major crush on her, he had mentioned that Sorrell woman. And try as she might, Jazzy hadn't been able to get woman off her mind.

"She was speeding, had a wreck, and Jacob brought her in this morning," Tim had said. "Boy, did those two not get along. I thought she was gonna hit him. And I figured he'd lock her up. But heck, Miss Jazzy, that lady looks just like you. Well, almost just like you. She's not quite as pretty as you. And I think she's a little taller." Tim had grinned sheepishly, deepening the boyish dimples in his cheeks. "I've never seen two people who weren't twins who looked so dang much alike."

"Well, we can't be twins," Jazzy had told him emphatically. "Maybe she's a long-lost cousin or something. Whatever." She'd shrugged. "Really doesn't bother me. She seemed like an uptight snob. Not our sort at all. So her leaving town is no loss to anyone."

"Yeah, that's the way Jacob saw her, too, as a real uppity sort. But she hasn't left town."

"She hasn't?"

"Nope. Jacob took her over to Cherokee Cabin Rentals, and he said she rented a place for three nights, so looks like we'll be seeing more of Ms. Reve Sorrell."

Jazzy groaned, then smiled and winked at Tim before he said good night and headed for the door. She lifted the hinged countertop and walked behind the bar where Lacy was cleaning up. "A really good night. Lots of customers and not one brawl."

Lacy dried off a glass and stacked it with the row of other clean glasses beneath the counter. "We haven't had many brawls in here lately. Not since Caleb took over as bouncer. Seems his reputation as a hard-ass has gotten around and nobody wants to mess with him."

"We did have a couple of macho idiots who decided they could best him." Jazzy smiled as she recalled those incidents. It would take some really tough dude to best Caleb, one with martial arts skills as subtle and expert as his. And there weren't many like that around Cherokee County—Jacob Butler, definitely, and probably Dallas Sloan.

"Yeah, well, it was way past time that somebody put Jimmy Carruthers and Ricky Lindsey in their place. I love the way Caleb handled each of them." Lacy settled her gaze on Jazzy. "You got yourself a heap of man there, honey. You don't want to do anything stupid and lose him, do you?"

Jazzy understood exactly what Lacy was trying to tell her. She wasn't just talking about Caleb's expertise as a bouncer. "I don't have Caleb. Not the way you mean. You can't lose what you've never had."

"He's a man, honey. A real man. He's not going to come begging, but he's put himself out there time and again and you keep shooting him down."

Jazzy glanced across the room to where Caleb was all but carrying a drunken customer out the front door, the guy's fairly sober girlfriend at his side. Caleb made it a point to not let anyone drive drunk. If a customer put up a fuss about Caleb calling a friend or relative to pick him or her up, he took them home himself. And the few times a mean drunk refused Caleb's help, he simply called the police. Although Caleb was a private man who didn't share anything personal and stayed out of other people's affairs, he was a responsible man who couldn't hide his take-charge, good-guy qualities.

"Maybe I should rectify that mistake tonight," Jazzy said aloud the moment the thought crossed her mind. "Oh, hell. You heard me say that, didn't you?"

Lacy laughed. "Thinking out loud will get you into trouble."

"You don't think giving things a try with Caleb would be a big mistake, do you? Let's face it, I've made so many mistakes already that I—"

"Your only big mistake was loving Jamie Upton," Lacy told her. "And believe me, Caleb McCord is nothing like Jamie. He's twice the man—make that ten times the man—that Jamie could ever be. You just gotta get Jamie out of your system, once and for all."

"He's out." When Lacy gave her a speculative look, she told her, "I swear I'm over Jamie. I just don't want to rush into anything where I could wind up getting hurt or hurting someone else."

"Life's a crap shoot." Lacy removed her apron, folded it, and laid it beneath the bar. "I'm heading out." She lifted the hinged countertop, then paused and said, "Jamie is snake eyes on the first shot. Caleb is definitely a seven or an eleven on the first roll of the dice."

Jazzy managed a smile. Just barely.

Only moments after Lacy left, Caleb came back in through the front entrance. His long, slightly shaggy, brown hair appeared windblown, making Jazzy wonder if the predicted springtime thunderstorm was already brewing.

"Is it raining yet?" she asked.

Caleb closed and locked the door. "Not yet, but I caught a glimpse of some heavy lightning back in the west. We just might get a gully-washer in a few hours."

"Why don't you head on home," Jazzy suggested. "I can finish locking up."

"I'm in no hurry." He moved with sleek, pantherlike grace as he came toward her. "Have you had supper?"

"Supper?"

"You know, the meal eaten in the evenings."

She shook her head. "I lost my appetite before I had a chance to eat over at Jasmine's. But come to think of it, I am a bit hungry."

"Unless you want to open up over at Jasmine's and fix us something, we could go upstairs"—he glanced at the ceiling, indicating her apartment above—"and I could whip us up some bacon and eggs. I'm not much of a cook, but I'm a whiz at bacon and eggs."

"I'm tempted. Especially if you add buttered toast to the menu. I haven't had a man cook for me in a long time. Not since I hired a male chef at Jasmine's about three years ago. He was a wizard in the kitchen, but he had sticky fingers. I caught him stealing and fired him on the spot."

Caleb eased closer and closer until he stood only a couple of feet away. "If I cook for you, I'll expect payment for my work."

Her eyes widened as her mouth gaped open. Well, that was blatant enough. Had he just told her he expected sex as payment for meal preparation? "I believe I told you once before that I don't put out on a first date."

"This won't be a date," he said. "Besides, I never do any bartering or trading when it comes to sex. The payment I was referring to is a date. A real date."

A smile played at the corners of her mouth. "Mm-hmm. You're being awfully nice to me tonight. I'm surprised, especially after the way you acted this morning when you introduced me to your new friend, Reve Sorrell. You accused me of sleeping with Jamie last night."

Caleb rubbed his cheek, the one Jazzy had soundly slapped this morning when he'd told her he didn't give a shit who she slept with. "And you most definitely set me straight."

"Not that I owe you an explanation, but . . ." She paused, hoping more talk about her much discussed, much bemoaned relationship with Jamie didn't ruin the nice and easy conversation she and Caleb were having. "Jamie came by last night and offered me a place in his life as his mistress, after he married Laura Willis."

"Damned stupid son of a bitch!"

"I refused his offer. He asked to stay and talk for a while. I agreed, as a good-bye gesture. He did not stay the night, and nothing more than a kiss happened between us."

"A kiss, huh?"

She nodded. "He's out of my life for good. I swear. I know I've said that before, and I've meant it. I have not given in to Jamie's demands since he came back to Cherokee County in January. Yes, I was tempted at first, but not anymore. I don't love him. I don't want him."

Caleb moved so quickly that she barely had time to catch her breath before he grabbed her face between his two large hands. "If you really mean that . . ."

"I do," she told him with breathless anticipation. God, how she wanted Caleb to kiss her.

"I don't like the idea that you even let him kiss you." Caleb ran his thumb over her bottom lip, then pulled her lip down, opening her mouth.

"Jealous?"

"Got that right."

He kissed her then. Kissed her like she'd never been kissed. And she was certainly no novice. He held her face, cupped between his strong hands, and took her mouth with gentle authority. No rushing. No roughness. But a powerful tenderness that took her breath away. As the tip of his tongue circled her lips, she swayed toward him, her body yearning for a closer connection. When he delved his tongue inside her mouth, probing with expert ease, she moaned deep in her throat. Her feminine core throbbed and moistened. With nothing more than a kiss, he had aroused her. And just when the kiss got even better, he lifted his lips from hers, raised his head, and slowly, provocatively slid his hands over either side of her neck, across her shoulders, and down her arms. Then he released her.

She stood there, staring at him, her pulse pounding frantically.

"You do have bacon and eggs in the fridge, don't you?" he asked.

"What?" It took her befuddled brain a few seconds to realize what he was talking about—the meal he'd offered to prepare for her. Good God, how could he kiss her like that, then stop so suddenly and act as if nothing had happened between them?

"Food," he replied. "Supper. Remember? I'm cooking. We're eating. And in payment for my services, you'll go on an honest-to-goodness real date with me."

"Yes. Yes, of course. I—I've got bacon and eggs in my refrigerator."

He grabbed her hand. "Then come on, woman, let's lock up and get out of here."

A feeling of excitement raced through Jazzy, a light, carefree exuberance that she hadn't felt in a long, long time. Without those heavy emotional chains that bound her to Jamie, she might actually have a chance at happiness. *Tonight,* she told herself, *is the beginning of the rest of your life.*

Jamie was always ready for an adventure, so he was looking forward to slipping away, just the two of them, in the dark of night, while the good citizens of Cherokee County slept safely in their beds, only dreaming of the kind of life he enjoyed. Whereas Jamie didn't just dream about excitement and danger, he experienced it first-hand. What man alive didn't fantasize about having a variety of females at his beck and call? Of screwing a different woman every night?

She had told him to pretend they'd never met. To act as if he was a hitchhiker she'd picked up on the road. Wouldn't it be fun, she'd said, to act out one of her fantasies? Hell, yes, it would be fun. He wasn't quite sure what she had in mind, but he was game.

Jamie crept quietly down the back stairs, hoping he

didn't awaken anyone. He sure as hell didn't want his future in-laws or his grandfather catching him sneaking off this way. And wouldn't they be surprised if they knew who he was going to meet? He had been more than a little surprised himself when she'd made the suggestion. It just went to show that you never knew a person, never really had any idea what they would and wouldn't do. He loved the idea that there was a wildly wicked side to her. Wilder than he'd ever suspected. And hopefully very, very wicked.

He punched in the security code at the back door and rushed outside, making sure to deadbolt the lock. He'd be home before anyone—even their housekeeper Dora—woke, and he could reactivate the security system then.

The early morning breeze penetrated his sport coat as he made his way around the house and down the long driveway.

"I'll pick you up at the gate," she'd told him. "Remember, you're a hitchhiker. Play your part well and I'll reward you."

The thought of that reward had his heart racing and his libido heading into overdrive. What nasty little games did she have in mind? His sex hardened when a very interesting idea entered his head. If she didn't take their playacting to where he wanted it to go, then he would take over and show her just what real sexual exploration was all about—the pain and the ecstasy.

As he neared the front gate, he spotted a car. Not the vehicle she usually drove. He smiled to himself. Hell, she'd even rented a car as part of their game. And not just any car. A snazzy little sports car. From where he stood, he couldn't quite make out the color and the model. As soon as he made his way through the walkway to the side of the massive gates, he all but ran toward the car. He grabbed the handle on the passenger side and found the door unlocked. After swinging the door open, he peered inside and took a long, appreciative look at the driver.

"What's with the wig?" he asked her, but suddenly realized who she resembled with the wig on.

She caressed the strands of the short, red hair that framed her face. "Don't you like it? I thought it might be more fun for you if we pretended I was Jazzy Talbot."

He chuckled softly as he got in and closed the door. "It just might be fun at that."

"So are you ready for our adventure?" she asked.

"Yes, ma'am, I'm ready, willing, and able." He patted his crotch.

"Hi there." She lowered her natural voice to a sultry, baby-doll whisper. "Can I give you a lift somewhere? I'm traveling all alone and sure would like some company. Masculine company . . . if you know what I mean."

"Yes, ma'am, I know exactly what you mean. And I'd love a ride. Just take me wherever you're going."

"Buckle your seat belt, handsome, and hold on tight."

The minute Jamie buckled the safety belt, she sped off in a flash. With her foot pressing harder and harder on the gas petal, the car zoomed up the mountain road.

"Are you in a hurry?" he asked teasingly.

"You have no idea how eager I am to make it to my destination as soon as possible."

"Can't wait for another kind of ride, huh?" He reached across the console and ran his hand up the inside of her leg, from knee to crotch.

"You're the one who should be eager. I promise you that it'll be the ride of your life."

Tiffany Reid knew she was an idiot for getting involved with Dillon Carson. The guy was years older than she and he had a reputation as a lady-killer. But heaven help her, she found him downright irresistible. It wasn't that he was drop-dead gorgeous, but he was interesting and exciting and was great in the sack. He'd waited around at Jazzy's Joint tonight until she got off work over at Jasmine's. Then, since he'd had a little too much to drink, she persuaded him to let her drive. She lived just outside of town, about two miles on the other side of the Upton Farm. When her stepmother died a couple of years ago, she had inherited the old home place. It wasn't much and needed a lot of work. But on the plus side, the rent was free.

Just as she turned off the main road onto the mountain road, a car came up quickly behind them. In her rearview mirror, she could see it was a small sports car of some sort and it appeared the driver's side of the hood was smashed in. Since not many people were out on the mountain road this late at night, she wondered who was in the car. Despite the fact Tiffany was doing the speed limit, the sports car's driver apparently was in a hurry. Only a couple of seconds later, the vehicle zoomed around them at breakneck speed and quickly disappeared up the narrow, winding road.

"Did you see who was driving that car?" Dillon asked.

"No, why? Did you recognize him?"

"Wasn't a him. It was a her. And even though I just caught a glimpse, I think it might have been your boss lady, Jazzy Talbot."

"No way. What would she be doing way out here? Besides, she drives a red Jeep."

"I'm not one hundred percent sure it was her, but the lady driving had short red hair and was wearing a pair of big gold hoop earrings like Jazzy wears a lot."

"Aren't you the observant one, paying attention to what kind of jewelry Jazzy wears."

"Hey, a guy would have to be dead not to notice a hot tamale like Jazzy." Dillon undid the seat belt she'd made him buckle, slid across the seat, and cuddled up to her. "But there's no need to be jealous. You're the woman I'm with tonight. You'll have my undivided attention every minute we're together."

"Is that a promise?"

"Just take me home with you and let me show you."

Yeah, she was most definitely an idiot for dating Dillon. He was a lot of fun, but for a girl who'd like to settle down, get married, and have a couple of kids, he was the wrong man. But most of the marrying kind who lived in Cherokee County were so boring. And that's one thing Dillon wasn't. She supposed that was the reason she kept coming back for more of his good loving.

"Where is this place?" Jamie asked as she stopped the car in front of what appeared to be little more than a hovel.

"It's my hideaway," she told him. "Come on. Get out. I have a surprise waiting for you inside."

"Have you had the place fumigated for varmints?" he asked jokingly.

"The only varmint around this place is you, Jamie, my love."

When she got out, he followed her quickly—up the dirt path, up the rickety wooden steps, and onto the partially rotted wooden porch. When she paused at the door, he came up behind her, slipped his arm around her waist, and nuzzled her neck.

She hated him. Hated him with a passion. It took every ounce of her willpower to endure his vile touch. Whenever she thought about how she might have to let him fuck her again, she wanted to vomit. *Don't think about it,* she told herself. *Just think about what you have planned, about all the delectable things you're going to do to him. When he's touching you, kissing you, concentrate on the revenge you will exact.*

The door opened easily, creaking on its rusty hinges. She led him into the interior, lit only by kerosene lamps and the logs burning in the fireplace. When she'd come up here late this afternoon to prepare the setting for Jamie's seduction and ultimate downfall, she hadn't been sure the fireplace was in good working order. They could have shown up and found the place burned to the ground. But she'd had to choose an out of the way place, somewhere miles from the nearest other house. After all, when Jamie was screaming in agony, she didn't want anyone to hear him and start snooping.

"Well, I'll be damned," Jamie said as he looked around the room.

"Cozy and private," she said.

She'd prepared a pallet on the floor with quilts she'd bought at various shops in Pigeon Forge, the kind that thousands of tourists bought every year. No way would anyone ever trace them back to her. A bottle of merlot she'd picked up at a local liquor store rested between two fat feather pillows directly in front of the fireplace. She moved away from Jamie and made her way over to the corner, where she'd placed a portable radio. After turning on the radio, she flipped through the stations until she found some soft, romantic music.

While he watched in fascination, she disrobed. Slowly. Doing a striptease for him. The sooner she subdued him, the sooner the fun would begin. Naked, her gaze focused on Jamie, she sat down on the pallet, opened the bottle of wine and poured the rich burgundy liquid into two green crystal flutes. What Jamie didn't know was that waiting in the bottom of one of the glasses was a potent sedative. Something that would render him helpless for a couple of hours. Long enough for her to prepare him for his so richly deserved reward for being a cruel, cunning, manipulative son of a bitch.

Jamie surveyed her naked body, then removed his own clothes and came over to accept the glass of wine she offered him. Before he put the glass to his lips, he grinned wickedly. "You've got a great body," he told her. "Despite . . . well, you know."

"So gentlemanly of you not to come right out and say it." She responded with a smile every bit as genuine as his and twice as wicked.

He sipped the wine. Some cheap stuff she'd picked up at a busy store where she was certain no one would remember her. She'd been wearing sunglasses and nondescript clothes, making herself look as forgettable as possible. Just another tourist.

Jamie finished off the wine quickly, then set the glass on the pallet and reached for her. Inside she cringed the moment he touched her, but outwardly she responded as most of the women he'd seduced had no doubt done.

When she pressed her naked body against his, he sighed loudly. "Oh, darlin', your heart's beating like mad and you're trembling. You're as excited as I am, aren't you?"

"You can't imagine how excited I am."

The anticipation was delicious. It was only a matter of time now. Of course she was excited. She could hardly wait until he passed out. Until he was rendered helpless and completely at her mercy. Oh, the marvelous things she had planned for him. Her little bag of tricks was hidden neatly away in the other room. Thick leather straps. Sturdy railroad spikes that would anchor so nicely into the old wooden floor in this room. Razors. Knives.

A poker that could be heated to a sizzling red hot in the fireplace flames.

When Jamie kissed her, she opened her mouth and thrust her tongue inside his parted lips. And all the while she thought about thrusting that hot poker up inside him.

Chapter 9

"Mm-mmm," Jazzy sighed as she placed her empty dish over Caleb's on the coffee table. "Those were the best scrambled eggs I've ever eaten." She looked over at him. He held his second cup of decaf coffee to his lips. "Tell me, Master Chef, what is your secret?"

Caleb downed the last drops of coffee and set his cup on top of their stacked plates. "If I told you my secret to perfect scrambled eggs, it wouldn't be a secret anymore, would it?"

She cuddled into the softness of her fat old sofa, sighed contentedly, and smiled at him. "Thanks."

"For what? All I did was fix you breakfast at two o'clock in the morning."

Jazzy loved his smile. A cocky, self-confident, closed-mouth smile that hinted of danger and mystery. He wasn't as pretty as Jamie, but he was far more appealing in every way. Damn! Why was she falling into that same old trap—comparing every man who came into her life with Jamie? *Ah, Jasmine, my dear, don't you realize what a*

*breakthrough you've made? You've actually found someone
who appeals to you more than Jamie Upton.*

Jazzy laughed, the warm, carefree feeling spreading
through her body rapidly. "You've done more than just
fix me breakfast. You've pampered me, which is something I'm not used to. And I think you've forgiven me,
too, haven't you?"

Caleb reached over from where he sat on the opposite end of the sofa and brushed toast crumbs from the
side of Jazzy's mouth. Without thinking, she ran the tip
of her tongue around the inside of her lips and accidently licked Caleb's index finger. Their gazes met and
held for an endless moment.

"I was wrong to judge you. It's not as if I've lived a
spotless life. What you did or didn't do with Jamie Upton
last night wasn't any of my business."

Jazzy grabbed Caleb's hand just as he pulled it away.
"I didn't have sex with Jamie last night. I haven't had
sex with him since he returned home in January. I haven't
been with another man since I've known you."

"Am I suppose to read some significance into that
statement?"

"Maybe one has nothing to do with the other. Maybe
it does. I honestly don't know."

"And that's suppose to make me feel better how?"

"Jamie is getting married in three weeks. We said our
good-byes last night."

"You've said good-bye to him before and—"

Jazzy drew Caleb's hand up to her face and pressed it
against her cheek. "Jamie isn't the man I want." She
paused, garnered up her courage and said, "You are."

He jerked his hand away and stared at her. "Don't
play games with me. I'm not the kind of guy who's willing to be second best. And I don't share. If you're mine,

you're mine alone. Whether it's for a night or a week or a month. Understand?"

Jazzy huffed. "Why did I know you'd be this way, all old-fashioned macho possessive?"

"Let's lay our cards on the table, so we'll both know where we stand."

She nodded.

"I've wanted you since the first time I saw you," he told her. "I want you now more than ever. But there are things about myself that I haven't told you. Things I won't tell you unless . . ." He clicked his tongue. "Let's just say I don't make promises to anyone that I don't keep. Do I want to fuck you? Hell, yes. Do I care about you? Yeah, I do. Will I make a lifelong commitment to you if we have sex? Not necessarily. But when I'm with you, I'm with you exclusively. And I expect the same from you. No lies. No games. And I swear I'll never hurt you."

Emotion caught in her throat. Tears stung her eyes. Jazzy glanced away, not wanting to face him until she was totally in control. She swallowed a couple of times, took a deep breath, and turned back around. Why couldn't she have met Caleb when she was sixteen? Why couldn't he have been her first love? If he'd gotten her pregnant, he would have married her. And if anyone— his parents or grandparents—had objected, he would have told them to go straight to hell.

"I want you, too," Jazzy admitted. "Since that first night. You'll never know how difficult it was for me not to . . . well, not to use you. And if I'm honest about it, I've been protecting myself, too. I've been hurt and dis- appointed so many times. I've believed promise after promise. But no more! I like you, Caleb McCord. I like you a lot. But I'm not ready to make a commitment to anyone. What I want—what I need—is for us to just take things one day . . . one night . . . at a time. Get to know each other. See if we really work well together. Don't push each other. Just let things happen naturally, on their own. If it works, we'll take the next step. If it doesn't, we'll part friends, with no hard feelings. No one hurt."

He studied her as if he were trying to gauge her honesty. "It would seem that we want the same thing."

"Yeah, it would seem so."

Caleb scooted closer. Jazzy held her breath. She'd been wanting another one of his devastating kisses. He slid his hand behind her neck and grasped gently, then pulled her forward, just enough to brush his lips against hers. Her breath caught in her throat. She wanted more. So much more.

He played with her lips, featherlight kisses at first. Then he used his tongue to paint a moist oval over her mouth. She sucked in her breath. His fingers reached up and splayed apart, forking through her short hair to cup her head. She sighed. And then he kissed her, really kissed her, curling her toes and making her heart pound faster.

This guy is a master at the art of kissing, she thought, and then ceased to think coherently.

When her breasts were tight and aching, her femininity clenching and unclenching in preparation, and he'd completely taken her breath away, he ended the kiss and lifted his head. She opened her eyes and stared into his whiskey-gold eyes. Puzzled that he'd stopped just as they were getting warmed up, she opened her mouth to ask him what was going on.

He laid his index finger across her lips. "This was our first date. You don't go to bed with a guy on a first date, remember?"

"Mm-hmm, I remember." Why the hell had she ever told him that? Even if it was the truth, somehow that rule just didn't apply to Caleb. He was different—not

only different from Jamie, but different from every
other man she'd ever known. Well, maybe he was a little
like Jacob, who was one of the best men in the world.
But there were no sexual sparks between her and Jacob.
And there were enough sparks between her and Caleb
to set off a major explosion.

"I'll clean up these dishes, then I'll leave." When
Caleb stood, he did nothing to try to hide the fact that
he had a magnificent erection.

"You're leaving?" Just like that, he was going away
when they were both aroused and needing relief in the
worst way?

"I'll be back," he told her as he gathered up their
dirty dishes. "You need some rest and so do I. It's"—he
glanced at the clock on the end table—"three-fifteen.
How about I come by this afternoon around two-thirty?
It's Sunday. My only day off. Let Tiffany take over at
Jasmine's. We'll drive over to Gatlinburg, meander
around through all the little shops, and then eat supper
at one of the nice restaurants."

"I see you've planned our second date." She rose from
the sofa and followed him into the kitchen. He put the
dishes into the soapy water where he'd cleaned the cooking utensils earlier. "Just leave them. I'll do them in the
morning."

He nodded and turned to go, but she blocked his
path.

Caleb grinned at her. "What?"

"You're a nice man, Caleb McCord."

He laughed. "You think so, do you? Just goes to show
how much you don't know about me."

She stepped aside, allowing him to make his way to
her front door. She followed behind him. "Okay, so
maybe *nice* was the wrong word. You're a good man."

When he glanced over his shoulder and frowned mockingly, she made one final correction to her original statement. "You're a man with a good heart."

He winked at her, then walked out and down the exterior stairs that led to the sidewalk. Jazzy stepped out onto the narrow stoop at the top of the stairs and watched him walk toward his car. As soon as he got in and drove off, she closed and locked the door, then danced back into the living room. She hugged herself and sighed.

She had a second date with Caleb tomorrow. An honest-to-goodness date.

Feeling an unfamiliar sense of happiness, Jazzy hummed softly to herself as she headed for her bedroom. Tonight she would dream of Caleb. And maybe tomorrow—no, later today—that dream might come true.

Andrea Willis couldn't sleep. She had tossed and turned for hours, but she had too much on her mind to relax. Besides, Cecil was snoring like a freight train. So like a man to be able to sleep soundly when his daughter was on the verge of making the biggest mistake of her life. It wasn't that his concern didn't run as deep as hers. It did. After all, he loved Laura in a way Andrea had never been able to, somehow able to overlook all her inadequacies.

When she had first suggested psychiatric help for Laura when she was twelve, Cecil had been livid, accusing her of wanting to find fault with Laura, of loving her less than she did Sheridan. But it was because she did love Laura that she'd wanted help for the child. Finally she'd been able to bring Cecil around to her way of thinking, but only after that terrible incident with the Roberts boy. He claimed she had tried to run over him with her car—her sixteenth birthday present. Laura had been unable to remember what happened that night.

After slipping into her house shoes and satin robe, Andrea crept out of the guest room and down the hall to the room their daughters were sharing this weekend. When she reached the closed door, she paused for a few moments, considering whether she should disturb them at this hour of the morning. Yes, she definitely shouldn't wait to talk to Laura. And if she woke Sheridan in the process, so be it. Maybe Sheridan could help her talk sense to Laura.

Andrea tapped on the door. No response. She tapped again. Still nothing. She didn't dare knock any louder for fear of waking Cecil, who was only a couple of doors down. The Upton family's quarters were in the other wing of the house, so no chance of bothering them. She tried the handle and found the door unlocked. She opened the door and walked into the dark room.

"Laura," she called as she tiptoed toward the bed where her elder daughter slept. "Laura, wake up, dear."

No answer.

When she reached the bed, she realized why no one had responded. The bed was empty. She glanced at the other twin bed. It, too, was empty. Andrea turned on a bedside lamp and searched the bedroom and adjoining bath. Where were her daughters? *Don't panic,* she told herself. *There is a perfectly good explanation for why neither of them are here.*

Wasn't it possible, even probable, that Laura was in Jamie's room, in his bed? Yes, of course, where else would she be? And Sheridan? God only knew where that wild young thing was. She was probably in some man's bed, too. Some fellow she'd met in town, some stranger.

Andrea shivered. Sheridan had the morals of an alley

cat, but she could hardly condemn her. After all, she'd had an adventurous streak when she'd been that age.

Andrea left the room and made her way back to her own bedroom. Cecil was still snoring. She went into the bathroom, closed the door, and turned on the light. After rummaging through her cosmetic bag, she found her prescription of sleeping pills. She averaged taking the medicine a couple of times a week lately. Not exactly addicted, but she was on the verge of becoming dependent on them. She popped the pill into her mouth, downed it with a small cup of water, then went back to bed. In about an hour, the medication would take effect and she would rest. Only when she slept could she stop worrying about Laura.

Jim Upton made his way down the backstairs at five o'clock. He had slept fairly well the first part of the night, but when he awoke around four, he'd started thinking about Erin. About how much he wished he was in bed with her. About how much he loved her. About how desperately he wished he could ask Reba for a divorce. But how did you ask a decent, caring woman who'd been your wife for over fifty years to give you a divorce? Reba had turned a blind eye to his indiscretions over the years, and God knew there had been quite a few. But he hadn't been in love before—not since he'd been a green boy and madly in love with Melva Mae Nelson, who had broken his heart when she'd married another man. He'd taken his parents' advice and married a suitable young woman from a good family, and although they'd shared a reasonably good life, Jim had never been truly happy. Not until this past year when a woman twenty-five years his junior had come into his life.

What the hell a gorgeous woman like Erin Mercer saw in him he'd never know. She didn't need his money, because she was rich in her own right. She had brought joy and excitement and sex back into his life. She had become everything to him, and he knew he couldn't go on this way, living a lie with Reba, when he wanted a life with Erin. At his age, he might not have more than a few good years left, and he wanted to spend that time with a woman who made him feel like a man.

When Jim entered his study, he left the overhead lights off and felt his way across the dark room until he reached his desk. He flipped on the banker's lamp and lifted the telephone receiver. He dialed her number and waited. The phone rang and rang and rang. Then the answering machine picked up.

"Erin, please answer the phone, sweetheart," Jim said. "We need to talk." He had come to a decision that would greatly affect both their lives. He waited, but she didn't answer.

He hung up, then dialed again and found himself repeating the procedure. He left a second message.

Why won't she answer? Maybe she's sick. Maybe something's wrong. Or maybe she isn't at home. But if she's not there, where is she? Could she be with another man? Damn! Don't think like that. She's not with another man. Erin loves you. Only you.

Jim all but ran back upstairs and into his room. He and Reba hadn't shared a room in years, so he didn't have to worry about disturbing her as he removed his robe and pajamas and dressed hurriedly. It had taken him months to come to this decision, and he couldn't wait another minute to tell Erin that he was going to ask Reba for a divorce. More than anything, he wanted to marry Erin.

Twenty minutes later, he pulled up outside Erin's

cabin. The porch light was on, but the house was dark. Then he noticed that her car wasn't parked at the side of the cabin. She wasn't here. Where the hell was she? He could try her cell phone, but since she seldom kept the damn thing on, he doubted he could reach her that way.

Should he stay and wait on her or just go home and try calling her later? *Go home, you old fool. Go home to your wife and wait for your mistress to explain why she was out all night.* Cursing loudly, Jim stomped across the yard and got back in his car.

Blood. Blood everywhere. Bright red. Fresh. It coated the wooden floor and dripped into the cracks. His body had been mutilated, sliced and diced and burned. His eyes rolled back in his head as he wept in agony. His throat was hoarse from screaming and begging. She brandished the hot poker over him. And then when he opened his mouth to plead, she rammed the fiery metal stick into his mouth. As indescribable pain silenced him, he passed out.

Genny screamed and screamed and screamed.

"Wake up, honey," Dallas pleaded with her as he held her securely in his arms.

Although he'd seen this happen to her before—too many times to suit him—he didn't think he'd ever get used to it. When they first met, he'd been a skeptic, the biggest skeptic of all time. But Genny had made a believer out of him. He figured it was fate's way of getting a good laugh at his expense. What could be more ironic than to have a guy who believed in nothing beyond his five senses to fall head over heels in love with a genuine psychic?

Genny's eyelids fluttered as Dallas rubbed her back

tenderly and kissed her temple. "That's it, Genny, come back to me. Come out of the dark fog. You're safe. I won't ever let anything bad happen to you."

She moaned deeply. Her eyes opened, then closed, then opened again. She gazed at Dallas. He could tell her mind was fuzzy, that a part of her consciousness hadn't returned from the other world she'd visited, from the mystical place that more than once had threatened to trap her and keep her there.

"It was bad, wasn't it?" he said in a matter-of-fact way. She nodded. "It was horrible."

"Tell me about it." He had learned that it was essential for Genny to share her visions, that she never had a vision they dared ignore.

She cuddled closer, burrowing her small body against him. "The vision was about Jamie again. Very similar to the first one, but . . . but more graphic." Reaching up to clutch Dallas's naked shoulders, she looked him in the eyes. "I can't be certain, but I believe either he's being tortured right now or he will be very soon. Within the hour."

"What did you see?"

"I saw him naked. His body mutilated. She—she . . . oh, God, Dallas, she rammed a hot poker into his mouth!" Genny fell apart then, tears filling her eyes as she trembled uncontrollably.

He hated it when these damn visions ripped her apart. Despite loving her and being there for her, there was only so much he could do. Sometimes he wished he could take away her powers so that she'd never have another vision, but he realized how selfish that would be and that without her special gift of sight, she wouldn't be his Genny.

He held her tight and let her cry. Often simply holding her was all he could do.

Several minutes later, she lifted her tear-stained face.

"We have to do something—you and Jacob and I," she said. "Jamie is in a house, an old and deserted house. I sensed that he and the woman were alone and they're here in the mountains somewhere, so that means it's Jacob's jurisdiction. Call him. Call him now!"

"I'll call him, if you promise to lie down and rest."

"I will . . . later. After we've made the phone calls and then found Jamie."

"The phone calls? Who else are we calling, other than Jacob?"

"Jazzy."

"Genny, you don't think that she—"

"No, of course Jazzy isn't the one torturing Jamie. But somehow this is going to hurt her. It's going to cause her great pain and threaten her life. Don't ask me how I know, I just know."

"That's good enough for me. And it'll be good enough for Jacob and for Jazzy." He scooted across to the edge of the bed and sat there, then glanced back at her. "I'll get the phone, call Jacob, and then let you talk to him. That is what you want, isn't it?"

"Yes, thank you."

Dallas reached over onto the nightstand and picked up the telephone receiver. He dialed Jacob's home number, then waited for the sheriff to pick up.

"Butler here," Jacob growled in a sleepy voice.

"Sorry to wake you," Dallas said.

"It's okay. I was half awake anyway. What's wrong?"

"Genny had another vision about Jamie Upton. This time she's certain that this mystery woman is torturing Jamie, either right at this very minute or within the hour."

"Let me talk to her."

Genny wriggled her fingers in a give-me-the-phone gesture.

"Yeah, sure. She wants to talk to you." Dallas handed her the phone.

"Jacob, she's insane. Totally insane. But she's clever. Devious. And she hates Jamie passionately. I can feel her hatred. It's thick and smothering and totally black. She doesn't just want to kill him, she wants him to suffer unmercifully before he dies."

"You have any idea where they are?"

"They're on the mountain, but not near. You need to call Sally and get the bloodhounds. Bring them here and Dallas and I will go with you. I'm almost certain that I can lead them in the right direction."

"We'll have to contact the Uptons in order to get a piece of Jamie's clothing," Jacob told her. "How the hell do I explain this to Big Jim?"

"It doesn't matter. Just do it and do it quickly. We don't have any time to waste."

"I'll be there in twenty minutes, twenty-five at most. Have Dallas call Sally and tell her to meet us at the Upton Farm. That'll save us some time."

"All right. We'll take care of the phone calls. I'll even have Dallas phone Big Jim." Genny paused, then looked at Dallas before she finished her telephone conversation with a startling revelation. "Jacob, she's done this sort of thing before. Jamie isn't the first person she's tortured to death. And—and he won't be the last one."

"My God!"

"Hurry. Please, hurry."

Dallas saw how weak Genny was when the phone slipped from her fingers and landed on the rumpled covers. He lifted the receiver and replaced it on the stand.

"I have to call Jazzy," Genny told him. "Use your cell phone to call Sally and tell her to meet us with Peter and Paul over at the Uptons as soon as possible. Then call the Upton Farm and ask to speak to Big Jim. Tell him we suspect Jamie's been kidnapped and we're putting Sally's bloodhounds on the trail. If he doesn't want to cooperate, tell him exactly what I saw in my vision."

Chapter 10

She stood over her handiwork and smiled with great satisfaction. Jamie's eyelids had been fluttering and he'd even tried to open his eyes, so it was only a matter of time before he awoke and realized his predicament. She walked around him, from his head along his body to his feet. He was heavier than he looked, and it had required all her strength to maneuver him into position. It hadn't taken the drug in the wine very long to render him helpless. His limp body had been as pliable as putty, cooperating fully as she laid him out on the wooden floor, spread-eagled. While she'd pounded the heavy metal spikes in to the floor alongside each arm and leg, he hadn't even moved.

Kneeling alongside him, she tested the thick leather straps that bound his wrists and ankles to the metal spikes. Then she loosened the gag in his mouth. Sometimes she derived more pleasure from a man realizing he couldn't speak, but with Jamie, she decided that she preferred to hear him beg and plead and scream. And he would scream. She removed the cloth gag.

Her hand skimmed his body from neck to navel. A perfect male specimen, a young man in his prime. But beneath all that exterior perfection existed a vile, cruel monster who preyed on women, making them promises he never intended to keep, breaking their hearts and destroying their lives. She intended to make him pay for his many sins—unforgivable sins. Everyone who knew Jamie Upton realized he didn't deserve to live. The world would certainly be a better place without him.

And her baby would be safe.

Jamie groaned. She rose from her knees, adjusted the plastic gloves she wore and picked up the curve-tipped iron poker. Jamie opened his eyes and closed them several times. *He's coming around,* she told herself. *Get ready to greet him in a special way.* She walked to the fireplace, where she'd kept the blaze burning for the past few hours. As she stuck the poker into the fire to heat it, she heard Jamie grunt and call out to her.

"Hey, what the hell's going on?"

She glanced over her shoulder and smiled at him. "I thought you'd never wake up, darling. I've been waiting for you to open your eyes so we could have a lot more fun."

"What?" He struggled against his bondage. "Hey, I didn't agree to anything quite this kinky. What did you do, drug me?"

"Yes, something like that," she told him, as she removed the poker from the fireplace and walked toward him, naked as the day she was born. Except for the protective gloves of course. She didn't want to leave behind any fingerprints.

Jamie's hazel eyes widened when she stood over him, the red-hot poker in her hand. "Hey, baby doll, I'm not into the slave part of rough S and M. This isn't my thing at all. I like to occasionally give a little pain, but, heck"—

he laughed nervously—"what you've got in mind could scar a guy for life."

She loved the fact that he still wasn't quite certain about her motives. He probably thought she was teasing him, titillating him, yet a part of him was just a little scared at the prospect of her branding him. She lowered the poker until it was almost touching the center of his chest. He looked up at her, real fear in his eyes. She let the tip of the poker barely touch him. He yelped in pain.

"Damn it, that hurt." He struggled against the leather ties that bound him. "Come on. Enough of this shit. Get on top and fuck me or untie me. I told you I'm not—"

She let the poker reply for her as she slid the hot edge down his body, from his chest to just below his navel. He screamed as the heat seared his flesh with third-degree burns.

With tears filling his eyes as the pain radiated through him, Jamie cried out, "What the hell's the matter with you? Are you crazy?" He tried his best to break free, but quickly realized struggling was useless.

"What's the matter? Don't you like the way I play, lover boy?"

Before he could respond, she carried the poker back to the fireplace to reheat it, then bent over the hearth and picked up a large, sharp butcher knife. When she turned and showed Jamie what she held in her hand, he cringed, every muscle in his body stiffening with fear.

"You're fucking insane, you bitch! If you know what's good for you, you'll let me go now. Otherwise you're going to regret the day you were born."

She knelt beside him and brushed his damp hair away from his face. "Oh, such a bad, bad boy. And so spoiled. Do you think your silly threat scares me? You're the one who should be afraid." She ran the tip of the butcher knife down his right cheek, just barely opening the skin. Blood oozed from the fresh wound. Jamie whimpered. "Such a pretty boy. The girls just love that handsome face, don't they?" While he continued struggling uselessly, she slid the knife down his left cheek so that he'd have matching scars.

"Okay, okay," he shouted. "Enough. Whatever it is you want, you've got it. Just tell me what you want from me."

"I thought that would be obvious." She hovered the knife over his chin. "I want you to suffer the way you've made so many others suffer." Laughter bubbled up inside her. "No, that's not true. Actually, I want you to suffer far more."

"What others?" he asked. "Who have I made suffer? I've never done something like this to anyone. Not ever."

She nipped his chin with the knife. "Physical torture is the only thing you understand, because someone has to have a heart and a soul to suffer mentally and emotionally. And we both know that you don't have either a heart or a soul."

"Don't do this. Whatever it is you think I've done wrong, however you think I might have hurt you, I'm sorry. Just let me go and I swear I'll make it up to you. Whatever you want, you—"

"I'm getting exactly what I want right now. You're begging. You're scared. And you're suffering." She reached down and cupped his scrotum in her hand. "But the fun has only just begun."

While Dallas drove toward the Upton Farm, Genny tried once again to call Jazzy. She'd been trying on and off for the past twenty minutes, but no one had answered. She'd just contacted the phone company and was assured the line was in proper working order and suggested that the phone might to be disconnected at the source.

Damn! Jazzy was in the habit of occasionally unplugging her phones when she didn't want her sleep disturbed. But why this morning of all mornings? If Genny had time, she'd go into town and wake Jazzy, but time was of the essence if they wanted to save Jamie's life. Genny could sense his life force beginning to drain from him.

"No luck?" Dallas asked.

"No. She's taken the phone off the hook again."

"Since Jacob has called in his deputies and I've got every available man on my force joining forces with Jacob's guys, I don't have anybody who can check on her. Why don't you call Caleb and see if he'll go over and let Jazzy know what's going on?"

"Good idea, but I don't know his phone number and all the Cherokee Cabin Rental numbers are unlisted. I'll have to wait until someone's in the office to get the number."

"It's not going to hurt to wait," Dallas said. "After all, maybe by the time you reach Jazzy, we'll have found Jamie and have his would-be killer behind bars."

"If only I could believe that . . ."

Dallas made a sharp turn as he kept the SUV on the road going down the mountain. "Are you picking up on something you haven't told me about?"

Genny shivered. "I'm getting strange vibes. Like I told you, I'm sensing Jamie's life force draining away. If we don't find him soon, he'll die."

Ten minutes later, they stopped at the open gates in front of the driveway at the Upton Farm. The roadway was lined with vehicles and Big Jim Upton stood beside Jacob's Dodge Ram, which blocked the drive. Sally stood by the truck bed, where she'd already placed Peter and

Paul. Jacob waved at Genny and Dallas as they pulled to a stop behind his truck.

Dallas got out, rounded the hood, and reached the passenger door of their SUV in time to help Genny onto the ground. "If I see you're getting too tired or if you get sucked into the darkness too deep, I'm taking you home. Understand?"

"Yes, Dallas, I understand." She loved him for being so protective.

Side by side, they approached Jacob and Big Jim. When they drew closer, Genny saw the strain on Jim Upton's face. Jamie had put his grandfather through hell for years, but the old man still cared about his only grandchild.

"We're all set," Jacob said. "Big Jim provided us with a pair of Jamie's socks. The ones he wore yesterday, so we're set to let Peter and Paul loose once you head us in the right direction."

Genny nodded.

"I can't tell you how grateful I am that you're willing to help Jamie," Jim said, his expression somber. "Considering how Jamie has treated Jazzy. I know she's your best friend."

Genny laid her hand on Jim's arm and squeezed comfortingly. "The only thing that matters right now is finding Jamie. And I'll do my best to help." She didn't tell the man that she wouldn't let any living creature die if it were within her power to prevent it, not even a sorry son of a bitch like Jamie.

"Is what Jacob said true?" Jim asked. "Did you . . . did you see him being tortured?"

Genny's gaze shot to Jacob's face, and she immediately understood that he'd had no choice but tell Big Jim everything, otherwise he wouldn't have believed Jacob.

"Yes, it's true. Someone is holding Jamie captive. She is torturing—"

"She? It's a woman who has him, a woman who is . . . God help him. It could be anybody. That boy has no conscience when it comes to taking advantage of women." Jim looked directly into Genny's eyes. "Do you know who she is?"

Genny shook her head. "No. I can't see the woman clearly." *Only her short red hair.*

Jim drew in a deep breath and nodded. "Then we'd better be off, hadn't we? It'll be daylight soon, and I don't want my wife or Laura and her family to know anything about this, unless it's absolutely necessary. Jacob was good enough to call me first before he showed up so I could meet him down here at the gate. If anything happens to Jamie, it'll kill my wife."

"We're ready." Jacob looked to Genny. "Which way?"

Genny turned back to Dallas, who stood only a couple of feet away. She wanted him near, in case she needed him immediately. Sometimes when she delved too deeply, she had difficulty reemerging. Dallas had become her lifeline to reality. He possessed the ability to draw her back from the obsidian depths.

With Dallas at her side, Genny closed her eyes and concentrated, praying that her sixth sense would pick up something on Jamie's whereabouts. Darkness descended quickly. Swirling, malevolent darkness that indicated evil.

Pain. So much pain. Unbearable suffering. She could hear Jamie's pitiful cries inside her mind and the gentleness within her could barely endure the knowledge of what was happening to him. The darkness turned a deep red, a thick, cloudy crimson covering everything. Blood. Blood. Oh, God, so much blood.

Concentrate on where Jamie is and not on what's happening to him, she told herself. *Connect with the place, not with Jamie.*

Although she was unable to visualize the exact location, she did recognize Scotsman's Bluff when she tried to picture the place where Jamie was being held. Only a few months ago, a vicious serial killer had murdered an innocent seventeen year old not far from Scotsman's Bluff. The place was deep in the forest, high in the mountains. Secluded. Dotted with caves. Plentiful with wildlife. And a few old, deserted cabins still stood here and there, within sight of Scotsman's Bluff. Jamie was in one of those cabins!

"He's somewhere close to Scotsman's Bluff." Genny opened her eyes. And although she had been able to return to the present moment without any difficulty, she felt a sudden and powerful weakness. When she swayed slightly, Dallas cursed under his breath. "I'm all right," she assured him.

"Okay, let's get organized here," Jacob called out. "Mr. Upton will ride with me, as will Genny and Dallas." He looked at Sally. "You take Genny's SUV and stay right behind us. Leave Peter and Paul in the truck with us." Sally nodded. Dallas tossed the old woman his keys. "Everyone else will follow us and stay in radio contact at all times. I don't want anybody doing anything without my specific orders."

Once they headed back up the mountain, Genny rested her head on Dallas's shoulder and tried her best to concentrate on where Jamie was located. Scotsman's Bluff could be seen from miles around, which meant it could take hours to search the vicinity. Genny felt certain that Jamie didn't have hours. She sensed that the woman who held him captive was growing weary of torturing him, especially now that he kept passing out from the pain.

*   *   *

She opened the thermos, tilted it, and poured water over Jamie's bloody face. He didn't respond. Damn, he was such a lily-livered weakling. A little pain and he passed out. Oh, well, she'd had her fun with him. He had suffered the torment of the damned. And his pretty boy face and perfect body were neither pretty nor perfect any longer. She stepped away from him and admired her handiwork. His face and body were covered with numerous cuts and burns. She had sliced his fingertips and toes with razor blades and nipped off his tiny male nipples with a pair of pliers. She had used the hot poker repeatedly; however, she had one final destination for that particular instrument.

Kneeling beside him again, she patted his face. Blood soaked her hands. The human face had so many tiny blood vessels that with a few cuts, it looked as if a person was bleeding to death.

"Wake up, darling. I've got another surprise for you."

Jamie's eyelids eased halfway open.

"That's a good boy."

He tried to shake his head, but couldn't manage. His burned mouth formed the word *No*. Using her fingers, she wiped the blood from his forehead where it was dripping into his eyes.

"It's almost over. All my fun. And all your pain. But then when you die, you'll go to hell, and the suffering there will last forever." She laughed at him, laughed with the giddiness bubbling inside her.

She got up and walked over to the fireplace. The poker should be red hot now. She lifted the poker from the flames and carried it with her as she stood at Jamie's feet. She knelt, picked up the sharp butcher knife, then eased up between Jamie's spread legs. She laid the poker aside for a moment while she lifted his scrotum. Then, in one swift slice, she took off his genitals. Tossing the knife aside, she picked up the hot poker and rammed it into his anus.

Leaving the poker imbedded in him, she crawled up beside him and took a good look at what was left of Jamie Upton. She forced his mouth wide apart and stuffed his bloody penis into his mouth. Then she stood, wiped her bloody hands off on her bloody body, and sighed.

"That's that. Job all done." If he wasn't dead, he would be very soon.

Now you have to clean up, she told herself. *Gather up all your things, put them in the garbage sack, and get ready to leave.*

Andrea Willis woke at six o'clock. Something was wrong. She could sense trouble. It was unlike her to wake so early, especially after she'd taken a sleeping pill. And whenever she got a sense of foreboding, it usually involved Laura. Suddenly she remembered that neither Laura nor Sheridan had come home last night. She didn't worry so much about Sheridan. That feisty young woman could take care of herself. But what about Laura?

Andrea got out of bed, slipped into her house shoes and robe, exited the bedroom where Cecil was still sleeping, and walked down the hall. She knocked on her daughters' door. No response. This time she didn't wait. She simply flung open the door and turned on the overhead light. Neither of the twin beds had been slept in. Both were still made up from yesterday morning.

What was that odd sound? Where was it coming from? She stopped dead still in the center of the room and listened. Someone was weeping, and the pitiful sobs were coming from the adjoining bathroom. Had one of the girls returned? Was Sheridan or Laura crying? If Jamie

Upton had done something to hurt Laura again, she didn't know what she'd do. Yes, she did. She'd make Cecil forbid Laura to marry the sorry son of a bitch and they'd take Laura home today.

When Andrea eased open the bathroom door, she gasped when she saw Laura, totally naked, standing in the shower. The shower was off, but Laura was soaking wet and shivering. Tears streamed down her face.

"Laura?" For a couple of seconds Andrea couldn't seem to move. "What's wrong? Why are you crying?"

Laura turned her head slowly and gazed at Andrea. That's when Andrea knew that Laura had had another spell. She rushed to her daughter, grabbed a large towel from the rack by the shower stall, and wrapped it around Laura.

"Come on, sweetie, let me help you."

With great gentleness, Andrea urged Laura into motion, helping her step out of the shower. She rubbed Laura's body dry, then took another towel and wrapped it around her head turban-style. Taking Laura's trembling hand, she led her daughter into the bedroom, where she eased her down on the edge of the bed. Laura continued weeping. Softly. Mournfully.

While she searched the closet for something suitable for Laura to wear, Andrea thought about what must be done. Cecil would fight her, but she didn't care how much he objected. Laura needed help. If she couldn't make Laura leave Cherokee County today and if Cecil wouldn't back her up, she'd call a local doctor and see if he could at least give Laura some medication. Something to soothe her nerves.

Andrea worked quickly, helping Laura dress in loose-fitting lounge slacks and top. Then she combed Laura's long blond hair, and all the while she spoke softly, soothingly to her troubled daughter. When Andrea sat down on the bed beside Laura and took her hand in hers, Laura stopped crying.

"Feeling better?" Andrea asked.

Laura nodded.

"What's wrong? Tell me about it. Why were you crying?"

"I don't know," Laura said. "I—I can't remember."

"Where were you last night and early this morning? I checked in here and both you and Sheridan were gone."

"I don't know." Laura squeezed Andrea's hand. "I remember Jamie kissing me good night and I came upstairs to get ready for bed. Sheridan wasn't here. I was alone."

"And then what?"

"That's all I remember until a little while ago. I—I was in the shower, scrubbing my body. And I was crying."

"Are you saying you don't remember where you were all night?" Andrea's heart caught in her throat. *Please, God, please, don't do this to us. Laura isn't to blame for the way she is. And Cecil, my poor Cecil, can't go through this again.*

"Oh, Mother, it's happening again, isn't it?" Laura flung herself into Andrea's arms. "I'm losing my mind. I'm having another nervous breakdown, aren't I?"

Andrea hugged her daughter fiercely. Protectively. "No, no, sweetie, you'll be all right. No one knows you weren't here all night. And you mustn't tell anyone. Everything will be all right. Trust me to take care of things, to take care of you."

"Oh, Mother, what would I do without you?" She laid her head in Andrea's lap.

Andrea stroked Laura's damp hair. *Help us, dear God, help us.*

* * *

They had let Peter and Paul loose the minute Scotsman's Bluff came into view. The sheriff's deputies and policemen had followed the bloodhounds, running at top speed to keep up with the lumbering dogs. Big Jim waited with Genny and Dallas outside Jacob's truck, parked on the side of the road. Jacob radioed to the truck several times, giving them updates, letting them know the dogs hadn't lost the scent.

Daybreak came quietly, all hint of bad weather vanquished. Last night's distant thunder that forecast rain hadn't kept the promise of a downpour. The few sprinkles that fell hadn't even settled the dust. Undoubtedly the clouds had bypassed Cherokee County and deposited rain farther north. The morning sky held no hint of red, which Genny's granny had said always predicted bad weather. Luscious pinks and lavenders streaked the edges of the sky.

"Dallas!" Jacob's voice came over the radio, easily heard through the pickup's open door.

Dallas jumped up in the truck and responded. "Yeah, Jacob, I'm here."

"We found Jamie."

"Alive?"

"No."

Dallas glanced at Jim Upton. The old man went chalk white.

"I'm sending a couple of our men back down to take Big Jim home," Jacob said. "But . . . I need Genny to come up here. I'm no forensics expert, but I'd say the killer covered her tracks pretty darn good."

"Please, I want to see my grandson," Big Jim said to Dallas. "Tell Jacob—"

"She tortured him to death. He's a sorry sight," Jacob said. "You tell Big Jim that he doesn't want to see Jamie this way. Tell him to take my word for it."

"Dear God!" Jim Upton crumbled before their eyes. A big, robust man, brought to his knees by grief. "Who would—" His voice broke as he wept.

Genny put her arm around him. "You must go home, Mr. Upton, and tell your wife that Jamie is dead. And you'll have to tell Laura and her family."

"Yes." Jim swallowed in an effort to stop crying, but tears still trickled down his cheeks.

"Jacob needs me to take a look at the crime scene and see if I can pick up on something." She patted Jim's back. "I promise that I'll do everything I can to help find out who killed Jamie."

Jim asked, "You don't think Jazzy would—"

"No! No, of course not. Jazzy isn't capable of such a thing."

Jazzy would never torture another human being, never inflict pain on any of God's creatures. She had a good heart. A kind and loving soul. But some people would suspect her. They would point fingers in her direction. Their accusations could hurt Jazzy, and if Jacob didn't find the real murderer, if Jazzy didn't have an ironclad alibi . . . Genny knew with a heart-wrenching certainty that even in death Jamie Upton would wreak havoc on Jazzy's life.

Chapter 11

Andrea Willis waited until the medication she had persuaded Laura to take took effect. Then she quietly left her daughter's bedroom, but not before glancing back to check on her one final time. She had been caring for and protecting Laura since she'd been a little girl, hoping beyond hope that some sort of miracle would spare their daughter from the curse she had inherited. Poor little Laura. If only she could have loved the child more. But she'd done her best. Even Cecil had often said that they had both done everything in their power to help Laura. But Andrea felt that she had failed Laura, that she hadn't done enough, hadn't pushed Cecil hard enough to admit the truth.

Andrea didn't stop by the guest bedroom she shared with her husband. Instead, she went straight down the back stairs to the kitchen. Startled at first by the housekeeper's presence, she paused on the bottom step and considered whether she should slip back upstairs before Dora saw her. But then she heard Sheridan's voice in the kitchen. Her younger daughter was laughing and talking to Dora.

Andrea marched into the kitchen. Sheridan sat at the table, a breakfast plate in front of her. One look at Sheridan reassured Andrea that she was perfectly all right.

With her mouth half filled with eggs, Sheridan said, "Morning, Mother."

"Good morning, Mrs. Willis." Dora looked up from where she busily prepared biscuit dough. "Coffee's made and I can fix you something to eat now if you're hungry. Biscuits won't be ready for another half hour, but—"

"Coffee will be fine. Nothing else for me right now, thank you." Andrea walked into the kitchen, poured herself a cup of fresh black coffee, then sat down at the table beside Sheridan. "Mind telling me where you've been all night?" she asked quietly.

"Where do you think?" Sheridan whispered her reply. "I met this really interesting guy last night while I was in town."

Andrea sighed. "I thought as much." She reached across the table and grasped Sheridan's wrist. "You were careful, weren't you? You made sure he used protection."

"Yes, of course, I did. I'm not a fool. I always take care of number one."

She hoped Sheridan was telling her the truth. Despite their closeness, her younger daughter had lied to her on more than one occasion. "Yes, you do. Usually. I only wish your sister . . ."

When Sheridan's eyes widened inquisitively, Andrea realized she'd already said too much. Although she loved Sheridan with all her heart—yes, more than she loved Laura—their older child had required the bulk of both

Cecil's and her attention. And over the years Sheridan had grown to resent Laura more and more. Andrea supposed she couldn't blame her, but the tension between the two girls only complicated an already complex situation.

"What's wrong with poor little Laura now?" Sheridan asked.

"Lower your voice," Andrea told her. "We do not air our dirty laundry in front of servants."

"God, Mother, get real. You've never fooled anybody. Not our servants at home. And not the Uptons' servants."

"Must you always—" Andrea cut her complaint short, realizing she was taking out her frustration about Laura on Sheridan. "If you need to shower and change clothes, shower in our bathroom. And I'll get your things out of Laura's room. She had a restless night and is just now sleeping peacefully. I don't want you disturbing her."

"What happened? Did she have another one of her crazy-as-a-Betsy-bug spells?"

There was no use denying it to Sheridan. She'd seen Laura at her worst. "I plan to speak to your father this morning about taking Laura home and putting her . . . placing her somewhere for treatment."

"Glory hallelujah. About damn time!"

Genny waited outside the dilapidated cabin, Dallas at her side and a handful of specially chosen lawmen scouring the area around the ramshackle old house for signs of any evidence. Jacob had ordered the inside of the cabin off limits to everyone until the crime scene investigators went over the entire place with a fine tooth comb.

"I'm using the most qualified of Dallas's people and

mine," Jacob had explained to the deputies and police-men on the scene. "And if they need help, we'll contact Knoxville."

When Jacob finished another phone call—only one of many he'd made in the past thirty minutes—he came over to Genny. "I might have missed something in there, but to the naked eye, it looks as if she cleared out any evidence that might have linked her to the scene."

"There's always something," Dallas said. "The prob-lem is that if our investigators find something, will it be anything useful? Without even one suspect"—Dallas paused momentarily—"or possibly with too many, un-less our people find DNA evidence that we can match—"

"That's one of the reasons I need Genny." Jacob looked to his cousin. "*I gi do*, I hate to ask you to look in-side the cabin at Jamie's body, but you could be our only hope of finding his killer."

Whenever he wanted to emphasize the importance of what he was about to say, Jacob called her sister in their ancestors' Cherokee tongue. "I understand," she told him.

"I don't want you to go inside. Just go to the door and take a look, then let me know if you pick up on any-thing."

"I'll go with her," Dallas said, keeping guard at her side.

"We'll both go with her." Jacob moved to her other side so that she was flanked by two large, overly protec-tive men who loved her.

The threesome walked up the rickety steps and across the porch. Then, using a gloved hand, Jacob opened the door. He moved aside just enough to give her a direct view into the shadowy room. The nauseatingly metallic odor of blood assailed her senses. And no wonder. The room looked as if it had been painted in blood.

She took a deep breath and willed herself to be strong as she focused on Jamie Upton's barely recognizable naked body. Nausea rose from her stomach and burned a trail up her esophagus. She turned and ran to the edge of the porch, then vomited violently. Dallas rushed to her and put his arm around her trembling shoulders. He jerked a handkerchief from his jacket and wiped her perspiring forehead and her damp mouth.

"She's not going to do this," Dallas told Jacob.

Genny grabbed Dallas's arm. "Yes, I am. I'll be all right."

"Damn it, can't you see what's it already doing to you?" Dallas glared at Jacob. "Tell her she doesn't have to do it."

"Genny, he's right," Jacob said. "You don't have to—"

"Yes, I do." She jerked away from Dallas's protective hold and marched straight back to the open front door. "Both of you stay away from me for a few minutes. Allow me to concentrate."

She looked into the bloody room, focused on Jamie's mutilated body, and let the darkness surround her. Thick, heavy darkness. Filled with anger. So much anger.

The moment Genny staggered, she felt strong arms holding her and knew that despite the dark evil encompassing her spirit, she was safe. Safe because Dallas would bring her back before she went in too deep.

Insane rage! The woman who had tortured Jamie had taken perverse pleasure in punishing him. She had wanted him to suffer as she had suffered, as others had suffered at his hands. Had she killed Jamie for revenge? Perhaps, but Genny got a sense of something as strong, perhaps even stronger than revenge. In the woman's sick mind, she had killed Jamie to protect someone. Herself? Or someone she loved?

Concentrate on this woman, Genny told herself. *Can you see her? See her body? Her face? Even a shadowy image?*

The darkness swirled faster and faster, sucking Genny deeper into a metaphysical realm. Evil. Tormented. *Do not be frightened away,* Genny told herself. *Seek deeper. Look beyond the veil and reach for the truth.*

Flashes of a human form danced through Genny's mind. A female form. Naked. Bathing herself in cool water, rinsing away the bright scarlet blood. It dripped from her fingers, ran in rivulets down her back and buttocks. The image was vague, unclear, unrecognizable. Except her short, stylish red hair.

Jazzy's hair!

Genny gasped. Her eyelids shot open. She grabbed Dallas's arm and held on tight. Unable to speak, she moaned, refusing to believe what she'd seen. *It wasn't Jazzy,* she told herself. *It was a woman who had hair the same style and color as Jazzy's.*

"Genny, honey, what's wrong?" Dallas caressed her face.

She shoved his hand aside and closed her eyes again. *Go back and take another look. Find the woman again. Prove to yourself that it wasn't Jazzy.*

"Genny, for heaven's sake, what do you think you're doing?" Dallas demanded. "Come out of it. Don't—"

"Let her go," Jacob told him. "I've seen this before. She needs to go back because something she saw disturbed her."

That's right, Jacob, soothe Dallas. Make him understand. Genny eased slowly—carefully—into that mystic realm, going just deep enough to connect once again with the woman's image.

Short red hair mussed by the morning breeze. The wind whipping around and about her as she traveled at high speed. Try as she might, Genny could not see the woman's face—only her hair, only a shadowy outline of her body. And then clearly, distinctly, she saw the car the woman was driving. A small, sleek green sports car with a tan interior.

Genny gasped for air as she brought herself back to the present moment. "Definitely a woman. I saw her washing away Jamie's blood. I couldn't see her face, couldn't make out who she was or if I knew her. She had red hair." Genny opened her eyes and looked first at Dallas and then at Jacob. "I think she was wearing a wig so that her hair was identical to Jazzy's. While she showered, she was also washing the blood from her hair . . . from the wig."

"Are you saying this woman was trying to pass herself off as Jazzy?" Jacob asked.

"No, I don't think so. I don't know. All I could make out was her hair. I sensed she wasn't really pretending to be Jazzy. Maybe she just wanted anyone who saw her at a distance to think she was Jazzy."

Jacob frowned. "Anything else?"

Jacob's inquiry seemed odd to Genny; she picked up some peculiar vibes from her cousin. "Yes, I saw the car she was driving."

"And?" Jacob came closer, his eyes narrowing as he approached her.

"It was a small, green sports car. Something new and sleek. The interior was tan. And there was something wrong with the car."

"What?" Jacob and Dallas asked simultaneously.

"The driver's side appeared to be damaged. And the glass surrounding the front headlight on that side was broken out."

"I'll be damned!" Jacob stormed off the porch and headed straight to his truck.

"Jacob!" Genny went after him, forgetting how much her psychic trips weakened her. When she stumbled, Dallas was there to catch her. She glanced up at the man she loved and told him, "I need to find out what's going on with Jacob."

Dallas nodded. "All right. Come on." He braced her with his strong arm as he helped her off the porch, across the yard, and down the gravel drive to where Jacob was talking on the radio.

"Get in touch with Roy Tillis and find out if that green Jaguar he towed in yesterday is still in his lot," Jacob said. "And check on a lady named Reve Sorrell. She's staying in one of the Cherokee Cabin Rentals. Just make sure she doesn't leave town. I want to question her personally."

Genny grasped Jacob's arm. "What's going on? Do you know someone who drives a green sports car?"

"Yeah. A very interesting lady who looks enough like Jazzy to be her sister," Jacob replied. "She had a wreck in her green Jaguar yesterday, on her way out of town. And it just so happens that she came to Cherokee Pointe because she'd met Jamie Upton at a party several months ago. She said she didn't fall for his pretty boy charm, but I had my doubts then and I've got even more now."

"Someone who looks like Jazzy?" Genny couldn't shake the overwhelming sensation that this mysterious woman and Jazzy were irrevocably connected. And not by their association with Jamie Upton. There was something else. Something basic. Something dangerous.

Dr. Galvin MacNair drove up to the open gates at the Upton Farm at nine-fifty. Jim had telephoned the doctor on his cell phone when one of Jacob's deputies had driven him home. He'd been waiting fifteen minutes here at the gate, not wanting to go up to the house and tell everyone about Jamie, not without a doctor in attendance. Reba was a strong, healthy woman, but she was also past seventy, had already lost both of her children, and her whole world revolved around Jamie. He was everything to her. Finding out that he had been murdered . . . Jim could hardly bear to think about it himself. Despite how much sorrow that boy had caused them over the years, he had been their only grandchild and they loved him.

Jacob hadn't let Jim see Jamie, had told him that his last memory of his grandson shouldn't be of his bloody body. Although Jacob had been honest enough with Jim to admit that Jamie had been tortured, as Genny had foreseen, Jacob hadn't gone into details. It was well enough. Some things an old man just didn't need to know. But he'd been fighting his imagination, doing his best not to visualize what the killer had done to Jamie.

Emotion so raw and painful that he was practically numb with it sapped Jim's strength. Although he realized that he would have to be the strong one, the one who'd support and care for Reba and Laura, he needed someone himself. He needed a shoulder to cry on. Loving arms to hold him. He'd telephoned Erin, but her answering machine had picked up again. Where the hell was she? Where had she spent last night? Why wasn't she there when he so desperately needed her?

Dr. MacNair pulled to a stop, rolled down his window, and called to Jim, "I got here as quickly as I could."

Jim nodded, then walked around the hood of MacNair's truck, opened the passenger door, and slid into the seat. "Thanks for coming. I don't know how Reba is going to be able to handle this. She loves Jamie. Loves him more than anything."

"Yes, sir, I understand. He is . . . was . . . your only grandchild. How are you holding up, Mr. Upton? Is there some-thing I can do for you right now?"

Jim looked at the doctor. MacNair, a stocky, ruddy-faced man in his thirties, had a kind face. He was new to Cherokee County, but in the few short months since he'd taken over Dr. Webster's practice after the older doctor had retired, he'd gained a reputation as a first-rate physician.

"Thanks, but I don't think it wise for me to take any-thing—pills or an injection," Jim said. "I'm the one who'll have to deal with the family, then make the arrange-ments and handle the local press. I'll need a clear head for all that."

"Yes, of course," MacNair agreed. "But if you think you'll need something to help you rest tonight . . . for the next few nights . . ."

"Mm-hmm. All right. That might not be a bad idea." Jim admitted to himself that he was unlikely to sleep much tonight or for many nights to come unless he did take a sleeping pill. It would be impossible to rest with images of Jamie's brutalized body flashing through his mind. Even though he hadn't actually seen the body, he had a pretty good idea what had happened from the bits and pieces of what he'd overheard the deputies say-ing. And not only that, but how did a man rest when his grandson's killer was on the loose?

"Mr. Upton . . . I'm deeply sorry about Jamie."

Jim nodded. "Thank you."

"Are you ready to go up to the house now?"

"No, I'm not ready, but it has to be done. No point in putting it off any longer," Jim said. "I called Dora and explained without going into details. I told her to make sure no one except she answered the phone and that no one made any calls out."

Dr. MacNair shifted his truck from park into drive

and headed the late model Ford up the long driveway toward the big house Jim had called home since the day he was born. A home was a place for a family, for children and grandchildren and . . . once he and Reba were gone, there would be no one. No more Uptons to carry on. No grandchildren and great-grandchildren to fill the empty rooms of the old home place.

When MacNair parked his truck in front of the house, Jim got out and he and the doctor walked up the steps together and onto the front veranda. Dora opened the door and came rushing out to meet them.

"I've had the devil's own time keeping everyone from making phone calls," Dora said. "And the phone's been ringing off the hook. Word's done got out about our Jamie. Neighbors have been calling. And the newspaper and . . . it's only a matter of time before there's a horde of people at the gate. You'd best figure out what to do about it."

"Close the gate," Jim told her. "And take the phones off the hook. All four separate lines. Once I've broken the news to Reba and Laura, I'll contact Jacob and have him send somebody out here to keep order. And if necessary, I'll hire my own private guards."

"Yes, sir." Dora looked up at Jim and he could tell she'd been crying. Dora had been with the family since she was a teenager, first as one of the maids and as the housekeeper for the past forty-five years. The woman was practically family.

Jim patted Dora's back. "We've lost him. Our Jamie's dead."

"Breaks my heart," Dora told him. "God help Miss Reba. This is gonna kill her."

"Is she down yet?" Jim asked.

"Yes, sir. She's in the dining room. Miss Reba and Mr. and Mrs. Willis are eating breakfast. Miss Sheridan is in the den, watching television. And Miss Laura is still up-stairs."

Jim ushered Dora back inside; Dr. MacNair followed them. Once in the massive foyer, Jim stiffened his spine. He'd done this twice before, when Jim Jr. and his wife were killed in an accident and when they'd received news about Melanie's death years after she'd run away. Each time he had wondered how he and Reba would survive. They'd been younger then . . . and they'd still had Jamie. Now, they had no one.

"Dora, ask everyone to come into the living room," Jim told her. "And send one of the girls upstairs to waken Miss Laura. I can't do this more than once. I want everyone assembled in ten minutes."

"Yes, sir. I'll see to it."

Reve Sorrell stepped out of the shower, dried herself off, and slipped into the white terry cloth robe which was one of the standard amenities at Cherokee Cabin Rentals. When she traveled, she never went tourist class, but even with her discerning tastes, she had to admit that this cabin wasn't half bad. Not luxurious by any stretch of the imagination, but clean, neat, and quite comfortable. On a scale of one to ten, she'd certainly give it a six.

Just as she removed the hair dryer from the wall unit, the telephone rang. Something else she liked about this cabin—there was an extension phone in the bathroom. She had placed a call to her personal assistant, Paul Welby, late yesterday to alert him that she would be re-maining in Cherokee Pointe a few days and to request he have another car—the dark blue Mercedes 300SL, her favorite, second only to her Jag—brought to her. She had instructed Paul to have whoever he sent with the Mercedes today pick up the Jaguar at the garage where it had been towed and take it back to Chattanooga for repairs. She didn't want any of these jake-leg body repair people in Cherokee Pointe touching her precious car.

When she answered the phone, she expected to hear Paul's soft, cultured voice on the other end. Instead she heard a rough, hillbilly redneck saying, "Ms. Sorrell, this here is Roy Tillis over at Tillis and Son Wrecking and Towing Service. I got some bad news for you, and I'm sure sorry about it. I done called Sheriff Butler and told him. And it ain't my fault. I ain't never had no car stolen from the lot. Not in all the years—"

"Mr. Tillis, exactly what are you trying to tell me?"

"Well, ma'am, I thought I told you. Somebody stole that green Jaguar of yours sometime after dark last night."

"What!"

"Yes'm, they just waltzed right in, got past old Worthless, and just drove right off with your car."

"How is that possible? They would have had to have the keys. And I'm sure you keep the keys locked up in your office, don't you?"

"Well, there's where you might figure it's my fault," Roy hemmed. "But it weren't my fault. You see, one of the boys left the keys in the car and—"

"Let me get this straight. You parked my car in an unguarded, unprotected area with the keys in the ignition. Then someone got past a dog called Worthless and just drove off with my wrecked Jaguar. Is that right?"

"Yeah, that's about it. But I figure it's no big deal, since you're bound to have insurance out the wahoo."

"What did Sheriff Butler say when you contacted him?" Reve asked, her patience almost at an end.

"He didn't say much except that he'd put an all-points-bulletin out on it," Roy replied. "Then he said something that didn't make no sense to me."

"What was that?"

"He said 'mighty convenient for her that the car got stolen.' He sort of mumbled it under his breath."

"I see." But she didn't, not really. What had Butler meant by that unfathomable remark? Although she hated that her car had been stolen, what she hated even more was the thought of having to deal with Jacob Butler again. The man was a Neanderthal.

"Well, Ms. Sorrell, I sure hope they find your car. And I'm real sorry about what happened. You ain't gonna sue me or nothing like that, are you? I figured you wouldn't, seeing how your insurance will cover—"

"I'm not going to sue, Mr. Tillis." She slammed down the receiver.

There was something about this town, Reve decided. Either the place was a jinx to her or it was the other way around and she was the jinx. She'd encountered a menagerie of odd characters yesterday morning—from her look-alike who'd gotten into a heated argument with a good-looking tough guy to a rawboned old kook who chewed tobacco. Then when she'd tried to make her escape and leave Cherokee Pointe, she'd had a wreck, which ended with the caveman sheriff all but locking her up. And now this—her Jag had been stolen. She couldn't help but wonder, what next? Maybe when the Mercedes arrived later today, she should forget satisfying her curiosity about Jazzy Talbot and simply go home to Chattanooga and forget all about the woman who might be her sister.

Chapter 12

"My goodness, Jim, what's this all about?" Dressed for church in her new suit and stylish hat, Reba pranced into the living room, her eyes alight with curiosity. She glanced at Galvin MacNair. "Well, hello, Dr. MacNair. What brings you out here on a Sunday morning?"

MacNair looked to Jim, who nodded, letting him know that he wasn't expected to reply to Reba's question. It was Jim's place to give his wife the heartbreaking news about Jamie.

Jim studied Reba for a moment. A fragile smile formed on his lips and vanished quickly. He thought that even past seventy his wife was still a fine-looking woman. She took good care of herself in a way only a wealthy woman could do. A personal trainer to keep her body toned and a tummy tuck, a boob job, and several face lifts had done wonders to make her look a good ten years younger than her actual age. No doubt about it, Reba Upton was a lovely, vivacious woman, and although she wasn't per- fect—who was?—she'd always been a basically good woman. And a better wife than he'd deserved.

Life had been unkind to Reba when it came to her personal life. Jim had married her, not loving her. And although he cared for her deeply and admired her greatly, the love that he had hoped would grow in his heart never took root. He had given Reba everything money could buy, but he'd been an unfaithful husband most of their married life. God knew she had deserved better. But even though he felt certain she suspected he'd had other women, she'd never confronted him about his affairs. Why she'd chosen to ignore his infidelity he didn't know for sure. Maybe she enjoyed being Mrs. James Upton. Or maybe she just loved him. Still. After all these years. After all the other women. She had loved him once, loved him as passionately as he had loved Melva Mae Nelson over fifty years ago. Maybe that kind of love never died. Truth be told, there was a part of him that would always love Melva Mae, even though she'd been dead for quite a few years now.

Reba had wanted more children after Jim Jr. and Melanie, but complications following Melanie's birth had made that dream an impossible one. The day they lost Jim Jr. and his wife, the only thing that kept Reba from dying of grief was Jamie. By that time, Melanie had already run away from her husband and her seemingly perfect life, but Reba never gave up hope that their daughter would one day return. Then, years later, the Memphis police had contacted them to let tell them their daughter was dead, and Reba had been forced to accept another loss.

Jim glanced around the room, counting heads, checking to make sure everyone was here before he shared the news about Jamie's death. "Where's Laura?" he asked when he noted the young woman's absence. He looked at Dora. "Didn't you ask her to join us?"

"Yes, sir, but—"

Andrea Willis interrupted. "I tried to explain to Dora that Laura didn't sleep well last night and—"

"Mr. Willis, go get your daughter and bring her downstairs immediately," Jim told Laura's father in no uncertain terms.

Reba gasped. "Jim, really. Is there any reason for such rudeness?"

"I apologize, my dear, but it's imperative that Laura joins us."

"Where's Jamie?" Sheridan Willis asked, a rather sly smile curving her full, pink lips. "Shouldn't he be included in this family powwow?"

"Mr. Willis, go now, please," Jim said, then gave Sheridan a scowling look that wiped the smile from her pretty face.

"Jim?" Reba came to him and placed her hand on his arm.

When she looked up at him, apprehension visible in her warm hazel eyes, he almost lost his composure. Only a few hours ago he had planned to leave this woman for his mistress. He'd had every intention of asking Reba for a divorce while Jamie and Laura were on their honeymoon. Now neither would happen. No wedding and honeymoon for their grandson. No divorce for Reba and him.

Jim pulled Reba into his arms and held her with great tenderness. She wrapped her arms around his waist and laid her head on his chest.

"Whatever it is, we'll see it through together," Reba whispered to him. "The way we've done so many times before."

He leaned down, tilted her face upward, and kissed her forehead. "I don't deserve you. I never did."

Cecil Willis returned to the living room, his face slightly flushed, his breathing a bit irregular, as if he'd run all the way upstairs and back down again. He had an obviously befuddled Laura in tow. She wore casual lounge slacks and top, slightly wrinkled. Her hair looked as if she hadn't brushed it this morning. And there was a dazed—maybe drugged—look in her eyes. Andrea rushed immediately to her elder daughter and put a supportive arm around her waist.

Jim eased Reba to his side and draped his arm around her shoulders, then looked at her for a full minute before he faced the others. "I received a phone call quite early this morning from Sheriff Butler."

Reba keened softly, the sound barely audible except to Jim because she stood at his side. He tightened his grip around her shoulders.

"There is no easy way to say this." Jim cleared his throat. "Jamie's dead."

He felt Reba dissolve, her whole body weakening instantly. He turned to her. "Do you want to sit down?"

She nodded, but seemed unable to speak. He led her over to the sofa and motioned for Dr. MacNair, who came immediately to Reba's side.

"You must be mistaken," Laura said, her words slightly slurred. "We were together last night. He was fine. He—he can't be . . . it's not possible. We're getting married."

"What happened?" Cecil asked.

"Was it a car accident?" Andrea inquired.

He glanced at Reba, who was now sitting. "Jamie was murdered," Jim told them.

"My God!" Cecil glanced from Andrea to Laura.

"No! No, no . . ." Laura pulled away from her mother and rushed toward Jim, her eyes wild, tears pouring down her cheeks. "He can't be dead. He can't be." She folded her arms across her belly and doubled over, whimpering loudly.

Andrea and Cecil hurried to Laura and together they

managed to soothe her momentarily. Jim sat down beside Reba and took her trembling hands into his own unsteady grasp.

"Who killed him?" Reba asked. "Did *she* murder him?"

"They don't know who killed him," Jim said.

"Was he with *her*?" Reba searched Jim's face, as if she thought he might lie to her and wanted to discern the truth. "She threatened to kill him. Everyone knows that she—"

"He wasn't with Jazzy." Jim glanced across the room at Laura and their gazes met for a millisecond. "They don't know who the woman was he was with, but his body was found in a deserted cabin up in the mountains, not far from Scotsman's Bluff."

"Who found him?" Andrea asked.

"Local law enforcement," Jim replied. "Both Sheriff Butler and Chief Sloan were together when they discovered Jamie's body."

"How did they find him if he was in a deserted cabin?" Cecil asked.

"Genny Madoc. She's a psychic who lives here in Cherokee County," Jim said. "Crazy as it sounds, Genny had a vision and saw Jamie being killed and got a sense of what area he was in. Sheriff Butler took Sally Talbot and her bloodhounds along to hunt for Jamie. I went with them. I didn't say anything to anyone until we knew for sure."

"How was Jamie killed?" Sheridan asked. "Was he shot? Did some jealous bitch shoot him? Did that Jazzy Talbot do it? I bet she did."

"Jamie wasn't shot." Jim wasn't sure how much to tell them, had no idea how they would react to the word torture.

Reba tugged on his hand. "Are you sure Jamie is dead?"

"Yes, he's dead."

"Did you see him?"

"Yes, I saw him." Jim swallowed. *A little white lie,* he told himself. Reba needed to hear him say that he'd seen their grandson dead; otherwise she would want to see the body herself.

"How did she kill him?" Reba asked. "I told him she was no good for him, told him to stay away from her, but she kept luring him back to her, seducing him." Reba clutched the front of Jim's shirt. "I want her arrested and prosecuted. I want her punished for what she did. Promise me that you'll see to it that Jazzy Talbot pays with her own life for what she's done."

"Reba, we don't know who killed Jamie."

"Who else would have done it? She knew she was losing him for good this time, that he was going to marry Laura and they were going to be happy and she couldn't stand it. She would rather see him dead than happy with someone else."

Jim realized his wife was on the verge of hysteria. She was obsessed with the notion that Jazzy had killed Jamie. "I want you to let Dr. MacNair give you something to help you relax. You're not doing either of us any good by getting so upset."

"Damn it, Jim, I know she killed Jamie, and I won't rest until she's punished." Reba jerked away from him and shot up off the sofa. "Bring her to me and I'll kill her myself."

"Has this Talbot woman been questioned?" Cecil asked.

Before Jim could respond, Laura's eyes widened and she cried out as she looked anxiously back and forth from her mother to her father. "What if Jazzy didn't kill him?" Laura grabbed her mother's hands. With a look of sheer terror in her eyes, she moaned. "I don't remember . . . I don't remember. What if—oh God, Mother, what if I killed him?"

"Oh, Laura, what nonsense. You're overwrought," Andrea said.

"Why would you think you killed Jamie?" Sheridan scowled at her sister.

Laura stared at Andrea as if transfixed. "Did I do it?"

"Of course you didn't. You were upstairs in your bed all night. Don't be silly. You had no reason to harm Jamie. You loved him."

"But I don't remember . . . and Jamie's dead. And there was blood. I think I remember the blood."

"Hush up. Don't say anything else. You don't know what you're saying."

"Jamie . . . Jamie . . ." Laura kept repeating his name, calling him, as she again escaped her mother's grasp and started wandering aimlessly around the room. She clutched her belly and cried out in pain, then fell to the floor in a dead faint.

Dr. MacNair rushed across the room and knelt beside Laura. "My God!" He murmured the words softly, then lifted her up into his arms. That's when Jim noticed Laura's slacks. Bright red and fresh, blood oozed through the soft cotton material.

Jazzy heard the knocking as she emerged from the shower. Someone was trying to bang her door down. Was Caleb that eager? It couldn't be much past ten-thirty. She'd awakened at ten, fixed coffee, downed one cup, then jumped in the shower. The pounding continued without letup. Jazzy rushed into her bedroom, grabbed her robe off the foot of the bed, and put it on as she ran into the living room.

"Jazzy, open the door!" Genny Madoc cried, her voice edged with panic. "Please, Jazzy, please be here."

My God, what was wrong with Genny? She sounded almost hysterical, and Genny wasn't prone to hysterics. Something terrible must have happened. Just as Jazzy finished tying her housecoat's cloth belt around her waist, she reached for the doorknob. The minute Jazzy flung open the door, Genny gasped. With tears sparkling in her black eyes, she grabbed Jazzy and hugged her fiercely.

"Thank God. What took you so long to come to the door?" Genny kept hugging Jazzy.

"I was in the shower." Jazzy pulled free and grabbed Genny by the shoulders. "Honey, what's wrong?" She glanced over Genny's shoulder and up at Dallas.

"Let's go inside." Dallas put one hand on Jazzy's shoulder and the other in the center of Genny's back, then he nudged them into the living room.

Once inside, Dallas closed the door. Genny grasped Jazzy's hands. She could tell by the expressions on Genny's and Dallas's faces that whatever brought them here on a Sunday morning was bad. Very bad. Terror clutched Jazzy's heart.

"Y'all are scaring me to death," Jazzy told them. "What is it? What's wrong? Is it Jacob?"

"No, Jacob is all right," Genny said.

"Caleb? Has something happened to Caleb? We—we have a date this afternoon. A real date."

"It isn't Caleb," Dallas said. "It's Jamie."

"Jamie?"

Genny nodded, then, tugging on Jazzy's hands, urged her toward the sofa. Jazzy allowed Genny to guide her until they sat side by side on the overstuffed old couch.

"Jamie's dead." Genny clutched Jazzy's hands.

"How? Was it a car wreck? Was he drunk?"

"He was murdered." Dallas moved across the room and sat down in the chair opposite from the sofa. "He was killed sometime early this morning."

"Murdered? Who? How? Why would . . ."

"We don't know," Dallas said. "We don't know who killed him, but we're pretty sure it was a woman."

Dry-eyed and feeling rather numb, Jazzy looked directly at Genny. "Did you see it? Is that how you know a woman killed him? You had one of your visions."

Genny turned Jazzy's hands over in hers, then squeezed reassuringly. Jazzy was her dearest friend, the closest thing she'd ever had to a sister. If only she could find an easier way to tell her what had happened. But there was no easy way. And Jazzy would want to know the truth—the whole truth. She would trust Genny to be completely honest with her.

"Yes, I saw Jamie being tortured in one of my visions," Genny admitted. "I couldn't see the woman's face. I got only blurry images of her."

"Tortured? She tortured him?"

"Yes. She wanted him to suffer. I felt her rage. She hated Jamie."

"How—how did she . . ." Jazzy jumped up off the sofa and turned her back to them.

Genny realized that the reality of Jamie's death—his murder—had just now actually registered in Jazzy's mind. Dallas glanced at Genny and she telepathically heard him say, "Shouldn't you do something? Get up and go to her? Hug her?" And Genny responded. "No, not yet. She needs time. Jazzy will want to get her emotions under control before she faces us." Genny knew her best friend like no one else did. They had shared everything—triumphs and tragedies, happiness and heartbreak, good times and bad—since they were small children.

The quiet in the apartment was deafening. Genny could hear her own heartbeat, could hear Dallas breathing. And the hushed sound of Jazzy weeping stirred Genny's caring, protective instincts. If this was all Jazzy would have to contend with, then she could deal with it. She would mourn Jamie and then move on. But Genny's sixth sense told her that Jamie's death would bring trouble for Jazzy and she would need all the love and support her friends and family could give her.

Jazzy sucked in a deep breath, then turned to face Genny. "Tell me. I need to know."

"She tormented him with knives, razor blades, and a hot poker," Genny said, the image in her mind as clear as when she'd envisioned it earlier today. She prayed that in time that image would vanish, that eventually she would not be able to recall it at all.

"Even Jamie didn't deserve to die that way," Jazzy said, her voice deceptively calm. Genny knew how badly Jazzy was hurting, how the thought of Jamie suffering and dying tore her apart inside. No matter what had happened between them over the years, there had been a time when Jazzy had deeply loved Jamie. And years ago, she had carried his child for a few brief months.

"No, Jamie didn't deserve to die such a horrible death," Genny agreed.

"You have no idea who she was? Jacob doesn't . . ." She looked at Dallas. "Any clues? Anything that can tell y'all who killed him?"

"We have our combined forensic teams going over the cabin and the area surrounding the cabin," Dallas said. "And we might call in Knoxville for some help. Big Jim is going to expect us to pull out all the stops to find his grandson's murderer. And when a man has the power Jim Upton does, he can get things done that even Jacob and I can't."

Jazzy nodded, then glanced at Genny. "What is it? There's more, isn't there? Something else you need to tell me."

"The woman who killed Jamie . . . I saw her hair."

"And?"

"She had short red hair. The exact color and style as yours."

Jazzy gasped. "Oh, God, Genny, you don't think that I—"

"No!" Genny bounded off the sofa and rushed to Jazzy. "I know you didn't kill him." She grasped Jazzy by the upper arms. "But this woman, whoever she is, wanted to resemble you for some reason. I don't know why. Maybe she wore a red wig and gold hoop earrings like yours so that, just in case someone saw her with Jamie at a distance, they'd think it was you. Or maybe she wanted to titillate Jamie by doing her best to look a little something like you."

"You know I didn't kill Jamie, but . . . tell me the rest." Jazzy pulled Genny's hands from her arms and clutched their hands together between them.

"I'm afraid that something will happen, that somehow you're going to be blamed for Jamie's death." Genny looked Jazzy square in the eye. "We have to be prepared for the worst. Dallas and Jacob will do everything they can, but you'll need a lawyer. A good lawyer."

"Aren't we jumping the gun just a little?" Dallas injected.

"Maybe a little," Genny agreed. "But I'm telling you"— she glanced at Dallas and then back at Jazzy—"this situation is going to get much, much worse before it gets better."

* * *

Jacob left Bobby Joe Harte behind at the cabin near Scotsman's Bluff while the combined forensic teams of the sheriff's department and the police department—three people in all—went over the area, inside and outside. He'd already put in a call to the Knox County sheriff and once the Cherokee County coroner, Pete Holt, gave Jacob a preliminary report, Jamie's body would be sent to Knoxville to the crime lab there. With only an on-site inspection, Pete had said that loss of blood alone or even heart failure from enduring prolonged, agonizing pain might have killed Jamie.

"No way to tell without a complete autopsy, although I'd say he bled to death," Pete had told them. "Whoever she is, the lady's damn vicious. I sure as hell wouldn't want to piss her off."

As he headed his Dodge Ram toward town, Jacob considered possible suspects—women who hated Jamie Upton enough to want to not only see him dead, but to see him suffer. Despite the gruesomeness of the case, Jacob found himself thinking that Jamie's demise was some sort of poetic justice.

Jacob snorted. Whoever killed Jamie was sick. Mentally sick in the worst way possible. Psychotic. And very dangerous.

Although Jazzy would be the first name on everyone's lips, Jacob knew that, as surely as he knew Genny had been born with Granny Butler's gift of sight, Jazzy hadn't killed Jamie. He'd known her all his life. She was not capable of torturing a man to death, not even Jamie, who probably deserved it more than anyone Jacob knew.

The list of Jamie's victims was probably endless, but only those now in the Cherokee County area could be considered suspects. Jazzy, of course. And Laura Willis. She might love Jamie, might have intended to marry him, but she had to have known what a bastard the guy was. And if he scratched the surface of the female population in these parts, he would no doubt come up with a few more women with reason to want to see Jamie dead. But as far as Jacob was concerned, his primary suspect was the lady who owed a green Jaguar and admitted that she not only knew Jamie Upton but had been romanced by him. The real clincher was the striking resemblance between Jazzy and Reve Sorrell. With a short, fire-engine red wig on, Ms. Sorrell could easily pass for Jazzy.

Had the woman come to town with the intention of killing Jamie? Had she sought out Jazzy to make sure they actually looked enough alike to be twins? Did she concoct the diabolical plot to torture Jamie to death before or after she arrived in Cherokee County?

But the one thing that didn't make any sense, the one piece of the puzzle that didn't fit, was why would Reve Sorrell be stupid enough to steal her own wrecked car and chance being seen in it?

If the whole town wasn't already hog wild over the news about Jamie's murder, it was only a matter of time. Before Jamie's body could be shipped off to Knoxville, reporters from MacKinnon media would bombard local law enforcement with a hundred and one questions that neither he nor Dallas would be able to answer. Not yet. And once the initial shock wore off, Big Jim Upton would start demanding answers. And action. If Jacob didn't make an arrest by this time tomorrow, there would be hell to pay. But how could a man make an arrest without any evidence?

A call came in over the radio from Tim Willingham, one of Jacob's deputies. "Better get over here and take a look," Tim said. "A Mr. and Mrs. Walker called in a report that something was on fire down the road from their cabin. When the fire department got there, guess what they found off in a ravine, burning like crazy."

Jacob's gut tightened. "A green Jaguar."

"Yeah, that's my guess. The vehicle is burned to a fare-thee-well. Right about the time the fire department showed up, the thing exploded. Sent sparks shooting up in the air. Ernie's crew is still working on making sure none of those sparks catch anything on fire in the surrounding area."

"Make sure nobody bothers anything until I get there," Jacob said. "And, Tim, make sure the people staying in the cabins within a two-mile area of the site don't run off anywhere. Somebody might have seen something."

Chapter 13

When Jacob made it to the site, the vehicle was still smoldering. The Jaguar was no longer green, no longer sleek, no longer classy. It was just a burned out hull of a once very expensive toy for a rich girl. Tim Willingham and Moody Ryan, another deputy, had the area sealed off, and Ernie Sweeney, the fire chief, had his squad hosing down the woods surrounding the ravine. A small crowd of onlookers had gathered, less than a dozen people, and no one Jacob recognized right off hand. Tourists, no doubt. Most had probably been just driving by. The cabins dotted here and there in the Cherokee County mountains rented by the day, week, or month and most folks were temporary residents, tourists who seldom stayed more than a week or two.

Using the rope that his deputies had installed into the ravine, Jacob inched his way downward, getting as close to the ruins as he dared. Once at the foot of the steep but relatively shallow gorge, Jacob released his hold on the rope and walked halfway around the Jaguar's remains. Enough of the car still existed to take an educated guess as to the make, if not the exact model. He'd bet his last dime that this was Reve Sorrell's Jaguar, the one stolen from Tillis's Garage.

"Keep this area corded off," Jacob called up to Tim and Moody. "As soon as they finish up over at the cabin, I'll send Burt, Dwayne, and Earl over here to work with Ernie to check the car over before we have it hauled in." Burt and Dwayne comprised the county's forensics team, and the Cherokee Pointe police had only Earl. They were all good at their jobs, but could do only so much, since neither the city nor the county had a state-of-the-art lab.

"Will do," Tim replied. "By the way, Jacob, we checked, and there are six cabins within a two-mile radius of here. One cabin is empty, but we spoke to the people in the others." Tim nodded toward the half dozen interested citizens keeping a respectful distance as they watched the firefighters and lawmen. "The folks who called in about the fire are over there. They're staying in the nearest cabin. It's a Fred and Regina Walker."

"Tourists?" Jacob asked.

"Yeah."

"What about the other four cabins? Tourists in them?"

"Tourists in two," Tim replied.

"Locals renting the other two?"

"Caleb McCord's in one and that lady painter, Ms. Mercer, lives in the other one."

Jacob grunted, then climbed back up the hill, using the rope to aid him in his ascent. When he reached the road, he pulled Tim aside. "Look, it'll save me time if you and Moody could round up—"

"Been done," Tim said. "I figured you'd want to question everybody, so I took it on myself to ask all the folks to come on over to Mr. and Mrs. Walker's cabin. They were real nice and said they didn't mind a bit." Tim cleared his throat. "It was all right that I just went ahead and—"

"Yeah, sure. Thanks," Jacob said. "I appreciate your taking the initiative. So let's go. The sooner I talk to these folks, the sooner we'll find out if anybody saw anything." Jacob focused his gaze on Tim. "Or have you already questioned them?"

Tim gulped. "No, sir. I figured you'd want to do that."

Jacob grinned, slapped Tim on the back, and headed toward the cabin that had been built way up in the woods, catercorner from the ravine. His guess was that, although the Walkers had seen the dark smoke rising into the clear blue sky, from the way their cabin was situated, it had been impossible for them to see this section of the roadway or the ravine itself.

With Tim at his side, Jacob approached the crowd. "Mr. and Mrs. Walker?"

"Yes, that's us." A short, stocky man in his mid fifties moved forward, a plump, rosy-cheeked blonde about the same age hugging his side.

"Where are you folks from?" Jacob asked.

"Nashville," Mr. Walker replied. "We come up here every year about this time. And we've been renting the same cabin the past five years."

"We sure do appreciate y'all contacting the fire department," Jacob told them. "I wonder if you might answer a few questions."

"Certainly, Sheriff. You are the sheriff, aren't you?" Mr. Walker asked.

"Yes, sir. Sheriff Jacob Butler." He held out his hand and he and Walker shared a brief shake. "We've had a homicide in Cherokee County, and there's a good chance the car down in the ravine is connected to that crime."

"Is there a body in the car?" Mrs. Walker asked, her eyes wide with wonder.

"No, ma'am," Jacob said.

"We'll answer any questions you have to ask," Mr. Walker said.

Jacob nodded. "Before y'all saw the smoke coming from the ravine, did either of you see or hear anything out of the ordinary? Did you see someone on the road? Or did you see the car—a green Jaguar—go by here any time this morning?"

Walker shook his head. "We slept late. I'd just walked out on the deck with my first cup of coffee when I saw the smoke. Regina was still in bed."

"I see. Well, thanks. And thanks, too, for allowing us to use your cabin to question the folks in the other nearby cabins. It shouldn't take long, and then we'll turn the place back over to y'all."

Jacob herded Tim toward his truck and the two got in and drove up the road and onto the drive leading to the Walker's rental cabin. As he pulled the Dodge Ram to a halt, Jacob noticed Caleb McCord sitting in a rocking chair on the wide front porch. The minute Jacob jumped out of his truck, Caleb bounded down the steps to meet him.

"What's going on with that car in the ravine?" Caleb asked. "I hope whatever it is won't hold me up for long. I've got a very important date at two-thirty this afternoon."

"With Jazzy?" Jacob asked.

"Yeah, with Jazzy."

"When did this come about?"

"Why so curious, Butler? I thought you two were just friends."

"We are," Jacob replied. "And as Jazzy's friend, I look out for her."

"I'm Jazzy's friend, too. Remember that."

Jacob barely knew McCord, but his gut instincts warned him there was more to the man than met the eye. And those same instincts that had saved his life more than once when he'd been a SEAL told him he could trust McCord. Jacob certainly didn't possess Genny's inherited sixth sense—her gift of sight—but he usually guessed right about people. He had his own kind of sixth sense. Like getting good vibes from Dallas Sloan when they'd first met. He got those same positive vibes from McCord.

"And you want to be more than friends with Jazzy, don't you?"

"I might." McCord's forehead wrinkled as he narrowed his gaze. "You got a problem with that?"

"Nope. Not as long as you treat her right. Jazzy needs a man who'll appreciate what a special lady she is. And she's going to need a man to stand by her whatever comes."

McCord's gaze centered on Jacob's eyes. "What's really going on and how is Jazzy involved?"

"What makes you think—"

"Cut the crap, Butler. Just lay it on the line for me, will you? You're talking in riddles."

"Jamie Upton's dead," Jacob said. "He was murdered sometime early this morning. In one of her visions, Genny saw the murderer—a woman who fits Jazzy's description—driving a green sports car"—Jacob nodded toward the road—"that we're pretty sure is the same one that was dumped in the ravine over there and set on fire."

"Genny thinks Jazzy killed Jamie?"

"No, Genny believes a woman wearing a wig to give her a similar took to Jazzy—"

"Reve Sorrell," Caleb said. "There was this woman

who came to town yesterday who drove a green Jag and looks enough like Jazzy to be—"

"Her twin. Yeah, I know. And believe me, as soon as I leave here, Ms. Sorrell is first on my list of people to question. But for now I need to know if you or any of the other residents around here saw anything earlier today."

"I can make it short and sweet. I didn't see or hear anything until your deputy came pounding on my door. I was up most of the night, so I'd planned to sleep all morning. And just so you know that Jazzy has an alibi— I was with her until nearly dawn."

"Jamie was probably killed after dawn," Jacob said. "But we figure he was with this woman most of the night. We think she drugged him, then—" Jacob cleared his throat. "She tortured him for hours. Cut him up with knives and razor blades and used a hot poker on him."

Caleb didn't so much as flinch. "Gruesome stuff. I'd say your lady killer is a real sicko."

"Yeah, I agree." Jacob glanced at the cabin. "I need to question the others. You're free to go."

"Has anyone told Jazzy about what happened?"

"Genny and Dallas are probably with her right now."

"I think I'll head on into town. Jazzy's going to need all her friends."

Jacob nodded, then turned and walked up the steps and onto the front porch. Yeah, his gut instincts were right on the money about Caleb McCord. He'd be real surprised if the guy didn't come through for Jazzy a hundred percent.

Four people waited for him inside the cabin. Three women and one man. He recognized Erin Mercer, of course. She was a wealthy amateur artist who'd come to live in Cherokee County over a year ago. Rumor had it that she was Big Jim Upton's latest mistress. Rumor also had it that Jamie had been sniffing around her since his return home this past January.

"How do you do," Jacob said as he entered the cabin. "I'm Sheriff Jacob Butler and I appreciate y'all volunteering to come here and answer a few questions."

"Your deputy was rather mysterious," Ms. Mercer said. "He told us only that you wanted to ask about a car that was set afire in a nearby ravine."

"Yes, ma'am, that's right." Jacob glanced from person to person. "Since y'all are staying in the cabins closest to the site of the fire, I was hoping one of you might have seen something—either the car or someone on foot along the road."

"I'm afraid I didn't see anything or anyone," Erin said. "I drove into Knoxville last night after dinner and just arrived home less than thirty minutes before Deputy Willingham knocked on my door."

"All right. Thank you, Ms. Mercer." Jacob turned to the lone man in the room. He had his arm around a young woman who seemed terrified. "And you folks are?"

"Tony and Mandy Landis. We're here on our honeymoon. And my wife"—he hugged her protectively—"is awfully upset about being questioned by the sheriff."

Jacob looked reassuringly at the pretty redhead, who wore no makeup and had her long, auburn hair pulled back in a ponytail. "Mrs. Landis, I'm sorry we had to bother you on your honeymoon and even sorrier that being herded over here has upset you. All I need from you folks is to know if you saw or heard anything that might help us find the person who dumped that car off in the ravine."

Tony Landis blushed profusely, and only then did Jacob realize that despite his black five-o'clock shadow and deep baritone voice, the guy probably wasn't a day older than his bride, who looked about twenty. If Mandy was indeed his bride. Jacob's guess was that these two twenty-something kids were not Mr. and Mrs.

"We—we didn't see anything. Honest to God, we didn't. We're on our honeymoon. You know how that is."

Jacob patted Tony on the back. "Yeah, son, I know how that is." Actually Jacob didn't know what it was like to be on his honeymoon since he'd never been married, but he sure as hell knew what it was like to spend a whole weekend in bed with a lady friend. "Why don't you two go on back to your cabin? And thanks for helping us out."

"Yes, sir. Thank you, sir." Tony grabbed Mandy's hand and all but dragged her toward the door.

Jacob then turned to the lone woman sitting quietly on the sofa, her hands resting in her lap, her ankles crossed in a ladylike fashion. Just looking at her, it was difficult to judge her age. She could be either a well-preserved fifty or a rode-hard-and-put-away-wet thirty-five. Jacob figured she was in her mid forties. For some reason she looked familiar, but he couldn't place her.

"Ma'am?"

When she lifted her head, he got a good look at her. A real pretty lady, with a warm smile, big blue eyes, and white-blond hair. "No, I'm afraid I didn't see or hear anything either. And I'm terribly sorry that I can't help you." She paused for a moment, then asked, "There must be something more going on than just a car set on fire for the sheriff himself to be questioning tourists."

"Yes, ma'am, there is," Jacob admitted. "And you'll hear all about it on the local news soon enough. We've had a murder in Cherokee County this morning. A young man was killed, and we have reason to believe that the murderer was driving the car that's burning over yonder in the ravine."

"My Lord! If you know the murderer was driving that car, then you must have an eyewitness."

"I'm afraid I'm not at liberty to say, ma'am. By the way, what is your name?"

"Oh, forgive me." Her small, delicate hand fluttered over her chest. "I'm Margo Kenley. I'm just a tourist. I rented a cabin for a month-long stay."

"Well, Ms. Kenley, you've just made it unanimous—no one saw anything."

"Sheriff?" Erin Mercer said.

"Yes, ma'am?"

"Can you tell us who the victim was? Is it someone I might know?"

"As a matter of fact it is. The murdered man was Jamie Upton."

Erin gasped, her eyes widening in shock. "Jamie's dead and—and someone killed him?"

"That's right."

"Does Jim—does his family know?"

"Big Jim was with us when we found the body," Jacob said.

"Oh, mercy. Poor Jim. That boy meant the world to him. And to Miss Reba, too. They must be devastated." Tears glistened in Erin Mercer's eyes.

Jacob thought Ms. Mercer's surprise and tears were genuine. He didn't peg her for the type of woman who would torture a man. But then again, he didn't really know the lady. Didn't know anything much about her.

"Ladies, thank you." Jacob tipped his Stetson, then turned and left.

He had another stop to make before heading back to his office and starting in on the mass of paperwork involved in a murder investigation. Maybe it was too much of a coincidence that Reve Sorrell's car had been driven by the killer, that Jamie had romanced her, and that the lady bore a striking resemblance to Jazzy. If so, did that mean the killer had set up Ms. Sorrell to take the fall and not Jazzy? Or could it be that the woman was as guilty as hell and just hadn't covered her tracks very well?

Galvin MacNair finished his examination, then removed his sterile gloves and shoved them into a plastic sack in his medical bag. Poor girl, Galvin thought as he glanced at Laura Willis. Small and delicate, with an ethereal beauty, she looked like a wounded angel. His heart went out to her. He knew he should control his emotions better when it came to dealing with patients, that he shouldn't agonize over telling this young woman her true condition. His ex-wife Nina had once told him that he cared too damn much and that fact would keep him from ever being a successful doctor. Maybe she'd been right. And perhaps the day would come when he could be totally objective when it came to dealing with patients, but he doubted it. It wasn't in his nature to doctor another human being without truly caring, without becoming emotionally involved to some degree.

"Would you like for your mother to come in now?" Galvin turned his back to allow Laura some privacy while she redressed.

"No. Not yet. I—I want to know if . . ." She burst into fresh tears.

Galvin rushed to her side, sat down on the edge of the bed, and put his arm around Laura's trembling shoulders. "Hush, hush. I promise that I'll do everything in my power to help you. I can't even imagine what you're going through, losing your fiancé and now . . . your parents will be here for you. Your sister. And Big Jim and Miss Reba."

Laura looked at him, tears glistening in her eyes. "Am I going to lose my baby?"

God, how he hated to tell her the truth, but he couldn't lie to her. *Sugarcoat the truth just a little,* he told himself. *What will it hurt?* "There's a chance you'll miscarry. You're bleeding heavily and . . . but there is always hope. We'll get you to the hospital right away and I'll—"

"No one knows I'm pregnant. I hadn't even told Jamie." She made a loud choking sound when she gasped.

"Laura, I want you to lie back and try to relax," Galvin told her. "I'm going to call the hospital and make arrangements. Then I'm going outside"—he nodded to the closed bedroom door—"and tell your parents and the Uptons about what's happening."

She grasped the lapels of his sports coat. "Please, Dr. MacNair, save my baby."

"I'll do everything humanly possible." For several minutes, he held her in his arms and let her weep softly. He lifted his hand and caressed her long, silky hair. When she calmed somewhat, he eased her down onto the bed, got up, and walked to the door. Once outside the bedroom, he was bombarded by the Willis family and by Big Jim.

"What's wrong with her?" Cecil Willis asked, his eyes filled with concern.

"I want to see her right now," Andrea said.

Galvin's gaze scanned the group, then zeroed in on Laura's mother. "Laura is pregnant. Probably six or seven weeks. But I'm afraid she's aborting the child and there isn't a great deal I can do to prevent it."

"My God!" Cecil gasped.

"Yes, I was afraid of this," Andrea said. "The minute I saw the blood, I suspected. You see, I've had several miscarriages myself."

"You say Laura is pregnant." Jim Upton came alive with hope.

Galvin hated to be the one to dash that hope, especially given the present set of circumstances, but he couldn't allow the man to believe that a great-grandchild was a possibility. It would take a miracle to save Laura's baby.

"I'm sorry, Mr. Upton, but I don't think there's any way we can prevent Laura from miscarrying."

Chapter 14

Numb, her mind barely functioning, Jazzy sat there staring off into space. She had felt so many things at first—grief, fear, anger, despair—that such a strong response, such a combination of feelings, had rendered her emotionally impotent. Mentally she accepted the fact that Jamie Upton was dead—brutally murdered by some sadistic person. The thought had registered in her mind, but not in her heart. Only last night she had believed herself free of him forever. She'd even celebrated that life-altering realization. But God in heaven, she should have known that she could never be free from Jamie. He was like some incurable disease. From time to time, she went into remission, but the illness doomed her happiness.

"Jazzy, can I get you something?" Genny asked. "More tea? Or a sandwich?"

Jazzy shook her head. Dear, sweet Genny, with her mother-to-the-world kindness. Jazzy glanced at the untouched cup of tea Genny had prepared for her over an hour ago, right after Dallas had left.

"It's cold." Genny followed Jazzy's line of vision to the teacup. "You need something warm and soothing."

When Genny picked up the cup of cold tea and headed toward the kitchen, Jazzy called to her. "I don't need tea or coffee or . . . I need to understand what happened, why it happened, and how it is that I'm involved."

Genny turned, set the cup on a nearby table, and faced Jazzy. "The most important thing we must concern ourselves with is how you're involved. And even though we both know you didn't kill Jamie, I keep getting these odd forebodings. Whoever killed Jamie wants you to be blamed for his murder."

"But who? Who would hate Jamie enough to torture him to death? And whoever she is, she hates me enough to want to see me blamed for a crime I didn't commit."

Genny came over and sat down on the sofa beside Jazzy. "We both know that the list of women in Jamie's life is endless. He's broken dozens of hearts over the years."

"So why would she focus on me to take the fall for Jamie's murder?"

"Because you're the only woman Jamie even came close to loving," Genny replied. "You're the woman Jamie kept coming back to, over and over again."

"I'd say it was Laura Willis, but I don't think she's capable of murder. Certainly not torture. She comes across as being a very nice young woman." Jazzy recalled their brief conversation in her office last night. She could hear Laura begging. *If he remains tied to you, in any way, he'll never be able to commit to me, to our marriage. Please, please . . . set him free.*

"Even so, we don't really know her, do we? And Dallas says that everyone is capable of murder, given the right set of circumstances."

"Yeah, he's probably right." Jazzy rubbed the back of

her neck. "I suppose I had more reason to kill him than anyone else did, and that's why I'll be the number one suspect."

"But there is no evidence against you. There can't be. You didn't kill Jamie. You were here in your apartment when he was murdered."

"Here all alone. I don't have an alibi."

"You have an alibi for part of the night," Genny reminded her. "Caleb was here with you."

At the mention of Caleb, Jazzy remembered their plans for this afternoon. A real date. So many hopes and dreams tied to a date that would never be. "Oh, God, I have to call him. We have a date for two-thirty. What time is it anyway?"

"It's almost noon." When Jazzy started to get up, Genny shoved her gently back onto the sofa. "Let me call him and tell him what—"

A loud, insistent pounding on the outer door stopped Genny mid sentence. She and Jazzy gasped and jumped simultaneously.

"I'll get it." Genny rushed to the door.

A couple of seconds later, Jazzy heard Caleb's voice. "How is she?"

"You heard about Jamie," Genny said in a matter-of-fact way.

"Yeah, I heard. I talked to Jacob."

Genny stepped aside to allow Caleb entrance.

"I came over as soon as I could." Caleb hurried past Genny and went straight to Jazzy.

The minute she saw him, the blessed numbness that had cocooned her from pain melted away. *Oh, Caleb, Caleb,* her heart cried. She'd never been so glad to see anyone in her entire life. On some deep, instinctive level she recognized him as her protector. She needed him. Needed him desperately.

"Caleb!" She shot up off the sofa and went right into his open arms. He held her, stroking her back, nuzzling the side of her face, whispering soft, incoherent soothing sounds into her ear. She clung to him for dear life.

"Hey, hey, honey, it's going to be all right." Caleb grasped her face with both of his hands. "I know you're hurting. I know how much you loved Jamie. It's all right to cry and even rant and rave, if that's what you want to do. I'm here for you. Lean on me."

"I—I used to love Jamie," she said, somehow needing to explain to Caleb that she hadn't been in love with Jamie for a long time. And last night—only hours before Jamie died—she had felt free of him for the first time since she was sixteen. Free of the past. Oh, God, what if she'd sensed Jamie was going to die and that's the reason she had felt so free?

"Tell me what I can do for you," Caleb said. "You name it and—"

"There's a problem you don't know about," Genny said.

Caleb snapped his head around and stared at Genny. "What is it?"

Jazzy reached up and clutched Caleb's hands and pressed them against her chest as she held them tightly. "Whoever killed Jamie wore a red wig—either that or she cut and dyed her hair to look like me."

"How did you find out about the woman? Did someone see her?"

"Genny did." Jazzy looked pleadingly at Caleb, hoping he wouldn't disregard Genny's gift of sight. "In one of her visions."

He turned to Genny. "Jacob told me about that, but not any details. Did you see anything else?"

"Only her hair. And the car she drove."

"Yeah, I know about the car. A green Jaguar."

"How do you . . ." Genny sighed. "Why would Jacob tell you about the car?"

"Because somebody set that car on fire and sent it over a ravine not half a mile from my cabin," Caleb replied. "The fire department is there and Jacob's got a deputy guarding the site. He questioned all the cabin residents nearby."

"By setting the car on fire, she hoped to destroy any evidence she might have left inside it," Genny said.

"Do you know who that Jag belonged to?" Caleb asked, but before either Jazzy or Genny had a chance to venture a guess, he went on, "Reve Sorrell, that woman who came to town yesterday asking about you, Jazzy. The woman who looks enough like you to be your twin."

The wheels in Jazzy's head spun haphazardly, creating a crazy scenario where the Sorrell woman had killed Jamie and wanted people to blame Jazzy for the crime. But then logic took over and she asked aloud, "If Reve Sorrell had intended to kill Jamie and pretend to be me so that I'd get blamed, why would she have driven into town yesterday, where a lot of people saw her? Why would she come looking for me?"

"Good question," Caleb said. "Who knows? Maybe she's crazy. Hell, if she tortured Jamie to death, then she's nuts."

"Is she a suspect?" Genny asked. "Jacob is planning on questioning her, isn't he?"

"He told me that as soon as he finished questioning the other cabin residents, talking to Ms. Sorrell was next on his agenda."

Holding onto Caleb's right hand—she didn't think she'd ever be able to let him go—Jazzy looked to Genny. "Could it be Reve Sorrell? Do you sense anything about her?"

Genny shook her head. "Nothing. Either there is no

link between her and Jamie's death or for some reason, I can't pick up on it."

When the telephone rang, they all three stared at it as if it were a slithering snake.

"I'll get it." Genny picked up the receiver. "Jazzy Talbot's residence."

When Caleb slipped his arm around her waist, Jazzy leaned against him. "I guess our date is canceled."

He hugged her to him. "Just postponed."

Genny held her hand over the telephone's mouthpiece. "It's Tiffany Reid. She said she needs to talk to you, that it's very important. What should I tell her?"

Tiffany was not just one of the waitresses at Jasmine's, she was a buddy, too. And only recently, Jazzy had given her a raise and promoted her to part-time hostess duties. "I'll talk to her."

"Are you sure?" Caleb asked.

Reluctantly Jazzy eased away from Caleb and walked over to take the phone. Genny gave her a concerned look. "Yeah, Tif, what's up?"

"Jazzy, you heard about Jamie, didn't you? I mean that's why Genny's there with you."

"Yes, I know that Jamie was murdered this morning."

"Look, there's something you need to know, something I'm not sure what to do about."

"Whatever it is, just tell me."

"Well, it's like this—I had a late date with Dillon Carson—" When Jazzy groaned, Tiffany laughed. "Yeah, I know. The guy's bad news, just like Jamie was—oh, God, sorry I said that. Anyhow, we were heading to my place sometime early this morning and this car came whizzing past us. Dillon said he thought it was a Jaguar. And—" Tiffany paused, as if reluctant to continue. "He thought the woman driving the car that turned off on the mountain road was you, Jazzy. So this morning when

I heard about Jamie and . . . I know you didn't kill him, but what do I do? I don't want to get you into trouble, so should I just keep quiet?"

"Did you see the woman?" Jazzy asked

"No, I was driving. But Dillon saw her. And unless I stop him from blabbing, he might tell folks that it was you in that car."

"It wasn't me."

"I know that, but—"

"You have to tell Jacob," Jazzy said. "He'll have to question Dillon."

"Are you sure that's what you want me to do?"

"Yes, Tif, I'm sure." Jazzy sucked in a deep breath, then exhaled slowly. God, what a mess. Dillon Carson had seen the woman who killed Jamie—and he'd thought it was her!

Jacob knocked on Reve Sorrell's cabin door shortly after noon. She responded quickly, but when she saw him, she started to close the door in his face. He grabbed the door and shoved it open.

"I've got a few questions for you," he said as he stepped into the cabin, his entry prompting her to move back quickly or be trampled by a man easily twice her size.

"Look, if this is about my car being stolen, I already know." She planted her hands on her hips and glared at him.

He glanced around the room, noticed her suitcase sitting by the sofa, and looked back at her. "Going somewhere?"

"I'm returning to Chattanooga," she told him. "If it's any of your business."

"Why the rush? I thought yesterday afternoon you'd decided to—"

"I changed my mind."

"Interesting."

"Look Dudley Doright, let me make this simple for you. I know about Jamie Upton being murdered. I know that the chief suspect is Jazzy Talbot. When I went out for breakfast this morning, people were talking about nothing else. I don't plan to stick around and try to find out if a murderess is related to me. As soon as my car arrives, I'm leaving Cherokee Pointe and I'm never coming back."

"I think you'd better stick around," Jacob told her. "We need to find out if Jazzy might be related to the murderess."

Reve gasped. "Just what do you mean by that? Surely you aren't implying that I—I . . . you're a moron if you think for one minute that I'm going to stand here and allow you to—"

"Pipe down, will you?" How the hell this woman could look so much like Jazzy and be so completely different he'd never know. "Nobody is accusing you of anything. But since we have every reason to believe that the killer was driving your car and that she set it on fire and sent it careening over into a ravine up in the mountains—"

"My Jag was set on fire?"

"Burned to a fare-thee-well. It's just barely recognizable. But we're ninety-nine percent sure it's your car."

"The killer stole my car, then burned it?"

"We think she used it to transport Jamie Upton to a deserted cabin up near Scotsman's Bluff. Then she drove it halfway back down the mountain, set it on fire, and—"

"I was right here, in this cabin"—she pointed to the adjoining room—"in that bedroom, in the bed asleep. I was not picking up Jamie Upton and taking him to some deserted cabin to kill him. Good grief, if I had planned to kill him, I'd have hardly been stupid enough to let someone see me driving my own car. A very distinct car, might I add."

"Maybe."

"Oh, you are a moron if you think I had anything to do with Jamie's murder." She flung her hands out in a gesture of exasperation. "I had no motive. Why would I want to kill Jamie?"

"You tell me, Ms. Sorrell. Did he love you and leave you? Did he make a fool out of you? Are you used to ending your affairs, not the other way around, and got pissed when Jamie broke things off?"

She shook her finger in his face. "I did not have an affair with Jamie, so there was no affair to end. We had a few dates. That's the extent of our relationship. It didn't take me long to figure out that the man was a charming Romeo who had only two interests in me. One, I looked like his teenage sweetheart. And two, he wanted me to be another notch on his bedpost. I was smart enough to see through him and not fall for his line of bull. Unlike your friend Jazzy."

"Lady, you're a real piece of work."

"And just what do you mean by that cryptic statement?"

When Jacob glared at her, she tilted her snooty little nose and said, "Would you like me to give you the definition of the world cryptic? I realize that as a backwoods sheriff you probably didn't go to college. Actually, you might not even have finished high school."

Jacob laughed. Damn infuriating bitch had not only implied he was an uneducated idiot, and therefore stupid, but she had referred to him—to his face—as a moron. Twice!

"Ms. Sorrell, don't leave town."

"Am I under arrest?"

"No, ma'am. But if you leave town, I'll put out a warrant for your arrest."

"On what charges?"

"I'm not sure. But I'll think of something."

She gritted her teeth. "I did not kill Jamie Upton. I had no reason to kill him."

"If you say so."

"I intend to contact my lawyer."

Jacob nodded to the telephone. "Go right ahead."

Oddly enough, the phone rang. Reve Sorrell jumped as if she'd been shot.

"Damn!" she mumbled the word under her breath, then walked over and picked up the receiver. "Yes, Reve Sorrell here." She paused, listening to the caller. "What did you say?" She listened again. "Yes, Sheriff Butler is here. Certainly." She held out the receiver to him.

"Who is it?" he asked.

"She didn't say." Reve placed her hand over the mouthpiece and said softly, "There's something funny about her voice."

"How's that?"

"It sounded muffled. Either that or she's got the worst case of laryngitis I've ever heard."

Jacob took the phone. "This is Sheriff Butler."

"You're questioning the wrong woman," the husky voice said.

"Who is this?"

"Someone who wants to help."

Jacob realized the voice was being disguised, probably by some type of device. His gut instincts told him that he was speaking to the killer.

"How can you help me?"

"You need evidence before you can arrest Jazzy Talbot, don't you?"

"And you have that evidence?"

"Of course not, but I know where you can find it."

"Where?" Jacob asked.

"In her office at Jasmine's."

"How do you—" The dial tone hummed in his ear. Son of a bitch.

"What's wrong?" Reve asked.

"Nothing you need to concern yourself with," he told her. "It's been interesting, Ms. Sorrell, but I've got to run. I have a murder case to solve."

"By all means, Sheriff. Don't let me stop you."

Jacob paused as he headed out the door, then glanced over his shoulder. "Remember not to leave town."

When she screwed up her face in a mocking smile, he tipped his hat and left. He had to talk to Jazzy and get permission to search her office for evidence he wasn't even sure was there. But if it was, he figured the real killer had planted it. And if that was the case, then things didn't look good for Jazzy. No, sir, things were looking worse for her with every passing minute.

Chapter 15

When Dr. MacNair entered the waiting room on the first floor of County General, Jim rose to his feet, but he stood back and allowed Laura's parents to meet the doctor. His heart lodged in his throat as he waited to hear his unborn great-grandchild's fate.

"I'm sorry," MacNair said.

Jim sighed. The only hope of an heir—a descendant with his blood flowing through his or her veins—had died with the miscarriage of Jamie's child. *Why now, God, why now? Wasn't it enough to take Jamie? Did you have to take his baby, too?*

"When may we see Laura?" Andrea Willis held her husband's hand tightly.

"Soon," MacNair replied. "We did a D and C and she's asleep and resting comfortably now. In a few weeks, she'll be fully recovered. There was no permanent damage, no reason she can't have other children."

It was good that sweet, little Laura would one day be able to have other children, Jim thought. But those children wouldn't be Upton babies. Jamie's child was dead.

Tears glistened in Cecil Willis's eyes. "Thank you, Dr. MacNair."

"I'll arrange for a grief counselor to speak to Laura," MacNair said.

"I would prefer that I be present when the counselor talks to Laura," Andrea said. "I plan on being here at the hospital with her day and night until she's released."

"Yes, of course." MacNair looked sympathetically at Andrea. "Laura will certainly need her mother with her."

After the doctor left, Jim walked over to Andrea and Cecil. During their brief acquaintance, Jim had formed an opinion of the couple. Basically he liked them. They seemed like good people. Reba sure set great store by them being wealthy and socially prominent. *Laura's from a fine family,* Reba had said. *The Willis family has been breeding Kentucky Derby winners for generations. They're old money.*

"I'm truly glad that Laura will be all right," Jim told them. "She's a dear girl. Reba and I were looking forward to her becoming a member of our family. And if the baby had—" Jim cleared his throat. "I'm going to head on back to the house. If the sedative Dr. MacNair gave Reba has worn off, she's probably worrying herself sick because I haven't called to let her know how Laura is."

Cecil shook Jim's hand, then patted him on the back. "Please tell Sheridan that we'll call her later."

"Yes, yes, of course," Jim replied. "I appreciate her staying at the house with Reba. It was kind of her to offer."

As Jim left the waiting room and walked down the hall toward the hospital's back exit, he thought about what he had lost today and how irrevocably his life had changed in the matter of hours. Less than twenty-four hours ago, Jamie had been alive. And Laura had been pregnant.

Just as the automatic exit doors opened and Jim

stepped outside, he came to an abrupt halt when he saw Erin Mercer rushing toward him. What was she doing here? How had she known where he was?

"Jim!" She ran toward him, her arms open wide.

He grabbed her hands to prevent her from enveloping him in a hug.

"I know about Jamie. I called your house and spoke to Dora. I asked to speak to you to give you my condolences, and she said you'd gone to the hospital." She looked up at him with concern in her eyes. "Are you all right? I was afraid you'd had a heart attack or—"

He pulled her aside, away from the glass wall that surrounded the hospital exit and exposed them to prying eyes. "I'm fine. I came to the hospital with Laura's parents. Laura just suffered a miscarriage."

"Laura was pregnant?"

Jim nodded. "She hadn't even told Jamie."

"Oh, Jim . . . Jim, I'm so sorry, darling. I wish there was something I could do."

He thought about demanding to know where she'd been all night, why she hadn't been at home early this morning when he'd stopped by her cabin. But somehow that didn't seem to matter right now. "I need you, Erin. God, how I need you."

Squeezing his hands, she leaned toward him. It was all he could do to stop himself from grabbing her and kissing her.

"I'm here for you," she told him. "Tell me what I can do and I'll do it. Anything. Everything."

Jim let go of her and stuffed his hands into his pants pockets. "I have to go home and tell Reba that"—he looked up at the clear blue sky, swallowed, and willed his emotions under control. "She's in pretty bad shape, as you can imagine. Finding out that we no longer have the hope of a great-grandchild . . ."

"I understand that you have to be with her, that she needs you." Erin offered him a compassionate smile. "And you probably need her, too. After all—"

"I need you," he told her. "Later today—will you be at home?"

"Yes, of course I will be."

"I'll try to come by. Just for a while."

"If you can't, it will be all right. Just know that if you need me, I'm here for you."

"I'll come by. I want to be with you." Without saying another word to her, he walked away, and all the while he wished he could turn around, go back to her, and pull her into his arms.

"I need your permission to search your office," Jacob told Jazzy.

"Why do you need to search her office?" Genny inquired at the precise moment Caleb asked "Why?"

"You have my permission," Jazzy said. "I have nothing to hide."

Jacob shifted uncomfortably. "Hell, Jazzy, I know that. Don't think just because I've got to search your office that for one minute I think you killed Jamie. Not even if we find evidence to the contrary."

Caleb snorted. "I don't see why you have to go searching for evidence against Jazzy just because some nut called you and said—"

"He's just doing his job." Jazzy grabbed Caleb's arm.

"Is it his job to help some crazy woman railroad you for a crime you didn't commit?" Caleb glared at Jacob.

"What will you do if you find some sort of planted evidence in Jazzy's office?" Genny asked. "You'll know that it was put there, that Jazzy is innocent."

Jacob removed his Stetson, then ran his fingers

through the back of his hair where it rested just above his shoulders. "I'm not trying to build a case against Jazzy, but as the sheriff, it's my job to share all the information I have with Wade Truman. Our ambitious young DA is already breathing down my neck hot and heavy about coming up with a suspect."

"And I'm the most likely suspect, aren't I?" Jazzy said.

When Jacob reached out and placed his hand on Jazzy's shoulder, Caleb tensed. Jacob could tell the guy wanted to knock his hand off her. He understood the other man's proprietorial, possessive attitude. He'd sensed the same thing in Dallas Sloan the very first time he saw him with Genny.

"You didn't kill Jamie," Jacob said. "We all know that out there somewhere is a very disturbed woman who will, sooner or later, give herself away."

"Yeah, but in the meantime, I may just wind up in jail." Jazzy crossed her arms over her waist and emitted a couple of nervous, mocking chuckles. "It's not as if Jamie didn't screw me over enough while he was alive. Now he's reaching out from the grave to do it."

While Jacob and Deputy Moody Ryan searched Jazzy's office, she waited outside in the hall with Genny and Caleb. She could feel the noose tightening around her neck. She didn't need Genny's psychic gifts to know that someone had intentionally framed her for Jamie's murder. But who? And why?

Someone had hated Jamie so much that they had tortured him to death. And that same person hated her enough to want to see her go to jail—oh, God, not just go to jail, but be sentenced to death for Jamie's murder. How could this be happening? And why now, when she had thought maybe she had a chance of finding happiness with Caleb?

When Jacob came out of her office carrying a plastic bag, she grabbed Caleb by the arm. Jacob held up the bag to show them the bloody knife it contained.

"Where was it?" Jazzy asked him.

"Hidden in the back of one of the file cabinets," Jacob told her.

"It's the knife she used on Jamie," Genny said. "But you won't find any fingerprints on it. Only Jamie's blood."

"I didn't put it there," Jazzy said, her strong survival instincts kicking in, forcing her to defend herself, even to her friends.

"We know that," Genny said. "Jacob, the knife was planted in Jazzy's office to make her look guilty."

"Yeah, I know," he replied. "But I'm afraid whoever put it there accomplished her goal."

"Are you going to arrest me?" Jazzy asked.

"Hell no, he isn't going to arrest you." Caleb moved between Jazzy and Jacob. "You and I were together last night and this morning. I'll swear in court that we were together whenever Jamie was killed." He glared at Jacob, his aggressive stance and determined expression issuing a warning.

Jazzy pushed Caleb gently aside and looked directly at Jacob. "What happens next?"

"Nothing right now," Jacob replied. "It could take a while to determine if this knife was used on Jamie, if this is his blood. Besides, if this is all the evidence that shows up—"

"She couldn't have killed Jamie," Caleb reiterated. "She was with me."

In that slow, easy way Jacob had, he turned and squinched his eyes as he focused on Caleb. "If you lie to try to protect Jazzy, you won't help her. You just might hurt her and get yourself in trouble to boot."

Caleb stared inquiringly at Jacob.

"Folks might think you two were in cahoots," Jacob said. "Maybe Jazzy lured Jamie up to that cabin where you were waiting for him. Maybe it wasn't a woman who killed him. Maybe it was a jealous lover. Maybe the two of you decided that the only way to get Jamie out of Jazzy's life permanently was to kill him."

Jazzy grabbed Caleb's arm, sensing he was on the verge of hitting Jacob. "No, don't. Jacob is only playing devil's advocate. Besides, he's right—you won't help me by lying about our being together when Jamie was killed."

Jacob's cell phone rang. He handed the evidence bag to Moody and told him to get it over to the sheriff's office immediately. Retrieving his phone from its belt holder, he punched the ON button.

"Butler here." He listened, then said, "Why am I not surprised?"

"What is it?" Genny asked, but Jazzy sensed that by the look on her best friend's face she already suspected what Jacob had been told.

"Yeah, Dallas, thanks. Meet me over at my office as soon as possible." He looked at Jazzy. "I know what I have to do, but I sure as hell don't have to like it." Jacob hit the off button and returned his phone to the clip holder on his belt.

"You know Dallas went back to the cabin and then to the site where the Jag was dumped, to oversee things there," Jacob said. "We've combined forces—the sheriff's department and the police department."

"What did Dallas tell you?" Jazzy asked, and when Genny slipped her hand over Jazzy's and squeezed, she knew the news was really bad.

"They found a book of matches at the cabin," Jacob

said. "They're from Jazzy's Joint. Got the logo on the cover."

"So? Big deal." Caleb all but snarled his statement. "Half the population of Cherokee County probably has a Jazzy's Joint book of matches."

"Yeah, I know, and the matches alone wouldn't prove anything. But coupled with the bloody knife and—" Jacob paused and cursed softly under his breath. "They found something in the woods only a few feet away from the burned out Jag."

Three sets of eyes focused on Jacob, but he looked only at Jazzy. "They found a red silk scarf with the initials J.T. monogrammed on it."

Jazzy laughed. "Whoever the hell she is, she's good. She didn't steal just any of my scarves. No, she had to steal the one with my initials on it—the one my friend the sheriff gave me for my birthday last year."

Chapter 16

"Is everything set for Miss Laura's return?" Reba asked Dora as the housekeeper served them afternoon coffee in the sunroom.

"Yes, ma'am. The florist delivered the fresh flowers you ordered, and I've placed the arrangements around the room," Dora replied. "I changed the bed linen as you requested and I moved Miss Sheridan's things into another room so that Miss Laura can have complete peace and quiet."

"Has the nurse we hired to look after Laura arrived?" Reba nervously rubbed her throat, the tremor in her hand a sure sign that the medication Dr. MacNair had prescribed to soothe her was wearing off.

Jim reached over and grasped his wife's wrist, then slipped his big hand around her small one. "Mrs. Conley went directly to the hospital to meet Andrea and Cecil. She suggested it was best if she speak to Laura's parents before bringing her home, as well as get instructions on Laura's care from Dr. MacNair and the hospital psychiatrist."

Dora placed the silver service on the wicker table, then lifted the silver pot and poured coffee into two china cups. "Will there be anything else?"

"No, that will be all," Jim told the housekeeper.

"I want everything possible done for Laura. That child has been through—" Reba's voiced cracked; tears pooled in her eyes. "She has lost everything, just as we have. Jamie. And the baby." She clutched Jim's hand tightly. "Oh, Jim, the baby. Jamie's baby. If only . . ."

Jim scooted to the edge of his wicker chair, leaned over, and draped his arm around Reba's shoulders. "Nothing can be done about it now. The baby's gone."

"Yes, the baby's gone." Reba dabbed the corners of her eyes with her fingertips. "It's as if we've been cursed, as if Fate—or God—is determined to take everything from us and leave us nothing. First Jim Jr. and then Melanie. Our children. Both such beautiful, fine people. And now Jamie, our only grandchild. If only Laura hadn't lost the baby, we would have—"

Reba broke down and cried. She'd been crying a lot these past four days, and Jim had done his best to be at her side. She deserved no less. As he patted her tenderly, he thought about Erin and how desperately he'd wanted to be with her, to find the comfort in her arms that he could find nowhere else. But how could he slip away— day or night—when Reba needed him so? And if he were totally honest with himself, he'd have to admit that as much as he wanted Erin, as much as he needed her, right now he needed his wife more. No one understood the depth of his despair the way Reba did. No one shared his grief and sense of hopelessness as she did. No one else had loved Jamie as much as he did, only Reba.

"We'll get through this somehow." Jim held her, and as she melted into him as if somehow absorbing his strength, he leaned his head over against hers and pressed his lips to her temple. A tender feeling swelled up inside him. He had never been in love with Reba, but he did care for her, perhaps even loved her in a way. "We've still got each other, for what it's worth."

Sniffling softly, she turned to face him. "Do we? Do I still have you?"

A nervous pang hit him in the gut. Did Reba know about Erin? Or did she simply suspect that there was another woman, that there had always been other women? "Of course you still have me. I'm here, aren't I?" With the utmost gentleness, he caressed her cheek. "We've been through a lot together in these past fifty-four years and somehow survived. We'll survive this, too."

"I don't know if I want to survive." Reba gazed into Jim's eyes, and what he saw frightened him. Utter hopelessness. The will to live fading away.

"I can't bear to see you like this. Please—"

Dora came rushing into the sunroom. "They're here. Miss Laura is home!"

Jim helped Reba to her feet and together they hurried to greet Laura. Andrea and Cecil flanked their daughter. A sulking Sheridan came in behind them, carrying Laura's overnight case. A tall, robust woman in her mid forties entered the foyer last. Jim assumed the tall brunette was Mrs. Conley, the psychiatric nurse that Dr. MacNair had highly recommended.

Reba walked quickly forward, then hesitated for a moment, searching Laura's pale, emotionless face. Jim moved in slowly behind his wife and put his hands on her shoulders.

"Welcome, home, my dear, dear girl," Reba said. "Your room is all ready for you."

"Thank you," Laura replied. "You've been so kind to me. Since the day Jamie brought me home and introduced me to y'all as his fiancée, you've been nothing but gracious and kind."

"Oh, Laura . . . sweet girl . . . you're everything we ever hoped for in a wife for our Jamie."

Andrea slipped her arm around Laura's waist. "If y'all don't mind, I think Laura should lie down for a while."

"Yes, of course." Tensing, Reba leaned backward into Jim. "How thoughtless of us to keep you standing here in the foyer when you—"

Laura pulled away from her mother, went straight to Reba, and held out her hands. "Would you walk me to my room, Miss Reba? And please sit with me, just for a few minutes. No one else will let me talk about Jamie. No one else loved him the way we did."

Jim glanced from Cecil Willis to Mrs. Conley, silently questioning them as to whether Reba should agree to Laura's request.

Mrs. Conley moved in and answered his question quite efficiently. She laid her hand gently on Laura's shoulder as she looked right at Reba. "Yes, Mrs. Upton, why don't you come with us and help me get Laura settled in? Her parents and sister can check in on us later."

Laura grasped Reba's hand and the two headed toward the staircase. Mrs. Conley took Laura's overnight bag from Sheridan, and after a quick glance at Jim— with an understanding passing between them that she would look after both Laura and Reba—she followed her charges.

"Am I dismissed?" Sheridan asked insolently.

Andrea sighed. "Why don't you—oh, dear, you're sharing a room with Laura. I didn't think—"

"We had Dora move Sheridan's things into the bedroom across the hall from Laura," Jim said.

"Thank you," Andrea replied.

"That's great," Sheridan said, an insolent, phony smile on her face. "Does anyone mind if I take a break from all this melodrama? I'd like to freshen up and then go into town, if I could borrow a car."

"Take Jamie's Mercedes," Jim said. "Ask Dora for the keys." He'd decided that he didn't like Sheridan Willis. She came across as a spoiled rotten, hateful little bitch. Actually she was the female equivalent of Jamie. Those two would have been a perfect match. And they probably had been, Jim thought. He didn't doubt for a minute that Jamie had scored with the younger Willis sister.

"That's very nice of you," Andrea said, "but—"

"You and Daddy take care of Laura," Sheridan said. "Don't worry about me. Laura comes first, doesn't she? As always." With a smirking, condescending grin, she whirled around and headed down the hallway toward the kitchen.

"I must apologize—" Cecil said.

"No need." Jim held up his hand in a stop gesture.

"We plan to take Laura home with us after the funeral," Andrea said. "The sooner she gets away from . . . well, from the reminders of Jamie, the sooner she'll start to heal."

"I understand," Jim said. "But it will be difficult for Reba to let her go. I think those two need each other right now. If y'all could stay on just a few days after the funeral, I'd appreciate it."

Cecil nodded. "We'll do whatever the doctors suggest is best for Laura."

"Yes, of course. Naturally Laura must be your first concern." An awkward silence followed. Finally Jim said, "If y'all haven't had lunch, we can get Dora to whip up something."

"I couldn't eat a bite," Andrea replied. "But a cup of tea would be nice." She turned to her husband. "Darling, why don't you come with me? We'll have Dora fix you a sandwich."

Jim watched as Andrea Willis led her husband away. It was apparent who the dominant partner in that relationship was. It wasn't that he thought Cecil allowed his wife to lead him around by the nose. No, he didn't think that. He suspected that Cecil found it comforting to be married to such a strong, capable woman. Jim almost envied the man. He wondered what it would be like, just once, to have a mate he could lean on instead of the other way around.

As he walked upstairs, he wondered how the visit between Laura and Reba was going. Jamie's doting grandmother and besotted fiancée. Two women who had loved Jamie deeply and overlooked his many character flaws. No doubt they would find Jamie, in death, to be a saint. Grunting, he shook his head sadly. When he reached the landing and started to turn toward his bedroom suite, he paused for a moment. Despite assuring himself that Mrs. Conley could handle two weeping, mournful women, he found himself walking in the opposite direction and straight toward Laura's room. The door stood open. He paused outside, feeling a bit like a voyeur as he looked in at a private moment. Mrs. Conley busied herself unpacking Laura's overnight case. Reba stood by the window, talking softly, telling Laura some silly little tale about Jamie's sixth birthday, and yet ignoring Laura completely. Jim could see that his wife had slipped away briefly into a world where Jamie still existed, that she was oblivious to everything and everyone around her.

His gaze traveled to Laura, who sat in the rocking chair, only a few feet away from the windows. One hand lay atop the other on her belly, as if she were protecting that spot. Her eyes appeared glazed. Apparently, she was completely unconnected to reality. Then, as she rocked back and forth, she looked down at her stomach and smiled.

A cold chill shot through Jim's body.

Wade Truman was as new at being Cherokee County's district attorney as Jacob was at being the sheriff. They'd known each other all their lives and had been friends just about as long, despite being total opposites and despite the fact Wade was several years younger. Wade was pure Scots-Irish, not a drop of Cherokee blood in his veins, which accounted for his ruddy complexion, sky blue eyes, and sandy hair. Where Jacob had joined the navy at eighteen, Wade had gone off to UT. Wade came from an upper-middle-class background. His father had been a state senator, his grandfather a federal judge. And Wade had ambitions to run for political office. Jacob suspected that he had his eye on the governor's mansion. On the other hand, Jacob's ambitions were modest in comparison. All he wanted was to learn how to be a good lawman.

While rubbing the back of his neck, Wade paced the floor. "Damn it, Jacob, I don't like the idea anymore than you do, but, my God, man, the evidence is right there in front of our eyes. Jazzy Talbot killed Jamie."

"No, she didn't," Jacob replied, trying to keep his voice calm, which was no easy task, considering how agitated he was. He'd spent the better part of the last hour doing his level best to convince Wade that somebody had framed Jazzy.

"I agree with Jacob," Dallas Sloan said as he poured himself a cup of coffee. "Jazzy's no fool. She would have covered her tracks better. She wouldn't have—"

"Let's say I agree with you two." Wade stopped pacing and faced Dallas. "I don't want to prosecute Jazzy. Hell, even if she did kill Jamie—"

"She didn't!" Jacob and Dallas spoke simultaneously.

"I was just going to say that I don't entirely disagree with the folks who say whoever killed Jamie should get an award. We all know the guy was a real son of a bitch. And the whole town knows the way he treated Jazzy. A sympathetic jury would go easy on her."

"If she's charged with first degree murder, the jury won't be inclined to let her off scot-free," Dallas said. "Whoever killed Jamie planned his murder down to the last detail. If you charge Jazzy, it will be for premeditated murder, won't it?"

"I don't know. Maybe not. As much as I'd like to, I can't ignore the facts." Wade grimaced. "Look, Big Jim called me this morning. He wants action and he wants it now. Miss Reba is calling for Jazzy's head on a silver platter."

"And you intend to serve Jazzy up to Miss Reba." Jacob knotted his hands into tight fists. He needed half an hour with a punching bag to work off some frustration. He knew Wade had little choice in the matter. If the Uptons wanted Jazzy arrested for murder, then her fate was sealed.

"Jazzy has no alibi for the time—"

"Caleb McCord says otherwise," Dallas told him.

"And who is Caleb McCord?" Wade frowned. "What do we know about this guy, other than he's Jazzy's lover and would lie for her? Hell, for all we know, he helped her kill Jamie."

"You're reaching," Jacob said. "And if Caleb needs a gold star for honesty and integrity, maybe I can help get him one."

Wade glowered at Jacob. "What the hell are you talking about?"

"We're running a check on McCord," Dallas said. "I've got some friends at the Bureau doing me favor."

Wade shook his head, then looked up at the ceiling. "Screw the Bureau. Even if you can give me evidence that McCord is a fucking saint, I can make a jury believe he'd lie to protect his woman. Any man on the jury will take one look at Jazzy and realize they'd do just about anything—lie, cheat, steal, maybe even kill—to get a piece of her ass."

"Is that what this is all about?" Jacob got right up in Wade's face and glared down at him. Although tall, Wade stood a couple of inches shorter than Jacob. "You had a thing for Jazzy a few years ago, and she wouldn't give you the time of day."

Snarling, Wade leaned toward Jacob, taking a defensive stance. "You know me better than that. Or at least I thought you did."

Dallas set his coffee mug on Jacob's desk, walked over, and clamped his hand down on Jacob's shoulder. "Cool off."

Jacob tensed the moment Dallas touched him. He wanted to smash his fist into Wade's handsome face. Jacob closed his eyes for a split second, then took a deep breath. He shrugged off Dallas's hand and stepped back, away from Wade.

"Let's just agree to disagree on this one," Wade said. "It's my job as the DA to take action when we have this much evidence against a person."

"And when Big Jim is breathing fire down your neck," Jacob said.

"Yeah, there's that, too," Wade admitted. "Look, I'm asking Judge Keefer to issue a warrant for Jazzy's arrest.

And it'll be your job as sheriff to send someone to pick her up."

Wade glanced from Dallas to Jacob, then headed toward the closed door. After he opened the door, he paused and, without glancing back, said, "You'll have that warrant before five."

Once Wade left, Jacob stomped across the floor, lifted the telephone receiver, and started dialing. Dallas pressed his finger down on the base, disconnecting the call in progress.

"Whoever you were calling, let it wait. You need to take some time to think calmly. Rationally. We knew before Wade Truman showed up that it was only a matter of time before you'd have to arrest Jazzy."

"Do you have any idea how fucking mad I am? At Wade. At myself! I'm the goddamn sheriff. It's my job to protect the innocent. And Jazzy is innocent. Plus, out there somewhere is a crazy woman who just might be thinking about whacking off some other guy's balls."

"We'll find her," Dallas said. "And when we do, Jazzy won't have to go to trial. But for now, you'll do what you have to do. We've already got a suspects list started—women we know for sure had motive to kill Jamie. And all of them might have been MIA the morning Jamie was butchered. We start by checking out their alibis."

"Erin Mercer says she was in Knoxville at the time, but wouldn't say where or with whom." Jacob could feel the tension draining from him. Dallas was right. He couldn't stop the inevitable—Jazzy's arrest. What he could do was put a bright spotlight on the other suspects. "Laura Willis's mother claims both of her daughters were asleep in their beds at the Upton mansion."

"Yeah, well what about Mrs. Willis?" Dallas asked. "If Jamie was diddling both Willis girls, their mother might have thought he deserved to die."

"We don't know for sure about Jamie and the younger Willis girl."

"Nah, we don't know for sure, but I'd lay odds that Sheridan Willis always wants whatever her big sister has. And that included Laura's fiancé."

Jacob glanced at the telephone. "By the way, I was going to call Genny. I thought maybe she should be with Jazzy when I arrest her."

Dallas nodded. "I thought you were calling McCord and I knew that if he was there when Jazzy was arrested, he might cause trouble and you'd have to book him, too. The guy's fuse is almost as short as yours. And he's as protective of Jazzy as I am of Genny."

"When do you think your people will have that in-depth report on him?" Jacob asked. "My call to the Memphis PD told us very little about him personally. All we know is that McCord was a cop whose partner was shot to death and that McCord almost died himself. According to the MPD chief, McCord was an okay guy, but he was a loner and nobody knew much about his personal life."

"Teri should get back to me by tomorrow at the latest. If anybody can find out the personal details of Caleb's life, Teri can."

Jacob frowned. Caleb McCord was hiding something. Jacob could feel it in his bones. "I'm telling you that there's something about that guy."

"Something that might affect Jazzy or in some way affect this murder case?"

"Maybe. Yeah."

"You know Genny is convinced that Caleb is the guy to make all Jazzy's dreams come true. She thinks we're wrong to distrust him."

"Yeah, I know. And Genny is usually right. But not always. Sometimes she lets that big heart of hers overrule both her common sense and her sixth sense."

* * *

When he opened the door and saw her standing there, Bobby Joe Harte wasn't sure whether he was glad to see her or sorry he'd ever met her. She was only a few years away from being jail bait. But she sure as hell didn't act like any nineteen-year-old he knew.

"Hey there, lawman." Sheridan Willis punched him in the chest with the tip of her index finger, urging him backward, into his apartment. "Miss me?"

He didn't budge, despite the fact his pecker throbbed just looking at her. "What do you want? Why are you here?"

She puckered her lips into a fake pout. "Now, is that any way to talk to a girl who knows how to give a guy a great blow job?"

"Is that right? Maybe if Jamie Upton was still alive, I could ask him." Damn, he hadn't meant to let that slip. When he'd heard Jacob and Dallas discussing suspects and they'd mentioned Sheridan, he had been more than a little surprised.

"What makes you think Jamie and I . . . that I ever gave Jamie—"

Bobby Joe grabbed her shoulders and jerked her into his apartment, then kicked the door shut. "I'm your alibi, you know. But how the hell do you think it's going to make me look to the sheriff if I have to tell him you couldn't have killed Jamie because you were too busy fucking my brains out that morning?"

"Why should the sheriff care what you do when you're not on duty?" Sheridan laid her hands over his where they gripped her shoulders. "I'm of age. I'm not married, and neither are you."

"Damn it, Sheridan, I should have said something to the sheriff when your name came up on his suspects list." Hell, Jacob was going to skin him alive.

"Why didn't you?" Sheridan pulled Bobby Joe's hands down her arms and around her hips, then placed them on her butt.

He swallowed as he gazed into her eyes. "I don't know. Stupidity I guess. Or maybe I was just out-and-out embarrassed that I'd had a one-night stand with a teenager. And not just any teenager, but Jamie Upton's future sister-in-law, who just happened to be screwing around with him."

Sheridan lifted her arms up and around his neck and rubbed herself seductively against him. "Why does it have to be a one-night stand?"

"Slow down, girl." Bobby Joe tried to push her away. "If you had a thing for Jamie, you sure are doing a good job of covering up your grief."

Sheridan shrugged, then smiled wickedly before she wandered around the living room, looking everything over as if she were considering buying the place. "I cared about Jamie. I'd have made a better wife for him than Laura would have. God, she's such a wimp. Miss Goody-goody. Daddy's favorite child." Sheridan whirled around and grinned at Bobby Joe. "But I'm not one to waste my time mourning a lost cause. Cut your losses and move on is my motto."

"You're a heartless bitch."

Sheridan lifted the edges of her long-sleeved cotton sweater up and over her head, exposing her upper torso. Her naked breasts all but screamed at Bobby Joe to touch them. Round, firm, and perky. He remembered how it felt to have one of those tight, puckered nipples in his mouth. His sex swelled and hardened instantly. She glanced down at his crotch and grinned.

"Why did you come here?" Bobby Joe asked her, knowing all along that he was a condemned man. He was going to fuck her. No doubt about it. And the devil could have his soul later.

"I should think that would be rather obvious," Sheridan told him as she unzipped her jeans, then rubbed her fingers over her mound while she licked her lips.

When he saw the dark triangle of curls between her thighs appear, he realized she wasn't wearing any panties. "How much is this going to cost me?"

She laughed as she shrugged off her jeans and held out her hands, beckoning him to her. Not giving a damn what her asking price was, Bobby Joe unzipped his pants and reached inside to free his penis. He'd pay the piper later, after he'd heard the tune.

When he shot across the room, grabbed her, and lifted her up on the wide sofa back, she spread her legs and gripped his shoulders. He lifted her just enough to accomplish his goal, then rammed into her without even a preliminary kiss. But hell, she didn't need any foreplay. The savage little bitch was already dripping wet.

Holding her hips securely, he maneuvered her back and forth. She went crazy, scratching him, licking him, biting him, as they went at each other. It didn't take long for him to come. While he jetted into her, she climaxed and practically climbed him like a tree.

When he was able to catch his breath again, he started to release her, but she held tight and toppled them over the back of the sofa and down onto the cushions. With him lying on top of her, she licked his ear. He shuddered. Then she whispered, "I don't think Jazzy Talbot killed Jamie." She paused, apparently giving him a minute for her statement to sink in. "I think my sister Laura killed him."

Chapter 17

Jazzy wondered if her imagination was working over-time or if what she suspected was really true—that some-one was watching her. Had some nutcase decided she was fair game because the whole town thought she killed Jamie? Was some lunatic stalking her? Maybe.

But thinking back, she'd gotten some peculiar vibes a week or so before Jamie was murdered. She hadn't thought much about it, had actually dismissed the no-tion, but she could no longer shake that eerie feeling that somebody was following her, watching her, keeping tabs on her every move. It wasn't that she'd actually caught anyone in particular, it was simply a feeling.

Okay, Jaz, admit it—people are staring at you, whispering behind your back, pointing fingers. A few locals had been cruel enough to call her a murderer to her face. That's why she had avoided mixing and mingling with the cus-tomers at her restaurant and at Jazzy's Joint and spent her time in her office at each place. But there had been just as many people who'd tried to be nice by saying things like, "About time somebody killed that SOB." Or a few even said, "I don't blame you for torturing that sorry asshole to death." The bottom line was that just about everybody in Cherokee County believed she had killed Jamie.

The evidence had certainly piled up quickly. A bloody knife found in her office. Forensic testing had shown it was Jamie's blood. Then there was the book of matches from Jazzy's Joint—with her fingerprints on it—and the red scarf Jacob had given her as a birthday gift. Add to those things Tiffany's and Dillon's testimony about seeing a woman fitting Jazzy's description on the mountain road only a few hours before Jamie died. *But don't forget the most damning evidence of all,* she reminded herself. The fact that numerous people could testify to the fact that she had threatened Jamie. More than once.

Jazzy sank down on the sofa in the living room, drew her legs up to her chest, and circled her knees with her arms. Although Genny, Sally, Ludie, and Caleb had been smothering her with attention, almost as if they were afraid to leave her alone, she'd managed to persuade them that she needed some time by herself. Just an afternoon holed up in her apartment to sort through her feelings. It was bad enough having to deal with Jamie's death, but knowing it was only a matter of time before she was arrested for his murder was terrifying.

I didn't kill him. Those words repeated themselves over and over inside her mind . . . and her heart. *But you could have killed him. You're capable of murder. That terrible night only a few months ago, you came damn near close to shooting him. To blowing his balls off!*

Jazzy shuddered as those haunting moments played vividly inside her head. She would have shot him, possibly killed him, if he hadn't backed off. But she wouldn't have killed him out of hatred or for revenge. Not ever. Only to protect herself.

She needed a good lawyer. A smart lawyer could show a jury that all the evidence against her was either circumstantial or had been planted. Everything was too neat, too pat, so obviously planned to frame her.

First of all, neither Tiffany nor Dillon could swear the woman they saw driving a sports car up the dark mountain road was Jasmine Talbot. All they could say was that it was a woman with short red hair who might have been Jazzy. A good lawyer could point out that a woman who could pass for Jazzy's twin had been in town when Jamie was murdered. All she—or any woman, for that matter—would have needed was a really good red wig.

And the book of matches didn't really mean anything. Her fingerprints were probably on a lot of the matchbooks, since she usually was the person who placed them beside the ashtrays on all the tables at Jazzy's Joint.

The scarf was damning evidence, as was the knife. But she kept the scarf in her Jeep to use whenever she rode around with the top down. And half the time she didn't lock her Jeep. Anyone could have stolen the scarf.

Then there was the bloody knife. No person in their right mind would have hidden the murder weapon in their own office. Anyone who knew Jazzy knew she was too smart to have done something so stupid.

She began rocking back and forth, her thoughts shooting off into a dozen different directions as she tried to make sense out of her life. Jamie was dead. The man she'd loved, the man she'd hated. *Oh, Jamie, you might have been unkind and selfish and downright good for nothing, but you didn't deserve to die the way you did.* Just the thought of how he must have suffered made her heart ache. It seemed strange that she would never see him again, never hear his voice, never have to send him away . . . not ever again.

Tears gathered in her eyes. Unwanted tears. She had spent a lifetime crying over Jamie Upton.

Think about yourself. Concentrate on what you need to do to protect yourself. Maybe she should find herself a lawyer now, before she was charged with murder. But who? What about Maxie? He was the best trial lawyer in Cherokee County. But Maxwell Fennel didn't come cheap. *So? You're not exactly poor. You've got a hefty savings account. We're talking about your life here, Jaz. You could wind up in prison or even be sentenced to death.*

She had wasted enough time worrying, feeling sorry for herself and trying to make sense of what was happening to her. It was past time she took action. She jumped up from the sofa and headed for her desk. After pulling out the phone book from the bottom drawer, she flipped through the pages until she found Maxwell Fennel's office number. Just as she lifted the telephone receiver, she heard someone at her door.

Damn! She groaned. Well, it was either Genny, Sally, Ludie, or Caleb.

Jazzy returned the receiver to the phone base and went to answer the door. There stood Genny, a somber expression on her face and a look of doom in her black eyes.

"What's wrong?" Jazzy asked.

"We need to talk."

"Come on in."

Genny entered the living room. Jazzy closed the door. The two friends faced each other.

"Whatever it is, it's bad, isn't it?" Jazzy said, really not needing a response.

"Wade Truman is having a warrant for your arrest issued," Genny said. "As soon as the judge signs it, Jacob will have to arrest you."

Nausea churned in Jazzy's stomach. A weak, sinking feeling swept over her. She had known this was inevitable and yet the reality of it hit her hard.

"I was just fixing to call Maxwell Fennel. I guess I should go ahead and do that."

"I'll call Maxie," Genny said. "Then I think we should go on over to the sheriff's department so you can turn yourself in."

Jazzy looked at Genny, not quite comprehending what she'd said. "You think I should turn myself in?"

"The local media is already in a frenzy about Jamie's murder," Genny explained. "Once word leaks out that there's been a warrant issued for your arrest, all hell will break loose. Newspaper and TV reporters will be swarming around here and around the courthouse like a bunch of killer bees. If we go on over to Jacob's office and wait, we might avoid the worst of it."

"Damn Brian MacKinnon. I'll bet he's enjoying this. As much as he dislikes me, you know he'll slant everything on his TV station and in *The Cherokee Pointe Herald* against me."

"Forget Brian. We can't do anything to stop him from doing whatever he wants to do. Our biggest concern right now is hiring Maxie and getting him to meet us over at Jacob's office."

"You're right. To hell with Brian Fucking MacKinnon. One of these days that maggot will get his."

"Jazzy, my Lord, will you stop shooting off your mouth? Everything you say is going to be scrutinized, and when you say something like that people will twist it around so that they can call it a threat."

"Well, shit, Genny, you might as well ask me to stop breathing. You know how I am. I say whatever pops into my head. And I didn't mean I'd personally see that Brian gets his."

"I know." Genny offered her a wavering smile. "Look, go freshen up, change clothes or whatever, then grab your purse and let's head out. In the meantime, I'll put in a call to Maxie and ask him to meet us over at the courthouse."

"Find out how much money he'll charge me up front," Jazzy said as she headed for her bedroom. "I might need to transfer some funds out of my savings account."

"I'll ask," Genny said. "And Jazzy . . . if you wind up having to hire a more high-powered lawyer than Maxie and need some help, financially, Dallas and Jacob and I want to—"

"Damn it, you're going to make me cry." Jazzy didn't dare turn around and face her best friend. If she had, she would have burst into tears. "If worse comes to worst, I can always sell Jasmine's and Jazzy's Joint."

"No, you won't. If it turns out Maxie can't handle this case, we'll hire you the best damn lawyer available, no matter what the cost."

Jazzy ran into the bedroom and closed the door behind her. With tears trickling down her cheeks, she leaned back against the door and thanked God for good friends. And while she was praying, she also asked God to help Jacob and Dallas find out who had really killed Jamie.

The room was quiet. The only sound was her own soft voice as she hummed to her baby. Her precious daughter. So tiny. So pretty. And so dependent on her. *Don't you worry, my little angel, I'll take good care of you.* It was a mother's duty to love and care for her child, to protect that child from the evil in the world. And there was so much evil, so much cruelty. Bad people doing bad things to her. Mean people plotting behind her back, saying terrible things about her.

As she rocked back and forth, cradling her baby in her arms, she whispered, "You're safe. No one can hurt you. And no one can ever take you away from me again."

He had said he loved her. He'd made her promises he never intended to keep. To love, honor, and cherish. But he had lied. Her feelings hadn't mattered to him, not as long as he got what he wanted.

She held her child close to her heart. "But he'll never have you. He'll never hurt you. They're all alike. Men who tell you they love you, then throw you away and pretend you never existed. And there is always a woman who lures them into evil. A wicked woman who deserves the same punishment for her sins."

Mustn't get upset, she told herself. *Everything is all right for now. I'm safe. My daughter is safe. Jamie Upton is dead. He can't hurt anyone ever again. Now all I have to do is bide my time and the law will punish Jasmine Talbot. She will suffer as we have suffered.*

She continued humming, a lullaby from long ago. Hadn't she sang this same song to another baby? Had there been another baby? No, of course not. There was only her little girl, the baby she held in her arms. The child who was safe. The child he couldn't hurt. The little girl he could never take away from her.

At the right moment, I will make him very, very sorry for what he did. He thinks he's safe. He has no idea that he will die soon. He shouldn't have let us down the way he did. I might have forgiven him and killed him quickly if he'd been a better father, if he had protected you and kept you from harm.

Not yet. Wait. There is no need to hurry. She had found him, and if he tried to escape, she would simply follow him. He couldn't get away from her. Wouldn't he be surprised when he saw her, when he realized who she was and that she was going to kill him?

Caleb flagged Genny down a block away from the courthouse. He stood in the middle of the street and waved his arms. She slammed on the brakes and rolled down the window. Before she could say a word, Caleb ran toward her Chevy Trailblazer.

"Let me in," he called out to her as he grabbed for the back door handle on the driver's side.

The minute Genny undid the locks, Caleb opened the door and jumped in the back seat. "Drive around to the rear entrance at the courthouse."

"What's wrong?" Genny asked.

Jazzy turned halfway around in her seat. Her gaze connected with Caleb's and held.

"Word's out that Jazzy is going to be arrested for Jamie's murder. There's a horde of reporters out front, along with TV cameras ready to follow Jacob when he leaves the courthouse or to catch you the minute you arrive to turn yourself in."

"How do you know?" Jazzy asked. "Did—"

"I told you that word's out all over town." Caleb leaned over the console and placed his hand on Jazzy's shoulder. "Jacob and Dallas have posted deputies and officers at the front and back entrances, but it's going to be a madhouse trying to get you into Jacob's office."

"Go ahead, Genny," Jazzy said. "I've got to face the reporters sooner or later. We might as well get this over with."

"Maxwell Fennel is waiting for you outside on the courthouse lawn and his presence is causing quite a stir," Caleb told them. "He's already pleading your case to the press."

"For what I'm paying him, he'd damn well better be doing a good job." Jazzy laughed, but there was no humor in the sound.

Caleb would like nothing better than to take Jazzy away from Cherokee Pointe, to run off with her to some tropical island and forget Jamie Upton ever existed. He hated what was happening to her and felt helpless to protect her against the injustice of being charged with a crime she hadn't committed. What she needed more than anything right now was a topnotch lawyer. Somebody who didn't know the word defeat, somebody with a reputation for always winning. The first name that came to mind was Quinn Cortez. Cortez was the premiere trial lawyer in the south and southwest. He had successfully defended a slew of accused murderers. But Cortez came with a high price tag. His retainer alone ran into six figures.

Caleb didn't have the kind of money it would take to pay Cortez's astronomical fee—and even if the guy did owe Caleb a favor, he could hardly ask him to work for peanuts. But Caleb knew someone who did have that kind of money, somebody who'd driven into town in a Jaguar, someone who was probably Jazzy's sister. But before he could approach Reve Sorrel, he needed some information on the lady. He still had contacts in Memphis who'd probably help him.

When Genny turned her SUV off the street and into the parking area behind the courthouse, reporters descended on the Trailblazer like a swarm of angry bees.

"Now what do we do?" Genny asked.

"We wait here, with the doors locked and the windows rolled up, until we get a police escort into the building," Caleb replied.

"This is Brian's doing," Genny said. "He's somewhere nearby. I can sense his presence. He's watching. And he's enjoying every minute of it."

"Sadistic bastard," Caleb grumbled under his breath.

Jacob came out the back door of the courthouse, Dallas at his side. Deputies Tewanda Hardy and Tim Willingham, working with a couple of Dallas's officers, parted the throng of reporters and curiosity seekers while Jacob and Dallas made their way to the Trailblazer. They came to the driver's side and motioned for Genny to open the door.

"Just park right here. Then I want everybody to get out on this side," Dallas said. "Genny, we'll put you and Jazzy between Jacob and me." He glanced in the backseat at Caleb. "You stay right behind them, and we'll put Tewanda in front so we can keep them surrounded until we make it to the office."

Caleb nodded and the minute both women were out of the vehicle, he hopped down to the ground and came up behind them to guard the rear. Moving as quickly as the encroaching horde allowed, they headed toward the back door. Reporters shouted questions. TV cameras rolled. And inch by slow inch, they came closer and closer to the courthouse back entrance.

"Don't nobody blame you for killing him, honey," a female voice in the crowd shouted.

"He deserved what he got," another woman yelled.

"You're a murderer," one man bellowed.

And another yelled, "You're a no-good slut. A murdering whore. You're going straight to hell."

Every instinct in Caleb demanded that he tear through the crowd and beat the hell out of everybody who dared say anything bad about Jazzy. But what good would that do her? None. Absolutely none. However, he knew what he could do for her. First, he'd post bond for her as soon as she was booked. He figured he had enough saved up to cover it. Second, he'd make a phone call to a man who owed him a favor. He'd never intended to call in Cortez's marker, but this wasn't for himself. It was for Jazzy. And after he got the info he needed on Reve Sorrell, he'd see if he could twist her arm into coming up with some cash. Even if Cortez did owe him, he doubted the man would take on Jazzy's case for nothing.

Caleb reached out, placed his hand on the small of Jazzy's back, and kept it there as they entered the courthouse and quickened their pace on their trek to the sheriff's department. He wasn't going to let her go through this alone. One way or another, he intended to take care of her.

Chapter 18

Jazzy was grateful for one thing above all else—that she had good friends she could count on. Otherwise she'd be spending the night in jail. Of course, it didn't hurt that two of those friends just happened to be the chief of police and the county sheriff. And with Maxwell Fennel, a man with more clout with the judges than any lawyer in the county, on her side, a reasonable bond had been set despite the charges being second degree murder. Jacob had explained that Wade Truman would have gone for first degree, but knew he'd never make those charges stick. The evidence against her, though plentiful, wouldn't hold up well under close scrutiny.

"If Big Jim hadn't put the pressure on Wade, we wouldn't have made an arrest so quickly," Jacob told her. "Seems Miss Reba wants her pound of flesh. Actually, to be more accurate, she wants a pound of your flesh."

Whatever Big Mama wants, Big Mama gets, Jamie had said numerous times.

Miss Reba. God, how that woman had fucked up her life. Jamie's grandmother had despised her from day one. If it hadn't been for Miss Reba, Jamie would have married her when they were teenagers and he'd knocked her up. But Jazzy hadn't been good enough for the Upton heir. Miss Reba had wanted him married and mated to a blue blood, to somebody whose folks had the kind of money and breeding the Uptons did.

At this precise moment, Jazzy felt nothing. No pain or anger or fear. It was as if something had shut down inside her and her ability to feel had gone into hibernation. An odd sort of numbness had settled over her once the booking process began. Of course, Maxie had earned his retainer when Jacob had questioned her. Wade Truman had been on hand for that, and, to give the devil his due, he'd appeared to be rather uncomfortable with the whole situation. Of course, the fact that whenever he was allowed anywhere near her, Caleb had continuously given the DA the evil eye might have had something to do with Wade's discomfort.

Jazzy walked up the outside stairs that led to her apartment above Jazzy's Joint, Caleb's strong arm around her waist. He hadn't left her all this time, during the seemingly endless hours it took for her to be fingerprinted and photographed and her personal information to be recorded.

Jacob and two deputies remained on the street below, fending off the reporters who had been lying in wait for Jazzy's return. As Caleb took her key from her and unlocked the front door, she could hear the newshounds shouting questions at her. She didn't care what they asked. Didn't care what they said about her in print. There were a lot of things over which she had no control, and the press was one of those things, as was being accused of Jamie's murder.

Once inside, Caleb gave her a gentle push toward the sofa. "Go sit down." He closed and locked the door. "It's nearly eight-thirty and you haven't had any lunch or supper. I'm going to fix you something to eat."

Jazzy shook her head. "I'm not hungry."

Caleb came up behind her, grasped her shoulders and walked her to the sofa. "Sit."

She sat.

He knelt down and removed her shoes. After easing her legs up on the sofa, he pulled a knitted afghan off the back and placed it over the lower half of her body. "You're eating something, even if it's just half a sandwich." He stuffed a couple of throw pillows behind her and urged her to lean back and relax. "If I don't take very good care of you, I'll have to answer to Genny and your aunt Sally."

"Believe me, answering to those two would be a fate worse than death," Jazzy told him and realized despite everything she hadn't lost her sense of humor.

"Don't I know it." Caleb grasped her chin and ran the pad of his thumb over it in a lingering caress. "Try to put all of it out of your mind. At least for now."

Jazzy nodded, knowing it was the response he wanted, even if it was a lie. She watched him until he disappeared into her small efficiency kitchen, then she closed her eyes and hugged herself. Although she hadn't cried a drop since being arrested, she felt drained. The numbness was wearing off and exhaustion was taking its place. She burrowed her head into the pillows and cuddled her body against the back of the couch.

Even with the doors and windows closed, she could still hear the rumble of reporters outside being kept at bay by the deputies. In the days and weeks ahead, they would hound her. Brian MacKinnon would see to that. Every aspect of her life would be put under a magnifying glass and written about in detail for the whole county to see. If—God forbid—the grand jury decided to bring down a ruling in favor of indicting her for Jamie's murder, she could lose her freedom. But she had already lost something as precious as freedom, actually a part of true freedom. She had lost her privacy. Everyone had secrets, things they would prefer the world never know. She supposed she had more skeletons in her closet than most. Yeah, sure, a lot of folks knew a little about her past history, but a great deal of what they thought they knew was nothing more than supposition. If you took a poll of the locals, sixty percent would tell you that Jazzy Talbot was the illegitimate daughter of Sally Talbot's baby sister. The other forty percent would swear Jazzy was Sally's child. Jazzy had a birth certificate that proved she was Sally's niece, born to Corrine Talbot on July twenty-first.

A local poll on what happened to Jazzy and Jamie's baby would end up pretty much a ninety-five percent agreement that Jazzy had gotten an abortion when she was sixteen. But a handful of folks knew the truth—she had miscarried in the first trimester. And everyone who knew her, except the ones closest to her, would swear that Jazzy Talbot was a good-time girl who had spread her legs for half the men in town. That was most definitely false. But no one would ever believe that she could count all her lovers on her fingers. Less than ten. Not lily-white by any means, but not exactly the harlot of the century, either.

Yeah, she liked to flirt. And when a woman looked like she did, men just naturally drooled over her. Was that her fault? Maybe. She had never done anything to dispel her bad reputation. Actually, she had done the exact opposite and fostered her town whore image. Just like Aunt Sally had often said, Jazzy sometimes cut off her nose to spite her face. It was that damn, mile-wide stubborn streak in her.

Sighing, she rubbed the back of her neck. Damn, she was tired. She closed her eyes. Weariness overcame her. Not just a physical and mental weariness. No, it was more than that. Jazzy was heart weary. Soul weary.

Dallas Sloan hung up the phone and turned to Jacob. "You are not going to believe this."

"Was that Teri?" Jacob asked. "Did she come up with something on McCord?"

"Indeed she did." Dallas mulled over the information his friend and old lover, who still worked for the FBI, had complied on Caleb McCord. The man was a real surprise on more than one count.

"Well, are you going to tell me or make me guess?" Jacob leaned back in his swivel chair and propped his big feet up on his desk. "It's been a long day and I'm really not in the mood for twenty questions."

"Sorry." Dallas shrugged. He couldn't help stretching out the suspense just a little, despite knowing what a short fuse Jacob had. In the few months they'd known each other, they had become friends. Good friends. And when Dallas married Genny, Jacob would practically be his brother-in-law. "We knew McCord was from Memphis and that he was a detective on the Memphis police force. But we didn't know he was one of the youngest men to ever make detective or that he was a well-respected, well-liked, multidecorated cop."

"What do you know." Jacob grinned as he lifted his coffee mug to his lips and downed the last sip.

"I know that wasn't a question, but I do just happen to have a lot more information." Dallas wondered if Jacob's take on this startling new info would be the same as his. He'd bet his last nickel that it would be.

"You're enjoying this too damn much. Whatever it is,

it must be good." Jacob eased his feet off his desk, shoved back his chair and stood. "Don't tell me. McCord turned out to be a dirty cop." Dallas shook his head. "He screwed up and got kicked off the force?" Dallas shook his head again. "Whatever this other information is, it has nothing to do with him being a policeman, does it?"

"Bingo!" Dallas walked over to the coffeemaker on the corner table, picked up a clean mug, and poured himself a cup. "Just to set the record straight, McCord was a topnotch cop."

"Just spit it out, will you?"

"Teri had no idea that just by checking simple things like McCord's birth records, his school records, and so on, that she'd blow McCord's cover here in Cherokee County," Dallas said. "You know what McCord's name is?"

"It's not Caleb McCord?"

"Yeah, but it's his middle name you might find interesting." Dallas paused for effect, then said, "The name on his birth certificate is Caleb Upton McCord. His father is listed as deceased. A guy named Franky Joe McCord."

"And the mother's name?"

"Melanie Upton McCord. Does that ring a bell? Is she related to Big Jim Upton?"

"Melanie Upton was Big Jim's daughter," Jacob said. "My God, that means—"

"Caleb McCord is Jamie's first cousin."

"And the sole heir to the Upton fortune now that Jamie is dead."

Caleb placed the tray on the coffee table in front of the sofa. When he turned to tell Jazzy that supper was served, he realized she was fast asleep. Worn to a frazzle. She lay there cuddled in the fetal position as if protecting herself. *Let me protect you,* he wanted to say. *Let me take care of you.*

There had been other women in his life, but not that many. He'd always been the type who preferred quality over quantity. And he'd never actually been in love. In lust several times, but never in love. And maybe he wasn't in love with Jazzy. He was smart enough to know that desperately wanting a woman and loving one wasn't the same thing. But damn it all, from the night they met at Jazzy's Joint—the first time he rescued her from Jamie—he'd realized that Jasmine Talbot was different from all the other women he'd known. It had been a gut-level reaction. A recognition. And despite the fact that she'd still been partly hung up on Jamie, Jazzy had felt it, too. He knew she had. The sexual tension between them had been electric. If he had just pushed a little harder that night when he walked her to her door, she'd have invited him in. He'd gone over that night a thousand times, and every time he mentally kicked himself for being such a damn gentleman. If only he had taken her to bed and fucked her like crazy, things would be different now. They'd be a couple, and she might not be the prime suspect in Jamie's murder.

Hell, maybe it was just his ego—or maybe it was part of that recognition thing between Jazzy and him—but he believed that once they made love, she would be his. Heart and soul. And that's what he wanted. Other men had possessed her body. And yeah, he sure as hell wanted that. But he wanted more. Only Jamie Upton had possessed her heart—ever since she was sixteen. He wanted her to love him like that, with all her heart. But what he wanted most, what he figured no other man had ever had, was a connection that went a lot deeper. Soul deep.

Just looking at her made his body hard and his mind

soft as mush. She was gorgeous. Classic features like an old movie star, like that sexy redheaded bombshell from the forties—Rita Hayworth. He knew she dyed her hair that shocking shade of bright red, but he figured that she was a real redhead, just a more subdued shade. And subdued was never a word anyone would associate with Jazzy. God, how that name suited her. She was sultry and sexy and seductive. And her sexuality and beauty was right out there, right in your face. During the three months he'd known her, he'd figured out that she wasn't the hot-to-trot little number most people thought she was. Unless she'd slept with Jamie—and he tended to believe her when she said she hadn't—there hadn't been a man in her bed since Caleb had known her. He suspected that her reputation as a tramp was grossly exaggerated.

Caleb lifted the afghan higher, enough to cover her to her shoulders. Then he leaned down and kissed her forehead. Leaving her to rest, he walked quietly over to the portable phone, picked it up, and carried it into the kitchen. He figured he'd try finding out what he could about Reve Sorrell on his own, and if his Memphis contact didn't come through for him, he'd go to Dallas Sloan. Although he liked Sloan and Butler well enough, he didn't know them any better than they knew him. He figured he could trust them where Jazzy was concerned, but he had a few secrets he'd rather keep hidden for the time being. If he got too chummy with them, they just might ask him too many personal questions.

Knowing Lieutenant Joe Donovan's cell number by heart, Caleb quickly punched the touch-tone keys and waited while the phone rang.

"Donovan here."

"Hey Joe, how are things in the River City?"

"Who the—McCord, is that you?"

"Yep."

"Where the hell are you, man? You just up and disappeared after you got out of the hospital."

"I'm in a picturesque little mountain town called Cherokee Pointe, Tennessee."

"Getting some R and R? Doing a little fishing?"

"Working as a bouncer in a juke joint."

Donovan laughed. "You're kidding me."

"The owner is a friend."

"A new friend?"

"Yeah."

"A lady friend?" Donovan asked.

"Yeah."

"You old dog, you."

"Think what you will," Caleb told him. "But I haven't called you to discuss my love life or lack thereof. I need a favor."

"Name it and it's yours."

"I want some information on a lady."

"Your lady?"

"No, not my lady. On a very rich, very stuck-up gal named Reve Sorrell."

"Sorrell . . . Sorrell. For some reason it rings a bell."

"How much do you think you can find out about her before morning?"

"Why the rush?"

"Because I figure the lady will be leaving town soon, probably tomorrow sometime, and I need that info fast."

"I'll see what I can do."

"I'd appreciate it."

"Hey, McCord . . . you all right?"

"Yeah, I'm all right."

"Glad to hear it. Some of us were . . . concerned, when you just up and left without a word."

"Call me as soon as you get anything on Reve Sorrel, okay?"

"Sure thing."

Jasmine Talbot had been arrested. The district attorney would present his case to a grand jury and then Jazzy would be turned over for trial. And she'd be found guilty. What a delicious thought: Jazzy suffering, paying for her sins. If there was any true justice, she would be sentenced to death. But if the charge was second degree murder, then imprisonment would be Jazzy's only punishment. If that happened, she knew what she had to do. But she wouldn't kill Jazzy, not until after she had suffered a great deal more. Not until after the trial. The way she had things planned, Jazzy would be the last to die.

Now that Jamie was dead and her plans for Jazzy were falling into place, she needed to do what she had originally come to Cherokee Pointe to do—take care of her baby and exact revenge on the others who had wronged her and her child.

It wasn't her fault that she had been separated from her baby. It was their fault. She would never have willingly let them take her away. How could anyone be so cruel as to separate a mother and child? But he hadn't cared—not about her and not about their little girl. If he had loved their daughter the way he said he did, he wouldn't have taken her away from a mother who loved her.

Tears moistened her cheeks. Was she crying? She didn't cry. Not anymore. There was no reason to cry. Everything was all right. Jamie was dead. Jazzy would be punished severely before she died. The others would pay for their sins. And her sweet baby was safe.

"You're safe, precious darling." She hurried across the room to where the baby lay sleeping in the middle of the bed. Beautiful baby girl. Safe. Safe with the mother who loved her. "You want Mommy to hold you and rock you and sing to you, don't you? That's what I want, too."

She lifted the child into her arms and kissed her sweet, pink cheeks as she carried her to the rocking chair. She sat down and began to rock and hum, the same lullaby she had sung to her other baby.

No, no, there was no other baby. Only this one. Only my little girl.

She stopped rocking and looked down at the child in her arms. "It's all right. Mommy's just a little confused. I thought you were my only baby girl, but . . . but she's my little girl, too. I killed Jamie to protect her. No, that's not right. I killed Jamie to protect you."

Sighing contentedly, she hugged her child to her breast as she began rocking and humming again.

Jazzy woke with a start, a scream frozen on her lips. She'd been dreaming. Crazy, mixed up things. Jamie's bloody hands reaching out for her, strangling her. *Don't panic,* she told herself. *It was only your subconscious mind telling you that Jamie is reaching out from the grave to destroy your life.* As if he hadn't done enough while he was alive!

Only a lamp in the corner of the living room gave off any light. A forty-watt bulb. She lifted her head and glanced around at the dimly lit area. Caleb sat in the chair across from her, his head bent, his breathing soft and even. He was asleep.

What time is it?

She threw off the afghan and swung her legs around so that her feet touched the floor. That's when she noticed the tray on the coffee table. Caleb had fixed her a sandwich and a cup of tea. Lifting her left wrist, she checked her watch. Eleven-eighteen. Jazzy's Joint would be closing soon and the rumble of jukebox music would fade away, as would the muffled sound of talk and laughter. One of the drawbacks of having an apartment over a bar was the noise at night. But since she was usually at Jazzy's Joint until it closed, the noise had never bothered her.

Jazzy's stomach rumbled, reminding her she hadn't eaten since breakfast. Wonder what kind of sandwich Caleb fixed? She leaned over and reached toward the tray. When she picked up the sandwich and discovered it was bologna and cheese on wheat bread, she smiled. He'd remembered her favorite.

She studied him as he slept, and everything female in her reacted to all that was so very male in him. For months now she had fought her attraction to Caleb, giving herself a hundred and one reasons not to have an affair with him.

Why did I fight so hard to resist him? Damn it, why didn't I just give in to what I wanted? Because you knew it would be more than sex with Caleb and you were afraid to love another man. Fucking is one thing, but loving is another.

Jazzy bit into the sandwich. Delicious. God, she hadn't realized how hungry she was. As she savored every bite, she groaned with satisfaction.

"If you react that way to eating a sandwich, I'm wondering how you react to real pleasure," Caleb said.

Jazzy gasped, then laughed and licked her lips. "I thought you were asleep."

"I was until somebody started moaning and groaning."

"You should have gone on home," she told him. "You didn't have to stay."

He yawned and stretched, then looked point blank at her. "Yeah, I did."

"Thanks. I'm glad you stayed. I really don't want to be alone."

"We're going to make sure you're never alone," Caleb said.

"We?"

"Genny, Sally, Ludie, and I. Whenever I can't be with you, one of them will be."

"Who decided I needed a full-time babysitter?" Jazzy gobbled up half the sandwich, then wiped her hands on the napkin beside the teacup.

"It was a unanimous decision. Even Jacob and Dallas voted in the affirmative."

Jazzy stood up and walked around the coffee table that separated the sofa from the chair where Caleb sat. She stood over him for a minute, then leaned down and placed her hands on his shoulders. "So does this mean you're spending the night?"

Caleb removed her hands from his shoulders, pushed her back, and stood. "Consider me your personal bodyguard."

Standing so close to him, she could feel his heat. And could almost hear the beat of his heart. Although she was five-eight, she had to look up at him because he was a good six inches taller. She draped her arms around his neck and gazed into his whiskey-golden eyes.

"Just who are you, Caleb McCord, and where have you been all my life?"

"Don't you know, sweetheart? I'm your prince charming, and I've been waiting for you to wake up from an evil spell so I could come riding in on my white horse and take you to live happily ever after with me in my castle."

Jazzy laughed. And God, it felt so good to laugh. She kissed him. Just a happy-to-be-alive kiss. A prelude to something more. He didn't take advantage, didn't press for anything else. Inside that rough and rugged exterior beat the heart of a true gentleman.

"I can sleep on the sofa," she told him. "Why don't you take the bed?"

"No, way. No white knight worth a damn would let a true princess sleep on the sofa."

"Is that the way you see me . . . as a princess?" Her heart fluttered wildly, as if it had never heard a compliment before tonight.

"Actually, Jasmine Talbot, you're not a princess." He caressed her cheek with the back of his hand as his gaze locked with hers. "You're a queen."

Tears misted her eyes. "Damn you, McCord. You're not real. You know that, don't you? You're too good to be true."

"Yeah, that's what all the ladies say."

With tears glistening in her eyes, she laughed again, and when Caleb put his arm around her waist and led her to her bedroom, she knew he wouldn't come in and stay. He was simply walking her to her door. He would sleep on the sofa. Like the true prince charming he was.

Chapter 19

When Caleb pulled his '57 Thunderbird, which he had personally restored a few years ago, onto the asphalt drive, he saw her putting her bag in the trunk of a dark blue classic Mercedes.

No doubt when she'd found herself ordered not to leave town, she'd sent someone from Chattanooga with another car. Odd how that at a distance she could easily pass for Jazzy, especially if her hair was shorter and a brighter red. At the same time, Reve Sorrell resembled Jazzy less from far away because she was probably a couple of inches taller—about five-ten, he'd say—and outweighed Jazzy by a good twenty pounds. He parked the car and got out. She ignored him completely as she headed back toward the rental cabin.

"Ms. Sorrell," he called to her.

She paused, but didn't turn around.

He'd made it here just in time. Another ten minutes and she'd have been on the highway headed back to Chattanooga. Of course, if he'd found her gone, he would have followed her—down Interstate 75, all the way home, all the way back to that big fancy house she owned on Lookout Mountain.

"We need to talk," he told her.

She glanced over her shoulder and pinned him with a don't-bother-me glare. "What could we possibly have to talk about, Mr. McCord?"

"Your sister."

"I'm an only child. I don't have a sister." She walked toward the cabin.

"You were adopted," Caleb said. "When you were an infant."

Her body tensed for a millisecond, barely long enough for him even to notice the pause in her quick steps.

"Spencer and Lesley Sorrell adopted a baby girl who had been thrown in a Dumpster and left for dead in Sevierville twenty-nine years ago. The birthday they gave you is only a few days different from Jasmine Talbot's birthday. Do you really believe it's nothing more than a coincidence that you two look enough alike to be twins?"

"We are not twins!" Reve halted and turned to face him. "I don't know how you found out such personal things about me, but I am not that Jazzy person's sister. I couldn't be."

"I think you are."

"Then you think wrong."

"When Jamie Upton told you about Jazzy, you were curious enough to hire a private detective to check her out. And once he provided you with information and pictures, you must have thought there was a chance you two were related or you wouldn't have come to Cherokee Pointe to see her, to check her out in person."

"I made a mistake," Reve said. "If you'll excuse me, I need to lock up before I leave."

"Why are you in such a hurry?"

"I have been delayed here for several days against my

will by that barbarian sheriff of yours because I bear a vague resemblance to a woman who murdered her lover and because I don't have an eyewitness to my whereabouts when the man was killed." Reve's cinnamon brown eyes flashed with anger. He'd seen that same expression on Jazzy's face countless times and couldn't help but wonder if, beneath those green contacts Jazzy wore, her eyes were as fiery dark as Reve's.

"Jazzy didn't kill Jamie," Caleb said. "She was with me part of the time that morning. She's been framed, and she needs a really good lawyer."

"What she does or doesn't need has absolutely nothing to do with me."

"Jazzy's blood type is AB negative." He paused to allow that bit of information to sink in, then said, "The same as yours."

She shrugged, but he caught a look of surprise she wasn't able to disguise. "So?"

"So that's a very rare blood type."

"It's just another coincidence."

"Jazzy's right handed and you're left handed. That's a trait many identical twins have."

"Go away, Mr. McCord. Nothing you say will persuade me to stay and become better acquainted with that woman."

"Is that why you think I'm here?"

"Isn't it?"

He shook his head. "Nope. Stay. Go. I don't care."

"Then why are you here? What do you want?"

"I want you to hire Quinn Cortez to defend Jazzy if the grand jury hands down an indictment."

She looked at him incredulously. "*The* Quinn Cortez?"

"Yeah, *the* Quinn Cortez."

"And why would you think I'd pay Mr. Cortez's enormous retainer for a woman I don't even know?"

"Because she's your sister."

"She is not—"

"Do you want all your highfalutin friends in Chattanooga and all your business associates to know that you were found in a Dumpster as an infant? Do you want them to know that your sister owns a honky-tonk, has a reputation as a loose woman, and is now on trial for killing her ex-lover? And do you want them to know that you hired a PI to check her out and, even after learning what sort of person she was, you still wanted to meet her?"

"Are you threatening to blackmail me?"

"I don't think I mentioned the word blackmail. I'm just telling you that if someone doesn't come up with the cash to pay Quinn Cortez, then—"

"What do you want me to do—write you out a check?"

Caleb grinned. Finding out how important the Sorrells' social standing was to Reve—and her own sterling reputation as well—had given him an advantage. He owed his old buddy Joe for coming up with the dirt on Ms. Sorrell so quickly.

"I'll call Cortez," Caleb said, "since I know him and he owes me a favor." When Reve opened her mouth to say something, Caleb shook his head. "Long story. No time for it now. Anyway, when I call Cortez, I want you to get on the phone, tell him who you are and that you'll be glad to pick up the tab for Jazzy. Then give him a credit card number or whatever the hell he requires."

"I could say no."

"Yeah, you could." Caleb's grin broadened into a wide smile. "But you won't."

"She must mean a great deal to you for you to resort to strong-arming me into paying you hush money."

"Don't look at it that way," he told her. "Just think of it as helping your sister."

"I told you that she is not my sister."

"Okay, have it your way. Jazzy is not your sister. But you two are definitely flip sides to the same coin. You pretend to be sugar, while Jazzy is definitely spice. You come across as being cold, calculating, snobbish, and unemotional. Jazzy's the exact opposite." Caleb walked over, grasped her arm, and said, "After we go inside and call Cortez and you put him on retainer, you can leave Cherokee County and never look back."

"And you won't tell anyone—"

He made a zipping-my-mouth gesture.

"Very well. Come inside and let's contact Mr. Cortez. The sooner we get this done, the sooner I can leave and put this entire nightmare behind me."

"Yeah, sure." Caleb loosened his hold on her arm and followed her into the cabin. Maybe she thought that once she went back to Chattanooga she could forget all about Jazzy, but he'd bet his old age pension—if he had one— that sooner or later Reve Sorrell's curiosity would bring her back to Cherokee County.

Jim Upton lay in the queen-size, pine sleigh bed, his breathing calm, his body relaxed. For the past hour, he had been able to forget that today was the day of Jamie's funeral, that this afternoon he would bury all his and Reba's hopes for the future. It was wrong of him to be here with Erin, to have made love to her with more passion than he'd felt in quite some time, when he was in mourning for his grandson. His wife was at home making preparations for the after-funeral reception at their home. Not only would three-fourths of Cherokee County's population wander in and out of their house later today, but friends and business associates—as well as the governor and both U.S. senators—would come by to pay their respects.

Erin caressed him, her slender fingers twining around the thick white hair on his chest. "It's all right, you know," she told him. "You mustn't feel guilty about our making love. The death of someone near and dear to us makes us need to reaffirm that we're alive." She propped herself up beside him, then leaned over and kissed his mouth in that sweet, tender way of hers.

"I can't leave her, you know," Jim said.

"Are you talking about Miss Reba?" Sighing, Erin lay back down alongside him and snuggled close. "You've told me before that you won't divorce her, so why bring that up now?"

He flipped over on his side and looked into her eyes. "That morning . . . before I found out about Jamie being murdered, I came here to talk to you."

"You came here? Why haven't you said—"

"You weren't here."

"No, I wasn't."

Where were you? Who were you with? Did you spend the night in another man's arms? "I came here to tell you that I had decided to ask Reba for a divorce. I wanted us to have a few years—however many I've got left—together. As man and wife."

"Oh, Jim. I—I don't know what to say."

"That's changed now. You see that, don't you? How could I ask her for a divorce now that we've lost Jamie? He was all—" Jim clenched his teeth. "I don't want to lose you, but I'll understand if you don't want to continue our affair."

Erin wrapped her arms around him and laid her head on his chest. "I'm not going anywhere. I love you. I want whatever you can give me."

He caressed her naked back. Soft, pale skin, dotted here and there with small, dark moles. He knew every inch of her. Had kissed those little moles, had memorized their locations. "Where were you?"

"The morning you came by here and I was gone?" She reached down and grasped his hand.

"If there's someone else—"

"Don't."

"You're still young and—"

"I went to Knoxville. I spent the night with a friend. And before you ask, the friend is female. She's a doctor."

Jim tensed, fear zipping through him like a fast-acting drug. "Are you ill?"

"No, my heath is fine. This friend is a gynecologist. I had called and asked her to put together some information for me about in vitro fertilization. About using a donor egg and a husband or lover's sperm."

"I don't understand." Jim rose into a sitting position.

Erin came up beside him, looked him in the eye, and said, "I'm too old to give you a child, as much as I wish I could. I knew how disappointed you were with Jamie, how much you wished there had been other grandchildren. I thought that if—"

"My sperm, a donor egg, and you'd carry the child in your body." Jim reached down and laid his hand over her flat belly. "You love me that much?" Tears misted his eyes.

"Now I have more reason than ever to want to give you—"

He cupped her face with his hands and kissed her. "You don't know what your offering to try something like that means to me. But you're not the only one too old to have a child. I'm seventy-five. Even if I'm not shooting blanks these days, do you know how old I'd be when

our child is ten? Eighty-five. Eight-five fucking years old.
It wouldn't be fair to the child."

"Yeah, I know." Tears trickled down Erin's cheeks.
"What ten-year-old would want a sixty-year-old mother?"

Jim hugged her to him, loving her more than he'd
loved anything or anyone, at this moment loving her
even more than he'd loved Melva Mae Nelson all those
years ago. He kissed her forehead and asked in a whisper, "Will you come to Jamie's funeral?"

"Oh, Jim, I don't know. How will I be able to bear
being there and not being able to comfort you?"

"Just knowing you're there, close by, will be a comfort. Please . . ."

"Yes, of course, I'll be there."

The Congregational Church was packed to capacity,
the sanctuary and the vestibule. A crowd had gathered
outside on the front steps and down the sidewalk. She
knew that these people weren't here to show their respects to Jamie. Not many people had liked Jamie. Quite
a few had despised him. And several had hated him, as
she had. The huge outpouring of sympathy was for Big
Jim and Miss Reba. Even people the Uptons barely knew
or didn't know at all had come together on this beautiful, sunny spring day. She suspected that even a few curious tourists mingled among the local citizens inside
and outside the church.

The sheriff and the chief of police were here, both in
their dress uniforms, making their presences official,
reminding everyone that Jamie had been murdered.
Tortured and tormented. Made to suffer. Punished for
his sins. She'd seen to that. She'd made sure he would
never hurt her, her child, or any other woman—not
ever again.

Jazzy Talbot was conspicuously absent. Good. She'd hate to think that worthless slut would dare to show her face.

As she watched while others paraded by Jamie's closed casket, she had to fight the urge to smile—even laugh. She had destroyed his pretty face and silenced his lying mouth. And now Jazzy was suffering.

But not nearly as much as she would suffer.

The woman had to die.

Deserved to die.

Would die.

But not yet.

When this all came to an end and everything was as it should be, Jazzy would be the last to die. After that, she and her baby would be safe. Safe and happy forever.

The Congregational Church choir stood outside the canopy covering the open grave as they sang an old spiritual, one the minister had said was Miss Reba's favorite. At least a couple of hundred people had come over directly from the church to the cemetery, while others were waiting to drop by the Upton house later.

Caleb had thought about going to the house, seeing what it looked like inside, getting an up close look at his grandparents. After being in Cherokee County for over three months, he still hadn't been able to work up enough courage to knock on the door and tell Big Jim and Miss Reba that he was their daughter Melanie's son. Hell, they probably wouldn't believe him. They'd think he was some opportunist out to sucker them. And who could blame them, especially now that they'd lost Jamie. Caleb knew that if his mother's revelation about her family hadn't been a deathbed confession, he probably wouldn't have believed her. Actually, at the time he *hadn't* believed her, had thought what she'd told him about her idyllic life as a rich girl had been nothing more than the ramblings of a drug addict, which his mother had been.

"You have a family," she'd told him. "My family. In Cherokee County, not far outside of Knoxville. I grew up there. On a farm. The Upton Farm. I had a wonderful childhood. Wonderful parents. Jim and Reba Upton. And I have a brother, Jim, Jr."

"Why are you telling me this now?" he'd asked her as he held her hand.

"Because you're just a boy and you need somebody to look after you. Go to my father and tell him . . . tell him I'm sending him a present. A grandson he never knew he had."

That had been fifteen years ago, right before he turned seventeen. He'd been a undisciplined kid, a boy who'd fended for himself most of his life, despite having a mother. When she'd been clean and sober, Melanie had been loving and kind and a halfway decent parent. But when she backslid into that drug-induced black abyss she couldn't escape for long at a time, he'd been on his own. The first time he stole food from the supermarket, he'd been seven and hadn't eaten in two days.

If it hadn't been for Joe Donovan's old man, a Memphis cop who'd taken an interest in a street smart kid with a penchant for getting into trouble, Caleb might be in the pen now. Instead, he'd wound up emulating his mentor and becoming a policeman. Then, six months ago, while on an undercover assignment, his partner had been killed and Caleb had spent weeks in the hospital recovering from gunshot wounds that had come damn near close to ending his life. That experience had changed him, and when he'd left the hospital, he'd known he didn't want to go back to his old job, his old life. While he was trying to sort through everything and decide exactly what he did want to do with the rest of his life, he got to thinking about what his mother had told him. She had a family in Cherokee County. *He* had a family.

Caleb figured that he could easily blend in with the crowd here at the cemetery, that nobody would even notice him. But he'd been wrong. Jacob Butler sure as hell noticed him. The six-five quarter breed had been eyeing him for the past few minutes, making Caleb feel very conspicuous. Was the sheriff wondering why Caleb would show up at the graveside of a man he'd loathed? Was Butler thinking that maybe there was some credence in what a few folks had speculated—that Caleb had either killed Jamie himself or at the very least had been an accomplice?

Ignore Butler, he told himself. *He's just trying to intimidate you.* Despite the sheriff's imposing size and tough-guy reputation, Caleb was more annoyed than intimidated. It would take a lot more than a killer stare to put the fear of God into him.

Caleb eased through the throng of mourners and away from Butler. He found a spot near a large, weathered oak tree that gave him a clear view of the family as they sat beneath the dark green canopy covering Jamie's open grave. His gaze traveled across the front row, seated closest to the shiny bronze casket. Big Jim Upton lived up to his reputation. He was big, robust, and physically fit for an old man. Although somber and quiet, he looked as if he was about to burst into tears. His big arm draped his small blonde wife's shoulders. Miss Reba had to be at least seventy, but she'd easily pass for sixty. If he'd ever doubted his mother's story about belonging to this wealthy, illustrious Tennessee family, taking a good look at Reba Upton erased those doubts. Although a taller, larger woman than Miss Reba, his mother had been the lady's spitting image.

Caleb studied the woman who was weeping quietly, doing her level best to remain dignified in front of the world while her heart was breaking in two. This was his grandmother. The woman who had given birth to his mother. The protective male side of his nature wanted to go to her, comfort her, tell her that she hadn't lost everything, that she still had one grandchild.

Laura Willis sat on the other side of Miss Reba, her body rigid, her eyes glazed. The poor girl was drugged senseless. Dr. MacNair stood at the side of Laura's chair, his hand on her shoulder. The Willis family—mother, father, and younger daughter—sat in the second row of folding chairs. Sheridan was staring a hole through her sister. *She hates her,* Caleb thought.

As his gaze traveled around the outer perimeter of the tent, he spotted Erin Mercer standing where she had a perfect view of Big Jim. As he watched her, he noticed how she seemed totally transfixed on something. He followed her line of vision straight to his grandfather and caught Big Jim staring straight at Erin. If he had noticed that intimate exchange, then others had, too. But it was no secret around town that the lovely middle aged artist was Big Jim's lover.

Caleb didn't know who to feel sorry for—his grandmother or Erin Mercer. Hell, maybe he should pity his grandfather. It wasn't as if he knew enough about his mother's family to understand his grandparents' marriage.

The choir sang a final hymn when the minister finished his tribute to the deceased. Big Jim helped his wife to her feet. Unsteady, tears dampening her perfectly made-up face, Miss Reba allowed her husband to lead her to the edge of the open grave as the casket was being lowered into the ground. With each passing moment, she wept harder and harder.

Poor woman, Caleb thought. *Poor Miss Reba. Poor Grandmother.*

Suddenly Reba clutched the front of her black suit and gasped loudly, then crumpled in her husband's arms. At first Caleb thought she'd merely fainted, but then he heard Jim call out for Dr. MacNair. After a quick examination, the doctor shooed everyone aside.

"We have to get her to the hospital immediately," MacNair said. Then Caleb thought he heard the doctor say something about a heart attack.

Big Jim swooped his wife up in his arms and stomped through the crowd, all but running toward the black limousine waiting at the head of the funeral procession. Caleb stood by watching, as did the others at the cemetery, while Jim placed his wife in the limo and issued orders to the driver.

Murmurs rose from the crowd, everyone speculating about Miss Reba's health, some making odds on whether she'd live to make it to the hospital. Caleb caught himself on the verge of shouting at those insensitive bastards. Instead he shoved his way through the thick, milling crowd and rushed to his T-bird, parked along the road outside the cemetery gates. He started the engine, revved the motor, and within minutes caught up with the speeding limousine. He wasn't going to let Miss Reba die without knowing she had another grandson, one who sure as hell would like the chance to get to know her.

Jacob drove to the hospital with Dallas, since the two had gone to the funeral together. Neither had missed Caleb McCord's reaction to Miss Reba's collapse. He'd acted like a man who cared—genuinely cared—whether the woman lived or died. En route to Cherokee County Hospital, they'd briefly discussed the possibility that McCord might have had something to do with Jamie's murder. After all, he'd had more than one motive.

When they inquired about Mrs. Upton's condition, they were directed to the ICU waiting area upstairs and were told that there was limited seating.

"Already a crowd here?" Dallas asked.

"If it was anyone other than the two of you, I'd have told you to go home and call back later for an update on Mrs. Upton," the receptionist said. "We've had to post a guard outside the waiting room, mostly to control the press. Would you believe that WMMK brought in TV cameras?"

"Yeah, I'd believe it," Jacob said, knowing firsthand that Brian MacKinnon would stop at nothing, would stoop as low as he had to, in order to sensationalize the news on his TV and radio stations, as well as in his newspaper. "That's the reason we're here—to make sure this situation doesn't turn into a three-ring circus."

"I'll coordinate efforts with your chief of security," Dallas said. "If you'll point me to his office, I'll check in with him while the sheriff goes on upstairs and assesses the situation there."

The receptionist shook her head. "Mr. Carruthers, our security chief, is upstairs personally making sure no one bothers Mr. Upton."

"I see," Dallas said. "Thank you, ma'am."

They headed straight for the nearest elevator. On the ride up, neither said a word. The minute the doors opened, they heard a ruckus and saw two guards escorting a TV cameraman down the corridor.

Jacob walked over to a burly gray-haired man in uniform. "Hey, Charlie, need a little assistance?"

Charlie Carruthers grunted. "I've never seen anything like it. You'd think the queen of England was in our ICU the way folks are acting."

"Miss Reba's heart attack is big news, considering it happened at Jamie's funeral," Jacob said.

"That poor old woman." Charlie shook his head sympathetically. "It's no wonder she keeled over at the graveside. Not many of us could go through losing both our kids and then our only grandchild."

"Yeah, you're right about that." Dallas nudged Jacob in the side and nodded to a spot to the left, a few feet behind Charlie.

Jacob glanced over his shoulder and scanned the area where two hallways intersected. Leaning against the wall near an alcove where several vending machines stood, Caleb McCord looked down at the floor, his hands stuffed into his pockets and his shoulders slumped.

Jacob left Dallas talking to Charlie while he casually made his way down the hall toward the alcove. When he approached, McCord glanced up and their gazes locked instantly.

"You got a reason for being here?" Jacob asked.

"I might."

"A reason I should know about?"

McCord gave Jacob a speculative look. "Maybe you already know why I'm here."

"Maybe I do."

"Why would it be any of your business?"

"Jazzy didn't kill Jamie and we both know it. That means somebody else did."

"Yeah, so? Genny said it was a woman who tried to look like Jazzy. What's that fact got to do with—"

"Maybe this woman had help."

"Are you accusing me of something, Sheriff?"

"Nope. Just speculating. It was no secret that there

was no love lost between you and Jamie because of Jazzy. Maybe you figured the only way to get rid of the competition was to kill him. That's one motive."

"And now you've figured out that I might have another motive as well."

"Seeing how you're Melanie Upton's son, now that Jamie is dead, you're the heir to the Upton fortune. I'd say that's a damn good motive for murder."

Chapter 20

As one of the maintenance crew for Cherokee Cabin Rentals, Stan Watson not only did yard work—mowing grass, trimming shrubs, and raking leaves—but because he was pretty much a jack-of-all-trades, he had keys to every cabin so he could keep a check on the heat and air systems, the plumbing, etc. Even though it was springtime, it still got chilly around these parts some days and just about every night, so tourists often used their fireplaces. Checking on the Honey Bear Trail cabin's fireplace was on his to-do list for this afternoon, but it was nearly six and he took off work about that time every day.

"The last tenants complained that the damper on the fireplace flu wasn't working right," his boss had told him. "Make sure you check it real good before the place is rented out again and somebody builds a fire and gets smoke all in the cabin."

When he parked his old Chevy truck in the drive, he noticed there wasn't another vehicle anywhere around, so he assumed that nobody had rented the place today.

Cherokee Cabin Rentals' policy was to do all inside maintenance work when a cabin was vacant.

Stan got out of the truck. Then, as he stepped up on the front porch, he fished around in his pants pocket for the key ring. Just as he pulled out the set of keys, he heard a peculiar noise. Could it be a bear? he wondered. The black bears had come out of winter hibernation and sometimes made it this far down the mountain. He'd come face-to-face with more than one bear since he'd been working on the rental cabins.

Damn, there the sound was again. Could be a bear scratching around out back, but it sounded more like somebody digging. There wasn't another cabin closer than half a mile, and he was the only maintenance man who was supposed to be up here today.

Figuring no matter whether it was a bear or a person making the racket, if he confronted him, he might attack. Best if he had some sort of protection. He went back to the truck and picked up one of the heavy metal rakes lying next to the lawn mower and gas-powered weed eater. Creeping around the side of the cabin, he felt his heart beating ninety-to-nothing. It wasn't that he was afraid. Not exactly. Just cautious. When he got to the back of the cabin, he paused. He could still hear the noise, but didn't see anything or anybody.

Following the sound, he made his way down the slope at the back of the house, then skidded to an awkward stop when he saw a woman down in the wooded section of the hollow. At this distance, he couldn't make out much about her, except that she was definitely female—and she had short red hair.

What the hell's she doing? Stan wondered.

Curiosity got the better of him, so instead of calling out to her and warning her that she wasn't alone, he decided to get a little closer so he could make out what she was doing. When he got about twenty feet from her, he realized she was digging a hole. With her back to him, he couldn't see her face, but he didn't think he knew her. Still, she reminded him of somebody. She wore blue jeans and a dark plaid shirt. And a pair of cotton work gloves. Guess she didn't want to put any blisters on her hands. Women were funny about stuff like that.

Just when he started to holler at her, ask her what she was doing on private property, she stopped digging. He took several slow, cautious steps in her direction and that's when he noticed two things: she'd already dug a pretty deep hole, about three feet or more, and there was a big black plastic garbage sack a couple of feet to her right.

She's going to bury that garbage sack, Stan thought.

"Hey, there," he called out. "You can't be burying your garbage down there. This here is private property."

The woman froze to the spot. For several minutes she didn't move, didn't respond at all. She sure was acting like somebody who'd gotten caught doing something they shouldn't be doing. Then all of a sudden she whirled around and smiled at him. Damn! She wasn't no bad-looking woman. He didn't know her, but she sure looked familiar. He thought maybe he'd seen her somewhere.

"Hello, yourself." She laid the shovel aside and waved at Stan. "Who are you?"

"I'm the one asking the questions," he told her. "Who are you?"

She laughed and when she did, he relaxed immediately. Hell, she was just a woman. All soft and round and downright friendly. Nothing to be afraid of, he told himself. And there sure wasn't no reason to be hateful to her.

"Call me Honey," she said. "All my friends do."

He started down the hill; she started up.

"What are you burying?" Stan eyed the plastic garbage sack.

"You'd never believe it if I told you."

"Try me."

She laughed again and he found himself smiling as she came closer. "Well, I just got a divorce from a lying, cheating son of a bitch. I came up here with some of his favorite things, and I intend to bury them where he'll never find them. I want to piss him off, make him pay for being such a lousy husband."

Stan chuckled. "Can't say that I blame you. That's what I should have done with my ex-wife's things."

The woman came up to him and laid her hand on his arm. "Well, handsome, you didn't tell me your name."

"Stan . . . Stanley Watson, ma'am."

She squeezed his arm and batted her eyelashes at him. Damn if she wasn't flirting with him. Looking at her up close, he realized there was quite a few years' age difference between them, but what difference did that make? None really.

"You know, Stan, I haven't been with a man since I kicked my husband out nearly a year ago."

"Is that right?" *Good-looking and horny. The perfect combination in a woman, no matter how young or how old.*

She ran her hand up and down his arm, then placed her open palm over the center of his chest. His prick twitched. He hadn't gotten laid in several months, so he was pretty horny himself.

"You could help me bury my husband's stuff. Then we could get better acquainted."

"I'd be happy to help you, ma'am."

"Honey. Call me Honey."

"Well, Honey, let's get that bag of stuff buried," he

said and started following her down the hill. "I got a key to that cabin back up yonder. And I know for a fact that there's a mighty fine king-size bed inside."

Stan couldn't get that damn plastic garbage bag buried fast enough. After he patted the dirt into a neat mound, she reached out and took the shovel from him.

"I'll take this," she said. "It's mine, not my husband's."

Stan nodded, then picked up the rake he'd set aside earlier. Together they climbed up and out of the wooded hollow behind the cabin. When they reached the driveway, Stan told her, "I'll put this rake in the back of the truck and then open up the cabin."

"Do you mind if I put my shovel in your truck?" She followed him toward the pickup. "I parked my car down the road apiece. Maybe afterward you could drop me off there."

"Sure thing." All he could think about was the fact that in just a few minutes he was going to be screwing a good-looking woman.

He dropped the truck's tailgate, leaned over, and tossed the rake onto the bed. Just as he started to turn around and take her shovel from her, he felt something hard and heavy hit him on the head. Stunned by the unexpectedness and the horrendous pain, he didn't have time to react before another blow struck him. And then everything went black as he lost consciousness.

Jazzy cloistered herself in the office at Jazzy's Joint. She couldn't deal with customers right now. Not when Caleb wasn't here. He'd called to tell her he would be running late for work, but that he'd try to be there by nine. Since the place seldom got rowdy in the early hours of the evening, especially on a weeknight, she was sure Lacy and the two waitresses, Sheri and Kalinda, could hold down the fort. But she did have a business to run despite presently being Cherokee Pointe's most notorious criminal.

Genny had spent the morning with her, then Aunt Sally had taken over around one. The only way she'd been able to get her aunt to go home was to promise she would stay put in here in her office until Caleb came in to work. As much as she appreciated their concern, having them hovering over her was already getting on her nerves. She figured they thought today would be especially difficult for her, considering Jamie Upton had been buried this afternoon. A part of her wished she could have gone to his funeral.

A soft rapping on the closed door gained Jazzy's attention. Hoping it was Caleb, she glanced up from the paperwork she'd been doing. "Yes?"

The door eased open and Reve Sorrell walked in. "May I speak to you?"

Jazzy inspected the woman from top to bottom. Damn, they did look a lot alike. Reve Sorrell was taller than she and plumper, but not by any means fat. She certainly didn't do much with what she had. Her hair was the same natural auburn Jazzy's would be if she didn't use that fabulous shade of Hussy Red, and her eyes were the same deep reddish brown as hers were without her green contacts. Not only could Ms. Sorrell use more makeup and a new hairdo—who the hell wore their hair in bun these days?—but she should invest in some stylish feminine clothes. The navy blue slacks and jacket she had on, albeit probably the best money could buy, were almost masculine.

"I figured you'd already left town by now," Jazzy said.

"I . . . uh . . . I'm on my way out of town, as a matter

of fact. I had intended leaving by noon today, but that was before your boyfriend showed up and threatened me."

Jazzy stared quizzically at the other woman. "My boyfriend?"

"Do you have so many boyfriends that I have to name the specific one?"

"If you came here to insult me, you can leave. I've heard all the insults lately that I want to hear."

"I apologize. I came here to ask you . . . well, to make sure that I have your word, as well as Mr. McCord's, that what y'all know about me—about the possible connection between you and me—will remain between us."

What the hell was she talking about? Caleb had threatened Reve Sorrell? And what was this connection between the two of them? "I don't know what you're talking about."

Reve gave Jazzy a you're-lying stare. "Do you expect me to believe that he didn't tell you he'd run a check on me . . . on my background, and is using that information to blackmail me?"

Jazzy grinned. So the snooty Ms. Sorrell had something to hide, did she? "It would seem I'm not the only one with a shady past. Just what are you guilty of, Reve?" She emphasized the woman's given name.

"He hasn't told you?" Reve inhaled and exhaled slowly.

"I haven't seen Caleb since early this morning, but I'm sure he'll tell me everything when he comes in to work later."

"Mm-hmm. Yes, I'm sure he will."

"Look, whatever it is, your secrets are safe with me. Whatever deal you worked out with Caleb"—and Jazzy intended to find out exactly what that was all about—"is okay with me. Besides, I'm hardly in a position to throw stones at anyone else."

Narrowing her gaze, Reve stared at Jazzy, her expression pensive and uncertain, as if she couldn't quite figure Jazzy out. "I haven't murdered anyone, if that's what you're thinking."

"Neither have I," Jazzy told her.

Reve nodded. "Perhaps not, but you were arrested for Jamie Upton's murder, and that's something I'd prefer my friends and associates not know."

"Why would you care if your—just what sort of information did Caleb dig up on you?" What was it that Reve had said a few minutes ago? Something about a possible connection between *us*. Between Reve and Jazzy? "What's the connection between us that you don't want anyone to find out about?"

"I'd prefer to think there is no connection, but your Mr. McCord believes that we are sisters."

"That's not possible. Aunt Sally told me that my mother gave birth to only one baby. Me."

"Yes, and I hope she's right." Reve's jaw tightened; a pained expression crossed her face. "I was adopted when I was an infant. I had been left to die in a Dumpster in Sevierville. And that's something very few people know. So you see, I have no idea who my biological parents are."

Oh, holy shit! A cold, unnerving sensation crept through Jazzy. Would Aunt Sally lie to her? Maybe. But why? Was it possible that this rich, classy, stuck-up woman was her sister? "That fact alone doesn't make us sisters."

"My adoptive parents gave me a birthday—they guessed the date since the doctors told them approximately how old they thought I was. My birthday and yours are less than a week apart."

"And?" There had to be more; Jazzy could sense that Reve hadn't shared the most damning evidence with her.

"My blood type is AB negative."

Jazzy gasped. Damn! Double damn! "So is mine."

"Yes, that's what Mr. McCord told me."

"Then . . ."

"Being completely logical here, I have to admit that there is a chance you and I are biological sisters. Possibly twins."

Jazzy didn't know whether to laugh or cry. "Well, honey, don't act like it's a fate worse than death."

"You must see how totally ridiculous it would be for us to be sisters . . . I mean in any other way than genetically speaking, of course."

"Of course."

"We have nothing in common."

"Oh, I wouldn't say that."

Reve stared at Jazzy in her damn aggravating, superior way.

Jazzy said, "It would seem we just might have a mother and father in common."

Reve tensed visibly, as if the thought was more than she could bear. "Did you know your mother?"

"Corrine Talbot?" Jazzy shook her head. "She died when I was only a few months old. She had come to live with Aunt Sally during her last month of pregnancy."

"How did she die?"

"She left me with Aunt Sally—actually deserted me— and she got involved with some guy who wound up driving drunk and killing both of them. It seems she didn't have much luck with men. Not with my father or—"

"Do you know who your father was?"

"Got no idea."

"Did your mother give birth at the hospital here in Cherokee Pointe?" Reve asked.

"Nope. She had me at home. Aunt Sally and Ludie delivered me."

"And your aunt says that her sister gave birth to only one child."

"Aunt Sally has been known to lie if it suited her purposes."

"Why would she lie about there being another baby?"

"I don't know. Actually I don't know if she is lying. Maybe we're sisters, but not twins." Jazzy clicked her tongue. "No, that's not possible, is it? We're the same age."

"Look, Ms. Talbot . . . Jazzy . . . I'm curious, naturally. But I think it best for me—perhaps for both of us—if we don't pursue this matter. I don't need to know more. I'm perfectly happy with my life the way it is. And surely, considering your present circumstances, you have more important matters to consider than the possibility that you and I are biological sisters."

"You're ashamed of me," Jazzy said, then shrugged. "Can't say that I blame you. Who'd want to claim me as a sister?"

"I'm sorry." Reve took a hesitant step toward Jazzy, then stopped abruptly. "I've insulted you again, and that wasn't my intention. I wish . . . well, I hope things work out for you and that you're acquitted of Jamie's murder. Having Quinn Cortez defending you should give you every chance of being—"

"The Quinn Cortez?"

"Oh, that's right, Caleb hasn't told you." Reve snapped open her leather handbag, reached inside, and pulled out a business card. "I've hired Mr. Cortez to defend you, if the grand jury hands down an indictment." She held out the card. "This is my office address, phone number, and e-mail. If—if there's anything else I can do to help you—"

"You're paying for Quinn Cortez?" Jazzy couldn't quite get a grip on what was happening here. "Caleb blackmailed you into hiring Mr. Cortez?"

"Let's say we struck a deal."

"Is it that important to you to keep my existence a secret—if I am your sister?"

"I thought it was," Reve replied. "Yes, I suppose it is. I don't know. Look, just because I'd prefer for us not to be a part of each other's lives doesn't mean I want anything bad to happen to you."

"You're not exactly what you seem, are you, Ms. Sorrell?"

Reve smiled faintly. "Neither are you, Ms. Talbot."

Jazzy took the business card and stuffed it into one of her front pockets. "Nobody will ever know about any possible connection between us. Not from me. And not from Caleb. I promise."

"Thank you." Reve turned to leave, then paused, glanced back at Jazzy, and said, "I meant what I said. If there's anything else I can do to help you, don't hesitate to get in touch."

Before Jazzy could think of a suitable reply, Reve was gone. For a couple of minutes she stood there as if her feet were glued to the floor. Then suddenly she broke into a run and raced down the hall. Just as she entered the bar area, she saw Reve going out the front entrance.

Let her go, Jazzy told herself. *She's right—you have more important issues to deal with right now than whether or not Aunt Sally has been lying to you your entire life and she knew all along that you have a twin sister.* But once this mess with Jamie's murder was cleared up—and she had to believe that the real murderer would be caught—then she and Aunt Sally were going to have a family powwow.

Chapter 21

When Stan Watson came to, he had the mother of all headaches and his vision was blurry. "What the hell happened?" he asked no one in particular.

Suddenly he felt someone on top of him—a woman's pussy sliding down over his pecker. Good God, was he unconscious and having some sort of sexual dream? When she started pumping up and down on him, he decided this was no dream. This was real. He tried to grab her hips, but he couldn't seem to lift his arms. He gave his legs a try and couldn't budge them. That's when he realized he was tied down, his arms over his head, his wrists bound together. What was going on? *Think, Stan, think. Try to remember. You'd come up here to Honey Bear Trail to check on the fireplace. It was nearly six o'clock—your usual quitting time.*

Although his vision hadn't cleared up much, he looked up at the sky and realized the sun had already set. It wasn't good dark yet, but he figured it was getting close to eight o'clock, maybe later.

Who was on top of him? Had he brought a woman

up here? No, that wasn't it. He remembered now. He looked up into the woman's face and saw a blurry image—short red hair was about all he could make out.

Honey. She'd said her friends called her Honey. He'd gone to put his rake in the back of the truck before they went into the cabin and—she'd hit him over the head. He couldn't think of any other explanation. When he'd had his back turned to her, she'd coldcocked him with her shovel. But why? Was she crazy?

"Why'd you hit me on the head?" Stan asked.

"Here I am fucking you like mad and you're asking stupid questions." She paused in her frantic humping. "How else was I going to get you in the back of the truck so I could tie you down? I sure do appreciate your having that big roll of duct tape in your tool box and that length of rope so I could secure the tape on your feet to the trailer hitch and the tape on your wrists to the lock on that big heavy tool box."

"Lady, what's your problem? Are you freaking nuts?"

Something sharp sliced across his chest. He yelped in pain.

"That wasn't very nice of you, was it, calling me nuts," she said in a syrupy sweet voice. "You mustn't be mean to me or I'll have to punish you again."

"Lady, I haven't ever done anything to you. Please, just untie me and let me go. We'll forget this ever happened."

He felt his dick softening. Fear could do that to a man. And he was scared shitless right about now. An odd feeling hit him right in the gut. What if Jazzy Talbot hadn't killed Jamie Upton? What if this crazy woman on top of him had killed Jamie? Now was a hell of a time to remember why the woman he'd caught trying to bury a plastic bag in the woods reminded him of someone. At a distance, she looked a little like Jazzy. It was the short red hair and the gold hoop earrings. Otherwise they didn't really look anything alike.

"Oh, Stan, I'm sorry, I can't let you go." She started moving up and down on him, apparently trying to keep him hard. "Don't go flat on me now. Not when this will be the last fuck of your life."

Every muscle in his body froze. What did she mean by that? Oh, God. Oh, God. She was going to kill him.

"Why me? I don't even know you."

"But you caught me burying my bag of goodies, and I knew it was only a matter of time before you told somebody else and they'd tell somebody and then the law would come sniffing around. So you see, Stan, I can't allow you to live."

"I won't tell a soul. I swear." His heartbeat drummed in his ears. Adrenaline created by pure terror zinged through his body.

"You've figured it out, haven't you?" She kept riding him, moving faster and faster. "You know I killed Jamie." She went wild, her movements frantic. Then she screamed when she came. Breathing hard, she said, "I thought the least I could do for you before I kill you was give you a good fucking." She started moving again.

Stan's vision cleared and he could make out her face plainly. There was a look of determination in her eyes as she leaned over and dangled her breasts in his face. How the hell was it possible for him to be aroused when the woman on top of him was insane? She was going to kill him. But his body didn't seem to care. Tension tightened as she rode him harder and harder. He climaxed suddenly. While the aftershocks of his release rippled through him, she climbed off him and ran her fingertips down his chest, over his belly, and across his navel.

"Are you going to torture me the way you did Jamie?" Stan prayed harder than he'd ever prayed in his life. *Please, God, please let her kill me quickly.*

"I could, I suppose," she told him, her fingertips sliding down his damp, sticky penis. "I'd enjoy it so much. But like you said, we don't even know each other. I have no reason to hate you, no need to punish you severely."

"Don't kill me. Please, please, don't kill me."

"Oh, Stan, you beg so nicely." She cupped his penis and scrotum and laughed. "You were just in the wrong place at the wrong time."

"No, please . . . don't . . . don't—"

"Hush up now. I promise to make it quick." She squeezed his genitals. "I'll have to take these off. I took Jamie's, you know. I always whack 'em off. It's sort of my trademark."

Stan keened. Fear ate away at him like an insidious acid. "No. God, no!"

"Don't get so upset. I'll kill you first, then take my prize."

The last thing Stan Watson ever saw was the knife coming down toward his throat.

Jim Upton sat by his wife's bed in the ICU unit, her small, fragile hand held securely in his tender grasp. She had regained consciousness nearly an hour ago, a little before eight o'clock, and they had called him from the waiting room. He had already sent the others home— Laura, Sheridan, and their parents. And he'd asked friends who'd stopped by to go home and pray. He'd wanted to wait alone.

When he'd first walked into the ICU, Reba had looked up at him and tried to speak. The only word that came out of her mouth was a hoarse, gasped, "Jamie." A lone tear had escaped her right eye and cascaded down her pale cheek. Although the usual visitation time in the Intensive Care Unit was twenty minutes every four hours from six in the morning until ten at night, no one had tried to make him leave. And they'd damn well better not, if they knew what was good for them.

He watched Reba as she slept, a drug-induced sleep to keep her calm and rested, Dr. MacNair had explained. The stress of dealing with Jamie's death, the knowledge that he had been tortured to death, and then the funeral to say a final farewell had all been too much for her. Although there was a good chance she'd live through this, there were no guarantees that she wouldn't suffer another heart attack, maybe a massive, lethal one next time.

Jim squeezed her hand. "Don't die on me, old girl. Don't you dare die on me."

If only he could give her something to live for—a reason to fight. Guilt unlike any he'd ever known weighed heavily on his shoulders. Reba knew he'd never truly loved her. She suspected, even if she didn't know for sure, that there had been numerous other women. She might even know about Erin. Asking her to live for him was a ludicrous thought. Why should she want to live for him after the way he'd treated her all these years? Maybe she did still love him, but a part of her had to hate him, too.

"I'm sorry, Reba," he told her. "I wish I could have been a better husband."

If only they hadn't lost both Jim Jr. and Melanie. If only there had been other grandchildren. Jamie had meant the world to Reba, and now she had lost him, too. Tears sprang into Jim's eyes.

If only I could give you a good reason to want to live.

* * *

Caleb arrived at Jazzy's Joint a few minutes past seven. After his confrontation with Jacob Butler, he'd left the hospital, had walked around alone, and had done a lot of thinking. His big secret was out, and if Jacob knew, it was only a matter of time before Jacob told Jazzy. And he didn't want her to know—not yet. She'd been the reason he had kept putting off making contact with the Uptons. He had come to Cherokee County to find his mother's family, but after meeting Jazzy and learning about her connection to his cousin Jamie, he'd decided to wait. Jamie had been a topnotch son of a bitch. What sort of family produced a rotten apple like that?

But today when he'd watched his grandmother collapse right before his eyes, everything had changed. She was an old woman who might not live. He'd mistakenly thought there was no need to rush into claiming his new family, that he could wait around and get the lay of the land, so to speak. He had wanted the chance to find out a lot more about the Upton clan before he revealed himself as their long-lost grandson.

Lacy motioned to Caleb the minute he arrived, so he made his way through the crowded, smoke-filled room and went straight to the bar. He leaned over the counter so he could hear Lacy without her having to holler.

"We've been having a problem with a guy who's been shooting pool with Dillon Carson," Lacy said. "I tried to handle things when I saw neither Sheri nor Kalinda could do anything with him. Even Dillon, drunk as he is, tried to reason with the man. I didn't want to ask Jazzy, but—"

"You're a murdering whore!" The man's cruel shout could be heard over the country music coming from the jukebox, the clinking of bottles and glasses, and the talk and laughter created by the other customers.

"Damn!" Caleb cursed under his breath.

"She came out a few minutes ago and has been trying to get him to leave," Lacy explained. "He hasn't been that loud before, but I could tell from her facial expressions that he's been giving her a really hard time."

Of all nights for some smart-mouthed asshole to hurl insults at Jazzy—the night Caleb had come in several hours late. After his long walk to think things through, he should have come straight to work. Instead he'd gone back to the hospital. When he'd peeked into the ICU unit, the door to Miss Reba's room had been open and he'd seen Big Jim sitting by her bed, holding her hand, his face damp with tears. He'd come close to walking in on them and telling his grandfather who he was. But he figured now was the wrong time. The Uptons had been through hell these past few days. Besides, he needed to tell Jazzy first. He owed her that much.

"I'll take care of things," Caleb told Lacy.

Her friendly smile deepened the wrinkles in her lined face. "I knew you would."

When Caleb arrived on the scene at the back of the room where the pool tables were set up, he found a tall, lanky guy in his late thirties right up in Jazzy's face. He could tell by her expression that she was on the verge of slapping the man's face.

"No wonder Jamie Upton threw you away," the man said, his words slightly slurred. "You're nothing but trash and this whole town knows it. But you're going to be prison trash pretty soon, when they put you where you belong."

"Look, buddy, why don't you leave?" Dillon Carson, a bit unsteady on his feet, patted the man on the back. "No one wants any trouble. Isn't that right, Jazzy?" When he turned to her, the other man knocked Dillon's hand off his back.

"Yeah," Jazzy said. "You've got a right to your opinion, but you're not going to badmouth me in my own bar."

"I'll say whatever the hell I want about you wherever I want to say it." The man put his face closer to Jazzy's, not two inches between their noses. "And you can't do a damn thing to stop me, 'cause everybody knows what I'm saying is the truth."

Jazzy punched him in the middle of his chest. "Look, you stupid jackass, either you leave now or I'll call the police and have you thrown out of here."

The man grabbed Jazzy and shook her. She shoved him, but he held onto her tightly with one hand and drew back his other hand into a fist. Caleb dived straight at them, shoving Dillon aside and knocking him to the floor in the process. The guy on the verge of striking Jazzy never knew what hit him. Caleb rammed into him and sent him back against the wall lightning fast, twisting his arm behind his back. Then, pressing one arm across the man's throat and applying pressure, he subdued him immediately.

The man gasped for air. Caleb eased up just a fraction as he said, "You want to apologize to the lady now before I take you out of here or do I have to whip your sorry ass?"

"I'm not going to—" He choked when Caleb added more pressure to his windpipe.

When his face turned red and his eyes bugged out, Caleb eased up again and asked, "Are you ready to apologize to Ms. Talbot?"

"That's not necessary," Jazzy said. "Just get him out of here."

"It's necessary," Caleb said, glaring at the man. "Apologize or—"

"I—I'm sorry." The man looked at Jazzy, his moist eyes pleading with her. "I'm real sorry."

"Get him out of here, will you?" Jazzy's gaze collided with Caleb's, and he realized that she was more than a little upset.

Without saying another word, he marched the man through the crowd that had been watching the entire exchange. After they stepped outside onto the sidewalk, Caleb released his tenacious hold on the guy.

"If you know what's good for you, don't ever come back here again."

The guy nodded and all but ran down the street to his car parked half a block away. Caleb waited until he drove away before returning to the club. When he got back inside, he couldn't find Jazzy. Lacy pointed toward the hallway that led to the ladies' room, the storage room, and Jazzy's office. He'd check her office first.

The door was closed. He knocked. No reply.

"Jazzy?"

Silence.

He tried the knob. Not locked. He opened the door. She sat on the front edge of her desk, her arms crossed over her chest. When he walked over the threshold, she glared at him.

"Are you all right?" he asked.

"No, I'm not all right!" Her voice held a steely, pissed-off edge. "Couldn't you have just thrown him out of here without threatening his life?"

"Is that why you're upset?" Caleb chuckled.

Bad move on his part. Jazzy huffed loudly.

"The guy was going to hit you." Caleb said.

"And I was fixing to knee him in the groin."

"Oh, so you're pissed because I interrupted before you brought the guy to his knees all by yourself, not because I nearly choked him to death."

Fuming, sparks flashing in her eyes, Jazzy slid off the desk and marched toward Caleb. This was the Jazzy he'd first met, all fire and spunk, taking names and kicking ass. This was the woman he was crazy about, the woman he wanted. She was as feminine as a woman could get, all round curves and beautiful face, but there was a toughness in Jazzy that overlay the softness beneath, the vulnerability she tried to hide.

Caleb waited for her, let her come to him. When she was a couple of feet away, she stopped and planted her hands on her hips. Now she was going to let him have it with both barrels.

"Where were you tonight?" she asked.

"What?" That was not what he'd been expecting her to say.

"When you called to tell me you'd be coming in late, you didn't mention why. Where were you? Or should I ask you who you were you with?"

Had he heard her right? She wasn't furious with him because he'd come to her rescue a few minutes ago. No, she was angry because she thought . . . she thought what? That he'd been with another woman? Was it possible she was jealous? If so, that had to mean she cared.

"I had some personal business to take care of. And before you ask, no, I was not with another woman."

She dropped her hands from her hips, huffed, and turned her back on him. "Why should I care if you were with some woman? It's none of my business."

"You could make it your business." He walked up behind her.

Knowing he was close—a hairbreadth away—she stiffened instantly, but didn't turn around. "I could have handled that loud-mouthed drunk, you know. I hired you as a bouncer to protect the customers, not protect me. I can take care of myself. I've been doing it for a long time. I don't need you or anyone else to fight my battles for me."

He clamped his hands down on her tense shoulders and pulled her back so that her body pressed against his, her back to his chest. Leaning over and putting his cheek against hers, he eased his mouth close to her ear. "You don't have to be alone anymore. You don't have to fight your battles by yourself. I want to be your friend . . . your protector . . . your lover."

She didn't melt into him all at once. Not his Jazzy. She had struggled a lifetime learning not to give in, not to say yes without putting up a fight. And that was all right with him. She could fight as much as she liked. Hell, she'd been fighting her attraction to him for three months now, hadn't she? He figured she was on the verge of giving in. Tonight.

Caleb swung her around and right into his arms. With her eyes wide in surprise and her mouth opened to protest, he grabbed the back of her head and pulled her face up and against his. Then he kissed her. Hard and demanding at first. Not allowing her a chance to protest. And the moment he felt her weaken, he softened his attack. When she began returning his kiss, her mouth as hungry and passionate as his, Caleb groaned, this prelude to real satisfaction arousing him unbearably.

Chapter 22

Holding her head in place, Caleb ravaged her mouth while his other hand slid down to cup her hip and press her intimately against his erection. For months now she'd been fighting her desire to be with him, to kiss him and touch him and lose herself in him. Instinctively she knew he wasn't like any other man she'd ever known. Nothing like Jamie.

Forget Jamie, she told herself. *Put him, his death, your arrest, and everything else out of your mind. Enjoy this night, savor every moment of being with Caleb.*

Jazzy wrapped her arms around his waist and rubbed herself seductively against him, loving the lean, muscular feel of him. Her pussy clenched and unclenched as tingles of sexual longing radiated through her body.

Caleb turned her around and, continuing the kiss, walked her backward until her butt collided with the wall beside the door. His lips lifted from hers, then skimmed her cheek, her chin, and down her throat, while his hands explored the outline of her body. She tugged on his shirt until she managed to pull the edges up and over his jeans. While he molded his hands to her buttocks and lifted her up and into him, enough so that her mound pressed firmly against his sex, she slid her hands up and under his shirt. His skin was hot, his belly washboard flat, his tiny male nipples tight and hard.

He licked a path from her neck to the vee created by her button-up cotton blouse, then undid the first two buttons and kissed the swell of her breasts above her bra. She ran her hands around either side of his waist and crawled her fingertips up his broad back. The feel of him was like some strong narcotic, drugging her into a stupor, making her want more and more in order to satisfy the insatiable craving.

He lifted his head and looked at her. Her gaze met his for a millisecond. They smiled at each other, then she unbuttoned his shirt and spread it apart. When she lowered her head and spread kisses from collarbone to collarbone, he reached over beside them and slammed the door shut. Only then did she realize that the door had been open and anyone could have walked by and seen them making out.

Hell, she didn't care. Nothing mattered except Caleb. Touching him, kissing him, being with him. In every way.

With trembling fingers, she yanked at his shirt until she managed to pull it off him. After tossing it on the floor, she started working on unbuckling his belt, which she did in no time flat. When she unzipped his jeans, he grabbed her hands and laid them flat on his naked chest.

"You're getting ahead of me." He finished undoing her blouse, then removed it and tossed it on the floor atop his shirt.

Kicking off their shoes, they tore at each other's remaining clothing, all the while looking and touching and pausing long enough to grab quick, wild kisses. When Caleb wore only his briefs and she her panties, he caressed her breasts, lifting them, flicking his thumbs over her sensitive nipples. Sexual excitement clawed at her insides, zinging along every nerve. When he lowered his head and sucked one breast and then the other, she whimpered with pleasure. He lifted her hips until she was able to wrap her legs around him. Then he carried her toward the desk while she kissed, nipped, and licked his shoulder. After placing her on the edge of the desk, he pulled her panties down her hips, over her legs, and off. She gasped when he slipped his hand between her thighs and shoved them apart. His fingers danced through her pubic hair and onto her feminine lips. When he inserted two fingers inside her, she lifted her hips to accommodate him.

"You're dripping wet, sweetheart."

He massaged her repeatedly until she began undulating against his hand. His briefs disappeared with one swift yank. She threw her arms around his neck as she spread her legs farther apart and welcomed him into her body. He accepted the invitation without hesitation, grasping her butt to position her before ramming into her full force. Clinging to him, wrapping her legs around his hips, she matched him thrust for thrust, as hungry for him as he was her.

So good, she thought. *So good.* Wilder, hotter, better than any sex she'd ever had before—because she wanted him more than she'd ever wanted anyone.

As their passion built, they went at each other savagely, desperate need controlling their actions. He murmured crude, graphic phrases as he screwed her. The more he talked to her, the more excited she got. She wanted this incredible loving to go on and on, but knew she was on the verge of an orgasm that couldn't be

stopped, couldn't even be slowed down. He was so big
and hard and every lunge hit all the right spots, bringing her closer and closer to fulfillment. And when it was
so good she didn't think she could stand it, it got better.
Her climax hit her like a tidal wave. She gasped, then bit
down on his shoulder to keep from screaming with pleasure. Her release triggered his. He hammered into her
until he came. While he trembled, he kept moving inside
her until he squeezed every ounce of pleasure from his
climax.

They clung to each other, their hearts beating loudly,
their breathing fast. He clasped her neck tenderly and
caressed her cheek with his thumb while he looked into
her eyes.

"It was even better than I thought it would be," he
told her.

"Yeah, it was, wasn't it?"

While he held her close, she wrapped her arms around
him and laid her head on his shoulder. They stayed like
that for quite a while. Naked. Their bodies damp with
sweat and smelling strongly of sex.

Finally he said, "Let's get dressed. Then I'll walk you
home."

"Will you stay the night?" she asked.

"I'll stay as long as you'll let me stay."

Everything was red. Bright red. Like a watery crimson veil coloring the whole world. Then suddenly black
clouds swirled around the scarlet liquid.

Genny had been in the kitchen, preparing herself a
cup of bedtime herbal tea when the vision hit her. At
the very first inkling of what was to come, she sat down
at the table and braced herself. She had no control over
these visions. They came to her awake and asleep. Day

and night. She hadn't called for Dallas because she knew that both he and her dog Drudwyn would sense her need for them and they would come to her.

As the darkness enveloped most of the red, Genny saw the starry sky overhead. Someone was looking up at the night sky. But who? As if viewing a camcorder recording an event, she watched while tall, eerie black trees came into view. Woods. Whoever this person was, they were in the woods. And probably somewhere nearby in these very mountains. Then a cabin came into view. A driveway. An old truck. Everything was dark—black and red and various shades of gray. Someone lay in the bed of the truck. A man. He was red.

Oh, God! Genny gasped and began trembling. The man was dead, his eyes staring sightless up at the night sky. His throat had been slit. He was naked. Genny screamed when she saw that the man's genitals had been removed.

"Genny? Genny?" She heard Dallas's voice as if he was far away and not right beside her as she knew he was. "Damn it, Genny, snap out of it."

Although she felt strong arms holding her, she couldn't stop screaming. But she didn't know if she was actually screaming or if the sound was only inside her head.

He's dead, she told herself. *You can't help him. Don't stay here. Leave this place. Leave now before the evil sucks you in.*

"Come on, Genny, don't do this. Get out of there now, while you still can." Dallas shook her. "I know you can do it."

The woman was there, too. Not in the truck. Beside it. Keys in her hand. She was going to drive the truck away, dispose of it and the body of the man she had just killed.

"Genny!"

I can't come back right now, she tried to tell Dallas telepathically. Although they were still working on strengthening their telepathic link to each other and hadn't quite perfected it, already he was able to connect with her nearly half the time. *I see the woman. She's killed again.*

"Be careful," Dallas told her, and she wasn't sure whether he'd spoken the words or simply thought them.

The woman was no more than a shadow. Not tall. Not short. Just a dark silhouette. Genny tried to focus on the figure as she opened the truck door, hopped up inside, and sat behind the steering wheel. Genny couldn't see her face, only the outline of head and shoulders. *Who are you? Who are you?*

Blackness hovered all around the woman, shrouding her in evil. No, the evil wasn't surrounding her, Genny realized, it was coming from her. So much anger and hate. And an insatiable thirst for revenge. But this kill hadn't been for revenge; it had been out of necessity.

Genny shuddered. She would kill again. And soon.

Suddenly and very clearly, Genny saw the back of the woman's head. She gasped. Short red hair. Jazzy's color and style. Without a doubt this was the same woman who had brutally murdered Jamie. And for whatever warped reason she was still trying to pass herself off as Jazzy.

Genny fought her way out of the darkness and back into the light. She opened her eyes briefly and saw Dallas's face as he knelt beside the kitchen chair in which she sat. He cupped her face with his big hands.

"Are you all right?" he asked.

"Jazzy." Genny's voice sounded weak, even to her own ears. These visions drained her of her strength, often weakening her for hours.

"What about Jazzy?"

"Call her." Drudwyn whimpered as he nuzzled Genny's knee with his nose. She lifted her hand, which felt as if it weighed a ton, and managed to stroke his furry head.

I'm all right, boy, she told him. She and Drudwyn had been communicating without words since the mixed-breed animal had been a puppy, sired by one of the mountain's few red wolves.

"You want me to call her now?" Dallas asked. "At this time of night? It's nearly midnight."

"She . . . she needs an alibi."

"Damn!" Dallas pulled Genny into his arms and pressed her head down on his shoulder. "What did you see?"

"She's killed again . . . the woman who murdered Jamie."

Their bodies moved in perfect rhythm, a mating dance as old as time. A man and a woman in the throes of a passion so powerful that they were oblivious to everything else. The sheets tangled about their arms and legs as they tossed and turned, rotating positions again and again. They had made love twice already, once downstairs in her office and once here in this bed, which they had nearly destroyed. The bedspread hung haphazardly half-on, half-off the bed, and the handmade quilt lay crumpled on the floor. One pillow hung precariously on the edge at the foot of the bed and the other rested vertically alongside the head of the bed.

They had explored each other's bodies thoroughly. Touching. Tasting. Pleasuring. Enjoying. He had known it would be good with Jazzy. The best sex he'd ever had. Because for them it was more than just two bodies experiencing physical gratification. Something inside him— something primeval—had recognized her as his mate the first time he laid eyes on her.

His other lovers didn't matter; neither did hers. Not even Jamie, and she had loved Jamie. There was a rightness to them that came once in a lifetime. That's what mattered—that soul-deep connection. It could be like this only with Jazzy. And he had to believe that she felt the same. Otherwise none of this made sense.

Caleb flipped her over on her back and took the dominant position. He lifted himself off her just enough so that he could look at her—that beautiful, flawless face; that silky smooth skin; those large, luscious breasts. His sex, buried inside her, throbbed. She lifted her hands to caress his chest. The moment she touched him, he pulled back, then thrust into her deep and hard. Gasping, she grabbed his shoulders and responded to his frantic, pounding lunges. He came first this time, the sensation making his ears ring and head explode as he jetted into her. While he climaxed, she moved wildly beneath him. Within half a minute she had an orgasm that went on and on and on, the aftereffects lingering. Just as he slid off her and onto his side, the telephone rang.

Who the hell? he wondered. It had to be well past midnight. They'd left Jazzy's Joint a little after ten. He'd noted the time right as they were leaving to come upstairs.

Jazzy groaned.

"Want me to get it?" he asked.

"Mm-hmm." She snuggled against him as he reached over her to the bedside table.

Caleb grabbed the receiver. "Yeah?"

Silence. Then a man's voice said, "McCord, is that you?"

"Who wants to know?"

Jazzy lifted her head and looked inquiringly at Caleb.

"It's Dallas Sloan," the voice on the phone said.

Sloan wouldn't be calling at this time of night unless something was wrong. "What's up?" Caleb asked, already aware that he didn't want to hear whatever it was.

Not tonight. Not when everything was so right between Jazzy and him.

"Genny had another vision," Dallas said. "Another man has been killed, his genitals whacked off. Genny is certain that it's the same person who killed Jamie."

A hundred thoughts fought for dominance in Caleb's mind. How would this affect Jazzy? Would she be blamed for the murder? Or would this remove suspicion from her?

"Has it already happened?" Caleb asked.

"Genny's not sure, but she thinks, yes, it's already a fait accompli. She wanted me to get in touch with Jazzy first before I call Jacob and we start searching for the body. Genny says that Jazzy needs an alibi. Genny saw the woman's hair again. Same color and style as Jazzy's."

"Holy shit! Not again." Caleb tightened his hold around Jazzy's slender waist. "Well, she's got one. We've been together since nine o'clock and before that dozens of customers saw her at Jazzy's Joint."

"Stay with her," Dallas said. "Don't leave her until we know for sure the deed's been done."

"Call us as soon as you know something, will you, Sloan?"

"Will do."

The minute Caleb hung up the phone, Jazzy rose up and over him, her face only inches from his. "That was Dallas? Why did he call? Is Genny all right?"

When Caleb sat up in bed, he brought Jazzy up with him into a sitting position, then draped his arm around her naked shoulders. "Genny had one of her visions. She saw another man murdered—his privates cut off the way Jamie's were. She's sure it's the same woman because she had short red hair, just like yours."

Jazzy took a deep breath. "I have an alibi this time. I haven't been alone all evening."

"If nothing else, this murder should give the district attorney second thoughts."

"Did Genny recognize the man?"

"Dallas didn't say, but probably not or he would have mentioned a name."

"They're going to start searching for the body, aren't they? Genny will go with Jacob and Dallas."

"They'll call us when they know something."

"Maybe we should—"

Caleb pressed his index finger over her lips. "No."

"No?"

"We are not going with them. We're staying right here."

"You're getting awfully bossy all of a sudden," she told him. "Just because we slept together, doesn't mean—"

"I don't think we've done any sleeping," he said. "At least not yet."

"Damn, you know what I mean. Just because we're lovers now does not mean you get to give me orders."

He grasped her face between his fingers and thumb, forcing her to look at him. "We're more than lovers, aren't we?"

She stared at him, neither agreeing nor disagreeing.

"Okay, I don't have the right to give you orders, even if you were my wife. But what we have, who we are to each other, does give me the right to protect you."

"You want to protect me?"

"Protect you, take care of you, make you happy." He released his tenacious hold on her face.

"You, Caleb McCord, are one of a kind." She kissed him. A tender, loving, grateful kiss.

Hugging her close, he rested his chin on the top of her head. "I was just thinking the same thing about you, sweetheart. There's nobody in the world like you."

* * *

She drove the truck to within half a mile of where she had dumped the green Jaguar. Along this stretch of road there were numerous steep ravines suitable for what she had in mind. She'd covered Stan Watson's body with a tarp she'd found in the massive steel toolbox attached to the truck bed. Luckily she hadn't run into another vehicle since she'd left Honey Bear Trail fifteen minutes ago. Before leaving, she had gone into the woods and buried the bloody knife she'd used on Stan—his own knife!—only a few feet away from where he'd buried her black plastic bag. It could be years—or maybe never—before anyone discovered that sack and its contents.

She hadn't wanted to kill Stan. She hadn't even known him. But once he'd seen her digging that hole in the ground, out in the woods, she'd had no choice. She had been merciful. She'd killed him quickly. And she'd even given him a farewell fuck. It was the least she could do for an innocent man.

Killing Stan screwed up her plans somewhat. If Jazzy Talbot had an alibi for tonight, then the sheriff and the district attorney might start questioning whether Jazzy had killed Jamie. But maybe, just maybe, there were enough differences in the two murders that the law would assume this was a copycat killing. She had left Jamie's body in the cabin. She would burn Stan's inside the truck. And if that weird mountain girl Genny saw any visions about Stan's death, she would report that he hadn't been tortured. At least not much.

I hope you're alone, Jazzy Talbot. I hope you don't have an alibi. If you don't, then this second murder will seal your fate.

Andrea Willis woke with a start. She heard voices. Sitting straight up in bed, she listened. Laura and Sheridan were arguing.

She glanced at the bedside clock. Twelve-twenty-five. Why were their daughters having a shouting match at this time of night? She got out of bed, slipped into her robe and shoes, then quietly made her way out of the room, leaving Cecil asleep. Whenever he took a sleeping pill, he slept like the dead. More and more often, he relied on medication in order to rest, just as she did. But tonight she'd left off her medication.

The girls were standing outside in the hallway, near the back stairway. Both were fully dressed. Odd, Andrea thought. Why would they be dressed? She hurried toward them and the minute they saw her, they quieted immediately.

"What in God's name is going on?" Andrea demanded. "What if someone overheard you?"

"Nobody heard us, except you," Sheridan said. "Big Jim stayed at the hospital and it would take a bomb exploding on his chest to wake Daddy."

"What about the servants?"

"The servants' rooms are downstairs," Sheridan reminded her mother.

"Who's going to tell me what's going on!" Andrea demanded.

Laura hung her head. Sheridan grimaced.

"Why aren't you two in bed asleep at this time of night? It's past midnight."

"I've been out," Sheridan admitted. "I had a date."

That fact didn't surprise Andrea in the least. She looked at Laura. "And you?"

"I was restless, so I went out somewhere . . . I think."

"You think?" Andrea's heart caught in her throat. "Where is Mrs. Conley?"

"I don't know. Asleep, I guess," Laura replied.

"She should have awakened when she heard you two screeching at each other." Andrea turned to Sheridan.

"Tell me in one or two sentences why you and your sister were arguing."

"When I came in, I caught her sneaking up the back stairs, so I asked her who she'd gone out and killed tonight," Sheridan said.

Acting purely on instinctive rage, Andrea slapped Sheridan, who jerked back and glared at her mother. Then she rubbed her cheek and grinned.

"Admit it, Mother, you think she might have killed Jamie."

"I didn't," Laura told them. "I—I couldn't have. I loved Jamie. We were going to have a baby."

Andrea put her arm around Laura's shoulders, then glanced at Sheridan. "Go to bed. And from now on, keep your opinion to yourself. Understand?"

"Yes, ma'am." Sheridan headed for her room.

"Come with me." Andrea led Laura into her bedroom.

The room lay in moonlit shadows. Andrea flipped on the overhead light. Mrs. Conley, snoring loudly, sat in the overstuffed chair in the corner. A empty cup rested on the floor beside the chair. Andrea left Laura standing in the middle of the room and went to check on the nurse. She called the woman's name. No response. She tapped on her shoulder. Mrs. Conley continued snoring. Andrea shook her. She grunted, but didn't awaken.

Drugged! The woman had been drugged.

Andrea whirled around and glared at Laura. "What did you give her?"

Laura hugged herself and looked everywhere but at her mother.

Andrea rushed over, grabbed Laura and shook her. "What did you give Mrs. Conley? Do I need to call an ambulance?"

"It was just a couple of Daddy's sleeping pills," Laura admitted. "I got tired of her watching me like a hawk.

She wouldn't even let me go pee without leaving the bathroom door open."

"Laura, Laura . . . what am I going to do with you?"

"Love me. Please, Mother, love me the way you do Sheridan."

Andrea wrapped her arms around her elder daughter and held her. "My poor little Laura."

Sally Talbot showed up at Jazzy's apartment promptly at six o'clock. Caleb was in the kitchen preparing coffee when she knocked on the door.

"How's our girl?" Sally asked.

"Still sleeping," Caleb said. "It was after four before she finally fell asleep again."

"Dallas called me right before I left the house." Sally glanced toward the closed bedroom door. "They found another vehicle burning down in a hollow, not half a mile from where they found that other one."

"When?"

"About an hour ago."

"I think I'll drive up there and see what they know."

"Figured you'd want to. That's why I'm here. To look after Jazzy. She don't need to go with you."

"I agree." He nodded toward the kitchen. "Coffee's on. I'll grab a mug before I head out." Caleb walked toward the bedroom.

"What are you doing?" Sally asked. " Don't wake her up or she'll want to go with you."

"I won't wake her. I just . . ." He felt awkward admitting his feelings to Jazzy's aunt. "I just want to take another look at her before I leave."

Sally grinned, then turned and headed for the kitchen.

Caleb opened the door and tiptoed into the semidark room. Jazzy lay under the sheet, curled in a ball on her side. He crept over to the edge of the bed and looked down at her. God, she was the prettiest thing he'd ever seen.

Admit it, McCord. You're in love with her.

Unable to resist the temptation, he reached out and ran the back of his hand gently across her cheek. She sighed and turned over on her back, but didn't wake up. He leaned over and kissed her forehead. She murmured something incoherent in her sleep.

"I love you," he whispered, knowing she couldn't hear him.

Her breathing was deep and even. Restful. Her lips parted and she said one word plainly. "Jamie . . ."

Chapter 23

While Genny slept on the cot in Jacob's office, recovering from their early morning search, he and Dallas sat in the outer office with a couple of his deputies, Moody Ryan and Bobby Joe Harte. Although Genny had been able to point them in the right direction and helped them find the spot where the truck had been abandoned and burned, she'd been unable to pick up the location where the murder had actually been committed. Before she'd passed out from exhaustion, she'd told them definitely that the murder hadn't occurred nearby.

"Farther up the mountain," Genny had said. "Near a thickly wooded area. Isolated. Maybe only one cabin anywhere close."

Jacob had left the forensics team going over the fiery truck site. And he'd put in a call to Knoxville. A second murder in a week's time was all too reminiscent of the serial killer that had stalked Cherokee County three months ago, so he was damned and determined to do his best to stop this killer before another man fell victim to her black-widow tactics. From the charred remains of the body inside the truck there was no way to tell for sure who the man had been, and Pete Holt had said it had definitely been a man. The body would be shipped out to Knoxville by noon today. Until then, they could only speculate as to who the victim was. But the truck was another matter. Although badly burned, the truck was still intact enough to make out the model. And as luck would have it, the car tag, which apparently had been held in place by a decorative plastic frame, had fallen off on the ground and escaped being blackened when the plastic frame melted. They'd immediately run a search on the tag and found the truck belonged to Stanley Watson, a maintenance man who worked for Cherokee Cabin Rentals.

Propped on the edge of Moody's desk, his legs crossed at the ankles, Jacob held the list of job assignments Stan's boss Hoot Tompkins, the manager of the rental cabins, had given them.

"Hoot said his men took their assignment sheets from him every morning, then decided for themselves which job to do first, unless told otherwise," Jacob said. "We've got a couple of guys from our department and from Dallas's going from cabin to cabin to find out if Stan finished up on all these jobs." Jacob tapped the assignment sheet he held. "If one was left undone, that might mean it was the last place he stopped before he was killed."

"Do you think it was her?" Bobby Joe asked and when all eyes focused on him, he swallowed hard. "Not Miss Jazzy. I didn't mean her. I'm talking about whoever really killed Jamie Upton. You think the same woman killed Stan Watson?"

"We're only guessing that it's Watson," Dallas said. "It

was his truck and the guy isn't at home and nobody's seen him since around lunchtime yesterday."

"If it is the same person—the killer, I mean . . ." Bobby Joe paced around the room as he spoke nervously. "Doesn't that put Miss Jazzy in the clear? If she's got—got an alibi this time, then maybe we should—should be looking elsewhere for Jamie's killer."

Jacob studied his deputy. Bobby Joe was stuttering and acting like a worm in hot ashes. He sure wasn't his usual laid-back, easygoing self. "What the hell's wrong with you?"

At the sound of Jacob's roar, Bobby Joe froze in his tracks. "Nothing's wrong with me."

"You sure are acting peculiar," Dallas commented.

"That's what I was thinking," Jacob said.

"Ah, his mind isn't on his job," Moody told them. "He's got himself a new sweetie. A real hot little number and—"

"Shut up, will you!" Bobby Joe glowered at Moody. "Hell, can't a man have a private life without everybody sticking their nose in his business?"

"You're overreacting to a little innocent ribbing," Jacob said. "That's not like you. Something is wrong or you wouldn't be acting this way."

Bobby Joe stormed out of the office, slamming the door behind him after he marched into the hall. Jacob glanced from Moody to Dallas and then back at Moody.

"Who's the girl?"

Moody grinned. With those big blue eyes and curly blond hair, he looked like an overgrown kid. "It's that Willis girl."

"Laura Willis?" Dallas and Jacob said simultaneously.

"Nah, the other one."

"The teenager?" Jacob asked.

"Yeah. Her name is Sheridan and she's only nineteen, but from what Bobby Joe says, she sure doesn't act like a kid, if you know what I mean."

Jacob nodded. So Bobby Joe was screwing the younger Willis girl. Considering that Bobby Joe wasn't exactly a ladies' man and not known for making the first move, Sheridan Willis must have put the moves on him. But why was he acting as if he'd committed a crime? If she was nineteen, she was legal.

"Maybe he's embarrassed about dating somebody that young," Dallas said.

Jacob shook his head. "I don't think that's it. There's something more. Something to do with these murders."

"You think Bobby Joe knows something we don't know?" Dallas asked.

"How's that possible?" Moody's smooth brow wrinkled.

"I'm not sure, but I'm going to find out," Jacob told them.

When he exited the office, he looked up and down the hall. He spotted Bobby Joe at the end of the corridor by the cola machine. As if sensing Jacob's presence, his deputy glanced up from where he'd just deposited coins into the slot. Their gazes met for an instant. Then Bobby Joe looked down to where the machine had deposited an ice-cold can of root beer into the metal bed. Jacob took some quarters out of his pocket so that when he reached the cola machine, he dropped the coins in the slot and hit the Orange Crush button. After retrieving his drink and snapping the tab, he lifted the can to his lips and took a long swig.

"I guess Moody told you who I've been sneaking around seeing." Bobby Joe deliberately didn't look at Jacob.

"Sheridan Willis." Jacob wiped his mouth with the

back of his free hand, then turned and put his hand on Bobby Joe's shoulder. "Is there something you want to tell me?"

Bobby Joe harrumphed. "Want to tell you—no. Need to tell you—yes."

"Just spit it out. Whatever it is, it can't be as bad you're making it out to be."

"It's not that. It's just I should have already said something to you about it, especially considering it might be something that could help Miss Jazzy."

"Tell me now."

"Well . . ." Bobby Joe shuffled, then motioned for Jacob to follow him. "Let's talk outside. Okay? I don't want nobody overhearing us."

When they walked out the back door of the courthouse, Bobby Joe looked around. After he saw that they were completely alone, he said, "Right after Jamie was killed, Sheridan said she thought maybe her sister had killed him."

"Laura Willis?"

"Yeah."

"What made her think that?"

"She said her sister had problems. You know, mental problems. It seems Laura had a nervous breakdown when she was sixteen."

"Any history of violence?"

"I don't know. Sheridan didn't say much more, but . . . she called me just a few minutes ago. You know . . . that personal call I took."

Jacob forced himself not to jump to any conclusions about Laura Willis. Not yet. Just because he knew Jazzy was innocent didn't automatically make Laura guilty. But if anyone other than Jazzy had a reason to hate Jamie, to wish him dead, it was probably Laura.

"So what about that call?" Jacob asked.

"It was Sheridan. She'd heard about the second murder. Seems it's already all over the TV and radio."

Jacob groaned. Yeah, Brian MacKinnon would see to it that the sheriff's department and the local police were held up to ridicule. That guy had it in for both Dallas and him.

"Go on. What did she have to say?" Jacob sipped on his Orange Crush.

Mimicking his boss, Bobby Joe took a couple of swallows from his root beer. "She said Laura could have killed this guy, too . . . that when I dropped her off last night and she was heading up the back stairs at the Upton house, she caught Laura sneaking up the stairs, too. Laura had been out somewhere for hours and hours and nobody knew where."

"Sheridan must really hate her sister to share this type of information with a sheriff's deputy," Jacob said. "Even if he is a deputy she's screwing."

Bobby Joe's face flushed. "What do you think?"

"I think we should ask Laura Willis to come in and talk to us," Jacob said. "And I want Wade Truman here when we question her. If he sees there's someone else with motive and opportunity, he might be persuaded to drop the charges against Jazzy."

Caleb pulled his T-bird in at a Dairy Bar, got out, ordered coffee, and got back in his car. When he'd left Cherokee Pointe this morning, he'd just started driving, and had ended up on Highway 321 and kept going all the way to Greenville before he realized where he was. Originally he had planned on meeting up with Dallas and Jacob to get all the info he could about the most recent murder in Cherokee County. His goal had been to help Jazzy.

I want to protect you and take care of you and make you happy, he'd told her. And he'd meant every word.

Why the hell had he gone back into the bedroom for one last look at her this morning? Why hadn't he just left as soon as Sally got there? If he hadn't touched her, kissed her, hadn't felt the overwhelming need to whisper that he loved her while she slept, he never would have heard her murmur Jamie's name.

God, it had been like a knife in his heart. He had just spent the most incredible hours of his life making love with a woman who had come to mean everything to him. He'd been stupid enough to think she felt the same way. But it wasn't his name she murmured in her sleep. He wasn't the man in her mind and in her heart. That sacred spot was reserved for a man who had never been worthy of her.

Maybe if Jamie were still alive, he'd have a chance to win Jazzy away from him. But how did he fight a ghost? Had he really thought he was such a stud that one night in bed with him and Jazzy would forget about all those years she'd been in love with Jamie?

Caleb squeezed the half full foam cup so hard that the contents sloshed out over the top and spilled onto his hand. He cursed loudly. The coffee was still hot. Hot enough to make him cringe, but not hot enough to burn.

What are you going to do, McCord? Just keep going. Don't look back. But what about his things back there at the cabin? *Okay, so go back long enough to get your stuff, then hit the road.*

You can't leave without checking on Miss Reba, without talking to Big Jim Upton and telling him who you are. After all, that's why you came to Cherokee County. To find out about your mother's family.

If he went to Big Jim with the truth, the odds were the man wouldn't believe him. *So show him your birth cer-*

tificate. Show him the pictures of you and your mother when you were a kid. Tell him you'll take a DNA test.

Is that what he wanted? Did he want to be Big Jim Upton's grandson—the heir to the Upton fortune? If he was filthy, stinking rich would Jazzy want him? Would she love him?

Caleb laughed at himself, at his own foolishness. He had known and pitied lovesick fools, never dreaming that someday he'd join their ranks.

If you love Jazzy so damn much, how can you desert her? How can you let your stupid pride keep you from being there to take care of her? You made her promises. You're a man of your word, aren't you?

He had unfinished business back in Cherokee County—with Big Jim Upton and Miss Reba. And with Jazzy.

Caleb got out of the car, dumped his smashed foam cup in the trash bin outside the Dairy Bar, and made a decision. If he went back and proved his identity to his grandparents and pursued a relationship with Jazzy, some people would say that he'd stepped into Jamie Upton's shoes and taken over the man's life. Hell, a lot of people would say it. But they'd be wrong. He didn't want any part of Jamie's life. *But you do want everything that had once been Jamie's,* an inner voice told him.

Jim and Reba Upton were his grandparents, too. He had a right to know them, didn't he? People might not understand that the Upton fortune didn't mean that much to him, but having a family did. And as far as Jazzy was concerned, he didn't want her to love him the way she'd loved Jamie. He wanted more from her because he was willing to offer her more.

To hell with Jamie. To hell with what people would think and say. He was not going to let one word—one name—that Jazzy had spoken in her sleep run him off and stop him from laying claim to everything he wanted. Everything that was rightfully his.

Caleb slid behind the wheel and started his Thunderbird. After backing out of the parking area, he turned the car southwest. He was heading home.

Mid afternoon, Dallas finished up a late lunch with Jacob, the two of them sipping coffee and enjoying Ludie's homemade pecan pie. As soon as Genny had finished eating, she'd gone to Jazzy's apartment to relieve Sally, who'd called to say that Jazzy was worried about Caleb. He'd left around six this morning and they hadn't heard a word from him. Dallas figured his Genny would be able to soothe Jazzy's concerns. He just hoped she didn't overdo. Genny had a way of putting everyone else first and herself last. As hard as he tried to look after her, to make her consider her own needs, she couldn't change who she was. By nature she was a caretaker. That loving, giving spirit was as much a part of her as those luminous black eyes and her remarkable gift of sight, all three inherited from her Granny Butler, a half-breed Cherokee.

Dallas's cell phone rang, pulling him from his thoughts of Genny. He removed the phone from its holder, punched the on button and said, "Yeah, Sloan here."

"Dallas, it's Teri. I've got a preliminary on Laura Willis and I'm still digging. It could take another day, maybe two, to get everything on her, her parents, and her sister."

"Keep digging," Dallas said. "Now go ahead and tell me what you've got."

"She did have some sort of mental collapse when she was sixteen. She spent nearly three months in a private hospital and was under psychiatric care for a couple of years."

"Any details on what caused the breakdown?"

"Haven't been able to find that out yet."

When Teri paused and didn't say anything for a couple of minutes, Dallas remembered how she'd always liked to build up to a big revelation with a long, silent pause.

"What is it?" he asked.

She chuckled. "Just an interesting little tidbit. It was easy enough to trace dates. You know, things like date of birth, date of marriage, and so on. Laura Willis is twenty-four, according to the records I was able to access—her driver's license info being one."

"So?"

"Andrea and Cecil Willis have been married only twenty-three years."

Dallas mulled the information over in his mind. "Did you double-check the dates?"

"Yes, I did. You should know that we FBI types always double-check."

"All that means is that Laura was born before her parents were married."

"Maybe."

"What are you dying to tell me?"

"Andrea Willis is not the first Mrs. Cecil Willis. His first marriage was annulled twenty-four years ago, so that means he was married to someone else when he fathered Laura."

"Interesting, but I don't see how it's pertinent to our case."

"I think there's more to it," Teri said. "Call it gut instinct, but—hey, why don't you ask Genny to do a—"

"No way."

"Not even if it would help her friend Jazzy?"

"You keep digging, find out all you can and if you

don't come up with something, then maybe I'll involve Genny."

"Whatever you say. I'll be in touch."

When Dallas replaced his phone in its holster, Jacob asked, "Anything?"

"Not really, but Teri's got a hunch and her hunches usually pay off," Dallas said. "She'll be back in touch with me soon."

"Well, I hope you're right about her hunches. We've got two unsolved murders and unless we can give the DA another viable suspect, Jazzy will more than likely be put on trial for Jamie's murder."

Chapter 24

Cherokee County Hospital seemed the most logical first stop for Caleb when he returned to town. He wasn't quite ready to face Jazzy, to confront her with his wounded masculine pride. If she told him that she still loved Jamie, he wasn't sure how he'd react. Was he willing to spend the rest of his life playing second fiddle to his dead cousin? Or if when she found out the truth about Caleb actually being an Upton heir, would she want him and put him in the position of always wondering if she loved him or the Upton millions? When he paused at the nurse's station down the hall from the intensive care unit, no one paid any attention to him. He cleared his throat.

A statuesque black woman in her mid fifties, with a warm smile, turned to face him. "May I help you, sir?"

"I was wondering if I could find out how Mrs. Upton is doing?" Caleb asked.

A petite middle-aged blonde—apparently the RN on duty—snapped around and glared at Caleb. "If you're another reporter, I suggest you leave before I call security."

"I'm not a reporter."

"Then what is your interest in Mrs. Upton? Are you family? A close personal friend?"

Caleb didn't know how to respond and before he could think of a suitable reply, the RN told him, "Since you're apparently neither, perhaps you should call Mr. Upton and ask for that type of information."

"I'm family," Caleb said boldly.

The RN eyed him skeptically. "I doubt that."

"Look, all I want to know is if she's better or worse."

"Check with the Upton family," the nurse told him, then picked up a stack of charts and walked off down the hall.

Just as Caleb started to leave, the other nurse called to him quietly. "Hey, young man."

Caleb stopped and faced her. "Yes, ma'am?"

"Mrs. Upton's condition has been upgraded. She's doing much better. So much better that they moved her out of ICU about an hour ago. Her husband arranged for her to have a suite on the fourth floor."

"Thank you." Caleb grinned. "And you should know I really am a member of the family."

"I thought so," the nurse replied. "I could tell right away that you were genuinely concerned about Mrs. Upton."

Caleb nodded, then rushed toward the elevators. After he entered and punched the fourth floor button, he thought about what the nurse had said about his concern for Reba Upton being obvious. Yeah, he was concerned, but he wasn't sure why. She was his grandmother, but he didn't know her, had never actually met her. Maybe just knowing she was his grandmother was enough to make him care. When Miss Reba's image flashed through his mind, he saw his mother. That was why he cared. At some point in her life, his mother had loved Miss Reba and Big Jim. Otherwise when she was on her deathbed, she never would have told him to go to them. Okay, so his mother had died years ago and he was a little late in fulfilling her dying wish. But better late than never, right?

When the elevator doors swung open, he hesitated for a moment. *Do it*, he told himself. *You aren't going to disturb her. You aren't going to tell her who you are. Not yet. But maybe you can just take a look and see for yourself that she's going to be all right.*

Caleb stepped out of the elevator and glanced left and right. Just how many private suites were up here on the fourth floor? And if there was more than one, how would he know which one Miss Reba was in?

If you run into anybody or if a nurse confronts you, just act like you know what you're doing and where you're going. And if there's a guard at Miss Reba's door, just walk on by.

It didn't take long for him to discover that the patient's name was posted on the outside of the door and there were only two private suites. One was empty. When he approached the other, the door stood halfway open. He took a deep breath and approached, then paused outside and looked into the room. A woman in a uniform—a private duty nurse, no doubt—sat near the foot of the bed, her back to Caleb. He had a clear view of his grandmother. Despite her blond hair and relatively smooth face, she looked old. A heart attack would age a person, he figured. But even though she was pale and looked terribly small and helpless in that hospital bed, she was still a pretty woman. Just like his mother had been. Years of drug use had taken a toll on his mother, but even at the end, when she'd been bone skinny, her once lustrous hair thin and dull, and with dark circles under her eyes, she had still been pretty. Or maybe he had just looked at her through a son's eyes. Melanie hadn't been the best mother in the world, but she'd been the only mother he'd had, and before the drugs took over her life completely, there had been some good times. Good memories.

He didn't know how long he stood there just staring at his grandmother, wondering how she would react when she learned that her daughter had left behind a child. Then, just as he decided it was time for him to leave, a big hand hooked over his shoulder.

"What the hell do you think you're doing?" Big Jim Upton's voice sounded like a rottweiler's ferocious growl.

Caleb turned around and faced his grandfather.

"If you're a damned reporter—"

"I'm not a reporter."

"Then what are you doing snooping around outside my wife's hospital room? Who told you where she was?"

"I wasn't snooping." Caleb jerked free of Jim's tight hold. "I stopped by to see how Miss Reba was doing."

Jim eyed him suspiciously. "Do I know you? You look familiar."

"You don't know me, Mr. Upton. But if I look familiar to you, it could be because I look quite a bit like my mother."

"Your mother? Do we know your mother? Is she a friend of ours?" Jim scanned Caleb from his overlong hair to his black leather boots.

If you're going to do it, do it! Caleb told himself. *Maybe this is the wrong time and the wrong place, but you've put it off long enough.*

"My mother was Melanie Upton McCord."

Jim glared at him as if he wasn't sure he'd heard him right. "What sort of game are you playing, boy? You here to try to take advantage of us when we're at our most vulnerable? Well, whatever you're up to, forget it. Our daughter died fifteen years ago of a—"

"A drug overdose in Memphis."

Jim frowned, squinting his eyes and scrunching his face. "How would you know that?"

"Because I was with her when she died. I'm the one who tried to save her. I'm the one who called for an ambulance."

Jim grabbed Caleb by the front of his shirt. "How old are you? Not old enough to have been her lover."

"I was sixteen when she died. She wasn't even forty, but she looked sixty. Drugs do that to people, even beautiful blonde women from good families. Beautiful blonde women who look just like their mothers."

Jim loosened his hold on Caleb's shirt, but didn't let go. He stared into Caleb's eyes— eyes that were not like his mother's. Jim studied his features. Slowly. Carefully. "You look a bit like her and I can see some of Jim Jr. in you—" Jim released Caleb abruptly and stepped away from him. "You can't be hers. If she'd had a child, the police would have told us when they notified us she had died."

"They didn't know about me," Caleb said. "When I knew she was dead, I split. I didn't hang around so some social worker could put me in a foster home."

"But if she had a child, why . . . why didn't she come home? She had a husband." Jim shook his head. "How old are you?"

"Thirty-two."

"She left here over thirty-three years ago. Left us, left a good husband—"

"He's not my father."

"And my Melanie is not your mother." Jim hardened his gaze. "Whoever the hell you are, don't you dare ever go near Miss Reba telling her your crazy lies. That woman has been through way too much already."

"I don't want to hurt her . . . or you."

"Then get the hell out of my sight. Leave Cherokee Pointe, and don't you ever come back. Do you hear me, boy?"

Caleb looked the old man right in the eye. "I'll leave whenever I get damn good and ready to go."

"You know who I am. You know what I can do to you if I've a mind to."

"Yeah, I know. I know that you've seen to it that the DA has railroaded an innocent woman, had her arrested for a murder she didn't commit. I know all about how powerful Big Jim Upton is." Caleb grunted. "Hell, maybe you're right. Maybe I'm not your grandson. If Jamie Upton was the result of your parenting skills, then I'm damn lucky I didn't do what my mother wanted me to do and come to you and Miss Reba when I was sixteen."

Jim's face flushed. For a minute there Caleb thought Big Jim might hit him.

"My mother's favorite color was blue. Her favorite fairy tale was Sleeping Beauty. You used to read it to her every night when she was a little girl. She had a pony named Ruffles. Her sixteenth birthday present from you was a yellow Corvette. And Miss Reba gave her a gold locket surrounded by diamonds on her wedding day. She wore it all the time when I was a kid. She hung on to that necklace for a long time, but finally in the end she sold it to buy drugs."

Caleb turned and walked away. Let the old man digest all that information. If he ever wanted to talk to Caleb, he'd have to come to him. He wasn't going to beg the man to believe him. And he sure as hell wasn't going to let Big Jim Upton intimidate him.

Andrea didn't like this one little bit. Although the sheriff had assured Cecil they didn't need their lawyer present, she felt uneasy walking into the sheriff's office without legal counsel. They had their murderer—Jazzy Talbot. Why did they need to question her family any further? She believed she could control Cecil. After all, she'd been doing it for years. But their daughters were another matter. Sheridan was headstrong, insolent, and might say anything. She'd taken her younger child aside before they left the Upton house and warned her to be on her best behavior. She probably had Sheridan under control, too. At least temporarily. But what about Laura? That poor child was so fragile that it wouldn't take very much pressure for her break into pieces. Pieces that might not ever go back together.

"Do not say anything about not remembering where you were the night Jamie died," Andrea had told Laura. "Do you hear me?"

Laura had nodded and promised to keep their secret, but Andrea knew that if she was pushed too far, Laura would crumble. And if that happened, there would be little that she and Cecil could do for the girl. God help them all if the whole truth ever came out.

What if she did kill Jamie? Andrea asked herself as the four of them entered the courthouse. *Heads high,* she'd told them. *We have nothing to fear.*

If Laura killed Jamie, no one must ever know. But what about the other man who had been murdered, that Watson man? Laura had been out again last evening. Sheridan had caught her slipping up the back stairs. Had she killed him, too? And if she had, why?

"Please come in." Jacob Butler met them at the door to the sheriff's department. "I sure do appreciate y'all coming in. I'll try not to keep you folks long. Just come on back to my office so we can talk in private."

Andrea nudged Cecil, who stood aside for his wife and daughters, then followed alongside the sheriff.

"I put in a call to Phillip Stockton, my lawyer, and he advised me as to what I should and shouldn't speak to you about," Cecil said. "But since neither I nor my wife and daughters have anything to hide, we're more than glad to cooperate."

"Just go on in and have a seat," Sheriff Butler said when they reached his office. "I've asked Police Chief Sloan and our district attorney, Wade Truman, to sit in on our conversation."

Andrea glanced at the other two men—the big blond police chief standing by the windows and Mr. Truman seated behind the sheriff's desk—but she didn't acknowledge their presence by speaking to them. Then she noted that four chairs were spread out over the room, so that no two people would be side by side. Had that been deliberate or just happenstance? She leaned over and whispered to Cecil, "Move one of the chairs next to this one"—she pointed—"where I'll sit."

He looked at her, a puzzled expression on his face, but did as she had asked. As soon as he placed the folding chair beside the one where Andrea sat, she called, "Laura, come sit by me, dear."

Sheridan eyed her mother, then grinned. She didn't like that cunning smile. What did Sheridan know? Probably nothing. But that girl had a mischievous streak a mile wide and seemed to enjoy causing trouble.

Jacob Butler crossed his arms over his massive chest and sat on the edge of his desk. "As you folks probably already know, we've had another murder here in Cherokee County."

"Yes," Cecil said. "A handyman of some sort, wasn't he?"

"A maintenance man for Cherokee Cabin Rentals," Jacob said. "His name was Stanley Watson. Did y'all by any chance know him?"

"Certainly not," Andrea replied. "Why would you ever think we might know such a person?"

"Just asking, ma'am. Just asking."

"Cecil could have answered that question over the phone—" Andrea stopped mid sentence, realizing she was overreacting.

"Stan Watson's murder has similarities to Jamie Upton's. Only this time the body was burned inside the vehicle, so we don't know whether she tortured him or not."

Laura gasped. Andrea put her arm around her daughter's shoulder. "Really, Sheriff," Andrea scolded.

"Sorry, ma'am, but you see, we figure that the person who killed Jamie killed Stan."

"Then you already have your murderer," Andrea told him. "Jazzy Talbot killed Jamie." She looked directly at the district attorney. "Isn't that right?"

"Jazzy's case will go before a grand jury, if we can't find the real murderer," Jacob said. "You see, Jazzy has an iron-clad alibi for the time Stan Watson was killed, so there's no way she could have committed the second murder."

Andrea swallowed. *Don't think about it*, she told herself. *If you think about it, something might show on your face that would make the sheriff suspicious.*

"We need to know exactly where each of you was between six yesterday evening and midnight last night."

"We were at the Upton home," Andrea replied.

"All four of you?" Jacob Butler asked.

"Yes—"

"Don't lie for me, Mother." Sheridan boldly stared at the sheriff. "I had a date that lasted for hours and hours. I was with this gentleman from about six-thirty until sometime after midnight."

Jacob cleared his throat. "We can verify your whereabouts, Ms. Willis."

Andrea snapped her head around and glared at her younger daughter. Good God, surely she hadn't been with the sheriff. No, not the sheriff, but certainly someone he knew. She scanned the room, studying each man, wondering if Sheridan had been with the chief of police or even the district attorney.

"Cecil and I were together during that time and Laura was either with us or with her nurse," Andrea said, wanting to protect Laura. The sheriff must never know that Laura had drugged Mrs. Conley and disappeared for hours yesterday evening. If necessary, she would pay off the nurse, give her an enormous bonus for keeping quiet.

Jacob walked over to Laura, squatted down in front of her and asked in a kind, gentle voice, "Laura, is there anything you can tell us that might help us solve Jamie's murder . . . and Stan Watson's murder?"

Laura looked to her mother, her blue eyes wide with fear and pleading for help. "I—I don't know . . . sometimes I can't remember things. I want to help, but . . ."

"Please, don't do this," Andrea said to the sheriff. "Laura is by nature very delicate and Jamie's death has unsettled her, not to mention the unfortunate miscarriage. She's under a doctor's care." Andrea looked at Cecil. "We should have Dr. MacNair here. He can explain how easily the least little thing might—" She cleared her throat. "Please . . . Laura can't help you. Believe me, she can't."

The sheriff eyed Andrea suspiciously and for a split second, she couldn't breathe. Fear smothered her. Butler rose to his full, impressive height. Andrea imagined that this man's size and savage features often frightened criminals into making a full confession. But she wasn't a criminal and she wasn't easily intimidated, especially by someone as inferior as this backwoods Indian sheriff.

Butler opened the office door and called to one of

his deputies, "Contact Dr. MacNair and ask him if he can come over here as soon as possible. Tell him we're questioning the Willis family and that I have some questions for Laura, but her mother feels questioning her any further might jeopardize her health."

Andrea felt the blood rush to her face, heard it pounding through her head. She stood, walked over to Cecil and said quietly, "Do something!"

"What would you have me do?" Cecil sighed. His shoulders sagged.

"Laura shouldn't be questioned." Andrea laid her hand on her husband's arm and squeezed tightly. "Do you understand?"

His eyes opened wide with realization. He nodded. "I'll call Phillip."

Just as Andrea started to respond, to tell Cecil they needed more immediate help than Phillip could give them since he was hundreds of miles away in Lexington, a telephone rang. She glanced around inside the sheriff's office and through the open door into the outer office and noted one of the deputies on the phone calling Dr. MacNair, as he'd been instructed to do. Then she saw the chief of police remove his cell phone from its belt clip and flip the phone open. She watched him as he hurriedly walked into the outer office area.

Andrea had an uncanny feeling that Chief Sloan's phone call had something to do with them, with Laura in particular. When he quickly came back to the open door and motioned for the sheriff to step outside, Andrea's nails bit into her husband's arm.

"Get on the phone and contact Jim Upton," Andrea said. "Tell him we're going to need a local lawyer as soon as possible."

"Why?" Cecil asked. "What haven't you told me?"

"It's about Laura—"

Before she could explain to her husband, the sheriff and police chief returned. Cecil rose to stand at Andrea's side. The two of them walked over and flanked their eldest child.

"We've just received some rather interesting information," the sheriff said.

Andrea held her breath.

When Sheriff Butler spoke again, he looked directly at her. "Why didn't y'all tell us that when Laura was sixteen, she tried to kill her boyfriend?"

Chapter 25

Caleb parked his T-bird in front of his rental cabin, alongside Genny's Trailblazer. He knew before he emerged from his car that if Genny was here, that probably meant one of two things: either Jazzy had sent her or Jazzy was with her. *Okay, so what did you expect?* he asked himself. He'd left Jazzy before she woke this morning and here it was late afternoon and he hadn't gotten in touch with her all day. She was bound to be wondering what the hell was wrong with him. After all, the two of them had shared an incredible night together. A lady had a right to expect certain things from a man after such an intimate experience.

If he was lucky, Genny was alone and he wouldn't have to face Jazzy. But when he approached the cabin and saw Genny and Jazzy sitting on the porch, he knew his luck had run out. Whether he wanted to or not, he was going to have to face Jazzy and explain his actions. He'd been having second thoughts about total honesty. He didn't think he was ready to come right out and ask her if she was still in love with Jamie. Actually, he wasn't sure he'd ever have the guts to confront her about that goddamn horrible moment he'd heard her whisper Jamie's name. And he certainly wasn't prepared to tell her that he was Jim and Reba Upton's grandson—that he was, as Jamie had been, an Upton heir. Only now that Jamie was dead, he was the only heir.

Just what *was* he going to say? What could he tell her?

"Afternoon, ladies." Caleb climbed the wooden steps leading to the porch that spanned the length of the house. He'd been renting this place from Cherokee Cabin Rentals since he'd gone to work as the bouncer at Jazzy's Joint back in January.

Not being one for subtleties, Jazzy hopped out of the swing and came charging toward him. "Just where the hell have you been?" Her bright green eyes squinted disapprovingly.

Caleb crammed his hands into his pockets and shuffled his feet. *Now what?* he asked himself. "I took a ride out of town." *Great response, McCord. Do you think she's going to accept that without any other questions?*

Jazzy crossed her arms over her chest and cocked her head to one side. "Wrong answer. Want to tell me what's going on?"

Genny rose from the rocking chair where she'd been sitting. "I think you two need to talk privately, without an audience."

When Genny walked past Jazzy on her way toward the steps, Jazzy grabbed her arm. "Don't go. Depending on Caleb's answers, I might need a ride back into town."

Genny glanced from Jazzy to Caleb, but didn't say anything. The intense expression in her black eyes spoke volumes. If Caleb had learned anything about Genny Madoc these past few months, it was that, by nature, the woman was a peacemaker.

"I'll drive you to town whenever you get ready to go,"

Caleb told Jazzy. "There's no need for Genny to hang around and listen to our argument."

Jazzy gave him an aha look. "So we're going to argue, are we?"

"Maybe. I don't know."

Jazzy released Genny. "Go ahead. And thanks for coming with me and sitting out here for two hours waiting on Caleb to finally come home."

"No problem." Genny hugged Jazzy. "Give me a call later. Okay?"

Jazzy nodded.

Two hours? They'd been waiting here for him for two hours, and that had given Jazzy more than enough time to work herself into a powerful hissy fit.

When Genny walked past Caleb, she patted his arm and smiled at him, then hurried on out to her SUV. Jazzy stood there on the porch, glaring at him. From several feet away, he could feel the pulsating anger inside her. She was pissed as hell. And he didn't blame her.

"Want to come inside and—" He didn't get the sentence finished before Jazzy barreled forward, reached out, and pounded on his chest.

"Damn you, Caleb McCord." She continued drumming her tight fists against his chest. "I thought last night meant something special to you. I thought we—" She gasped when he grabbed her wrists and drew her hands up between them.

"I just took a drive to clear my head this morning," he told her. When she struggled against him, he increased the pressure, holding her wrists securely. "I had some things to think about and I needed to be alone—somewhere away from Cherokee Pointe." What he told her wasn't a lie, at least not completely.

She calmed enough so that he felt safe to release her. She stood only inches from him and looked up at him, their gazes clashing as she searched his eyes for the truth.

How the hell did you admit to a woman that you were jealous of her dead lover?

"What did you need to think about—you and me?" she asked, hugging herself as if she'd suddenly gotten a chill.

"Come on inside and—"

"Did I get it wrong?" she asked. "Did I read more into what happened between us than was actually there?"

"If you thought something special happened, it did," he told her. "If you think it was the most incredible experience of my life, you're right. It was."

"Then I don't understand—"

Caleb walked away from her, pulled his key chain from his pocket, inserted the house key in the lock, then turned the knob and opened the door. When he glanced back at her, he said, "Let's talk inside. I need a drink. How about you?"

"Is what you have to tell me that bad?"

Her voice held a touch of humor, which he thought was a good sign. They'd both need a sense of humor and a whole heap of understanding and forgiveness if they were going to weather this storm. Just how honest should he be? Diplomatically honest? Brutally honest?

"I'm not sure how to answer that question," he told her truthfully as he headed for the kitchen and the bottle of whiskey he kept in the cupboard above the sink.

After closing the door, she followed him through the living room and into the small kitchen area. He set two glasses on the table, then filled each with a shot of Crown Royal. He picked up one glass and held it out to her. She looked at him and then at the glass. As soon as she accepted her drink, he picked up his.

"What are we drinking to?" she asked.

"How about to happiness in the future," he said. "And to burying the unhappy past."

She examined his face, his expression. "I thought that's what we did last night. You helped me bury my past and gave me a reason to think I had a chance to be happy in the future."

"Did we bury your past last night?" Caleb gulped down the liquor, slung back his head and let the whiskey sizzle down his throat. One drink wouldn't be enough to erase the memory of Jazzy whispering Jamie's name. Hell, a hundred drinks wouldn't be enough.

Jazzy set her glass down on the kitchen table, the liquor untouched. "I don't know what's going on. Stop avoiding giving me a direct answer. Cut to the chase."

Caleb finished off his drink and poured himself another. "How do you feel about Jamie Upton? And I want the truth."

She stared at him, a puzzled look in her eyes. "Where is this coming from? I thought I made myself perfectly clear last night. Jamie is my past. Before he died, I'd set myself free from him. I knew that I didn't love him, that whatever fragments of caring were left in my heart I could deal with and move on."

Caleb took a sip of whiskey. "Was last night about Jamie? Or was it about me?"

She stared at him, her gaze transfixed, as if his question stumped her. After a long, torturous silence, she finally said, "Both, I guess."

Caleb nodded, then downed the second shot of whiskey.

She reached out and took the glass from his hand, then recapped the liquor bottle and set it aside. "Being with you was unlike anything I'd ever experienced. Better than anything."

God, how he wanted to believe her. Not just for his

masculine pride. He loved Jazzy. He wanted her to love him. Love him best. Love him more.

She put her arms around his neck. His body stiffened, and he knew he couldn't resist her. "After being with you last night . . ." When he continued looking away from her, she kept one arm around his neck and, with her free hand, grasped his chin and forced him to look right at her. "Even if Jamie were alive, you'd have no reason to be jealous. If he were here right this minute, I'd choose you."

Caleb cupped the back of her head and brought her face up to his. And while he kissed her, he tried to forget about Jamie Upton. What difference did it make whose name she whispered in her sleep? It didn't mean she loved Jamie.

Keep telling yourself that and maybe one of these days you'll believe it!

While the Willis family met with Dr. MacNair and the young hotshot lawyer Jim Upton had supplied them, Jacob and Dallas waited in Jacob's office. Despite Andrea's cool, uppity attitude, Jacob had seen below the surface and figured Andrea Willis had something to hide. His first guess was that she was trying to protect her elder daughter, that she either knew Laura had killed Jamie or suspected she had. His second supposition was that Mrs. Willis was the one who'd killed Jamie.

"So who's this lawyer?" Dallas asked.

"Trent Langley," Jacob told him. "He's young and eager. And from what I hear, pretty darn sharp. He's from Jefferson City and was recommended by the most prestigious law firm in Knoxville. Hobart, Richards and English."

"Mm-hmm."

"Big Jim would have sent Maxie, if we hadn't already hired him for Jazzy. Maxie's the best lawyer in Cherokee Pointe."

"But not Big Jim's business attorney?"

"Nope. That would be Hobart, Richards and English."

"Out of Knoxville."

Jacob grinned. "Yeah."

Dallas walked over to the open door and glanced across the outer office to a quiet corner where Dr. MacNair sat holding Laura Willis's hand and talking to her, soothing her. The young lawyer, Langley, stood several feet away, deep in conversation with Mr. and Mrs. Willis. Dallas's gaze scanned the room and found the younger Willis daughter perched on the edge of Deputy Bobby Joe Harte's desk. Bobby Joe looked downright mortified.

Glancing over his shoulder at Jacob, Dallas said, "What about Sheridan Willis? Think there's any chance she might actually know something? She told Bobby Joe she believes her sister might have killed Jamie, but that could be conjecture on her part."

"She might know something. But my guess is that Mrs. Willis told her to keep her mouth shut. And I'd say Mama rules the roost."

"I agree." Just as Dallas started to close the door, his cell phone rang again. His gaze met Jacob's. He retrieved the phone and hit the on button. "Sloan here."

Jacob waited patiently, something not easy for him. Dallas didn't say much, just "uh-huh" a few times and "interesting" twice. Then Dallas's eyes widened in surprise and he looked at Jacob. Something was up. Something more important than the fact Laura Willis had attempted to run down her high school boyfriend with her sixteenth birthday present—a Mustang convertible.

"Thanks, Teri," Dallas said. "I can't tell you how much

Jacob and I appreciate your unearthing this information so quickly." After he replaced his cell phone on its belt clip, he faced Jacob. "You might want to ask Mr. and Mrs. Willis to come in here alone."

"What's up? What did Teri find out?"

"She found out why Laura was born a year before her parents married."

Jacob frowned. "I don't see how that information could affect Jamie's murder case, not the way knowing Laura tried to run down her teenage boyfriend could go to prove she might be unstable enough to kill someone."

"What if I told you that Laura's mother was declared legally insane when Laura was an infant and it's possible Laura inherited her mother's mental illness?"

Andrea hesitated when the sheriff asked to speak to Cecil and her. She didn't want to leave Laura. But seeing how calm Laura was, what a soothing effect Dr. MacNair seemed to have on her, Andrea agreed. However, she insisted Trent Langley accompany them. She didn't trust Sheriff Butler. He suspected Laura had killed Jamie and since he was Jazzy Talbot's friend, he would no doubt do everything possible to lay the blame elsewhere.

"Have a seat." The sheriff indicated the two chairs in front of his desk.

Cecil looked to her before doing anything. When she sat, he sat. Their lawyer stood directly behind the two of them.

"What's this all about, Sheriff?" Mr. Langley asked.

"First, I need to preface what I'm about to say by telling y'all that Laura is a suspect in both murders," Jacob told them.

"See here, Sheriff Butler, you can't really believe that my Laura"—Cecil's voice broke. "She is the sweetest, dearest child. She loved Jamie. She wouldn't have . . . she's not capable of such a heinous crime."

"Maybe not, but her mother was capable of it, wasn't she?" Jacob Butler made the profound comment and waited for a reaction.

All color drained from Cecil's face. Andrea tried her best not to gasp or cry out a denial. She laid her hand over her husband's, then looked from the sheriff to the police chief. "Exactly what do y'all know?"

"We know that Cecil Willis was married to a woman named Margaret Bentley and that she gave birth to a daughter named Laura," Dallas said. "And we know that Margaret Bentley was found guilty of attempted murder, but instead of going to jail, she was placed in a private sanitarium when the judge ruled her legally insane."

"Laura doesn't know," Andrea said. "She must never know."

"Laura doesn't know that you aren't her biological mother?" Jacob asked.

"No." Andrea shook her head. "I suppose we should have told her, but . . ." Andrea looked at the sheriff, hoping he was capable of great understanding and compassion. "Would you want to know that your mother was criminally insane? That she had tried to kill your grandfather by torturing him to death?"

"No, ma'am, I wouldn't."

"Then you can understand why we wanted to keep the truth from Laura, why we've lived in fear all these years that the truth would come out. Very few people know about Cecil's first marriage. He and his father had a falling out when Cecil married Margaret. She wasn't . . . she wasn't our kind."

"My first wife came from trash, Sheriff Butler," Cecil said. "She was a beautiful woman determined to escape from poverty, and she saw me as her escape route. I was young and foolish, and although I was in love with Andrea and we were practically engaged, one night I succumbed to Margaret's rather considerable charm. She came to me a couple of months later and told me she was pregnant. Naturally, I did the honorable thing and married her. Against my parents' wishes.

"We moved to Louisville and were living there when Laura was born." Cecil sighed heavily. "My parents cut off my funds, and I was ill-equipped to make a living on my own. Margaret discovered that I could offer her very little without my father's money, and it was then that I realized my wife had severe mental problems. She . . . she . . . uh—" Cecil cleared his throat. "I took Laura, left Margaret, and went home to my parents." Tears trickled down Cecil's cheeks. "My parents arranged for the marriage to be annulled and we—I—gained full custody of Laura."

Andrea couldn't bear seeing her husband this way, so totally defeated, in so much pain. She had never loved anyone but Cecil. She had forgiven him, loved him, married him, and adopted Laura. And she had never regretted those decisions.

"Margaret somehow managed to abduct Marshall Willis, Cecil's father," Andrea said. "She blamed him for everything at the time. She had intended to kill him, after she tortured him. She took him to the Willis hunting lodge and only by mere chance a couple of hunters heard Marshall's screams and investigated."

"Margaret had tortured my father for hours," Cecil said. "If those hunters hadn't . . . he almost died."

"You must see that our knowing Laura's biological mother's background sheds new light on Jamie's murder case," Jacob said.

"Just because Margaret was capable of doing something so terrible doesn't mean Laura is," Cecil said. "You tell them, Andrea. Tell them that Laura would never . . ."

"You have absolutely no proof that Laura had anything to do with Jamie's murder." Andrea held her head high and looked the sheriff right in the eye. "Yes, our elder daughter is emotionally fragile and it's possible she inherited a mental weakness from Margaret. But Laura is, as Cecil told you, a kind, sweet young woman, incapable of murder."

"Is that what her psychiatrist told y'all after you committed her for treatment a few days after she tried to run down her boyfriend when she was sixteen?" Dallas asked.

Andrea glared at the police chief. "That was nothing more than an accident. No charges were ever filed."

Andrea looked to their lawyer and the minute he noticed her staring at him, he cleared his throat and said, "I suggest that instead of tormenting the Willis family and pointing fingers at Laura Willis, you make some inquiries about Margaret Bentley's whereabouts. Is she still confined to the mental hospital? If not, then I'd say she could very well be your—"

"Shut up!" Andrea huffed. Damned stupid young man!

"Ma'am?" Wide-eyed and mouth agape, Trent Langley gulped as he looked at Andrea.

"The sanitarium where Margaret Bentley resided for nearly twenty-two years burned to the ground two years ago," Dallas explained. "She and nearly two dozen other patients died in that fire."

If only Margaret were alive, Andrea thought. If only that insane bitch had been the one who'd killed Jamie. But Margaret was dead. And the truth about Laura's maternity was no longer a well-kept family secret. She had spent twenty-four years trying to protect Cecil's little girl, but now she feared the time had come when there was very little she could do to protect Laura from a tragic past that had come back to haunt them all.

Chapter 26

Andrea Willis slapped the morning edition of *The Cherokee Pointe Herald* down on the table in front of her husband. Jim Upton glanced up from his plate, littered with the remnants of ham and red-eye gravy, scrambled eggs and Dora's homemade biscuits. Cecil Willis looked like a damn whipped dog. Jim wanted to shout at the man, tell him to grow a backbone—hell, to grow a set of balls. Only recently he'd envied Cecil being married to a strong, take-charge woman, but that was before he'd realized just how pussy whipped the guy was. He'd take a clinging vine like Reba any day of the week over someone like Willis's wife.

"Look at the headlines!" Andrea shouted. "How are you going to deal with this?"

Cecil lifted the newspaper off his plate. A wad of scrambled eggs, which had stuck to the back of the paper, dropped off, leaving a greasy spot on the newsprint. He read the headlines, sighed, and looked up at his wife, who hovered over him like a vulture.

"It was to be expected," Cecil told her.

"Is that all you have to say?" Andrea demanded.

"What's the problem?" Jim asked. "I assume the reporters have gotten wind of Laura's past history . . . her emotional problems when she was a young girl."

Cecil folded the paper and handed it to Jim. "Now that Laura is a suspect in Jamie's murder, if you'd prefer we find somewhere else to stay, I'll understand."

Jim took the paper, scanned the headlines:

IS JAZZY INNOCENT?

DID JAMIE'S FIANCÉE DO IT?

then tossed the newspaper aside. "Rubbish. Laura didn't kill Jamie any more than I did. Brian MacKinnon likes to sensationalize everything. If I thought it would do any good, I'd call Farlan and tell him to rein in that son of his."

"Are you saying that there's nothing we can do about what the newspaper prints about Laura?" Andrea asked, her gaze focused on Jim.

Jim glanced at the discarded newspaper. "My bet is that the reporter who wrote that piece of trash stopped just short of slander. The facts are probably correct, even if they've been distorted a bit."

"I've read the entire article," Andrea said. "Either someone in the sheriff's department has been talking or that reporter has done some digging—deep digging—into Laura's past."

"My God, do they know about—" Cecil shut up the minute his wife glowered at him, making Jim wonder what he'd been about to say.

"Yes, they know that the Roberts boy accused Laura of trying to run him down with her car when she was sixteen." Andrea glanced quickly back and forth from Cecil to Jim. "I assure you that Laura did not try to harm that boy. It was an accident."

Jim figured there was more to the story than either

Andrea or Cecil was letting on, but at present his biggest concern wasn't Laura. He knew the girl, knew how gentle and kind she was. The very idea that she had tortured Jamie to death was ludicrous. Of course, he didn't really believe Jazzy Talbot was capable of such cruelty, either.

I know that you've seen to it that the DA has railroaded an innocent woman, had her arrested for a murder she didn't commit. I know all about how powerful Big Jim Upton is. Hell, maybe you're right. Maybe I'm not your grandson. If Jamie Upton was the result of your parenting skills, then I'm damn lucky I didn't do what my mother wanted me to do and come to you and Miss Reba when I was sixteen.

He had heard Caleb McCord's words repeating themselves in his mind, again and again, ever since yesterday when he'd confronted that young man standing outside Reba's hospital suite.

Jamie's murderer was probably still at large, free to kill again. Hell, she'd already killed again, if the sheriff's guess was right, that the same person had killed that Watson man. Neither Laura nor Jazzy was guilty, he felt certain of that fact. If he did what he knew was right, he'd make a phone call to Wade Truman and see if it was too late to get the charges against Jasmine Talbot dropped.

Why now? Jim asked himself. *Are you willing to go against what Reba wants just because of what that young pup McCord said?*

"We'll make sure Laura is taken care of," Jim told her parents. "How is she this morning?" He glanced around the room. "Didn't she feel like coming down for breakfast? And what about Sheridan?" Jim was beginning to dislike Sheridan more and more. There was something decidedly unappealing about the girl. His guess was that the younger Willis daughter had been *The Cherokee*

Pointe Herald reporter's source of information about Laura. It was plain to see that Sheridan despised her older sister.

"After the terrible time we had at the sheriff's office yesterday afternoon, Dr. MacNair came home with us and instructed Mrs. Conley to keep Laura sedated so that she'd get a good night's rest," Andrea explained. "And Sheridan has already gone out this morning."

Or never came home last night, Jim thought.

"If there's anything Laura needs, you just let me know." Jim finished off the last bites of his breakfast, washed them down with coffee, then scooted back his chair and stood. "Please excuse me. I have some business to attend to."

"Yes, of course." Andrea offered him an artificial smile.

"Thank you, Jim," Cecil said. "We appreciate your kindness."

Jim nodded, then headed straight for his study. The minute he was alone and the door locked, he sat behind his desk and lifted the telephone receiver. He punched in the number and waited as it rang.

"Powell Investigations," the receptionist said.

"Griffin Powell, please. Tell him it's Jim Upton."

"Yes, sir."

In less than a minute a man's deep baritone voice said, "Morning, Jim."

"What do you have for me?"

"Not a lot," Griffin replied. "After all, we just started on this investigation late yesterday afternoon."

"Do you have anything at all?"

"There is a marriage record for Melanie Upton to a Franky Joe McCord—six months before the birth of a child named Caleb Upton McCord—thirty-two, almost thirty-three years ago."

"My Melanie?"

"That's what we're checking on," Griffin said. "I should have a more detailed report for you by late today. Two of my best men flew into Memphis last night."

"I want everything they can dig up on my daughter during her years in Memphis. If she married this Franky Joe McCord, the marriage wasn't legal. She was already a married woman. Byron didn't get a divorce for several years after Melanie left him."

"I don't suppose that fact matters any now, except that would make Caleb McCord illegitimate."

"I want to know every detail of Caleb McCord's life. And if he is my grandson, I don't give a rat's ass that he might be a bastard."

"It'll take time to get the info you want."

"Do a rush job. You know that money is no object."

"I do have the guy's blood type, if that will help."

"How'd—no, don't tell me. I don't need to know how you get the information, just get it," Jim said. "So what's his blood type?"

"Type O."

"Humph! Half the world is type O. I'm type O. So were Melanie and Jim, Jr. No great revelation there, but at least it doesn't rule the boy out. He might be my grandson."

"Tell me this, Jim—do you want him to be your grandson?" Griffin asked.

"I've thought about that all night. Couldn't think of much else. Do I want Caleb McCord to be my grandson? Yes, I do, if he's a decent human being. If he won't break Reba's heart a dozen times over the way Jamie did."

"McCord was a Memphis cop and his record with the MPD is admirable," Griffin said. "So far we haven't found one dark blot on his record since he joined the force at twenty-two. From what we've uncovered so far, McCord is someone any father or grandfather could be damn proud of. He resigned from the police force after his partner was killed and he was severely wounded."

Jim swallowed. A grandson he could be proud of! Damn it, he couldn't get his hopes up, couldn't start making plans for a boy who might turn out to be a fraud. "If you find solid proof that Caleb McCord's mother was my Melanie, you call me. And send that proof by courier on the next plane out of Memphis."

"We'll do the very best we can."

"I want this kept top secret for now. You understand."

"Yes, I understand," Griffin replied. "And you have my word that we'll keep this under wraps."

When Jim heard the dial tone, he returned the receiver to the base, then leaned back in his desk chair and cupped his hands behind his head. Was it possible? Was it honest to God possible that he and Reba had another grandchild? Was God going to be merciful to them after all?

In a fit of rage she tore the morning newspaper into pieces and threw them in every direction all around her. How dare they print such vicious lies! How dare they accuse Laura Willis of Jamie's murder. This was wrong. All wrong! Jazzy was the woman who should be punished. She was the one who had been Jamie's true partner in wickedness. Laura was an innocent child. Her parents should have taken better care of her. They shouldn't let bad things happen to her. This was all Cecil Willis's fault. If he'd been a better father . . . but some men didn't know how to be good husbands and good fathers. Her baby's father had been a bad man. A bad father. She couldn't allow this to happen. There had to be a way to turn things around, to take the suspicion off Laura. But how?

Kill someone else and make sure Laura has an alibi.

This was all that man's fault. That Stan Watson. If he hadn't seen her digging a hole in the woods to bury the weapons she had used to kill Jamie and the other items from the cabin, none of this would be happening. Watson had been another man who had ruined her plans, as others had in the past. But she could fix things. Laura Willis hadn't been arrested. The sheriff had no solid evidence against her. For the time being Laura was safe.

But what about Jazzy? If they didn't prosecute her for murdering Jamie, she wouldn't suffer. She wouldn't endure the torment she deserved.

Then it will be up to you to make sure she suffers terribly before you kill her.

It was time to revise her plans, to consider her options. She could still accomplish most of what she'd set out to do, torture those who deserved to be punished. Torture and kill them. She would kill him slowly and painfully. She had dreamed of killing him, of making him pay for what he'd done to her and her baby.

No, that's not right. Think, damn it, think. You've already killed Jamie. Your baby is safe. He can't hurt her. You made him pay.

But what about him? What about him?

Who? an inner voice asked.

"You know who!" she cried. "Yes, of course. I'll kill him first. And then I'll kill Jazzy. It's her fault. It's all her fault. If it hadn't been for her, he wouldn't have left me. She wouldn't let him go. It's her fault that he was so mean to me, that he didn't love me."

Was that her name—Jazzy? It doesn't sound right. That's not what he called her.

Of course it's her. Jasmine Talbot. He loved her. Never me. Never me.

She would kill him first. And anyone else who got in her way. And then she would kill that horrible woman who had taken everything away from her. *Kill them together. Do it at the same time. Let him hear her scream. Make her watch him die.*

Jazzy hadn't pressed Caleb to tell her why he'd disappeared yesterday morning, why he'd run away from Cherokee Pointe—from her. They'd made love at his cabin after Genny left. Wild, crazy, animalistic monkey-fucking. And it had been good. Hell, it had been great. But it had been different than when they'd made love the night before, when Caleb had been both passionate and tender. There had been no tenderness in their lovemaking yesterday afternoon. She had felt that he'd been trying to brand her as his property, to consume her completely, to prove something either to himself or to her. Maybe to both of them. And she knew that Jamie was the reason.

She had heard the doubt and fear in Caleb's voice when he'd asked, "How do you feel about Jamie Upton? And I want the truth."

Damn! Would she never be totally free of Jamie? Here she was accused of Jamie's murder—despite suspicion falling on Laura Willis now, the DA hadn't dropped the charges against her—and when she'd finally found a man she thought she could love, Jamie's ghost stood between them.

How could she convince Caleb that he had no reason to be jealous of Jamie? How could she prove to him that he was the only man she wanted?

After they'd spent the afternoon in bed together yesterday, Caleb had driven her into town and she'd show-

ered and changed clothes before coming to work here at
Jasmine's. She had thought things were okay between
them, that whatever had been wrong with Caleb, they
had worked it out in bed. But last night when she'd
thought he would go home with her after they left Jazzy's
Joint, he'd surprised her and said good night at the door.

"I need some time to think," he'd told her. "I've already called Sally and she's on her way. I'll wait in the
car until she gets here.

"Caleb, what's wrong?"

He'd kissed her, but hadn't answered her question
before he walked away, down the stairs and to his car.
She'd wanted to go after him, to demand some answers.
Instead she'd gone inside her apartment and had herself a good cry.

She hadn't seen him all day today. If he needed time,
she'd give him time. Her days of running after a man,
begging for his love, were long gone. She'd made a fool
of herself over Jamie Upton when they were teenagers.
Once he realized how much she loved him, he'd walked
all over her. But she would never let another man do
that to her. Not even Caleb. If he didn't want her, if
he'd decided he couldn't handle his stupid jealousy of a
man she didn't love anymore, then so be it.

The phone on Jazzy's desk rang. Without thinking
she lifted the receiver, then thought, *What if it's Caleb?*

"Jasmine's," she said. "This is Jazzy Talbot. How may I
help you?"

"You're a bad woman. You deserve to die." The voice
over the phone sounded strange. Muffled.

"Who is this?"

"Someone who is going to make sure you pay for
your sins."

"Look, whoever the hell you are, get a life, will you?
And don't bother me again."

Jazzy slammed down the receiver. When she saw her hand trembling, she balled it into a firm fist and pounded her fist on the desktop. Pain radiated from her hand to her wrist and tingled up to her elbow.

It's just some nutcase, she told herself. *There's no need to get all torn up about a silly phone call.* But it wasn't silly. It was threatening. The person had said that he—or she—was going to make Jazzy pay for her sins.

She jerked the phone into her still unsteady hand, then punched in the numbers hurriedly. As she waited for him to answer, she made herself breathe in and out slowly, hoping to calm her nerves.

"Sheriff Butler," Jacob said when he answered his phone.

"Jacob, it's Jazzy. I—er—I just got a crank call. At least I think it was a crank."

"Okay. Tell me about it."

"The voice sounded muffled, maybe disguised. I don't know."

"Man or woman?"

"I couldn't tell."

"What did this person say?"

"He said—or maybe it was a woman—that I was bad, that I deserved to die and that he—or she—was going to make sure I was punished for my sins."

Jacob was silent for what seemed like forever, then he said, "I want to put a tap on your phones."

"Why? What good would that do? He didn't talk more than a minute, if that."

"If this person calls again, you can try to keep him on the phone long enough for a trace."

"You don't think it was a crank call, do you?"

"Could have been," Jacob said. "But it just might have been Jamie's murderer."

"Oh, my God!" Jazzy's mind wrapped itself around

the thought that Jamie's killer had called to threaten her. "Then it was a woman. And she said . . . she'd make me pay for my sins."

"Where's Caleb?" Jacob asked.

"Caleb? Over at Jazzy's Joint."

"Where are you?"

"At Jasmine's, in my office."

"Go over to Jazzy's Joint and tell Caleb about the phone call. Do it now. And make sure he keeps watch over you. I don't want you alone from here on out. Not even alone in either of your offices."

"You think it really was her and that she—"

"Let's not take any chances. Okay?"

Jazzy nodded, then realized she hadn't spoken. "Yeah, okay."

When she hung up, she sat there for a couple of minutes and let the realization sink in. If her caller was Jamie's killer . . .

She had to tell Caleb. Jacob had told her to make sure Caleb kept watch over her. But with the tension between Caleb and her right now, could she go to him? Did she have the right to expect him to stand by her side?

No time like the present to find out, she told herself.

Caleb felt her presence the minute she entered the bar. God knew it wasn't that he could smell her perfume in this smoky jungle. Too much smoke, liquor, and human sweat to ever distinguish one distinct odor. And he couldn't see her from where he was standing, but more than one set of male eyes focused in a particular direction—straight at the most gorgeous woman in the world. Jazzy Talbot. His Jazzy.

Yeah, that was right—his Jazzy. Damn Jamie Upton to

hell. Caleb chuckled to himself. That was just about where Jamie was right now—burning in hell. Or maybe because he'd suffered through torment before he died, the good Lord had taken pity on him. Who knew? Who cared? He sure didn't. But one thing he did know, one thing that did matter to him was not allowing Jamie's ghost to come between Jazzy and him. He'd never been the kind of guy who gave up when he wanted something bad enough. And he had never wanted anything more than he wanted Jazzy's love.

When he turned around, their gazes met across the room and he felt as if he'd been hit in the head with sledgehammer. If this wasn't love—honest-to-goodness, forever-after love—he sure as hell didn't know what else it could be. He held her gaze, silently beckoning her to him. She took several tentative steps, then paused. Was she waiting to see if he'd meet her halfway? Knowing Jazzy as he did, he figured that's why she'd stopped. Okay, no problem. He'd do his part. Caleb walked toward her, then waited when about ten feet separated them.

She smiled and, heaven help him, he wanted to run to her, grab her and . . . tonight he wouldn't say goodbye at her door the way he'd done last night. He'd needed time to think, time to clear his head. And being near Jazzy made that impossible. All he had to do was look at her and he wanted her.

Be honest, McCord, a part of you wanted to punish her for daring to whisper another man's name in her sleep. Yeah, okay, so that was part of it. But who had he really punished? Jazzy, maybe. But he'd punished himself, too. There was no place on earth he wanted to be except with her.

She moved toward him slowly. He headed in her direction, one easy, unhurried step at a time. They came together in the middle of the bar, between the dance floor and the tables scattered throughout the room. From the jukebox, Willie Nelson and Julio Iglesias crooned about all the girls they'd loved before. Beer bottles and frosty glasses clinked. Pool balls clanged together. The din of hushed voices blended with rowdy laughter.

Caleb and Jazzy stayed focused on each other, not breaking eye contact for even a millisecond. She smiled at him again. He grinned at her.

"Want to dance?" he asked, desperately needing to take her into his arms.

She nodded.

He held out his hand. When she placed her hand in his, he walked her across the bar to the dance floor and eased her into his arms. They moved to the music, a couple of inches separating their bodies.

"I missed you last night," she said.

"Yeah, I missed you, too."

"Do we need to talk about it?" she asked.

"Probably." He pulled her closer, aligning her body to his. "But not tonight."

"No, not tonight."

She seemed to melt into him, all soft femininity and womanly heat. He brushed his chin against her temple and thought he'd lose it when she sighed. This was where she belonged, in his arms. They were right for each other, and he figured she knew that fact as well as he did.

One song ended and another began, this one a loud, bawdy melody not meant for slow dancing. Caleb kept his arm around her and whispered in her ear. "Want to sit this one out?"

She nodded. He released his hold on her, but she didn't move away. She stayed close, her shoulder brushing his arm. "How about later tonight, after this place closes, we dance on upstairs to my place?"

He wanted to touch her again, but figured they'd already brought enough attention to themselves without him doing more to prove what a fool he was over Jazzy. "There's nothing I'd like better."

Her broad smile said it all. Everything was going to be all right. Whatever lingering problems Jamie's memory might cause, they'd deal with them. Together.

Caleb slipped his arm around her waist and led her toward the bar where Lacy stood smiling as she watched them approach. "How about a Coke?" he asked.

"With lemon," Jazzy said.

"Two Cokes," Caleb told Lacy. "One with lemon. One straight."

"Coming right up." Suddenly Lacy looked beyond them to someone or something on the far side of the room. "Well, I'm be damned. I never thought I'd see the likes of him in here."

"Who are—" Jazzy turned around to see who Lacy was talking about. "Big Jim Upton in Jazzy's Joint. If that man's here to cause trouble, I'll—"

"Let me handle it," Caleb said, his gut telling him that Big Jim was here to see him.

"I can fight this particular battle myself," Jazzy told him as she marched away from the bar.

Caleb grabbed her shoulder. "Wait up, honey. I don't think he's here to see you."

"Who else would he be here to see?"

"Me."

Jazzy eyed him curiously. "You? Why would—"

"Evening," Jim Upton said as he came up to Caleb and Jazzy.

Jazzy glowered at Jamie's grandfather. "What do you want?"

"I want to speak to Caleb," Jim said.

Jazzy looked at Jim, then at Caleb. "What's going on here?"

"Look, honey, I need to talk to Mr. Upton alone, if you don't mind?"

"Well, what if I do mind?" She fixed her gaze on Big Jim. "So who's going to tell me why you're really here? Why do you want to talk to Caleb?"

"Personal business," Jim told her.

She looked at Caleb. "Tell me now or tell me later, but if we've got a snowball's chance in hell of making it, we can't keep any secrets from each other."

"I know, honey. And I swear, I'll tell you everything. Later."

"Okay." Jazzy nodded and started to walk away.

"Are you and Jazzy a couple now?" Big Jim asked.

"Yes," Caleb replied. "We are."

"Then why haven't you told her that you're my grandson?"

Chapter 27

Jazzy whirled around, her eyes huge with astonishment. "What the hell did you say?" She glared at Big Jim Upton.

Caleb rushed to her, grabbed her arm and said, "Let's not do this here." He scanned the room hurriedly. "This is private business. Personal."

She stared at Caleb. "Did you hear what he said?"

Damn, why hadn't he already told Jazzy? Why did she have to find out this way?

"Yeah, honey, I heard what he said, but before everybody here at Jazzy's Joint starts wondering what the hell's going on—"

Jazzy looked back at Jim. "You have some nerve coming in here, in my bar, and spouting off such stupid nonsense. I know you've been under a lot of stress since Jamie died and Miss Reba had a heart attack. But you don't have the right to go shooting off your mouth with some wild notion you've concocted about Caleb."

"I apologize," Jim said, his gaze fixed on Caleb. "Look, son, I didn't mean to cause a problem for you with . . .

are you two really together? I mean is she . . . important to you?"

Jazzy tensed. Her eyes flashed green fire. Caleb tightened his hold on her arm. "May we use your office?"

"What?" She stared at him, a dumbfounded expression on her face.

"Let's go to your office—you, me, and Mr. Upton," Caleb said. "So we can finish this conversation without an audience."

"By all means." Jazzy got right up in Jim's face. "Follow me, Mr. Upton." She emphasized the *Mr.* when she spoke.

When Jazzy sashayed off toward the back of the building, Caleb motioned for Big Jim to follow her, which he did. Within a couple of minutes, the three of them were cocooned in Jazzy's small, cluttered office. Caleb closed the door, then glanced from his grandfather to the woman he loved. She was going to be mad as an old wet hen when he told her the truth. God damn it, why had he kept her in the dark about why he'd actually come to Cherokee Pointe in the first place?

"Start anywhere," Jazzy said as she sat down on the side of her desk and crossed her arms over her chest. "Start with Big Jim's crazy statement. Or start with who the hell you really are. Or even start with telling me you haven't been lying to me for months now."

"Jazzy, honey . . . please—"

"Don't you 'please' me," she told him. "Somebody had better start talking right now!"

Jim cleared his throat. "I believe that's your cue, son."

"Stop calling him son!" Jazzy screeched at Jim.

When Caleb tried to approach Jazzy, her deadly glare warned him off. He threw up his hands in a gesture of surrender. "Okay. Who am I? My name is Caleb Upton McCord." The moment Jazzy heard his middle name, her shoulders stiffened and she sucked in her breath.

"My mother was Melanie Upton, Big Jim and Miss Reba's daughter."

Speechless, her mouth parting on a silent gasp, Jazzy sat there staring at him.

"I had no idea my mother had any family," Caleb said. "Not until right before she died fifteen years ago. She told me about her parents, but . . . well, I was a wiseass kid who thought he didn't need or want a family. It was only a few months ago, after I resigned from the Memphis Police force, that I decided I wanted to find my mother's family."

"That's the reason you came to Cherokee Pointe—to find the Uptons?" Hugging herself nervously, her eyes downcast, Jazzy shook her head in disbelief. "You're Jamie's first cousin. And you knew all along who he was, who Big Jim and Miss Reba . . . you've been lying to me since the first night we met." Lifting her head, she glared at him. "Damn you, Caleb. Damn you for making me care about you, for letting me think things would be different with you."

"Things are different with me. I swear, honey. I swear—"

She flew off the desk, rushed toward him, and slapped him soundly. "What was it? Did you want everything Jamie had—including me? Was getting me in the sack some sort of prize?"

"Stop talking like that." Caleb ignored the stinging pain throbbing through the left side of his face. "I wanted you the minute we met. Before I knew anything about your relationship with Jamie."

Jazzy zeroed in on Big Jim. "How long have you known?"

"This is all my fault. I didn't know that you and Caleb had anything serious going on." He looked to Caleb. "I didn't mean to—"

"How long?" Jazzy demanded.

"Caleb told me yesterday," Jim said. "But I didn't believe him. Not at first."

"Apparently you believe him now." Jazzy kept her gaze fixed on Jim. "Got yourself some sort of proof, didn't you? You wouldn't have come here to claim the new heir to the Upton fortune if you weren't pretty damn sure he was your blood kin."

Jim glanced at Caleb. "I hired the best PI firm in Tennessee, Powell Investigations, to do a thorough check on you, boy. Every indication is that you're definitely our Melanie's son. My grandson."

"Well, isn't this nice?" Jazzy crossed her arms over her chest as she smiled sarcastically. "A warm and fuzzy reunion in my office. Aren't I lucky to be witnessing such a heartwarming event?" Jazzy gasped mockingly. "My God, I'll bet Miss Reba is thrilled. Lose one grandson, gain another." Narrowing her eyes to mere slits, she fixed her gaze on Caleb.

"And once she finds out about me—" Jazzy laughed. "She'll be fit to be tied. You see, I'm not good enough for an Upton. Jamie would have married me years ago if it hadn't been for his grandmother."

"Jazzy, don't do this," Caleb said.

She tapped him in the center of his chest, each punch a little harder than the one before. "It doesn't even matter if you really do care about me. Hell, it doesn't matter if you love me. And you know why? Because you're the Upton heir now. You're Miss Reba's grandson and she'll move heaven and earth to keep us apart."

"It won't be like that." He looked to his grandfather. "Tell her. Tell her that Miss Reba doesn't even know and that when she does—"

"Miss Reba doesn't know yet?" Jazzy shouted the question.

"No, Reba doesn't know," Jim said. "I had hoped Caleb would meet me at the hospital in the morning so we could tell her together."

"Ah . . . how sweet." Jazzy marched across the office, swung opened the door, turned and aimed her gaze on Caleb. "Take your grandfather and get out of my office. And while you're at it, get out of my bar. You're fired."

"Jazzy, we can work through this. It's not as bad as you think." Caleb held out one hand to her.

"Get out. Now! Out of my office. Out of my bar. Out of my life!"

"Jazzy . . ."

She stood there trembling, her cheeks flushed, anger boiling over inside her. He knew when to accept defeat. But this was only one battle, the first skirmish. This battle might be lost, but, by God, he intended to win the war.

"Let's go." Caleb laid his hand on his grandfather's shoulder. "I think the lady has made her feelings perfectly clear."

Without saying another word, Jim exited the office and Caleb followed. The very second they entered the hall, Jazzy slammed the door shut.

"Jazzy's always been high-strung and temperamental," Jim said. "The girl's got grit."

"You sound as if you almost admire her."

"I do, in a way."

"Then why—"

"Miss Reba hates Jazzy," Jim admitted. "If you've got serious intentions where she's concerned, you might as well know your grandmother isn't going to like it one little bit."

"Meaning no disrespect to Miss Reba, but my relationship with Jazzy—or any other woman—is none of her business."

Jim slapped his hand down on Caleb's back and laughed. "Damn, boy, you sound just like me."

"Is that good or bad?" Caleb asked.

"Neither. It's just a fact." Still chuckling, Jim walked down the hall beside Caleb.

Once they reached the smoke-filled hub of Jazzy's Joint, Caleb said, "Wait for me outside, will you? I need to talk to Lacy, the bartender, before I leave."

Jim nodded, and as soon as he headed for the door, Caleb walked over to the bar.

"What's up?" Lacy asked when he leaned over the counter.

"Jazzy and I just had a major falling out," he said. "She fired me. And she kicked me out of her life. For the time being."

"All because of Big Jim Upton? What's that about anyway?"

"Big Jim is my grandfather," Caleb told her.

Her eyes round and wide, Lacy whistled loudly. "And you didn't bother mentioning that fact to Jazzy? Good God, man, you must have a death wish."

"Listen, this thing isn't over between us by a long shot, but until she cools off . . . you understand. She shouldn't be alone tonight. Give Sally a call and tell her what's happened. Tell her to come on over to Jazzy's apartment and spend the night. Once Jazzy's had a chance to cool off and think things through, I'll talk to her again."

"That could take a while."

"I'll give her until noon tomorrow."

Lacy rolled her eyes toward the ceiling.

He leaned over and kissed her on the cheek. "Keep an eye on her, will you?"

"You really do love her, don't you?"

"Yeah, I'm afraid so," Caleb admitted.

* * *

Jazzy swept everything off the top of her desk in one angry pass, letting things hit haphazardly against the wall and scatter over the floor. Lifting her foot, she kicked the swivel chair and sent it sailing halfway across the room and into a file cabinet.

"Damn him! Damn him to hell and back!" she shouted.

Once a fool, always a fool!

How could she have been so stupid? Why did she think she could actually be happy? *You were born under a damn unlucky star,* she told herself. *Hell, a witch must have placed an evil spell on you the day you came into this world.*

The last time she'd been this angry, she had threatened to blow off Jamie's balls. She hadn't thought any man could ever hurt her the way Jamie had. Boy, had she been wrong. Putting so many hopes and dreams for the future into her relationship with Caleb had been a huge mistake. She should have known better.

When will you ever learn that happily ever after isn't for you?

Of all the men on earth to have fallen for—another goddamn Upton! Oh, his last name might be McCord, but he had Upton blood flowing through his veins. High society, Miss Reba blue blood. Rich, powerful Big Jim blood. Just like Jamie! She'd gone and traded in one Upton grandson for another.

He should have told her. She'd had a right to know. Why had it taken him all these months to approach Big Jim? Why had he waited around, working as a bouncer at Jazzy's Joint, when he was the heir to a vast fortune?

Maybe she should give him a chance to explain. Surely it hadn't all been an act. If he'd been pretending to care about her, then he deserved an Academy Award. Just thinking about the way things had been between them—all hot and wild—upped her body heat a few degrees and moistened her inside as if his big hands were stroking her naked flesh.

No, no, no! You aren't going to give in to him, allow him to weave some believable tale to explain away his behavior. You can't trust him. Even if he swears on a stack of Bibles that he loves you, you cannot believe him.

Okay, Jazzy, stop and think about what you're telling yourself. Just who are you talking about anyway? Caleb or Jamie?

Caleb might be Big Jim's grandson, but he was not Jamie. Caleb and Jamie had very little in common. Caleb was totally different. Everything Jamie hadn't been.

But he'd change now that Big Jim had declared him an Upton. All that money and power would get to him sooner or later. *Give him a few months and you won't recognize him.*

Hey, girl, what makes you think that in a few months he'll even want you? Add wealth and social standing to all of Caleb's other fantastic qualities, and there wasn't a woman anywhere who wouldn't jump at the chance to belong to him.

Jazzy poured herself a drink and downed it in one long swallow. The whiskey burned a sizzling streak down her throat and set her belly on fire. She coughed and spluttered a few times, then poured herself a second drink. As she lifted the glass to her lips, she thought about how she'd been so sure she could count on Caleb, how she'd believed he would see her through the nightmare her life had become lately.

"What are you going to do now?" she asked herself. "Now that Caleb isn't going to be looking out for you?" She downed the second shot of eighty proof and wondered just how much liquor it would take to get riproaring drunk.

Chapter 28

Cecil had wandered out into the garden seeking solitude from not only his wife, but from everything incomprehensible that his life had become recently. How had he reached this point? What had he done to deserve such misery? Wasn't every man entitled to a few mistakes?

All the old nightmares had returned. He'd dreamed about Margaret last night. Vivid, ugly dreams. It had taken him years to put the past behind him, to live without fear that someday the truth about Laura's biological mother would be revealed to the world. His sweet, precious Laura. Except for the pale blond hair, she actually resembled him much more than she did her mother. That alone had been a blessing. If every time he'd looked at his elder daughter he'd seen the madwoman who had almost destroyed his life nearly twenty-five years ago, he wasn't sure he could have loved her. But he did love Laura. And oddly enough, so did Andrea. Oh, he knew she didn't love Laura the way she did Sheridan, but the fact that she loved his child at all never ceased to amaze him. It had been Andrea who had defended Laura time and again. It had been Andrea who had insisted Laura receive the psychiatric help she'd needed as a young girl. And it had been Andrea who had cared for and protected Laura during these black days following Jamie's brutal murder.

Cecil finished off his tea, then set the china cup and saucer on the glass and metal patio table. Herbal tea often soothed his nerves, but he suspected that tonight he would have to take another sleeping pill if he wanted to rest.

He wished he could stop thinking about something that had been tormenting him since Jamie's death. If he didn't know for a fact that Margaret was dead, that she had died in the fire that swept through the private mental hospital where she'd lived, he would wonder if she had been the one who'd killed Jamie. Margaret had tortured his father, had almost killed him. And at her trial, a gruesome truth had been revealed. Margaret's own father had been found brutalized—castrated—when Margaret was only fifteen. Although there had been no proof that Margaret had killed her own father—and the judge couldn't consider that crime evidence against her—everyone involved, from the police officers to the district attorney, had been convinced that Margaret was a psychopathic killer.

Laura. His poor Laura. She must never know about Margaret. Although Laura had always been emotionally fragile, Cecil had never seen any evidence that she had inherited her mother's evil sickness. Not until that Roberts boy had accused her of trying to run him down with her car.

But that was only one incident, he reminded himself. *Until Jamie's murder.*

No! Absolutely, unequivocally no! Laura is incapable of such cruelty. You can't allow yourself to think, even for one minute, that she has killed two men.

"Daddy?"

Jumping at the sound of her voice, Cecil gasped and turned to face his elder daughter.

"Yes, Laura, what is it?"

"Are you all right?"

He offered her a smile as he walked toward her. "Just concerned about you. You've been through so much lately. Jamie's death. Losing the baby. And now this asinine attempt to blame you for Jamie's death."

"Do you think I killed him?"

She looked at him, her heart in her eyes, and Cecil wanted to pick her up and set her on his lap as he had done when she'd been a little girl.

"Of course not. I know you didn't—"

"I don't remember where I was the night Jamie was killed."

"What?"

"Mother told me that I mustn't say anything to anyone about it. But I had one of those odd spells, like the one I had when—"

Cecil grasped Laura's shoulders. "Your mother is right. Don't ever repeat to anyone else what you just told me. If the sheriff were to find out . . ." Cecil shook his head. "No, no, that mustn't happen. He wouldn't understand. He could use that fact as evidence against you."

"But, Daddy, what if I did kill Jamie?"

Cecil shook her gently. Tears welled up in her eyes. "You didn't kill him. I know you didn't."

"Your father is right, Laura. You didn't kill him," a female voice said. "I did."

Cecil searched the darkness for the source of the voice, a voice that seemed oddly familiar.

"Who said that?" Laura clung to her father as she looked all around her.

A small gray shadow moved out of the tall shrubbery that lined the back garden wall.

Cecil held his breath as she came into view, the soft patio torchlights casting a golden glow over the woman. He stared at her for an endless moment.

"My God, it can't be."

"But it is," she said. "I've come for you. And for Laura. Surely you knew that I would." She lifted her hand and aimed a sinister-looking gun directly at him.

"How?" It was the only word Cecil managed to say.

"How did I get inside the locked gates of the Upton compound?" the woman asked, smiling wickedly. "I used Jamie's remote control, of course. I found it in his pants pocket when I stripped him."

"Who are you?" Laura managed to ask.

"Didn't your father tell you about me? No, of course he didn't. He's ashamed of me. But he should be ashamed of himself, because he hasn't been a very good father. A good father never would have allowed you to become involved with Jamie. He was a bad man. A bad man like you, Cecil. He deserved to die."

"Daddy?" Trembling from head to toe, Laura clung to Cecil.

"It'll be all right Laura," he promised her, praying fervently that he could keep that promise.

"He's right, Laura. Everything is all right, now that I'm here. I'll make sure no one ever hurts my baby. I'm a good mother. I was always a good mother, but they took my little girl away from me. That wasn't right, was it? And Jazzy raised my little girl and told her she was her mother. Jazzy and Jamie were so . . ."

She stared from Laura to Cecil as if she couldn't quite remember who they were. If only he dared to jump her, Cecil thought, dared to go for the gun and try to stop her. But what if she accidentally shot Laura?

"That's not right, is it? Jamie was mean to you——" She pointed the gun at Laura and Cecil gasped. Then she pointed the gun back at him. "I killed him because he was mean to my baby. And you've been a bad father, Cecil. A very bad father. And Jazzy was a bad mother. It was wrong of her to take you away from me. She had no right to tell my baby she was her mother."

"Daddy, what is she talking about? Do you know her?"

"Yes . . . Daddy . . . tell her what I'm talking about. Tell her who I am."

Andrea swung open the French doors and marched out onto the patio. She had given Cecil more than enough time to brood on his own. It was time they talked, time they made plans to protect themselves and their daughters. Whatever it took to keep the truth hidden, they must do it. If anyone in their circle ever found out about Margaret, it would ruin them. And it would destroy Laura. She hadn't invested twenty-four years of her life in Cecil's daughter to let it be for naught. She loved Laura, as much as it was possible to love another woman's child, and for Cecil's sake she had protected the girl. Of course, loving Laura hadn't been difficult at first, not when she'd been an infant and toddler.

"Cecil, where are you?"

No response.

Damn, had he gone off for a walk and not told her? She glanced around and suddenly noticed two rather odd things——Cecil's empty teacup and saucer lay scattered in broken pieces on the brick patio floor. And only a couple of feet away, one of Laura's house slippers rested upside down, as if she'd lost it while running.

An unnerving sensation fluttered through Andrea's stomach. Something was wrong. Terribly wrong. Laura wouldn't have taken a walk with her father without her slippers. She had such sensitive feet that she'd never been able to play barefoot as a child the way Sheridan had.

"Cecil!" Andrea shouted. "Laura!"

Oh, God! Oh, God! She had no idea what had happened, couldn't even imagine why she felt so panicky. But her instincts told her that her husband and daughter were in danger. Serious danger.

Andrea rushed back inside and screamed, "Dora!"

The housekeeper came running as fast as a woman her age could. "Yes, ma'am, what's wrong?"

"Have you seen my husband and Miss Laura?"

"No, ma'am, not since Miss Laura came by the kitchen and asked me where her father was. I told her he'd taken a cup of tea out on the patio."

"Call Sheriff Butler immediately and tell him that Mr. Willis and Miss Laura are missing."

"What?"

"You heard me. Call the sheriff right now. Something terrible has happened to my husband and daughter."

She tried to be gentle with Laura, but the girl was afraid of her. That was his fault, of course. In order to keep from hurting Laura, she'd been forced to use the chloroform on her as well as on Jamie. No, not Jamie. Cecil. Cecil Willis. A bad husband. And a bad father.

She had taken them back to her cabin. Since she would be leaving town as soon as she finished what she'd come here to do, there was no reason she couldn't kill them here in the cabin she'd been living in for quite some time. After all, she'd used an alias and a phony ID. And once she left Cherokee County, no one would be able to trace her. She had new identities chosen for herself and her baby, with all the necessary papers to prove they were who they would say they were. And she could do as she'd been doing for two years now, charge everything to credit cards, pay a little along, and then change identities and disappear. She had been waiting and planning, knowing that she would eventually be able to punish the ones who had hurt her, the ones who had taken her baby away from her.

Her baby. Where was her baby? She'd left her sleeping when she'd gone to get Cecil, but when she brought him and Laura back to her cabin, her baby was gone.

Think, think, think. She tapped herself on the temple. *Jazzy has your baby. She's been pretending to be her mother. Jamie gave your baby to Jazzy.*

No, that wasn't right. It hadn't been Jamie.

But Jazzy had taken her baby. Jazzy had to pay with her life. She'd hurt . . .

Who had Jazzy hurt?

Laura.

Jazzy had hurt Laura.

She leaned over Laura Willis, who lay sleeping on the sofa, and caressed the girl's soft cheek. It hadn't been too difficult to drag the girl from the car. She was small and slender. Getting Cecil into the cabin had been more difficult because he was bigger and heavier. But she had managed by sheer determination.

"I'm going to get Jazzy and bring her back here. I want her to watch me kill him, but before I end his life, I want him to hear her screams. I'll make them pay, baby, I promise. I'll make them pay for everything they've done to us."

Jazzy staggered around in her office. She was a bit tipsy. Not drunk, just feeling very little pain. That third shot of whiskey had soothed her. And the fourth had numbed her. What she needed now was to get upstairs to her bed and sleep for about a hundred hours. Once she'd slept, once she'd erased both Caleb and Jamie from her mind, she would be able to decide what to do. Tomorrow.

Lacy could close up shop without her. She'd done it numerous times. And there was no need to bother her. *I'll just sneak out the back way and go home. Don't want nobody making a fuss over me.*

"Who the hell would do that, Jazzy, you damn fool?" she hollered.

She placed her index finger over her lips. "Sh—be quiet. You're talking too loud."

What if when you go home you can't sleep? What if you're not drunk enough to pass out? You'll be in the bed where you and Caleb made love for the first time. Will you be able to lie there and not think about him? Hell, no! You'll wind up crying, that's what you'll do. Because you're in love with him. In love with another damn Upton.

So don't go home. You're part owner in a couple of dozen cabin rentals. Choose one that's empty and spend the night there. But which one? The one where Reve Sorrell stayed. I don't think anybody has rented that one again.

Jazzy stumbled across her office, back to her desk, stepping over scattered debris on the floor. She rummaged around in the desk drawers until she found a set of master keys to the rental cabins.

Now what was the name of the cabin where Reve had stayed? Pines something or other. Two Pines. No, Twin Pines. That was it.

She dragged her sweater off the clothes rack in the corner, inadvertently crashing the rack into the wall. Ignoring the total mess she'd made of her office, she stuffed the huge key chain in her sweater pocket and headed for the door.

Music mixed and mingled with other honky-tonk sounds and drifted down the hallway. Jazzy glanced up the hall, saw no one, and then went straight toward the back door that led into the alley. Her car was parked at the end of the street, on the corner by the alley near the outside stairs that led to her apartment over Jazzy's Joint. She felt in her jeans pocket for her car keys and sighed when she felt them there.

She'd taken only a few steps when she thought she heard something. *Hearing bogeymen again?* Ignoring the sound, she kept walking up the alley, toward the street ahead. When she'd almost reached the street, she heard a noise again.

"Is somebody there?" she asked as she turned around, then gasped when she saw the dark figure step out of the shadows. "What do you want?"

"I want you, Jazzy," the woman said. "I've come to take you to your lover."

"Who are you? What the hell are you talking about?"

"I'm the mother of the child you stole. I'm the wife of the man you seduced."

Jazzy tried to get a better look at the woman, but all she could see in the shadowy darkness was the shimmer of blond hair. "You're crazy. I've never fooled around with a married man. And I sure as hell never stole anybody's baby."

"Lying won't help you. Not now."

The woman moved closer, close enough for Jazzy to see her face clearly and to recognize the wild-eyed creature pointing a gun right at her.

"We're going to take a little ride."

"I don't think so," Jazzy said.

"We can do this the easy way or the hard way," the woman told her.

"I'm afraid it's going to have to be the hard way."

Before Jazzy realized the woman's intent, she aimed her gun at Jazzy's midsection and fired. The bullet entered Jazzy's belly like a hot serrated knife, ripping her apart with fiery pain.

When Jazzy dropped to her knees, the woman came closer and stood over her. Jazzy couldn't believe this had just happened, couldn't believe this crazy bitch had actually shot her. Gripping her belly with both hands, she felt the warm stickiness of her own blood. *Oh, God, please help me.*

The woman grabbed Jazzy by her hair. Jazzy yelped. She took hold of the nape of Jazzy's sweater and started dragging her down the alley. *Damn, for a small woman, she was strong as an ox.*

"Where . . . where are you taking me?" Jazzy asked, knowing that she was on the verge of fainting.

"Back to my cabin, of course. I have Cecil and Laura waiting for us."

Cecil and Laura? Laura Willis and her father? Jazzy realized she was fading fast and her thought processes probably weren't working all that well, but none of what this woman had said made any sense.

You're going to die if you don't do something, Jazzy told herself. But what could she do? She was bleeding profusely and about half a minute away from passing out. *Leave a clue. It's only a matter of time until somebody misses you and comes looking for you.*

While the woman continued tugging on the neck of Jazzy's sweater, pulling her along the rough alleyway, Jazzy managed to muster enough strength to ease out the big key chain from her sweater pocket and slide it quietly down on the ground.

Chapter 29

Dallas Sloan knew the signs. It hadn't taken him long to recognize both the subtle and the obvious clues when Genny's mind left this temporal plane and moved into a spiritual realm. Whenever one of her visions took her away, she often became very still and very quiet and her eyes would glaze over. Then when she became fully immersed in that place out of time and space, where she witnessed either the future or events occurring somewhere else at that very moment, she often fainted dead away. If she was asleep when a vision happened, her body would become rigid only moments before she began tossing and turning. And more often than not, she would wake screaming.

Tonight she'd been wide awake. They'd been removing items from the dishwasher and placing them in the appropriate cupboards and drawers before turning in for the night. They had been talking and she'd just made a comment to which he had replied. When she didn't respond, he'd looked at her and realized she was fading away, leaving him.

"Genny?" He grasped her arm and shook her gently.

The ceramic dish she held slipped from her hand and crashed onto the floor. Dallas shook her again. No response. Damn, he hated it when this happened. Hated it because it scared him just a little. *Admit it, Sloan, sometimes it scares the bejesus out of you.* Even now, after months of knowing and loving Genny, of day by day becoming more and more telepathically linked with her, he still felt overwhelmed by her psychic abilities.

Suddenly he knew, without a word being spoken and a split second before it happened, that Genny needed him to catch her before she fell. As she swayed unsteadily on her feet, he reached out and grabbed her, then lifted her up into his arms. Using his foot, he slid one of the kitchen chairs away from the table, then sat down with Genny in his lap. Holding her rigid body securely, protecting her with every ounce of his strength, he spoke to her inside his mind, hoping he could reach her and give her his support. He'd found that if he could link with her while she was in that other world, she was able to draw power from him so that when she came out of her trancelike state, she wasn't quite as physically weak and emotionally vulnerable as she otherwise would have been.

Stay with me, Dallas, Genny pleaded telepathically. *It's bad. Really bad. Oh, God . . . oh God. Jazzy!*

"What is it Genny?" he said aloud. "What are you seeing? Is something wrong with Jazzy?"

Silence.

I can't lose the connection. Dallas told himself. *I have to stay focused on Genny, on helping her.*

For what seemed like an eternity, he couldn't sense what she was experiencing and it made him wonder if something or someone had severed the link between them. Then, with a tidal wave of sensation, she touched him, touched his mind and drew him closer and closer. He held her tighter and shut his eyes. Darkness. Utter and complete blackness.

Hang on to me, she told him. *Keep calling my name so that I can find my way back to you.*

Dallas saw nothing. He heard and felt only Genny. She was all around him and inside him, a part of him. Her body trembled involuntarily, then she began moaning. When she thrashed about in his arms, he trapped her in his embrace, cocooning her. Her moaning turned to sharp, high-pitched keens. And then she dissolved like ice in the snow—slowly, languidly—her body going limp and her mouth silent.

He held her all the tighter, poured all his mental and emotional strength into her, quite certain what would happen next. Genny's eyelids flew open and her black eyes stared sightlessly off into space. A millisecond later, she opened her mouth and screamed.

"It's all right, sweetheart," he told her. "You've come back to me. You're here in my arms."

She turned her head and looked at him. "Oh, Dallas, we have to find Jazzy before it's too late."

"Tell me everything."

"She—she . . . the woman who killed Jamie is going to kill Jazzy. She shot Jazzy. I could see Jazzy clutching her stomach, her hands covered with blood. And this woman was dragging Jazzy down an alley."

"Is this happening now?" he asked.

Genny shook her head. "I think it's already happened. I think this woman has taken Jazzy somewhere to kill her."

"Do you have any idea where?"

"No. Not yet. But . . ."

"But what?"

"I'm going to try linking with Jazzy. We haven't done

that in years, not since we were kids." Genny grasped the front of Dallas's shirt. "And Jazzy was never . . . never—" Tears glistened in Genny's eyes, like stars in the black night sky. "She was never very good at it, at linking with me."

"I'll call Jacob and we'll form a search party."

"How could this happen? Caleb was supposed to be with her. And I didn't feel his presence anywhere near Jazzy. All I felt was Jazzy's pain and fear." Tears trailed down her cheeks. "She felt alone. So alone."

Dallas kissed the top of Genny's head, loving her beyond all reason, wanting desperately to comfort and reassure her. "We'll find Jazzy. I swear we'll find her before . . ."

He shouldn't be making promises to Genny that he wasn't a hundred percent sure he could keep. But damn it all, if Jazzy died, it would destroy Genny. And he couldn't—wouldn't—let that happen.

When she regained consciousness, Jazzy realized she must have passed out sometime between when the crazy bitch forced her into a car and when she woke inside this cabin. Jazzy glanced around in the semidark room and realized she was indeed inside a Cherokee Cabin Rentals. And she was lying on the sofa. When she tried to move, pain ripped through her body, radiating from her stomach and outward. Oh, God, now she remembered. She'd been shot. That wild-eyed woman who looked vaguely familiar had shot her. Jazzy tried to feel her wound, and suddenly realized she couldn't move her hands. Damn it, her hands were tied behind her. She tried to lift her legs and couldn't. Her feet were bound together. Not good. Actually bad. Very bad.

Jazzy glanced around the room, searching for the

woman. That's when she saw the naked man lying on the floor, spread-eagled, his hands and feet tied to some sort of metal spikes in the floor.

Holy shit!

When she managed to roll over just enough to get a better look, she recognized the man. Cecil Willis. The crazy bitch had not only kidnapped her, but Laura's father, too.

"Please, why are you doing this?" a soft, quivering voice asked.

Who said that? Jazzy wondered. From where she was trapped on the sofa, she couldn't see the entire room, only the expanse of floor where Cecil Willis lay spread out like a sacrifice to some ancient god.

"Oh, Laura, my sweet baby girl," the crazy bitch said. "You must know that everything I've done, everything I will do, is for you. To protect you."

"I—I don't understand," Laura said.

Jazzy closed her eyes and uttered a silent prayer, pleading with God for help. This nutcase had kidnapped Laura, too. But why? *I don't understand any of this.* Okay, so maybe she wasn't thinking straight. Maybe a combination of the liquor she'd consumed and the pain and loss of blood from the gunshot wound had made her delirious. Maybe she was hallucinating. Maybe Cecil Willis wasn't really manacled to the floor, buck naked and gagged. And maybe Laura wasn't really here.

A shadow passed by the sofa. Jazzy closed her eyes and pretended to still be unconscious.

"I think your father should explain to you who I am and why I care so much about your happiness," the woman said.

Jazzy eased one eye open. When she saw that the woman had her back to her, Jazzy opened her other eye. The woman's hair was blond. Jazzy tried to put the face she'd seen in shadows in the alley behind Jazzy's Joint with blond hair. *Think. Try to remember where you've seen her before.*

As Jazzy watched, helpless to do anything else, she saw the woman drag an unbound Laura Willis with her toward the pitiful man lying on the floor. When the woman released Laura's hand and dropped to her knees alongside Cecil Willis, Laura stood there shivering and whimpering.

Run, you damn fool, run. Get away now, while you've got the chance, Jazzy screamed silently. What the hell was wrong with Laura? Didn't she understand this might be their only chance to survive?

The woman removed the gag from Cecil's mouth, letting the cloth rag nestle around his throat. Smiling cruelly, she caressed his cheek. "Tell her who I am."

With terror in his eyes, he looked up at his daughter. "This is Margaret. My—my first wife."

She stroked his cheek again. "That's a good boy. Now tell her why I love her and why I've come for her."

"Laura, darling . . ." Cecil looked pleadingly at his daughter.

The woman kicked him in the ribs. Hard. He groaned in pain.

"Daddy!"

When Laura started to go to her father, the woman flung a restraining arm out in front of her. "Tell her, Cecil." She whirled around and caught Jazzy staring at her. "Or had you rather your whore tell our daughter the truth—that she seduced you, that she took you away from me, that she stole my baby!"

"Margaret, please—"

She kicked Cecil again to silence him.

"Lady, you're fucking nuts," Jazzy said. "I told you before that I've never seduced a married man"—least of all Cecil Willis—"and I've never stolen a baby. Certainly not yours."

"Lying whore!" She propelled herself across the room in a flash and slapped Jazzy soundly. "He was my husband. Mine! And Laura was mine, too. My baby."

"Margaret, for pity's sake," Cecil called. "This woman didn't take Laura away from you. Look at her. She's only a few years older than Laura. You've confused her with—" Cecil gulped. "Please, let Laura and Jazzy go. Do whatever you want to me, but don't hurt Laura."

The woman looked at Jazzy and smiled. A cold shiver shocked Jazzy's body as she suddenly realized who this woman was. She was the small blonde woman who had eaten dinner at Jasmine's often during the past month or so. What was her name? Not Margaret. No, but something similar. Margie. Marj. Margo! Margo Kenley!

"Margo, I'm Jazzy Talbot. Don't you remember me? You've eaten at my restaurant several times. I'm not the person who stole your baby." Jazzy looked to Laura for help. *Snap out of it, girl, and do something—anything. And do it now.*

"I know who you are. You're the slut that Jamie Upton couldn't leave alone," Margo/Margaret said. "I had to kill him, to punish him for hurting my baby."

"You—you killed Jamie?" Laura's blue eyes widened in shock, as if she'd only now realized that this woman was a deadly viper, a murderess who enjoyed torturing her victims.

"I did it for you, Laura," Margo said. "He betrayed you, just as your father betrayed me. Men are weak creatures, really. They put their filthy hands all over you and make you feel like nothing. They fuck you and hurt you and . . . but I made them pay. My father. He raped me the first time when I was eleven. But I cut off his pecker and rammed it down his throat. And then there was my first boyfriend, who cheated on me with a perky little cheerleader. I killed him, too. Killed them both when I found them together."

"Daddy . . . why does she . . . keep saying . . . I'm her baby?" Laura gasped the words between frightened, confused sobs.

"You are my baby." Margo turned and reached for Laura, who shrank away from her. "Don't be afraid. I'd never hurt you. I love you. I always loved you."

"Daddy!"

"Let her go. Please." Cecil struggled fruitlessly against his restraints.

Margo looked at Laura, who stood frozen to the spot. Then she patted Laura's cheek. "See how he begs me to let his whore go free? He doesn't love me. He never did. And he doesn't love you. He only gave you to that slut of his because he wanted to punish me."

"Daddy, please tell me the truth—is she my mother?" Laura dropped to her knees beside her father.

"Yes. Your biological mother." Sweat coated Cecil's pale face and body. "But you're nothing like her, Laura. I swear. You're gentle and kind and loving."

As if in a trance, Laura rose to her feet and stared at Margo. "If you love me the way you say you do, you won't hurt my daddy."

Laura glanced at Jazzy, who knew she was on the verge of passing out again. God only knew how much blood she'd lost. Jazzy figured that if she didn't get to the hospital soon, she'd die long before this crazy bitch sliced her to ribbons. And she was pretty sure that's what this Margo broad had in mind. Doing some slicing and chopping on Cecil Willis and her, the same as she'd done on Jamie and Stan Watson.

"Please, let Daddy and Jazzy go. And if you want me to, I'll stay with you."

"No, Laura, no!" Cecil cried.

Amazing, Jazzy thought. What had happened to that pitiful, helpless little girl who'd kept whimpering and calling for her daddy? It was as if Laura Willis had turned into a mature, capable woman in the blink of an eye.

Wooziness suddenly overcame Jazzy. Her head spun around and around. The pain wasn't so bad anymore. Sort of a dull ache now. *That's a bad sign, isn't it?*

And that was the last coherent thought Jazzy had before she passed out again.

Jacob and Dallas had taken every precaution to make sure the search party stayed under their control, and that meant bringing along Jim Upton and Andrea Willis. Mrs. Willis had threatened to call everyone from the local TV station to the governor. Jacob had told Big Jim that it was his job to keep Mrs. Willis calm, which he'd been doing—up to this point. But the real problem wasn't Andrea Willis, it was the wild card in the deck, a man Jacob figured nobody could control. Caleb McCord had been with Jim when Mrs. Willis had called him to tell him about Cecil and Laura's disappearance. And when Jacob had confided in Jim that Jazzy, too, was missing, he'd shared the news with his newfound grandson.

Living closer to the Uptons, Dallas had gone there, with Genny in tow, to speak to Mrs. Willis and search the house and grounds for clues. He'd found nothing of any significance, other than Laura's bedroom slipper and a broken teacup. Except one other peculiar item— a remote control to the Uptons' massive front gates. Big Jim had identified it as Jamie's.

"Each of us has a different color remote," Jim had explained to Dallas, who had later told Jacob when they'd been trying to put all the pieces of this missing persons' puzzle together. "Reba's is white. Mine is dark green. Dora's is purple. Laura's is red. Jamie's was blue."

It didn't take a rocket scientist to put two and two together and come up with the inevitable four. The woman who had killed Jamie Upton had somehow managed to kidnap Cecil and Laura. And probably Jazzy, too, if Genny's sixth sense was correct. And it was, a good ninety-eight percent of the time.

While Dallas had taken charge of the investigation at the Upton mansion, Jacob had gone in search of clues in and around Jazzy's Joint—the last place anyone had seen Jazzy. He'd found Lacy in tears, and while he'd been questioning her, Sally had stormed in, along with Ludie.

"I'm heading home to get Peter and Paul," Sally had told him. "I'm gonna find that gal, and when I do, whoever's got her had better run like hell."

Jacob had managed to rein Sally in by explaining the entire situation to her and promising her that she and, if necessary, her bloodhounds, would play a significant part in searching for Jazzy and Laura and Cecil.

"I don't give a shit about that Willis fellow and his daughter," Sally had said.

He'd sent her off to pick up her dogs and told her to meet him at the Uptons. In the meantime, he and his deputies had scoured the alley behind Jazzy's Joint. What they'd found had chilled him to the bone. Blood. Probably Jazzy's blood. That meant she had been shot, just as Genny had seen in her vision.

"Look here, Sheriff," Moody Ryan had called after he'd picked something up off the ground. After holding it up in his gloved hand so that the glow from the nearby streetlight illuminated the object, the deputy had bagged the evidence. "It's a set of keys. Got blood on them."

"Let me take a look." Jacob had reached for the plastic bag and studied the red-stained keys. Turning the bag this way and that, he'd noticed something written on the oval key ring. "Cherokee Cabin Rentals," he'd said aloud.

Was it just a coincidence that what was probably Jazzy's set of master keys to the cabin rentals had been found in the alleyway? With blood on the keys? He didn't think so. It was as if Jazzy had deliberately left the keys behind, as a clue. What had she been trying to tell him? Jamie Upton had been killed in a cabin, albeit a deserted cabin. But wasn't it possible, maybe even probable, that the woman who had kidnaped Jazzy—as well as Laura and Cecil—had taken her to a cabin? One of the Cherokee Cabin Rentals.

Scrunched together in Jacob's Dodge Ram—he, Genny, and Dallas in the front seat and Caleb and Sally in the backseat—they drove up the long, lonely stretch of highway, toward the site where Reve Sorrell's Jag and Stan Watson's truck had been burned. He and Dallas had compared notes and discovered they both had a hunch the woman they were tracking might be in one of the nearby cabins. And if she was, that meant her three captives were probably with her.

"Wait!" Genny cried.

Jacob slammed on the brakes. Everyone took a collective deep breath and waited for Genny to continue. She'd been trying for the past hour to mentally connect with Jazzy, but without success.

"Did you do it?" Caleb lurched forward, his hand gripping Genny's shoulder. "Did you make contact with Jazzy? Do you know where she is?"

Dallas knocked Caleb's hand aside and growled at him.

"Nearby," Genny said. "She's drifting in and out of consciousness. We must hurry. If we don't get to her . . . if we don't help her soon, she'll die!"

Chapter 30

Caleb listened while Jacob and Dallas issued orders to the search party, comprised of their combined personnel. Pairing up, the officers and deputies were to check each cabin in the vicinity and radio back after each check. Since the number of searchers was limited, they'd be able to check only half the cabins at a time, even with Jacob and Dallas joining the hunt.

Big Jim and Andrea Willis stood nearby, Mrs. Willis bravely holding it together, with Jim at her side for support. Jacob rattled off the names of the present occupants in each cabin, one cabin empty. But he instructed his men to include the unoccupied cabin, also. When Jacob said the name Margo Kenley—that her cabin would be one of the cabins checked on the second round of inspections—Mrs. Willis gasped, but no one other than Caleb and Jim heard her.

Caleb eased closer to his grandfather and asked, "Did Mrs. Willis recognize the name Margo Kenley?"

Jim laid his hand on Andrea Willis's shoulder. "Did you recognize the name? Do you know the woman?"

"No, I don't know anyone by that name, but . . . forget it. It can't be."

"Please, Mrs. Willis, tell us," Caleb said. "Whatever your first thought was when you heard the name, tell me. It might help us find your husband and daughter." *And my Jazzy.*

"It was a ridiculous thought." Andrea sighed. "But if you think it might help."

Caleb reached out and took her hand in his. "Tell us." He knew only too well what Andrea Willis was going through. The same hell he was because he was scared out of his mind about the safety of the person he loved more than anything in this world.

"My husband was married to another woman before we got married," Andrea explained. "Her name was Margaret Bentley. I thought the names sounded similar. Margo Kenley. Margaret Bentley. That's all it was."

"Would this Margaret Bentley have any reason to want to harm your husband and daughter?" Caleb asked, grasping at straws with his question.

"Yes, she would. If she were alive."

"She's dead?"

Andrea nodded. "She died in a fire about two years ago."

"You know without a doubt that she's dead?" Caleb's training as a police detective resurfaced immediately. "The body was recovered and identified?"

"Yes, I . . . I suppose so. We never asked. We just assumed. I mean they notified Cecil and said Margaret was dead."

"So it's possible that she didn't die in that fire, that somehow she escaped." Caleb's policeman thought processes went into action, putting pieces of an unknown puzzle together. "Is there any reason this woman would have wanted the fact she was alive kept secret?"

"I—I . . ." Andrea stared at Caleb, fear and uncertainty in her eyes. "Yes. The woman spent years in a mental institution. That's where she died. You don't really think it's possible that—"

"Which cabin did Jacob say this Margo Kenley was staying in?" Caleb asked. "Eagle's Nest, wasn't it?"

"Yes, that was it," Jim replied.

Andrea grabbed Caleb's arm. "It can't be Margaret. It just can't be!"

"You have no real proof she died, right? The woman must have had severe mental problems to have spent years in an institution, right? Sometimes in a case where there's a fire in a place like that, with numerous casualties, they do a body count and figure anybody missing is dead. And you said yourself that this woman had a reason to want to harm your husband and daughter."

Clutching her throat, Andrea gasped. "Oh, God. If Margaret is alive and she has Cecil . . . she . . . she tried to kill his father, years ago. She tortured him."

Caleb's blood ran cold. "Excuse us a minute, will you, Mrs. Willis?" He nodded to his grandfather, indicating for him to come with him. Big Jim followed Caleb, about ten feet away, out of Mrs. Willis's earshot. "You wouldn't happen to have a gun with you, would you?"

Big Jim eyed him speculatively. "Don't do anything foolish, son. Let the law handle this."

"Jazzy Talbot is my woman," Caleb said. "Do you understand?"

"Yes, but—"

Caleb clutched his grandfather's arm. "I'm not some rank amateur who doesn't know what he's doing. I was a police detective."

Jim nodded. "I keep a pistol in the glove compartment."

"Is your car locked?"

"No."

"You wait here with Mrs. Willis and Genny. When Jacob and Dallas return, tell them where I've gone and why. If this Margo Kenley turns out to be Margaret Bentley, I just might need backup."

"Damn, boy, I wish you wouldn't—"

Caleb was halfway to Big Jim's Cadillac before Jim finished his sentence, so he didn't hear the rest. He opened the door, leaned inside, and opened the glove compartment. There, atop various other items, rested Jim's Heckler and Koch 9mm. He picked up the pistol and inspected it. A P7M8 automatic, with an eight-shot magazine. After rummaging through the other items in the glove compartment, he found an extra clip, which he stuffed into his shirt pocket, then headed toward the road leading to the Eagle's Nest cabin.

Jazzy kept fading in and out of consciousness. Every time that crazy bitch, Margo, decided it was Jazzy's turn for a little sadistic torment, she would slap Jazzy's face and pour water on her to try to rouse her. Luckily, her wounds, other than the bleeding bullet hole in her belly, weren't life threatening. Mostly small, superficial knife wounds on her arms and legs, just enough to inflict pain and keep her alive for prolonged torture. But from what she could tell, Cecil Willis wasn't fairing as well. The sound of his tormented screams had been what brought Jazzy back to consciousness this time. She turned her head and stared at the pitiful man on the floor, blood oozing out of countless cuts on his body, from shoulders to feet. God, the man was a bloody mess.

Margo stood over him, a hot poker in her hand and a wicked, maniacal look in her eyes. Bringing the poker down again, she ran it up one leg, across his lower belly and then down the other leg. Cecil bellowed with pain.

Where the hell was Laura, and why wasn't she trying to do something to help her father?

Using what little strength she had left, Jazzy maneuvered herself just enough so she could scan the room to search for Laura. Jamie's fiancée wasn't saying or doing anything because she couldn't. Sometime while Jazzy had been out of it, this Margo bitch had tied Laura to a wooden chair and gagged her.

Jazzy's gaze met Laura's, and she wondered if the same terror she saw in Laura's eyes was reflected in her own. Probably. Because she sure as hell was terrified. If somebody didn't do something to help them—and soon—they were going to die. Maybe Laura, too, even if she really was this insane woman's daughter.

All Jazzy had been able to figure out was that Margo's real name was Margaret, that she'd been married to Cecil Willis and Laura was their child. But Laura hadn't known that little fact, hadn't had any idea that this Margo/Margaret even existed. From what Cecil had said and from Margo's nearly incoherent ranting, Jazzy had figured out that Cecil's first wife had somehow, in her deranged mind, gotten Laura and Jamie all mixed up with Margaret and Cecil. That meant the woman she really wanted to kill alongside Cecil was probably Andrea Willis.

When Margo walked across the room and placed the poker back into the fireplace, its tip heating in the blazing fire, Jazzy studied her, careful not to alert the woman that she was awake and aware. As Jazzy lay there on the sofa, helpless to do anything except watch and wait, Margo disappeared into the bedroom. If only she could figure out a way to get loose. There was a telephone on the table in the corner, a good twelve feet from her. If she could manage to get to the phone . . . she could at least knock it off the hook, maybe use her nose to dial 911. *Do it,* she told herself. *It's now or never.*

Jazzy rolled herself off the couch, hitting the wooden floor with an agonizing thud. Pain radiated through her whole body, every muscle and bone and nerve ending screaming. For a second, she almost passed out again. With supreme effort and determination born from a will to survive, she managed to roll over several times, each time a torturous ordeal. But she was closer to the phone now. Six feet away.

Come on, you can do it. She rolled over a couple of times. Oh, God, the pain! She clutched her belly and felt fresh blood oozing from her wound.

Don't give up now. You're close, so close. Reaching out, she could almost touch the telephone cord. Almost. One more roll, just halfway, over on her side. That should do it.

What was that sound? Jazzy wondered, then realized that someone was singing—humming actually. Margo was humming. Jazzy glanced back toward the open bedroom door and prayed for just a few more minutes. She held out her hand. Her fingertips grazed the phone cord. She inched her way closer, grabbed the cord, and yanked. The receiver jerked off the base and came tumbling down to the floor, making a rather loud thump. Jazzy held her breath and waited. Margo kept humming, as if she hadn't heard anything. *Thank you, God!*

Jazzy placed her face close to the touch-tone digits on the receiver, then tried to use her nose to punch a number. It didn't work. *Okay, so try something else.* She used her tongue. That didn't work either. *Now what?* Teeth! She tried to focus on the numbers, but her vision blurred. *Hell, just punch in some numbers—any numbers.*

Just as Jazzy used her teeth to press what she hoped was 911, Margo came out of the bedroom. Jazzy glanced over her shoulder. Damn! But Margo seemed oblivious to Jazzy and to Laura as she glided across the room to where Cecil waited, abject terror on his face when she approached him.

What the hell was Margo holding in her arms? Was that a doll of some kind? It was. The crazy bitch was holding a life-size baby doll, wrapped in a pink blanket.

Margo knelt on the floor beside Cecil and held out the doll to him. "Isn't she pretty? Look at her, Cecil. Our little Laura."

Cecil didn't respond; he simply lay there, stunned and suffering.

She looked at the doll and smiled. "Daddy's been very, very bad and we have to punish him. He tried to give you away to that awful woman. But you mustn't worry. You're with your real mommy now. And no one will ever take you away from me again."

"Margaret." Her name croaked from Cecil's throat.

"Yes, Cecil, what is it?"

"That—that isn't Laura," he said. "That's a doll. Look at it. Can't you see it's not a real baby? Laura—our Laura—is a grown woman. That's her, over there." He inclined his head in the direction of the chair where Laura sat bound and gagged.

Gazing lovingly down at the blanket-wrapped bundle, Margo said, "She is a doll, isn't she? So pretty. She looks like me, don't you think?"

"Margaret, please . . . listen to me. Laura is an adult. She's twenty-four. Look over there at that young woman. She's our daughter. Look at her carefully and you'll see that she has your blond hair and—"

"Shut up! Don't talk to me. I hate you!" Margo whirled around and looked from Laura to Jazzy and back to Laura. "Who are you?" she asked Laura.

Unable to speak, Laura shook her head. Margo quickly turned her attention to Jazzy. "Who are you?"

"I'm Jazzy Talbot." *God, please, please help us!*

"Do I know you?"

"No, not really." *Soon, God. Real soon.*

"What are you doing here? Did you come with Cecil?" Margo gasped. "You're her, aren't you? You're Cecil's lover. You want to take my baby away from me."

"No!" Jazzy cried. "I'm not Cecil's lover. I don't even know him. And I don't want your baby. I swear!"

Margo started crooning to the bundle in her arms and once again totally ignored Jazzy and Laura as she meandered back to the bedroom.

The phone, damn it, the phone! Jazzy scooted just enough to be able to place her ear over the receiver. She listened. No 911 response. Just the repetitive voice of a taped message telling her to hang up and try again. *Okay, try again,* she told herself, but before she could do more than adjust her head, Margo came flying out of the bedroom, brandishing two large, shiny knives.

Laura wriggled and moaned, her eyes wide with fright. Cecil mumbled softly and Jazzy realized he was praying. *Good idea,* she thought. *Okay, God, looks like it's now or never. So how about making it now? How about putting me in touch with Genny? Yeah, that might work. We used to be able to connect mentally when we were kids. Could you help us do that again? Just this once?*

Genny. Can you hear me? If you can, let me know. I need help. I need help now.

Caleb approached the Eagle's Nest cabin with caution. If Margo Kenley was Margaret Bentley and she was holding Jazzy, Laura, and Cecil prisoners, the last thing he wanted to do was alert her of his presence. A nondescript older model Ford Taurus was parked in the drive, so that meant somebody was probably here. Caleb crept over to the car and checked the right back door. Unlocked! He eased open the door and looked around inside, able to see the interior fairly well since the vehicle was parked under the bright security light to the side of the driveway. Immediately his gaze paused on the red streaks smeared across the beige cloth backseat. He wiped the red with his fingers and brought them to his nose. Blood. Partially dried blood. Fairly fresh. Jazzy's blood!

He closed the door and made his way toward the side of the house, his actions silent and vigilant. After removing the pistol he'd tucked beneath the waistband of his jeans, he leaned forward just enough to peep through the front windows. The room lay in shadows, lit only by the roaring fire in the fireplace and a lone lamp burning on a corner desk. His gaze traveled speedily over the room. A man whom he was pretty sure was Cecil Willis lay on the floor, naked and spread-eagled—and covered in blood. To the man's right, Laura Willis sat bound and gagged. Caleb's heart pounded loudly in his ears, his pulse racing, sweat breaking out on his forehead. Jazzy? Where was Jazzy?

Raking his gaze from right to left, from ceiling to floor—the floor! Jazzy lay on the floor, her hands tied behind her, her feet bound. As best he could make out, she appeared to be unconscious. *Please, dear God, let her be alive.* The thought of losing Jazzy rendered him temporarily immobile. *Snap out of it! Get moving!*

While he studied the situation and his mind worked to form a hasty plan of action, a small, blond woman rose from the fireplace and lifted a red-hot poker in her hand. This must be Margo Kenley, who might be Margaret Bentley. At this precise moment, her name didn't matter, didn't mean a damn thing to Caleb. He watched in horror as she walked over to Cecil Willis and stuck the poker into his navel. The man screeched in agony. Salty bile rose up from Caleb's stomach. He wiped the perspiration from his face with his palm, then aimed Big Jim's 9mm. But before he could get off a shot, his target moved straight toward Jazzy, the poker she'd used on Cecil still burning hot. Margo punched Jazzy with her foot. Jazzy didn't respond. The bitter, salty liquid reached Caleb's mouth. He turned his head and spit.

Using her foot, Margo rolled Jazzy over and aimed the tip of the poker toward Jazzy's face. Caleb repositioned himself and took aim again. Just as the poker came down . . . down . . . nearer and nearer Jazzy's beautiful face, Caleb fired his weapon. The bullet blasted through the window, sailed through the living room, and entered the side of Margo's head. Blood spurted from her right temple. She dropped to the floor like a lead weight sinking into the river.

Caleb rushed to the front door, grasped the knob, and flung open the unlocked door. Margo lay halfway on top of Jazzy, the woman's bloody, tattered head and slender shoulders resting on Jazzy's legs. When he reached them, he rolled Margo over and out of the way. She was dead. She wasn't going anywhere, wasn't going to do anything. Kneeling, he reached out and felt for Jazzy's pulse. It was weak and thready, but she was alive. He examined her from head to toe and found the bloody bullet wound in her belly. She needed medical attention and she needed it now!

After ripping open Jazzy's blouse, he tried his level best to remember his first aid training as he examined the entry wound, then he searched but didn't find an exit wound. That meant the bullet was still inside her.

* * *

The light hurt her eyes. *Turn it off. I'm trying to sleep.* But no one responded. Jazzy's eyelids fluttered.

"Wake up, beautiful. You've been asleep way too long."

She recognized that voice. "Caleb?"

He squeezed her hand. "Yeah, honey, it's me."

When she opened her eyes, she barely recognized him. "You look like hell," she told him.

He grinned. "Guess I do look pretty rough. I haven't shaved in a couple of days and I've been taking a whore bath in the men's room down the hall."

"Why . . ." She glanced around and realized she was in the hospital. Pale green walls, white sheets, and a strong medicinal smell were sure signs, not to mention the nurses she saw at the their station just outside her door. "Am I in ICU?"

"You're in SICU. Surgical Intensive Care." He leaned over and kissed her forehead. "Do you remember what happened?"

Did she remember? Flashes of a woman holding a doll. Fragments of memory about someone shooting her. Then it all came back, one horrific incident at a time. "That crazy bitch tried to kill me. And Laura and Cecil Willis, too!"

"Calm down, honey. She's dead. Margo Kenley, whose real name was Margaret Bentley, is dead. She won't ever hurt anyone again."

"How . . . who?" Jazzy wanted to know details.

"Laura Willis is all right, physically. She's in the psychiatric unit of the hospital here."

"And Mr. Willis?"

Caleb remained silent for a minute, then heaved a deep sigh. "I'm afraid he didn't make it. The doctors said he suffered a massive heart attack."

"That poor man."

Caleb nodded. "It seems Margo was once Cecil's wife and was Laura's biological mother. She was insane, of course. Spent most of her life in a mental institution."

"Poor Laura. Oh, God—Jamie."

"Yeah, Margo probably killed him because she thought she was protecting Laura."

Someone cleared their throat. "Is she awake?" Genny asked from the doorway.

Caleb glanced over his shoulder. "Yeah, our girl's awake. Come on in."

"I've got Dallas and Jacob and Sally and Ludie out here with me," Genny said.

"All of you, come on in here." Jazzy tried to lift her head, but found she didn't have the strength. Not yet.

Within a minute, her bed was surrounded and one of the SICU nurses came in and scolded them for breaking the rules. Two visitors at a time. Jacob walked the lady out, reminding her that he was the sheriff. Jazzy could hear the RN informing Jacob that his authority didn't extend to her domain.

"You're damn lucky Caleb found you when he did," Sally told her. "He shot that crazy woman right in the head. One shot."

"Sally!" Genny scolded.

"Hell, gal, our Jazzy ain't no hothouse flower who needs to be shielded from the truth. She's got a right to know who saved her life."

Jazzy lifted her hand and discovered just how difficult that simple task was for her. Caleb leaned over her. She caressed his scruffy face. "Is that right? Are you my white knight?"

"You bet he is," Ludie added her opinion.

"We're so grateful that you're all right." Genny's gaze went to Jazzy's side, the side bandaged beneath her hospital gown.

Jazzy looked at Caleb and saw tears in his golden eyes. "I guess I am lucky to be alive."

"Got that damn right," Sally agreed.

Jazzy kept staring at Caleb, deeply touched by his tears, knowing how unlikely it was that a man such as he cried easily or often. "Thank you for saving me," she said quietly, then added, "I'm so glad you came into my life."

Caleb cleared his throat, then swallowed. "There's something I want you to know," he told her. "Something I want your family and friends to hear. It's something I promised myself I'd tell you, if you . . . if you lived. Actually, I swore to God that if he kept you alive, I'd tell you exactly how I feel. As a matter of fact, I tried making all kinds of bargains with the Lord if he'd just let you live."

"This sounds serious." Sally grinned. "Making an oath to the Almighty and all."

"Jazzy, I love you," Caleb said quickly and without hesitation. "And if you'll give me a second chance, I'll prove to you just how much."

A hush fell over the room, as if everyone was holding their breath. She looked from one person to another and was met with smiles. They all knew that Caleb McCord just might turn out to be the best thing that had ever happened to her.

Jazzy swallowed tears of happiness, grateful to be alive and loved by so many people.

She smiled at Caleb. "I think maybe you and I both need a second chance."

He kissed her then. Warm and tender, with a hint of passion. "Thank you," he whispered against her lips.

Epilogue

Of course the day was perfect. Genny and Dallas deserved nothing less than true perfection on the most special day of their lives. Sunshine in abundance. Blue sky overhead. Green grass beneath their feet. Wild flowers blooming profusely. Birds chirping. Fiddlers playing alongside flutists. The melodies ancient. Celtic. Cherokee. Sometimes a subtle blending, just as the bride herself was a mixture of the two noble people.

Genny had never been more beautiful than she was this spring afternoon in June when she exchanged vows with the man she loved. Of course the groom was handsome. In his simple black suit and gray-striped tie, his attire complimented his new wife's unadorned antique white sheath of sheer organdy over an aged silk underlay. Genny's granny, Melva Mae Nelson, had wed her true love, Jacob Butler—the present day Jacob's grandfather—in the dress Genny wore today. Her long shiny black hair hung loosely to her waist, unfettered by jewelry or a headpiece and veil, the sparkling diamond on her finger, now mated to the simple gold wedding band, her only embellishment.

Jazzy joined the group of unwed women as Genny prepared to toss her bouquet of pale pink wild roses. Jazzy's life had changed unbelievably in the past six weeks since she'd nearly died at the hands of a madwoman. Nothing would ever be the same again. Her views on life in general had altered. She was stronger, wiser, far more cautious. And she was happier than she'd ever been, mostly due to her relationship with Caleb McCord. She hadn't told him she loved him. Not yet. It wasn't that what she felt for him wasn't love, but after what she'd gone through with Jamie, she wasn't ready to commit her whole heart to anyone. Not until she was sure. Not only of the man, but of herself.

She trusted Caleb and believed he loved her. But she couldn't forget that he was now the Upton heir or that Miss Reba, despite Big Jim soundly defending Jazzy to his wife, still disapproved of her. Caleb hadn't moved into the Upton mansion, but everybody knew who he was now. She'd told him that he couldn't put off the inevitable for much longer and he hadn't disagreed with her. He still lived in the rental cabin and still worked as the bouncer at Jazzy's Joint. But even he admitted that he was considering Big Jim's offer to come into the family business empire.

Jazzy supposed she didn't quite trust Caleb to choose her, to put her first, if it came to a choice between her and what his grandmother wanted. And someday soon, it would come to that. He understood that she would want marriage and children. And Miss Reba would oppose their union. They hadn't discussed marriage. Not yet. But they would. She'd been the one who'd suggested they take their relationship slow and easy and give themselves plenty of time to be sure. Reluctantly, Caleb had agreed.

Maybe things would work out for them. It was what she wanted, what he professed he wanted, too. But she needed time. She was barely on the mend after her long hospital recuperation. And there was another relationship she had to work out first—the relationship with Reve Sorrell.

Reve had called her while she'd been in the hospital. And in the weeks since her release, they had talked on the phone several times. Jazzy had questioned Aunt Sally about her birth and her aunt had told her the same old story again and again. No twins. No second child. Corrine Talbot gave birth to one baby girl. Jazzy had no sister. No twin. But a part of Jazzy doubted her aunt. Her gut feelings told her that Reve was her sister—her twin.

Before she could move forward with her life and make a commitment to Caleb, she had to find out the truth. And from some things Reve had said recently, Jazzy was pretty sure she felt the same way. If Aunt Sally wouldn't help her unearth the truth, then she'd have to find another way to discover who she really was. Caleb had promised her that he'd do everything he could to help her. For the first time in her life, she had a strong, reliable man at her side.

All the bridesmaids fluttered and giggled as they lifted their arms and reached for the bouquet that sailed toward them. Maybe it was because she stood a couple of inches taller than the others, or maybe because Genny aimed directly at her, Jazzy wasn't sure, but the bouquet of wild roses landed in her uplifted hands. She clutched the fragrant nosegay to her bosom and laughed. Would she be the next Cherokee County bride? Would she and Caleb truly find their happily ever after? With bubbly happiness warming her heart, Jazzy glanced around the crowd and her gaze connected to Caleb's, who stood alone, away from the crowd.

Barefoot, as were Genny and her other attendants, Jazzy ran across the field at the back of Genny's house where the outdoor ceremony had taken place. She raced straight into Caleb McCord's open arms. Life was good. And the future looked bright.

Dear Reader,

Now that you've finished reading the second book in my Cherokee Pointe trilogy, I hope you're curious about what's coming up next. In September 2004, the third and final installment of this series will be released. You can expect to see more of Genny and Dallas, as well as Jazzy and Caleb. Picking up where THE LAST TO DIE left off, AS GOOD AS DEAD reintroduces Jazzy's look-alike, Reve Sorrell. Are these two women really twin sisters who were separated at birth? If so, why was the infant Reve thrown into a Dumpster and left for dead? Would a mother really keep one child and dispose of another so heartlessly? And do the recent murders in Cherokee County have anything to do with the mystery surrounding Reve and Jazzy? The upcoming third book in the trilogy will put Sheriff Jacob Butler in the forefront and pit him in a deadly game against a brilliant killer. Also, look for sparks to fly between Jacob and a certain lady he intensely dislikes. For a hint of what's to come, check out the prologue for AS GOOD AS DEAD in the back of this book.

In 2004, I have seven new books tentatively scheduled, two from Zebra and five from Silhouette. For those of you who have been following my "The Protectors" series, you'll be pleased to know that four of my five Silhouette novels this year will be part of this on-going series. Coming in February, look for my next "The Protectors" book from Silhouette Intimate Moments, DOWNRIGHT DANGEROUS. The book picks up where the June '03 single title, GRACE UNDER FIRE, left off and has Rafe Devlin and Elsa Leone as the protagonists. Using her position as the manager of WJMM radio and TV stations in Maysville, Mississippi, Elsa founds the Maysville Good Samaritans, an organization of concerned citizens determined to clean up the seedy area of the town where crime goes unchecked. But someone wants to stop the MGS and zeroes in on Elsa. After an attempt is made on Elsa's life, her boss hires Dundee agent, Rafe Devlin, to protect her.

Look for my very first "The Protectors" DESIRES in April and June. Both stories have reunited lovers as the protagonists and deal with a parent's worst nightmare—child abduction. Look for the return of FBI agent, Dante Moran, from GRACE UNDER FIRE, who'll show up in both of these DESIRES. When Moran leaves the FBI, his first case as a Dundee agent turns out to be much more than he bargained for in my November '04 novel. I'll be taking part in the launch of Harlequin's new mainstream romance line, HQN, with Moran's "The Protectors" book tentatively titled WORTH DYING FOR. I'm excited about the opportunity to move my Dundee agents from series romance into mainstream romance fiction.

In May, my contribution to the "Family Secrets" continuity series, CHECK MATE, Book #12, will be on the stands. This book wraps up all the loose ends of the series and gives readers the long-awaited Jake Ingram story.

I truly treasure each of my readers and enjoy hearing from you. You can write to me in care of Kensington Books. And please check out my Web site at www.beverly-barton.com, sign my guest book, and sign up for my monthly e-mail newsletter.

Warmest regards,
Beverly Barton

Please turn the page for an
exciting sneak peek of
Beverly Barton's
AS GOOD AS DEAD.
Coming in September 2004 from Zebra Books!

Chapter 1

Reve Sorrell closed the lid on her suitcase, lifted it off the foot of her bed and set it on the floor. She'd been up for over an hour, after waking at three, unable to sleep. Her decision to return to Cherokee Pointe had been made after a great deal of deliberation. She'd spent months unable to put Jazzy Talbot out of her mind. Back in the spring she'd driven up to the mountains to seek out the woman Jamie Upton had told her was her spitting image, a woman who looked enough like her to be her twin. She'd met Jamie at a party here in Chattanooga, back before Christmas last year. He'd been a charming jerk, the type of man she usually avoided. But he had piqued her curiosity when he'd mentioned that his teenage sweetheart, a bar and restaurant owner in Cherokee Pointe, would easily pass for Reve's twin.

If she hadn't been an abandoned child, adopted in infancy by wealthy socialites, Spencer and Lesley Sorrell, she'd have passed off Jamie's comments without a second thought. But since she knew nothing of her birth parents, she wondered if it was possible that this Jasmine

Talbot Jamie had mentioned could be her sister. So she'd disregarded what her common sense had told her—not to go digging around in the past—and had gone to Cherokee Pointe. Her first encounter with Jazzy had been less than pleasant. She'd found the woman to be rather crude and vulgar. They had disliked each other on sight. And Reve would have returned home that very day, if she hadn't been involved in a minor car accident.

As if wrecking her Jag hadn't been bad enough, following the accident, the local sheriff had treated her abysmally. Sheriff Jacob Butler was an old friend of Jazzy's and took offense at an offhand comment Reve had made about the woman. It had seemed to Reve as if half the men in town were Jazzy's friends, a fact Reve had learned both firsthand and from local gossip.

To complicate matters now that she was returning to Cherokee Pointe, she'd been plagued by thoughts of the big, surly, half-breed sheriff. He was a thoroughly unpleasant sort. A real ruffian. After their initial encounter, she had hoped she would never see the man again. But when Jamie Upton was murdered while she was still in town and a witness had identified a woman fitting Jazzy's description—and therefore her description—as having been seen with Jamie shortly before his death, Sheriff Butler had come knocking on her door. He'd had the gall to practically accuse her of the murder, had in fact assumed—erroneously—that Jamie and she had been lovers. Naturally, it hadn't taken the authorities long to realize she wasn't involved in the crime, so she had, thankfully, been able to escape from Cherokee Pointe and the watchful eyes of the Neanderthal sheriff.

Upon returning to Chattanooga, to her home on Lookout Mountain and her set of friends and business associates, she'd tried to put her less than pleasant experiences in Cherokee Pointe behind her. She hadn't wanted

to think about Jazzy or the fact that they did in fact resemble each other in a way only twins did. But try as she
might, she hadn't been able to erase from her mind the
image of her double, a woman of dubious character.

Reve sighed heavily. Would she regret going back to
Cherokee Pointe and joining forces with Jazzy to seek
the truth about their possible sisterhood? They had spoken on the phone several times recently. Somewhat reluctantly, Reve had made that first call. Thirty years ago,
someone had thrown her into a Dumpster in Sevierville
and left her for dead. She'd been an infant, possibly
only days or weeks old at the time. However, Jazzy's aunt
Sally, who had raised her from a baby, swore that her sister Corrine had given birth to only one child. Was Sally
Talbot lying? Or was there some other explanation?
Reve knew she'd never have any peace of mind until
she found out the truth—the whole truth.

She hadn't intended to leave Chattanooga this early. It
wasn't quite four-thirty. But why not go ahead and get on
the road? If she left now, she'd be in Cherokee Pointe by
the time Jasmine's opened and she could have breakfast
at the restaurant before meeting Jazzy at Dr. MacNair's office around nine. They had agreed that DNA testing was
the first step in discovering the truth about their past.

Not wanting to bother any of the servants at this un-
godly hour, she heaved her suitcase off the bed. As she
walked through the house and out to the garage, she
couldn't help wondering if she was making a monu-
mental mistake. She and Jazzy Talbot had nothing in
common, other than a strong physical resemblance—
and possibly the same birth parents. Did she really want
to form a familial connection with this woman who was,
by all standards, socially beneath her and morally inferior? *God, Reve, listen to yourself. You sound like the biggest
snob in the world.* All right, maybe she was a snob. No

maybe about it. She was a snob. But she'd been trained by her parents and peers to look down her nose at her inferiors. *There you go again, assuming just because she grew up poor, has a reputation as the town tramp and owns a honky-tonk, that Jazzy isn't your equal.*

Reve unlocked the trunk of her Jaguar, dumped the suitcase inside, then slid behind the wheel and started the car. Even if Jazzy and she turned out to be twin sisters, that didn't mean they had to become friends. She seriously doubted that Jazzy wanted to build a relationship with her any more than she wanted one with Jazzy. But there was a need deep inside her to find out the truth—who had thrown her in that Dumpster and why? Had her birth mother thrown her away? If so, why had she disposed of one baby and not both? And if she and Jazzy were twin sisters, why had Jazzy's aunt Sally lied to her all these years? After their DNA testing confirmed their relationship, the likely place to start their search for the truth was with Sally Talbot. And what a place to start—with a nutty old woman the whole town thought of as a kook.

Reve hit the button to open the garage door, backed out and then closed the door. As she entered the street, she stopped the car and took a long, hard look at her home. This house had belonged to her grandparents, Spencer Sorrell's parents, and the plush mansion held only happy memories for Reve. If only she weren't adopted. If only the Sorrells had been her biological mother and father. But her adopted mother had pointed out to her on numerous occasions that she *was* a true Sorrell in every way that counted. Except by blood.

As she drove along the steep, twisting street leading off Lookout Mountain, Reve compared the similarities between this road and the one where she'd had her car accident outside Cherokee Pointe. Damn! Why had she thought about that wreck again? Automatically her mind

brought Sheriff Butler to the forefront—a vivid image of
his hulking six-five frame, his green eyes, his hawk nose,
his fierce frown. She intended to do her best to avoid
Jacob Butler while she was in Cherokee Pointe. Not only
did the man annoy her, but he unnerved her. His nature
was a bit too savage to suit her. He'd been more than just
downright unfriendly toward her; he'd shown no respect
whatsoever for who she was—one of the richest and most
powerful women in the state of Tennessee.

Jazzy's orgasm exploded inside her, eliciting a loud,
guttural moan from deep in her throat. The powerful
sensations went on and on until they finally tapered off
into delicious aftershocks. Hot, damp, completely sated,
she smothered Caleb with deliriously exuberant kisses.
He toppled her off him and onto the bed, his hard penis
slipping out of her during the maneuver. Before she
had a chance to catch her breath, he thrust up into her.
Deep and hard. Once. Twice. And then he came.

Roaring like the male animal he was, Caleb shuddered with release. Moments later, their bodies damp
with sex-induced sweat, they lay on their backs, their
bodies not touching, only their entwined fingers.

She loved holding hands with Caleb. A sweet, senti-
mental gesture, but it said so much about their relationship. About who she was when she was with him.
About the type of man Caleb McCord was.

Jazzy looked up at the ceiling, stretched languidly and
smiled. Sex with Caleb was always like this—explosive
and fully satisfying. But there was so much more to their
relationship than great sex. They were friends as well as
lovers. And they were madly in love, too. Honest to
goodness in love.

She didn't know what she'd done to deserve a fabulous guy like Caleb, but she thanked God for him. And with each passing day, she trusted Caleb and the love they shared more and more. Maybe one of these days soon she would be able to accept his marriage proposal. He had asked her to marry him so many times it had almost become a joke between them.

Almost.

Even now, months after Jamie Upton's death, his memory haunted her. But not in the way Caleb thought it did. On some basic, totally masculine level Caleb was still jealous of Jamie, of the fact he'd been her first love and her first lover. There was no reason for him to be jealous. She didn't love Jamie. Only the distrust and fear Jamie had instilled in her kept him alive and allowed him to stand between her and Caleb, between her and happiness.

"Jazzy?" Caleb said her name in that lazy, sexy Memphis drawl she loved so well.

"Hm-m?" She turned sideways and looked at the silhouette of his long, lean body there in the semidarkness of her bedroom. She knew his body as well as she knew her own.

"Marry me."

Her smile widened. She reached over and ran her fingertips up and down his body, from throat to navel.

He grabbed her hand. "I mean it. Marry me. Let's get a license tomorrow and just do it. We'll elope. No fanfare, no—"

"No Miss Reba throwing a hissy fit until it's over and done."

"Do not bring my grandmother into this equation. I've told you a thousand times that I don't give a damn what she thinks." Totally naked, Caleb jumped out of bed and grabbed his jeans up off the floor.

Damn it, she'd hurt his feelings by questioning his loyalty to her. Her mind told her that he would never do as

Jamie had done and allow Miss Reba to dictate who he could and couldn't marry. But her heart had been broken once by an Upton heir, by the charming, worthless, womanizing Jamie. And her heart was afraid to trust, afraid to believe that Miss Reba didn't wield the same power over Caleb that she had over her other grandson.

"What are you doing?"

"I'm putting on my clothes," Caleb told her.

"Why? You aren't leaving, are you? Please, Caleb, don't go."

He pulled on his jeans, and then felt around on the floor until he found his shirt. "I'm just going outside for a few minutes. I need some early morning air to clear my head. I'll be back in a little while."

"I'm sorry."

"It's okay," he said. "Just remember, I'm not Jamie. I'm not walking out on you or giving up on us. Not now or ever. You couldn't beat me off with a stick, honey."

"I know you're not Jamie." When she sat up, the sheet dropped to her waist, exposing her breasts.

"Then stop assuming I'm going to treat you the way he did. I can't stand it when you project his actions onto me."

Caleb turned from her and hastily left the room. Jazzy flipped on the bedside lamp, then got up and headed for the bathroom. Usually they didn't get up this early—and seven-thirty was early for people who didn't go to bed until two in the morning—but she had an appointment to meet Reve Sorrell in Dr. MacNair's office at nine. Galvin had explained to them that the results of the DNA test might take a few weeks, but Reve had informed him that she would pay any extra costs necessary to facilitate a speedy response.

Jazzy turned on the water, waited a couple of minutes for the water to heat, and then stepped under the showerhead. As the warm spray doused her, she thought about her future. Her first concern was Caleb. She couldn't keep putting him off. Sooner or later he'd get tired of waiting for her to marry him. The thought of losing him was too terrible to consider, yet she wasn't ready to say yes. There were too many unanswered questions in her life, too many loose ends she had to tie up before she could build a solid future with the man she loved. And she did love Caleb. More than she'd ever thought possible to love a man. But she had to convince him that he was the only man she loved. In order to do that, she had to let go of Jamie completely.

Since Caleb spent most nights at her apartment above Jazzy's Joint, they usually closed the bar together and came upstairs for a late night meal and then went to bed. She loved being with him, making love with him, sharing her life with him.

So why don't you marry the guy? she heard Lacy Fallon's voice inside her head. Lacy, the bartender at Jazzy's Joint, treated Jazzy like a kid sister, giving her advice and watching out for her.

Don't let what Jamie did to you keep you from finding happiness with Caleb, Jazzy's best friend, Genny Sloan, had told her repeatedly.

Even her own heart advised her to reach out and grab the happiness Caleb offered.

Jazzy bathed hurriedly, washed her hair and emerged from the shower, fresh and clean, and clear-headed. By the time she dried her hair and dressed, Caleb would probably be back in the apartment and in the kitchen fixing their breakfast. She smiled to herself. Her Caleb was a man of many talents.

The telephone rang. *Who on earth would be calling so early?* Everyone knew they slept late. After wrapping a towel around her, Jazzy rushed into the bedroom to answer the phone.

"Hello."

"Jazzy, this is Reve Sorrell. I got an early start so I'm already in town. I'm over at Jasmine's and have just ordered breakfast. Any chance you can join me?"

"Ah . . . I just stepped out of the shower. But—" Maybe it was a good idea to touch base with Reve before they went to see Galvin. After all, if it turned out they really were twin sisters, as they suspected, they'd be spending a great deal of time together in the upcoming weeks. They had agreed that if the DNA tests proved they were siblings, they would work together to discover the truth about their parentage.

"If you'd rather not—" Reve said.

"No, it's okay. I'll hurry and dress." Jazzy peeked through the open bedroom door and into the living room. No sign of Caleb. She listened for any sound of him in the kitchen. None.

"It's okay if I bring Caleb along, isn't it?"

"Sure. After all, he is your fiancé, right?"

"He most certainly is. Unofficially."

"Have you two set a date?"

"Not yet." Everyone assumed that sooner or later she'd accept Caleb's proposal—everyone except Caleb's grandmother, one of Cherokee County's grande dames, Reba Upton. Damn the old bitch!

"Bring him along," Reve said. "I'll go ahead and eat, then have coffee when y'all arrive. Or would you like for me to order for you two and wait?"

"Yes, do that. Just tell Tiffany that Caleb and I will be eating at the restaurant this morning. She knows our usual order."

"See you soon."

"Hm-m." The dial tone hummed in Jazzy's ear.

Reve Sorrell had been pleasant enough, but not overly friendly. The woman had erected some sort of emotional barrier around herself, one that effectively kept people at bay. If they were twin sisters, how was it possible that their personalities were as different as night is from day? She supposed it all boiled down to the old question about which dominated a person's physical, mental, and emotional makeup more—nurture or nature.

Reve Sorrell was a class act. A real lady. Jazzy Talbot was a dame, a broad, a good old gal.

"Jazzy?" Caleb called to her as he entered the living room.

"Huh?"

"Want me to put on some coffee?"

Caleb might get upset with her, he might storm off in a rage, but he always came back. He never left her for more than a few minutes, an hour or two on a few occasions. He meant what he'd said about not ever leaving her. Not the way Jamie had done, time and time again.

"Reve Sorrell just called," Jazzy said. "She wants us to meet her for breakfast over at Jasmine's."

"She got in early, didn't she?"

"Yeah, she did. I guess she's as anxious as I am to get our DNA samples sent off to the lab."

Caleb appeared in the bedroom doorway. "Give me a couple of minutes to grab a quick shower." As he moved past her, he paused, leaned over and kissed her cheek, then yanked off her towel before he went into the bathroom.

Jazzy hugged herself and sighed contentedly. Reve Sorrell might be a lady—a very rich and important lady—but who cared? Caleb didn't. And it didn't matter to him that Jazzy wasn't some blue blood with a lily-white reputation. He loved her just the way she was. And Caleb's opinion was all that mattered.

* * *

Sally Talbot stood on her front porch, a tasty chaw of tobacco in her mouth. Peter and Paul, her old blood-hounds, lounged lazily under the porch, their heads barely peeking out as they snored. She wished she could sleep as easy as them two varmints did, but if they had the worries she had, they wouldn't be sleeping so soundly either. After spitting a spray of brown juice out into the yard, Sally wiped her mouth and took a deep breath of autumn mountain air. There weren't nothing like autumn in the Appalachians. The crisp, clean morning air. The bright colors nature painted the earth this time of year. No, sirree, weren't no place on earth as near God's heaven as these here mountains.

All her life—some seventy-one years now—she'd spent here in Cherokee County, most of it in this same old house her pa had built for her ma before he up and died of TB back in forty-nine. And all these years she'd been an oddball, different from folks hereabout. Not crazy, mind you, but not quite all there either. She had book learning. She could read and write and add up figures. And she knew these hills as well as anybody, better than most. She'd always been poor and hadn't never cared a hoot about money. Not until Jazzy came into her life. She'd wanted to give that gal everything her little heart desired, but she'd failed miserably. She'd done the best she could. If she'd had a man bringing in a living, things might have been better, but she and Jazzy had made out all right. They'd had a roof over their heads and they'd never gone hungry. Jazzy had grown up to be a fine woman, a real smart woman who'd done all right for herself. Her gal owned a restaurant and a bar in Cherokee Pointe and she was a partner with some other people in Cherokee Cabin Rentals. Yep, she was damn proud of her niece.

A chill racked Sally's body. "Winter's coming," she said to no one in particular.

But it wasn't the cool morning breeze that had chilled Sally. It was thoughts of Jazzy. Her little Jasmine. She'd named Jazzy for them beautiful flowers that her sister Corrine had loved so. When she'd put Jasmine in Corrine's arms thirty years ago, she'd never dreamed that within a few months Corrine would be dead—her and her lover—and she'd be left to raise Jazzy all alone. But there hadn't been a day pass that she hadn't thanked the good Lord for that gal. She loved Jazzy as if she was her own and Jazzy loved her like a mother.

"God, forgive me and please help me," Sally said softly. "You know I didn't have no idea there was another baby, that Jazzy had a sister."

Reve Sorrell might not be her sister, Sally told herself. *Could just be a coincidence that they look so much alike.* But if the DNA test they was having done proved them to be twins, then Jazzy was going to be asking a lot more questions. She'd want to know how it was possible that her aunt Sally hadn't known nothing about another baby.

All the lies she'd told Jazzy from the time she'd been a little girl would come back to haunt her—if that Sorrell gal turned out to be Jazzy's sister. She knew what Jazzy would say to her, could almost hear her.

"You told me that my mama came back home to you right before I was born, that her boyfriend had run out on her and she had no place else to go. You told me that you delivered me and that you sent for old Doc Webster a few days later to record my birth and check me and mama to make sure we were all right. Isn't that so? Tell me, Aunt Sally, did you or did you not deliver another baby? Were you the one who threw my sister away?"

Them there DNA tests wouldn't lie. If they proved them gals to be sisters, then Sally had some explaining to do. *If I tell Jazzy the truth, will she hate me? I just couldn't bear it if that gal hated me.*

* * *

Genny Sloan stopped suddenly on her morning trek from the greenhouse to her back porch. Although she'd seldom been able to control the visions that came to her, she had learned what signs to expect, signs that forewarned her.

Drudwyn paused at her side, and then licked her hand.

"It's all right, boy. I think I can make it to the porch." Genny stroked the half-wolf dog's head. "But if I don't make it, you let Dallas know that I need him."

Drudwyn hurried ahead of her, then paused and waited at the door. Genny made it to the porch. Barely. She slumped down on the back steps and closed her eyes. She'd been born with the gift of sight, a God-given talent inherited from her grandma. More times than not, she'd found the gift could be a curse.

Lights swirled inside her head. Colors. Bright, warm colors. And then she heard Jazzy's laughter mixing with softer laughter. Another woman's laughter. Happiness. Beautiful happiness. Genny sensed a togetherness, a one-ness, almost as if Jazzy and this other woman were a single entity. As that knowledge filled Genny's consciousness, she understood she was receiving energy from Jazzy and from Reve Sorrell. She didn't need to see the results of a DNA test to know they were twins. Identical twins. Individuals, yet forever linked from the moment of conception.

Suddenly the bright, cheerful lights inside Genny's mind darkened. Black clouds swirled about in her con-sciousness, completely obliterating the beauty and hap-piness. Fear. Anger. Hatred. Jealousy! An evil mind concealed by a mask of normalcy.

Danger! Jazzy and Reve were in terrible danger.

But from whom? Who possessed this dark, viciously cruel heart? Who feared the truth? Who was willing to do anything—even kill—to keep the truth hidden?

Genny delved deeper into the black abyss, seeking the identity of this person, searching for any link between this evil and her dearest friend, Jazzy.

Oh, God, the hatred. Pure wicked hatred.

"Genny!"

She heard Dallas's voice as if it came from far away.

"Damn it, Genny, come out of it. Now! You're going in too deep."

He shook her soundly.

Genny groaned. Her eyelids flew open. She gasped for air.

Dallas pulled her into his arms. "What the hell happened? I thought you promised me that you wouldn't go in that deep without my being there to—"

"I had to go as far as I could," she said as she rested her head on her husband's chest and wrapped her arms around his waist. "I had a vision about Jazzy and Reve Sorrell. I know they're twins." She lifted her head and looked at Dallas. "That was a vision filled with joy and light and beauty. But suddenly the darkness came. I— I'm not sure if there's a connection between Jazzy and Reve and the evil I sensed."

"The two visions might have nothing to do with each other," Dallas told her as he caressed her cheek with the back of his hand.

"Maybe not, but usually, when two visions overlap that way, they're somehow connected."

"But not always."

"No, not always."

Dallas lifted Genny into his arms and carried her into the house. She snuggled close, loving the protective feel of this man she loved above all others, more than life itself.

"You're awfully quiet," Dallas said. "Are you sure you're all right?"

"Yes. I'm all right. But Jazzy and Reve may be in grave danger."